THE DEBT

INSTALLMENT SIX

THE DEBT

Installment One: Catch the Zolt

Installment Two: Turn off the Lights

Installment Three: Bring Back Cerberus

Installment Four: Fetch the Treasure Hunter

Installment Five: Yamashita's Gold

Installment Six: Take a Life

THE DEBT

TAKE A LIFE

INSTALLMENT SIX

PHILLIP GWYNNE

Kane Miller
A DIVISION OF EDC PUBLISHING

First American Edition 2014
Kane Miller, A Division of EDC Publishing

Copyright © Phillip Gwynne 2013
Cover and internal design copyright © Allen & Unwin 2013
Cover and text design by Natalie Winter
Cover photography: (boy) by Alan Richardson Photography,
  model: Nicolai Laptev; (helicopter) by Getty Images; (Gold Coast)
  by Shutterstock

For information contact:
Kane Miller, A Division of EDC Publishing
PO Box 470663
Tulsa, OK 74147-0663

www.kanemiller.com
www.edcpub.com
www.usbornebooksandmore.com

Library of Congress Control Number: 2013953415

Printed and bound in the United States of America
1 2 3 4 5 6 7 8 9 10
ISBN: 978-1-61067-308-2

Sept '14
to
Abernthie #6

To Lizey

DON'T ROCK THE BOAT

The stench of flesh – my flesh.

The outrage of pain.

My pain.

When I looked down there were five letters *PAGAT* branded on my thigh, the last one still raw molten skin.

Only one more letter, one more installment, to go.

I was almost there.

But I knew that my grandfather had the same letters on his thigh. I knew that many years ago he was "almost there" too. But he'd failed at the last installment. And instead of the branding iron searing the final letter, it was a scalpel that sliced off his leg.

I looked over at my father. And I knew that he had the word *PAGATO* branded on his thigh.

He hadn't failed. He'd paid back the installment. Not only that, he'd prospered, becoming the rich and successful businessman he was today.

But then I reminded myself that when I broke into his offices they were all empty and cobwebby.

So how successful was he, exactly? And if he wasn't successful at business, where did all his money come from? Had it come from making people disappear, for example? But I quickly banished those thoughts from my mind – he'd repaid the last installment, and that was all that mattered to me right now. Like him, I wasn't going to get all this way only to fall at the sixth, and final, hurdle.

"We're finished here," said Dad, putting the equipment away in the drawer in Gus's desk. He moved over to me and put his arm around my shoulders. "Let's not get ahead of ourselves, but there's only one to go."

I nodded, and suddenly I felt incredibly close to my dad, like our skin, his skin, my skin, had melted away and we were one person, one blood, one DNA, one ambition.

He'd done it and so would I.

And when my eyes took in Gus, all old and wrinkled, he and his stumpy leg seemed so far away, like I was looking at them through the wrong end of a telescope.

Dad and Gus wanted to discuss something between themselves, so I left by myself.

One to go. One to go. One to go, I repeated as I walked home, hurrying upstairs to my bedroom.

I got into bed, crawling under the covers.

One to go.

Until The Debt contacted me I was going to keep really, really low.

One to go.

No digging.

One to go.

No rocking the boat.

Only one to go.

No nothing.

Just keeping low.

I burrowed deeper into my bed and concentrated on one thing and one thing only: the pain from my thigh. Concentrated so that it seemed to become tangible. Something hard and brilliant. Like a diamond.

A FEW MONTHS LATER

INTO THE VALLEY

A knock on my door.

Go away.

"Are you in there, Dominic?" came Mom's voice from the other side.

It was what my English teacher, Mr. McFarlane, would call a rhetorical question – of course she knew I was in here.

"Hi, Mom," I said. "What is it?"

"Do you mind if we have a talk?"

How could I say no? I'd been behaving weirdly. I knew it. She knew it.

"Okay, Mom, you can come in."

"The door's locked." I got up, unlocked the door, and let her in.

The little talk was her asking questions, which I couldn't help but think were from some pamphlet on teenage depression she'd picked up. Or maybe

7

she'd been on the phone to Dr. Juratowitch, the mint-sucking psychiatrist.

Do you feel like other kids don't like you?

Do you feel like you can't start anything new?

Finally, I said, "Mom, I assure you, I'm not depressed, okay? I'm just taking it easy until school starts."

"That's not for another couple of weeks," she said.

I looked at her. She looked at me. And suddenly I had this huge feeling of – I'm not sure how to explain it – I'm-totally-over-this-ness.

Really, wasn't it about time we stopped kidding each other?

"I've got one more installment to The Debt to pay back, okay?" I said. "I don't intend to muck it up. So I've been, like, keeping myself wrapped in cotton wool."

Mom actually recoiled, as if this mention of The Debt was some sort of physical thing, a real slap on a real face. She recovered quickly, though, and not for the first time it occurred to me that my mother was a pretty tough sort of person.

"Dom, I hear what you're saying," she said.

A handful of words, but it was an absolute breakthrough: the first time my mother had ever acknowledged the existence of The Debt.

"But can you do something just for me?" she said. "Can you start running again? I don't necessarily mean competitively – a run in the morning would be enough to make this particular mother very, very happy."

My first thought: *Running – pah phooey!*

But there was such a look of concern on Mom's face I couldn't help but say, "Okay."

She smiled her California – or was it Italian? – smile, tousled my hair.

"That's the spirit," she said.

Ω   Ω   Ω

The next morning it was the Baha Men who woke me from my slumber. I burrowed my head under the pillow but it was no good, their despicable canine-related lament found its way through. I had no choice: I got out of bed, hurried across the room, turned off the alarm. I was about to hop back into my now Baha-free bed when I remembered the look on Mom's face and the promise I'd made her. I got dressed in my running gear.

As usual, I took the quietest route out of the house, making sure I didn't make any noises that would wake my sleeping family.

Sitting on the front step, I laced up my runners.

Fingers of light were poking up over the wall as I made my way down the driveway. Stepping from behind a bush – a figure.

Looming, threatening.

I stifled a scream.

"But it's only me, Mr. Silvagni," said the figure, in a slightly sarcastic tone.

Roberto!

"What the blazes are you doing?" I said, my heart finding its way back to its normal position somewhere in my chest.

"I work here, remember?" he said.

Is that all you do here, Roberto? I remembered that time when Toby had gone missing, I'd seen him and Mom in conversation in the kitchen, their noses practically touching. It was Roberto Mom had turned to. And Dad had definitely not been happy.

"Yes, of course," I said, which sounded so pathetic. I turned on my heel and took off.

When I got to the entrance of Halcyon Grove Samsoni, the Tongan security guard, was all smiles. "Mr. Silvagni, you're running again!"

"Yeah," I said, trying not to buy into his enthusiasm, but I had to admit to myself that even the short jog here had felt sort of nice.

There was no advice from Samsoni as to where I should run this time, either. Only a very sincere "Good luck!"

I followed my old route around the Halcyon Grove wall, up Chirp Street, and then over the bridge into Chevron Heights.

I half expected to see the diminutive figure of Seb Baresi jogging outside Big Pete's Pizzas, ponytail bouncing. He wasn't there, of course, and I wondered where, and how, our paths would cross again, because I knew that they would.

Up the Gut Buster, heart rate spiking, and then down the hill towards the sea, the smell of salt now in the air. As I ran along the edge of Preacher's Forest, it occurred to me that I should stop calling it that now that the Preacher was dead. Ibbotson Reserve, its proper name, was so boring, though. I guessed it was going to be Preacher's Forest for a bit longer, anyway. Or maybe even Dead Preacher's Forest?

As I turned back into Chirp Street, the resident birds were, as usual, in full song. Again I had that feeling – *this running thing actually feels pretty good* – but immediately I dismissed it. If it wasn't going to help me pay the final installment, then what use was it?

Chirp Street was never a busy street, especially so early, and I was surprised when out of the corner of my eye I noticed a white vehicle approaching from behind. I was getting some pretty major flashback now – this was pretty much how The Debt had started. It was a white van, streamlined, sort of futuristic-looking, and seemed to make no noise at all. And because the sun was glinting off the windshield, I couldn't make out who was driving.

Just as I was about to get both terrified – what did they want? – and excited – could this be the final installment? – I realized that my mind was playing tricks on me. It wasn't a van at all, and definitely not a streamlined, futuristic-looking one. It was Gus's ancient truck.

I stopped, letting him drive up next to me.

"Not looking too bad," said Gus through the open window.

I noticed an old cocoa tin sitting on the passenger seat. I'm sure it wasn't intentional, but it actually looked like the seat belt was fastened around it.

"Where you off to this early?" I said.

"Berang Valley," said Gus.

"Where Dad grew up?"

"Exactly, where your dad grew up," said Gus, and then he added, "and me too."

Dad had often threatened to take us kids to Berang Valley. "I'll show you kids the shack I grew up in and then you'll be grateful for what you've got!" That sort of thing.

He'd threatened, but he'd never carried through with any of his threats and we figured that was because Berang Valley wasn't so bad after all. We even used to make jokes about it.

"It's like this luxury resort," Miranda would say.

"Basically Palazzo Versace, but with sugarcane," Toby would add.

"You wanna come along for the ride?" said Gus.

Actually, I did want to see where my father grew up, but I was also determined not to rock the boat.

But it was just a little ride, I reasoned. No real danger of rocking any boats.

"What about your passenger?" I said, indicating the cocoa tin.

"He can sit on your lap," said Gus, going along with my excellent cocoa-tin-as-a-person joke.

"Why not?" I said, moving around to the passenger side, opening the door.

It was only when we were on our way, the cocoa tin between my legs, that something occurred to me.

"So what's inside?" I said, tapping the tin.

"The Preacher," said Gus.

"Very amusing," I said.

"Well, what's left of him."

Suddenly I got it: the Preacher had been cremated and these were his ashes.

Yes, I jumped. Well, as much as my seat belt would let me.

"That's your brother in there," I said, shocked at how unsentimental Gus seemed.

"My brother died," said Gus. "That's what's left of the vessel he inhabited during his time here on earth."

I took his point, but it was still pretty weird to have a dead Preacher in a tin between your legs.

We were climbing now, Gus's ancient truck making wheezing sounds as it came to uneasy terms with the steep gradient.

"Old girl's just like me," said Gus. "Doing it tough."

"Yeah, so what did you bench press this week?"

It was a tactic, tried and true: whenever Gus started doing that old-is-me thing, I got him on to his bench press, the thing he was most proud of in the world. His arm muscles flexed; it was if the mere mention of the words "bench press" got them working.

"Now you come to mention it ..." he said, smiling.

See what I mean?

For the rest of the trip up he talked "pumping tin" as he called it, why it was so good for you, especially as you got older.

Then the truck stopped complaining and we were in the hinterland.

Just after one of those camera signs – *You must take a photo!* – Gus pulled into a turnout.

Some Japanese tourists were getting into a bus and when they left we were the only people there. From here we could see the whole sweep of the coast, from Southport in the north all the way down to Coolangatta in the south. Arc after arc of white sand, and beyond that the ocean, blue and brilliant, stretching out to the horizon.

It was incredibly beautiful, and I felt this sort of awe. I actually got to live down there, in that paradise. It made me realize something: as much as I made fun of the Gold Coast, I did actually love where I lived; I really couldn't imagine living anywhere else. And it was my dad, empty cobwebby office or not, who had done that for me.

"Pretty spectacular," said Gus, echoing my thoughts.

We got back into the truck and continued on our

way, turning down a small road I'd never been on before.

We passed a winery, an organic farm, and then the road wound down into a valley. That's when it started to get a bit weird. At first there was rain forest, but this gave way to land that was cleared – or had been cleared, because there was a profusion of tangled vegetation.

"What's that stuff?" I said.

"Lawyer vine," said Gus, and I could tell from the way he spat the words out that it probably wasn't his favorite plant. "This used to be some of the best sugarcane country in the state, but it's all wait-a-while now."

"Wait-a-while?" I queried.

"You'll find out when you get caught in some," said Gus, laughing.

Deeper into the valley we went. When we came to a crossroads, a dilapidated bus shelter on our side, Gus turned down an even narrower road. There were no people around, no animals; it was a pretty spooky sort of place. We pulled off the road and into a rutted driveway, passing a couple of old tractors, before drawing up outside a tumbledown shed. The wait-a-while had taken this over, too, vines twining through the missing windowpanes and over the roof.

"My God, what is this place?" I said.

Gus smiled. "Actually, it's where three generations of Silvagnis grew up."

I wouldn't say that all of a sudden I totally got my dad, but right then something did definitely change in my opinion of him.

Palazzo Versace with sugarcane?

Hardly.

Okay, maybe there hadn't been so much lawyer vine when he'd lived here, but I couldn't imagine it as anything but a dump.

It was dump, Berang Valley was a dump – it was dump, dump and more dump. I wanted out.

"Would you like to take a look?" said Gus, opening the driver side door.

"Not really," I said.

Gus sighed, and not just a normal sigh; this was the sort of sigh that only somebody who had seventy-four years of living under their belt – and a seventy-five kilo bench press – had the right to muster.

"You know what, neither do I," he said, closing the door. "It was a fricking dumb idea to come here."

"What about the Preacher?" I said, indicating the cocoa tin.

Gus's eyes flicked between the tin and me. Eventually he said, "We better do the right thing by him."

He dropped the clutch and we followed the dirt road deeper into the valley until we came to a small church. Or the shell of a church, because all that was left were broken stone walls. I hadn't thought of churches going out of business, but I guessed it had to happen. And for the same reason other places close down: lack of customers.

"This is actually starting to freak me out a bit," I said.

Gus took the cocoa tin from me and said, "You can stay here, no problem."

Which was what I intended to do.

Even when he got out of the truck, cocoa tin in his hands, it was what I intended to do. But as he walked towards what was left of the church, the engine of the truck tick-tick-ticking as it cooled down, I changed my mind.

Not sure why – maybe the same thing that had killed that cat.

But by the time I got out of the truck Gus had disappeared from view.

The day had become very still, very humid, the air so thick you could poke holes in it with your finger.

"Gus!" I yelled as I hurried towards the church.

There was a loud fluttering sound from within its ruined walls. Were there ghosts? Spirits? Other things that didn't even have names? The appearance of pigeons, at least twenty of them, taking for the sky, put paid to these possibilities.

My heart, I noticed, was fluttering too.

"Gus, you there?" I yelled.

"Over here," came his voice from behind the church.

I walked quickly – okay, I ran – in that direction. After I rounded the corner of the church I could see him, standing, staring.

"You okay?" I said as I approached.

Gus turned and there was an expression on his face I hadn't seen before. I pretty much thought nothing scared Gus – after you've had your leg taken away at fifteen, what's going to faze you? But right then he looked scared, really scared.

"You okay?" I said again.

"Memories," he said. "Too many for an old codger."

Don't rock the boat.

No more digging.

But I really couldn't help myself – this was my family, my history. In a way it was my inheritance.

"Was your father a cane farmer?" I blurted.

"For all of his working life," said Gus.

"So you used to come to this church?"

"All the time," he said. "My parents were great believers."

Great believers – it was a strange choice of phrase, but I guess Gus was about as atheist as an atheist could get. From great believers to a great non-believer in only one generation – that was something worth considering.

"Is that where the Preacher got all that stuff from?"

Gus nodded. "He was a strange kid – the Bible was pretty much the only book he ever read."

I thought about this for a while: okay, he'd been a strange kid, but lots of kids were strange – it didn't mean they ended up like the Preacher.

"And he, like, just got stranger?" I said.

Gus responded with that sigh, the one he earned by being around for seventy or so years and bench pressing seventy-five kilos.

"The death of his twin sent him over the edge."

I thought of two photos: the family portrait in the drawer of Gus's desk and the photo in the Tabori crypt.

"How did his twin die?"

Gus hesitated before he answered, a sure sign that he was lying. "He got sick. Lots of kids died in those days."

With that, Gus marched off. I followed him. By that time we were right at the back of the church, surrounded by that now-familiar tangle of lawyer vine.

It was only when I saw a lopsided gravestone that I realized we were in a graveyard.

I stopped, waiting for the coimetrophobia to hit.

But it didn't; the only thing I felt was a slight wobble.

Have I been cured? I recalled what Dr. Juratowitch had said, that my phobia was about being reminded of my mortality. When I thought about it, it seemed pretty obvious: I didn't need graveyards to remind me of my mortality because The Debt was doing an even better job of it.

Gus stopped in front of another gravestone.

Luigi Silvagni, it said. *1915 – 1956*.

Gus's father, my great-grandfather. I quickly did the math.

"He was only forty-one when he died," I said.

"Bad ticker," said Gus, bringing his hand up to his own heart. But then it dropped down again. "Actually, he died a long time before that."

I sort of knew what was coming next, and I wanted to hear it but didn't want to hear it.

Gus continued, "They took his arm."

"When he was my age?" I asked, though I already knew the answer. Gus nodded and I waited for it to come – a Tristanesque pile-driver to the guts – but it didn't. Maybe it was because I'd already seen that photo in Gus's drawer – the hidden arm, or hidden lack of arm.

"A one-armed cane farmer?" I said.

"About as useful as a one-legged track coach," said Gus, sounding sorry for himself.

"Almost," I said, not buying into it.

"A one-armed cane farmer could get by, but a one-armed piano player was never going to cut the mustard."

"Sorry?" I said.

"Your great-grandfather was a gifted musician. Completely self-taught, mind you, but when he was a kid he could play just about anything, especially piano. That Jelly Roll Morton stuff."

Jelly Roll who?

"And then they took off his arm and he never played again."

"Nothing?"

"Occasionally he'd blow some mouth organ. But never in public. I'd go down the back of the shed and he'd be playing to himself. If he knew anybody was listening he'd stop."

It was about the saddest thing I'd ever heard, and tears were welling in my eyes.

"Can we go back home?" I said.

"Just one thing to do," said Gus, taking the lid off the cocoa tin.

"You're going to just toss them out here?"

"It's what he wanted," said Gus, and he launched into a pretty good impression of his strange Bible-obsessed brother: "That I may die in mine own city, and be buried by the grave of my father and of my mother."

"Buried, not just tossed out," I said.

"You're getting pedantic now," said Gus, tipping the cocoa tin over.

At first there was just a puff of dust, but then the ashes themselves started tumbling out. I knew that Gus was right: what I was seeing was what was left of the vessel the Preacher had inhabited during his time on earth. But I couldn't help but think it was more than that, that what had made the Preacher the Preacher was also coming out of that cocoa tin, turning the wait-a-while ash-gray.

And it was freaking me out.

I started walking away, but some lawyer vine attached itself to my sock – now I totally got the wait-a-while thing. As I removed it another gravestone caught my eye.

Elizabeth Pandolfini. 1943 – 1955.

"Didn't anybody in this stupid valley live to a proper age?" I said.

Gus looked at the gravestone and shook his head slowly, tears forming in the corners of his eyes.

Dom, stop digging! Stop it! Stop it! Stop it!

"I'll wait for you in the truck," I told him.

Once inside I switched on the radio and turned up the volume as loud as it went; I needed to drown out all these questions that were whizzing around my head, demanding answers.

Gus returned a couple of minutes later, still holding the cocoa tin.

"What are you going to do with that?" I said.

He looked at it, as if he wasn't quite sure what the answer was, and then he walked over to the church and placed it somewhere inside.

"At last, a real preacher," he said when he returned.

The pigeons were returning to their roosts.

"With a congregation of pigeons."

Gus didn't seem to be in a talking mood as we

wound back out of the valley. Which was fine with me – neither was I.

By the time he dropped me back home it was midday. Time for a swim. Or maybe take in a movie. Open those emails from Imogen.

Or time to turn the air-con to arctic and crawl back into bed.

Which, as you may have guessed, was exactly what I did.

JRLO, HWKP AND HRLP

My phone beeped.

So what? I thought. *I've got about a million unopened emails and you think I'm going to stress about a piddling text?*

It beeped again, seemingly more insistently.

Phone, didn't you hear me last time?

A third beep.

Obviously not.

And then, nothing.

I'm not sure why leaving an email unopened is sort of okay but not reading a SMS is unbearable. Maybe Dr. Juratowitch or some other expert on adolescent behavior could explain that. I grabbed my stupid phone and I read the stupid texts.

jrlo, said the first one.

hwkp, said the second one.

hrlp, said the third one.

They were all from the same person: PJ.

I checked the keypad on my iPhone – it was just as I thought: "jrlo," "hwkp" and "hrlp" were all what you might come up with if you were trying to type "help" but couldn't see the keyboard.

So, basically, PJ was saying "help." Three times.

So what? I thought.

What's it got to do with me? I thought.

I went with this for maybe five minutes before the hard reality kicked in: it had everything to do with me!

Somebody as tough and resourceful, as streetwise, as PJ wasn't going to ask for help unless she really needed it. And I kind of felt flattered that she'd asked me and not some other street kid. So I texted her back.

Although I waited for ten minutes I got no answer. I thought about calling her, but decided against it. The three misspelled "helps" suggested that her phone was hidden somewhere, in a pocket maybe. If I called it maybe I would give the game away.

So the conventional methods of finding PJ weren't going to work. Fortunately for me, and thanks mainly to The Debt, I had some other less conventional means at my disposal. Like triangulating her phone. Which is what I did. ClamTop came up with this address: 45 Frank Condon Drive, Mermaid Waters. I'd been to Mermaid Waters once before and I remembered it as a typical Gold Coast suburb, crisscrossed with canals.

I shoved ClamTop into a messenger bag and made my way downstairs.

It wasn't far to Mermaid Waters – a short taxi ride and I was there. I wasn't sure who Frank Condon was, but the street named after him was a pretty ordinary-looking one full of pretty ordinary-looking houses.

I walked, eyes flicking from one mailbox to the next until I came to number 45. There was nothing about this house that disrupted the pattern – yes, it was also very ordinary. Nothing about the exterior gave any indication as to who its occupants might be.

So what to do?

It took me all of a second to arrive at the answer to that – I had to get inside. But if I was going to just rock up and knock on the door to 45 Frank Condon Drive, I needed to have a story.

So what sort of random people knock on random doors?

Because I lived in a gated community, pretty much nobody knocked unexpectedly on our door. Occasionally Samsoni would call on the intercom and say something like, "There's a couple of young men here who are interested in discussing the state of your eternal soul with you."

They never seemed to get any farther than the front gate.

And then it came to me: I was knocking on the wrong door! I'd met this girl on the bus and we'd gotten to talking and found we had a lot in common. She'd given me her address and I'd put it in my iPhone. So here I was.

Okay, this story had several thousand holes in it – for a start, why would a girl give you her street address in this day and age and not her email address? – but it was all I had, so I decided to go with it.

I approached the front door. All very suburban. All very normal.

But when I got close enough to knock, I noticed something that wasn't quite so suburban, quite so normal: a CCTV camera. Thanks to the visits I'd made to Hanley's shop I knew what model it was: a wireless Boscan 165Y, the same as those seriously cashed-up bikies had bought that day.

Although my knocking wasn't getting any response, I had this feeling there was somebody inside the house and right now they were looking right at me.

Okay, it was only a feeling, a hunch, but that's yet another thing I'd learned from The Debt; sometimes that's what you go with. I made my retreat, but already a plan was forming in my head.

There weren't many hiding places on Frank Condon Drive, so I sat in the gutter, took ClamTop out of my bag and opened it. It was just as I'd expected: there was a wireless network within range. I set ClamTop to work, the little red devil waving his trident about. It took much longer than it normally did and it occurred to me that this particular wireless network had more security than usual for a suburban home. I'd been suspicious before, but now I was pretty certain there was something nasty going on in 45 Frank Condon Drive. And maybe that something nasty was happening right now.

Hurry up, Dom!

Eventually the network was hacked, and I had a cloned desktop to look at. Again it was just as I'd expected: the CCTV feeds were open.

I'd been right – somebody had been looking at me when I'd knocked on the door, because the first feed was the view from the camera I'd seen. I couldn't help noticing how clear the image was. Hanley was right: quality hardware. The second feed was from the back door, giving a view of a nondescript backyard: a patch of lawn, a clothesline, not much more. But the third feed caught my attention immediately – it was a brightly lit room. There didn't seem to be any furniture, but in the corner I could make out a figure, wearing jeans and a face-concealing hoodie.

Is that PJ?

The figure moved closer to the camera – yes, it was PJ!

A cold shiver moved up my spine, jumping from vertebra to vertebra.

One word popped into my head: *police*. This was pretty creepy, pretty serious, no job for some fifteen-year-old kid with a jumped-up idea of his own capabilities. I even took out my phone, ready to give the cops a call.

But I stopped. I was so close to the final installment; could I afford to have the cops snooping around in my life? And I knew that PJ was certainly no fan of the constabulary.

Cops or no cops?

If I went with the no-cops option I needed a plan; how to get inside that house?

It seemed logical to me that somebody who had that much CCTV, who was that paranoid, would most probably have other hardware as well, like a gun.

I couldn't risk just breaking in.

I remembered the work I'd done for Hound during the third installment. How, as he had put it, we'd flushed the rat out. We'd tricked Nitmick into leaving his apartment and then we'd nabbed him.

I needed to flush the rat out.

But how?

How?

And then it came to me.

As far as plans went it wasn't my best work, not by a long shot, and already I could see that it had lots of problems. But it was the only one I had.

First I had to get on to YouTube, find some footage. That wasn't as easy as I thought it would be. Yes, there were a lot of clips of cops, but mostly they were from films, and the cops were film cops, doing very spectacular film stuff – definitely not what I wanted.

But eventually I found this program called *The Force*. It was actually shot in Victoria, and the cops wore Victorian cops' uniforms. They were different, but not that different. I fast-forwarded through several clips until I found what I was looking for: cops bashing on a door. I saved a few minutes of this clip to an AVI file.

It took me a while to find out how to do what the next part of my plan needed. But, as with most things in life, the answer was on Google. Now I was ready to go.

Seriously, is this going to work? I asked myself again. The plan had so many holes you could strain spaghetti with it.

But I had no choice – I had to go with it.

So I did.

I got as close to the house as I could without being captured by the CCTV. And then, ClamTop in my hands, I switched the feed from the first CCTV to the AVI file I'd created.

I put ClamTop back in my bag, raced up to the door and started thumping on it, channeling every beefy, burly cop on every cop show I'd ever seen.

My theory was that the combination of the knocking and the footage would cause whoever was inside to panic and exit via the back door. Just like, so Dr. Chakrabarty reckoned, the god Pan had caused the Persians to panic in the Battle of Marathon.

It worked – *Dom Silvagni, you are a genius!*

I watched as a figure hurried out the back, through the backyard and then out of sight.

But I didn't watch for long, because when I tried the front door it was locked! I hurried along the side of the house, to the back.

The back door, as I'd hoped, had been left open. I slipped inside.

"PJ!" I yelled over and over again as I raced from room to room to room.

But none of them was the brightly lit room I'd seen on the CCTV.

How could that be? Was the feed from another house close by?

But as soon as I'd posed that question I knew what the answer must be: the feed was from a hidden room. I retraced my steps through the rooms, looking more carefully this time. In the third room, the living room, I found what I was looking for: the rug, some hideous gold-and-blue thing, didn't seem to be lying completely flat. Again, this was nothing more than a feeling.

But when I grabbed the edge of the rug and pulled it up there was a trapdoor underneath.

The rest was pretty straightforward: using the ring, I pulled up the trapdoor. Steps led down. I followed them into a storeroom, but there was another door, locked with a dead bolt from the outside. I undid the lock.

"PJ?" I said as I pushed the door open.

She rushed to meet me.

"I knew you'd come," she said, wrapping her arms around me, squeezing tight. "I told him you would."

I'm glad she knew it, because I sure hadn't been so certain.

"Let's get out of here!" I said, and we made for the stairs. I followed her.

"Take the back door," I said when we'd reached the top, but PJ said nothing.

The man I'd seen fleeing through the back door – short, chubby, maybe in his fifties – was sitting in a chair, like he'd been waiting for us all along.

I'd been right about one thing: he had a gun, a very serious-looking one, too. And it was pointed at me.

"Do you really think I would fall for such an amateurish effort?" he said.

I felt ashamed – he'd nailed it: totally amateurish.

"Don't take any notice of him," said PJ.

How couldn't I? As far as creepy went, this dude was right off the creepy meter. Creepy and smart, a dangerous combination.

But as soon as I had that thought I knew it was the wrong one. *Yes, he's smart, but so are you, Dom.*

"And do you really think I'm that amateurish?"

I said, trying to get some 'tude back into my voice. I saw the tiniest flicker of something cross his face and I knew I was on the right track. *Keep talking, Dom. And keep it smart.*

"You think I would come into a place like this without a backup plan?" I said. "Without a contingency?"

Another flicker across his face.

"You don't think I told somebody where I was?"

"Really?" he said, and I wondered if I'd overplayed my hand.

"I can show you the text if you like?" I said, reaching for my pocket.

"Actually, I'd quite like to see that," he said.

I took out my iPhone, and held it up so that he could see the message: *dad if i'm not home by 12 then come to the 45 frank condon drive, mermaid waters.*

The man sat there, silent.

The gun, I noticed, was now pointing to the ground.

"There is no criminality here," he said. "Priscilla came here of her own free will to sort out her family's finances. Isn't that right, dear?"

PJ nodded. "That's right."

I looked hard at PJ – what the blazes was going on here?

"Brandon owes him money," she said.

"Quite a lot of money," said the man, smiling like he'd just had some victory. Then he lifted the gun up, pointed it at me and pressed the trigger – a small flame appeared at one end.

It was a cigarette lighter.

He laughed and said, "Get out of my house."

I didn't need any further invitation: I grabbed PJ's hand and made to get out of his house.

PJ wouldn't budge, however.

"Where's my stuff?" she said.

"You've got some cheek, haven't you?" said the man, and I was pretty much in agreement with him on this one.

But like I said, PJ wasn't about to budge.

"My phone?" she said.

It took a while but eventually the man got up out of his chair, went over to the kitchen. He opened a drawer, and held out a phone.

PJ took it from him. "My spray?"

He handed her a can of what looked like pepper spray.

"And my money?"

"You know how much your brother owes me!" he said.

"Him, not me," said PJ.

But the man still had a you've-got-to-be-kidding look on his face.

I picked up the gun/cigarette lighter. "Give my friend her money," I said, trying to get some of that Hound-style menace into my voice.

It didn't really work.

"Or what, you going to light a smoke?" he said, laughing.

I moved over to the control panel for the CCTV, pointed the gun at the circuit.

"They're a good unit, the Boscan," I said. "But I'm just not sure they're fireproof."

Immediately the man took out his wallet, pulled out some bills and handed them to PJ.

"You tell your brother I want my money," he said.

I grabbed PJ's hand and pulled her towards the door.

Once outside, once beyond the gate, once safely in suburbia's bland but safe embrace, only then did I allow myself to relax, my shoulders to drop back from where they'd been, up around my ears.

"What was all that about?" I asked PJ as we hurried up the street and turned into a main road.

I expected, and reckoned I deserved, a pretty major explanation.

"It's complicated," she said.

"But –" I started, but PJ leaned towards me and placed her finger on my lips. "Trust me, it's better if you just leave it, Dom."

I'm not sure why I did it, but I bit her gently on the finger.

"You really are crazy," I said.

"Taxi!" screamed PJ.

Which would have been a pretty weird response,

except that a vacant taxi had just passed us. It stopped, and in no time at all, PJ had the back door open and was in the backseat.

"Well, what are you doing?" she said.

I looked up and down Frank Condon Drive. So ordinary. So creepy.

"I'm coming with you," I said.

"Well hop in then," she said, sliding over.

"Mater Hospital," she said, once I was next to her.

"Please," I added.

The taxi driver, I could see, was giving her the once-over in the rearview mirror.

"So you got the money for the fare?" he asked.

"Of course I've got the –" I started, but I didn't get to finish my sentence because PJ took out a fifty-dollar bill and tossed it onto the front seat.

"I reckon that might do the trick," she said.

The driver snatched up the money and did what he was supposed to do – he drove his taxi.

In the meantime PJ was leaning against me, and I felt the weight of her head on my shoulder. In about five seconds flat, she was asleep. Again I could see the taxi driver clocking us, his face a cartoon of disapproval.

I was just about to say something to him when I thought, why bother? PJ was safe. I was safe.

WEIRD HAPPENS

It had occurred to me, quite a few times actually, that as far as learning stuff went, The Debt had been a much better teacher than my incredibly expensive school. Without The Debt I wouldn't have learned about the generation of electricity, about the legend of Yamashita's Gold, how to hot-wire a bulldozer, how SMS messages are sent; without The Debt I wouldn't have learned lots of stuff. I reckoned The Debt had taught me a lot about the future – not what was going to happen, nobody knew that, but how to cope with the future. Because, let's face it, as exciting as the future is, it can do your head in. The Debt had taught me to expect anything, and everything, and while it was good to be prepared it wasn't good to be too prepared, to expect it to go logically, or smoothly. The Debt had taught me that weird happens, and weird happens often.

So as we sat in the taxi, PJ's sleeping head on my shoulder, my first impulse was to wake her up, fire off a whole lot of questions: who was the creepy man you told me not to ask about, why are we going to the hospital, who's at the hospital, and so on. But I had learned to keep my mouth shut; I knew these questions would be answered soon enough, that the best thing I could do right now was exactly what PJ was doing: relax. Let my adrenaline levels return to something like normal. I put my arm around PJ's shoulder, and leaned into her. It felt nice. It felt calm.

"Hospital," announced the driver.

Actually he said "hospedal," but I wasn't going to hold that against him.

PJ woke up.

She looked at me, puzzled, as if she couldn't quite recognize me. Then it must've all clicked into place, because she said, "Grammar Boy, let's go."

"How about the change?" I said to the driver.

"Fixed rate," he said.

"Fifty bucks?"

"Let him have it," said PJ. "Obviously he needs it more than I do."

PJ sure had a strange attitude to money, but she was already out of the door, so there was no time to argue.

I followed her into the hospital. From the way she negotiated the elevator, and the corridors, she'd obviously been here many times before.

When at last we stopped at a ward I wasn't surprised to see Brandon in one of the four beds. What did surprise me was how sick he looked.

He'd been thin for as long as I'd known him, but now he was, what was the word – emaciated. And white. Boy, was he white! Compared to him, sheets were grubby. Snow was dirty.

"Sis," he said, his voice soft and lispy. "What took you so long?"

"I had to see a dog about a man," she said.

This was obviously some sort of family joke, because he smiled; his teeth were scummy brown.

Then he noticed me.

"What's Grammar doing here?"

Not even a "boy" to go with it; for some reason it felt really insulting.

"He's helping," said PJ.

She turned to me. "Can you stay here? I've got to sort something out."

I didn't really want to stay with Brandon, but I didn't see that I had much choice. When PJ left, I took the opportunity to check out the ward.

Although there were three other beds in the room, only one of them was occupied. A man, maybe in his fifties, with lank long hair, was watching *Who Wants to be a Millionaire* on a portable television.

"So, you and my sis are an item or something?" said Brandon, in that winning way he had.

To think I had actually gone to the bother of saving him from drowning once.

"No, we're just friends," I said, and then, because I was feeling sort of angry that PJ had left me with her loser brother, I said, "what's wrong with you, anyway?"

"I've got an incurable disease," he said, in that typical joking tone. "I call it Paris Hilton, after Paris Hilton."

"Well done!" I said, happy to go along with the joke.

"Yeah, well, some of us are just born lucky, I s'pose."

"So let me guess," I said, going into a spooky voice. "You've got only six months to live."

His voice was even spookier. "Only two months to live, and then my brain is going to pretty much explode."

The *Who Wants to be a Millionaire* man looked over at us.

"Hey, can you delinquents keep it down?" he said. "This is a shared ward."

Brandon and I smiled at each other – him with his scummy teeth, me with my hopefully not scummy teeth, united in our delinquency.

PJ returned.

"They don't want you to leave," she said.

"They never want me to leave," said Brandon brightly. "But I always do."

"Is that your final answer?" asked the host on *Who Wants to be a Millionaire*.

TAVERNITI'S

Although everybody was waiting in the kitchen when I got home, it didn't really register that it was me they were waiting for.

"Der, like movie night," said Toby when I asked why they were all there.

"Der, and it's like your choice," added Miranda.

I considered losing movie night, but when I thought about it, getting totally involved in a movie didn't seem like such a – der – bad idea.

And when I thought about it even further, an after-movie dinner at Taverniti's didn't seem like such a – der – bad idea, either. Because I was sure the Tavernitis had something to do with The Debt. So by going there, maybe something would happen, maybe I would finally get the last installment. Maybe.

When the five of us arrived at the cinema I scanned the board, before finally deciding on an action movie called *Full Throttle!*

Miranda was appalled at my choice. "I can't watch something called *Full Throttle!*"

"Respect!" said Mom, which was shorthand for the cardinal rule of movie night: we must respect each other's choices, no matter how crap they were.

"Well, at least it's not subtitled," said Dad, throwing Miranda a look.

The last movie she'd chosen had been Korean and pretty much half the screen had been taken up with subtitles. It was like having to read a book where you didn't get to turn the pages.

Actually, *Full Throttle!* ended up being a pretty good action film.

But it was a really bad choice. Because instead of just letting it all wash over me, it got me thinking.

People die really, really easily in action films.

They get blown up.

Sharks eat them.

They get shot.

But as I watched these people getting blown up, eaten by sharks and shot, I couldn't help but ponder how, in real life, people don't die so easily.

After the movie was finished, we made our way outside. It was time for something to eat.

I could see it in everybody's faces: *not Taverniti's again. We're sick of the calamari fritti and the garlic bread and the spag bol.*

So when Dad said, as he always did after the

movie, "Where shall we put on the nose bag, then?" there were plenty of suggestions.

"There's supposed to be this great new Mexican at Broadbeach," said Toby.

"I'd just kill for some sushi," said Miranda.

"Just no carbs for *moi*," said Mom.

Dad held up both hands as if he was under siege and said, "Hold on, this isn't looking much like a consensus to me."

I said just one word: "Taverniti's."

My siblings looked at me like I'd totally betrayed them.

"Looks as if everybody's keen on somewhere different tonight, champ," said Dad, slapping me on the shoulder.

"May I remind you all of the rules of movie night," I said. "Not only does the person get to choose the movie, they also get to choose where to eat."

"But we always go to Taverniti's," said Toby, shifting into petulant mode.

"Good, then you'll be pretty familiar with the menu," I said.

"I guess rules are rules," said Dad, smiling at me. "We're going to Taverniti's, then."

We walked there in silence; well, a sort of silence, because there was a lot of low-level grumbling going on. But everybody seemed to brighten up when we arrived and got the same excellent service we always

43

did, maybe even better. And when the waiters insisted that Toby try some special bocconcini that had just come in from Italy he seemed to quickly forget how spagged out and totally bolled he'd been just a few minutes ago. Miranda just wasn't the type to bear a grudge, though it was her movie choice next week and I was pretty sure it would be death by subtitle. Mom still didn't seem happy, though. And it wasn't as if there weren't any carb-free options on the menu, either.

We had our entrees and it was all very normal, so I figured a visit to the bathroom was in order. Like the last time I was here, I walked past the bathroom to the door that led to the alley at the back, pushing it open.

There were cats everywhere, but no sign of old Mr. Taverniti. I'm not sure why I was so certain he'd be here, but I sure was disappointed that he wasn't. So disappointed I kicked the cooking oil drum he usually sat on. Which sent it rolling, rattling, down the alley, the cats skedaddling in all directions.

"*Sto arrivando!*" came a voice from down the alley.

And then old man Taverniti appeared from the gloom, buttoning up his fly.

"Sorry," I said, picking up the large oil drum and putting it back in its place.

He looked at me for a while before he finally said, "*Il corridore.*"

I remembered from last time that this was Calabrian for "the runner."

"*Si*," I said. "That's me."

Mr. Taverniti sat down on the drum and took some salami and a knife from his pocket.

What there was of his hair was all over the place, and he hadn't zipped up his fly completely; I wondered if he was starting to lose it a bit. Even before he'd started cutting up the salami, the cats had reappeared and were taking it in turns to rub against his legs, to purr encouragingly.

"*Essere paziente gattini*," he said to them. "*Voi tutti ottenere un pezzo.*"

Now that I was right in front of him, I knew my hunch had been right: it *was* Mr. Taverniti behind Mr. Havilland in the photo on Imogen's computer. Yes, it was a long time ago, but he hadn't really changed that much.

"Did you know Mr. Havilland?" I asked.

"Mr. Havilland?" he said, his accent as thick as the salami he was slicing. "*Il politico.*"

Even I recognized that word. "*Si*," I said. "*Si.*"

"*Ha avuto troppo avidi, quello.*"

"Sorry, I don't understand Calabrian," I said.

I took out my iPhone, turned on the Voice Memo function.

"Mr. Havilland?" I prompted. "*Il politico?*"

"*Ha avuto troppo avidi, quello,*" he repeated. "*Stava per rovinare tutto per tutti.*"

"What happened to Mr. Havilland?"

Again he answered in Calabrian: *"Ho ottenuto i ragazzi a prendersi cura di lui. Gli hanno dato un'altra bocca. Rocco e Ron e Gnocchi."*

But this time his words didn't just disappear into the salami-scented air, this time they ended up in the phone's memory.

"Is Mr. Havilland dead?" I asked.

There was no answer; instead the old man's eyes seemed to be focused on a point beyond me, behind me.

And he was now holding his knife by the blade.

His wrist flicked.

And the knife flew out of his hand.

My first thought was that it was headed for me, that I'd asked too many questions and was now going to be de-questioned, to have my larynx sliced open by a steel blade.

But the de-questioner flew past my nose and continued on its way.

I was able to twist my head quickly enough to see it hit its target: a huge glossy rat sitting on the top of a stack of crates. The rat squealed, staggered, and seemed to fall in slow motion.

Whoosh!

Another knife – slimmer, sharper looking – passed my face, almost trimming my eyebrows, and skewered the rat just before it hit the ground.

I turned back.

Rocco Taverniti, standing behind his father, had this look on his face – he was pretty pleased with himself.

And I couldn't blame him – that was some throw!

Old man Taverniti got off the drum, walked over to the rat, pulled both knives out and swiped them a couple of times on the side of his trousers, leaving the material smeared with fresh rat blood.

He held out the slimmer of the weapons to his son.

Taking the knife, Rocco flicked his wrist and this time I thought I really was a goner, that I was about to join the shish-kebabed rat on the stained concrete.

But the knife didn't leave his hand.

Instead the blade disappeared into the handle with the tiniest of *clunks*, and he put it back into his pocket.

He had a short conversation with his father in Calabrian before he turned to me. "He's an old man, my papa. These days his tongue is loose."

"He only talks in Italian," I said, not wanting him to think that old man Taverniti told me anything – all the knife play had left me unnerved.

Rocco smiled at that. "Calabrian, not Italian. But you're right."

He then steered me back to our table, taking the opportunity to have his customary conversation with the parental units, the usual blah blah blah old-people stuff, before he went off to greet some other customers. But later, after dessert, Dad disappeared for a while and I caught a glimpse of him up at the bar, talking with Rocco.

This conversation looked like anything but blah blah blah, however.

As if the evening hadn't been weird enough, later, as we drove home, Dad was in this strange, strange mood. He couldn't stop talking; we were going to do this, we were going to do that. As we pulled into the main gate of Halcyon Grove, he even said, "You know what, I reckon I might even get that plane I've been promising myself all these years."

As we got out of the car I could tell from the looks that Toby and Miranda were exchanging that they had picked up the same vibe.

But I had more pressing things to do than discuss our father's weirdness with my siblings.

I hurried to my room, where I transferred the mp3s from my iPhone to my computer's hard drive.

But how on earth was I going to translate it?

Yes, there was voice-recognition software available on the net, and lots of it, but I couldn't find any that understood Calabrian. Especially not the Calabrian spoken by an old man, in a dingy alley, with cats meowing like crazy in the background.

I downloaded TalkTrans, an open-source program that translated spoken Italian into English and tried that, running each of the mp3s through it. And all I got was a single word: "gnocchi."

Obviously, in order to really get somewhere, I needed to find somebody who spoke Calabrian fluently.

Dad?

Yeah, right.

And for sure anybody who spoke Calabrian on the Gold Coast would be connected to the Tavernitis somehow – they were that sort of family, like a mutant octopus, hundreds of tentacles creeping everywhere.

IM-O-GEN

Sleep: it just wasn't going to happen. Way too much stuff going on in my head. PJ. Old man Taverniti. The final installment.

I tried counting sheep – that didn't work. So I tried googling them instead. That didn't work, either, but I sure got to see some really woolly critters.

Then I got this idea in my sleep-deprived head that I needed to see Im-o-gen, she of the three syllables. Yes, the very same Im-o-gen who had sent me that terrible text message, and all those emails I'd been ignoring. I read the emails, and they all said basically the same thing: *I didn't mean to send that text message – we need to talk.*

So I tried texting her: *hi im, you awake?*

There was no reply, but given it was after 1 a.m. that didn't surprise me.

Leave it, Dom, I told myself.

But Dom, stubborn pig, wouldn't leave it.

Dom, stubborn pig, actually got out of bed, got dressed, and padded his way down the corridor.

At ten past one in the morning you don't really expect other family members to be awake. So when I heard noises coming from behind the closed door to Dad's office I was pretty surprised. I was also pretty intrigued, intrigued enough to stop right next to the door and bring my ear closer to the polished wood.

"I'm telling you, Roc, he's a loose cannon," I heard my father say.

There was silence, during which Roc obviously said something to my dad.

"No, but something needs to be done."

Again silence, during which I assumed Roc was talking to Dad. There was quite a lot of silence, so there must've been quite a lot of talking.

Eventually Dad said, "It's for the best, Roc. Let Art take care of it."

I'd heard enough, and as I made my way downstairs and out of the house there was plenty to think about.

Were they talking about old man Taverniti?

Was he the loose cannon?

When I reached Imogen's house, dark and forbidding, I realized how stupid my original plan had been. Did I really think I was going to sneak into a girl's house while she, and her mum, were sleeping?

Hello, pervert anybody?

I'd already decided that the best thing to do was just to go back home and go back to bed and try to sleep, when my phone beeped. The belated message from Im said: *yes awake*.

I texted her back: *can I see you?*

now?

i'm outside

ok, come through the back door

That's exactly what I did: ninja-ing along the side of the house, I entered through the unlocked back door. As I sneaked up the stairs, I was feeling excited. I hadn't really seen Imogen for ages, and here I was about to slip into her bedroom in the middle of the night.

Her bedroom with all its girl things, all its girl smells.

I knocked softly on her door.

There was a response from inside: "Come in."

I came in and Imogen was in her nightie, on her bed, the bedside lamp throwing a soft blanket of light over her.

And sitting cross-legged on the floor was Tristan.

I'm sure I'd been as surprised as this before in my life, in my previous fifteen and something years, but I just couldn't remember when.

What the blazes was Tristan doing here?

And more than that, what the blazes was he doing

looking like he was always here, that it was normal for him to be in Imogen's room in the middle of the night?

And if Tristan was surprised to see me rock up like this, he certainly didn't show it.

"How you doing, matey?" he said, reaching out his hand, going for one of those complicated sideways dude handshakes.

I'm not sure who got it wrong, me or him, but we ended up clashing knuckles.

"I'm cruisy," I said, not wanting Tristan to know just how cruisy I wasn't.

I noticed now that there was a huge version of that photo from her desktop, the one of her dad taken after the election victory, spread over the floor. And there were papers with lists of names, which I guessed was the stuff Joyless Joy Wheeler had sent her.

The faces in the photo were highlighted in yellow or green highlighter, and I wondered what those colors meant.

I studied them closer, and realized that I knew one of them – the green-highlighted man just to the right of Mr. Havilland was a younger version of Art Tabori.

Tristan must've noticed me looking, because he said, "We're getting closer."

We're getting closer?

"Tristan's been a great help," explained Imogen.

There are certain one-celled animals that have more brain power than Tristan Jazy – how could he possibly have been a great help?

If anybody had been a great help, it was me – I was the one who had blackmailed Joyless Joy into sending Imogen that material.

There's more stuff, I wanted to tell her. *In fact I've got a hard disk full of it!* But how to possibly explain that? Explain why I hadn't sent it to her earlier?

No, I needed something better, bigger, less complicated, more spectacular.

"I know who that is," I said, pointing to the face I had recognized in the blown-up photo.

"Arturo Tabori," said Tristan. "Born in Siderno, Italy in 1952. Immigrated to Australia in 1974, and –"

"Yes, okay," I said, talking over him. "You're obviously all over it."

Imogen gave me a look, a look I knew well – *Play nicely, you two!*

I scanned the faces again, concentrating on those highlighted in yellow. Something better, bigger, less complicated, more spectacular.

But then Imogen yawned in a theatrical sort of way.

I was the first to pick up on the cue. Looking at my watch I said, "Well, I guess it's time to go home. We can talk at another time, eh?"

Tristan also looked at his watch, but said nothing.

Now I felt like an idiot – I'd just committed myself

to leaving and Tristan hadn't. But surely Imogen wouldn't let him stay here, would she? It was almost 2 a.m.!

I stood up.

Again, Tristan didn't shift.

Surely.

I thought about saying something, something along the lines of: *We better let Im get some shut-eye*, or *Tristan, old chap, there's something private I'd like to discuss with you on the way out.*

But they sounded so absolutely naff I knew I couldn't.

I had no choice, I was committed to leaving, and Tristan wasn't. So I said good-bye to both of them and traipsed down the stairs, one agonizing step at a time.

It was only when I'd reached the door that something occurred to me.

I retraced my steps.

Re-knocked on the door.

"Dominic?" came the reply.

I pushed it open and – relief! – they were in exactly the same position as when I'd left them.

Imogen looked at me, a look of puzzlement and anger.

I had no choice.

"I can identify another one of those people for you," I said.

"You can?" said Imogen.

Tristan scoffed at that. "Really," he said. "Then why didn't you tell us that before?"

Though the question had come from Tristan, in possession of less brain power than certain single-celled organisms, it was actually a reasonable one – it deserved a reasonable answer.

I looked at Imogen – I would like to say that I looked into her eyes, but her eyes were impenetrable – and said, "Because I was scared."

"Scared of what?" said Tristan.

I couldn't quite believe that all this was getting played out in front of Tristan, of all people.

I looked at Imogen – the same question was on her face – *Scared of what?*

"My father was a member of the Labor Party," I said, and then I pointed to the obscured face in the photo, to the ear and curve of jaw that was highlighted yellow. "That's him right there."

FIRST DAY OF THE NEW SCHOOL YEAR

Mom dropped Toby and me off and suddenly we were in the middle of it, the craziness that was the first day of the new school year. There were kids gang-tackling other kids, desperate to tell them what a great/average/crap vacation they'd had. There were the new Year 7s, lost in their two-sizes-too-big uniforms, giving their mums one last lingering hug before they were chewed up by the monster that is high school. And there were the newly promoted seniors, the Year 12s, swaggering around, looking for the right target to terrorize.

And there was me, making slowly for the gates, thinking the same thing I'd thought for weeks: when was I going to get the last installment? Here we were, school had already started, and I only had those five letters branded on my thigh.

It really did feel like my life was on hold until The Debt had been repaid.

57

There was a thump of footsteps from behind, and Tristan appeared at my side, towering over me, putting his very heavy arm around my shoulders.

"So maybe you've got some more stuff for Im?" he said.

If he was going to persist in calling Imogen by my name for her I had to come up with something else, something that proved I was inner circle and he wasn't.

"Well, actually I've got quite a lot of stuff, but I just need to find it on my hard disk."

Any normal person would come up with a whole lot of questions: what stuff? Where did you get it?

Not Tristan, however.

"Okay, mate," he said. "But how about you put some effort in? Me and Im, we're on fire these days." He then made some very unnecessary smooching noises. "I practically sucked her face right off her head the other night."

Even if he was lying – which of course, he was – I still wanted to pretty much punch his head right off his shoulders.

"First base only," said Tristan, utilizing a really unnecessary sports analogy. "If you play your part, I reckon we'll be hitting a homer before the end of the term."

After I'd pretty much punched his head right off his shoulders, I imagined it rolling along the ground. And then – what fun! – some Year 7s playing soccer with it, smashing it into the back of the net!

With that, Tristan took off.

As I walked through the gates, Coach was waiting for me.

Okay, maybe she wasn't waiting for me, maybe she just happened to be standing there and I happened to be walking through. Maybe. But unlikely.

She was waiting for me.

"Coach?" I said.

"Champ," she said, though that word sounded as hollow as the cicadas I sometimes found on our front lawn; I hadn't run competitively for months now. "You ready to start training again?"

I looked at Coach standing there, and the lines that furrowed her brow seemed even deeper than they had been last year.

I remembered the story she'd told me, how she'd been a top-rated runner, but for some reason her career had gone nowhere. I even remembered what she had said then: *there's not a day that passes when I don't think about it; when I don't imagine what I could've bloody well been.*

Every now and then it had occurred to me that what The Debt was doing, above everything else, was taking me away from what I really loved in the world. And when I put everything else aside – the doctored photo, Mrs. Jenkins, all that stuff – what was left was one truth: I loved running. So why let them take that from me?

"I'm ready," I said.

It was as easy as that – I was running again.

The next person I ran into was Mr. Ryan, dressed as usual in chinos with creases so sharp you could slice cucumbers with them.

"Hi, Mr. Ryan," I said.

This time I really did think he just happened to be there, because he had nothing in particular to say except, "Welcome back, Dominic." And after that, "How's your dad doing?"

"He's good," I said, and then I made my way to the classroom.

My Year 10 class wasn't that different from my Year 9 class: Tristan was in it, and Bevan Milne, that bit of a turd, was in it, and Charles Bonthron was in it. No surprises there.

But when I saw who else was in it, I was pretty shocked.

"Rashid!" I said.

After he'd run in Afghani colors in the World Youth Games I guess I thought he'd have to live in Afghanistan now. Maybe even join the Taliban. Obviously not.

"That was some race in Rome!" he said, his voice full of excitement.

"Yeah, you were awesome," I said, and I really meant it.

"But you still recorded the best time," he said. "Four minutes exact."

Only Rashid would remember somebody else's time.

"I'll see you at training," I said.

We had the same homeroom teacher as last year: Mr. Travers.

He looked at me. I looked at him. He was about to say something, but he bit his tongue. We both knew that I wasn't going to forget what he'd posted on Facebook.

"Back at the moron factory, then?" I said, keeping my voice low.

He glared at me, but that's all he did.

There was the usual first day of term housekeeping, and then it was time for a welcome assembly.

We all filed into the Great Hall, took our seats. So far, so last year. But I guess it was sort of cool to be closer to the back now, to the seniors and their swagger.

Mr. Cranbrook looked the same as usual in his Italian suit. Sounded the same as usual with the care he gave to pronounce every syllable clearly. And if the speech he gave wasn't the same as last year's it was pretty darned close. Yes, Coast Grammar had a responsibility to every boy here. But likewise every boy here had a responsibility to Coast Grammar, to live up to the example that its former students had set. It was all about rights and it was all about responsibility.

Like Thor? I wondered, thinking of the former dux of the school who was now an ecoterrorist.

"And this year," Mr. Cranbrook enunciated, "we would like to welcome quite a number of overseas students to our school, a record total I believe."

Some lukewarm applause.

Mr. Cranbrook continued, "If those students would like to stand up, we can all have a better look at you."

The overseas students stood up. I wouldn't say Coast Grammar was a racist place, but put it this way: if you didn't surf, nobody really trusted you. And the blonder your hair, the more chance there was that you surfed.

"Come on, Coast Grammar, surely we can do better than that," said Mr. Cranbrook, switching into jolly mode. "A big round of applause for our overseas students!"

The applause was probably much warmer and much luker than before, but I wasn't really in much of a state to notice. Because standing just across the aisle from me was Droopy Eye.

At first I was sure I must be imagining this; how could Droopy Eye, somebody who belonged to the subterranean spaces of San Luca, possibly be in my school, as an *overseas student*?

But even when I kept looking, blinking a few times to make sure my eyes weren't clouded or anything,

Droopy Eye continued to be Droopy Eye.

He looked over at me, and I saw the smallest smile play on his lips.

It *was* Droopy Eye.

He brought his hand to his neck. Maybe he was adjusting his tie – after all those weeks of vacation, of wearing nothing but T-shirts and board shorts, a lot of kids were adjusting their ties – but maybe he wasn't, maybe he was drawing an imaginary knife across his neck.

AFTER-SCHOOL ACTIVITY

I was supposed to find my own way home after the first day of school, but I thought hey – why didn't I have me a coffee!

So instead of heading back to Halcyon Grove I went in the opposite direction, towards Cozzi's. I wasn't sure if I was feeling really adult or really try-hard – an after-school latte when you're only fifteen?

But the Droopy Eye thing had rocked me, and my body was telling me that it wanted caffeine and how can you argue with your body? Which, it occurred to me, is probably the same line of reasoning that millions of addicts all over the world use.

I caught a bus I didn't usually catch, one that was crowded with kids from Miami State High. They did the usual you-private-school me-public-school thing and I copped lots of smart-aleck comments and a few stray elbows in the ribs. Maybe, once, and not so long ago,

I would've been pretty scared. Not now, however. I'm not bragging or anything, but if you've been through what I've been through, if you've been stabbed, locked up underground, dropped in the middle of the sea, had half your fin bitten off by a great white, then you just don't scare so easily anymore.

Hey, my dad actually went to your high school, I wanted to say to them.

But I knew that would probably antagonize them even further – if Miami State was good enough for him, why wasn't it good enough for me? That sort of thing.

Once I got off the bus, I started walking.

As I did I had this sense that somebody was watching me. In this age of CCTV that's not unusual, somebody probably was watching me! But this wasn't a CCTV-type somebody-is-watching-me feeling, this was a real somebody-is-watching-me feeling.

The street I was walking along was busy, and there were a lot of people around. If you knew what you were doing it wouldn't be that difficult to follow someone and remain anonymous.

There wasn't much I could do – it was just a feeling, after all – but keep on walking.

It was a relief to reach Cozzi's, to slalom my way through all the people sitting on chairs outside and join the line inside. It was the same man serving as before, he of the perpetual five o'clock shadow. I mentally rehearsed my order. But there was no need, because when it was my turn he looked me up and down and said, "Triple espresso, right?"

Compared to this dude, elephants were forgetful.

Actually, I was going to order a latte, but once you've been pegged as a triple-shot-espresso sort of guy it's not easy to go all milk-based.

"You got it," I said in my best triple-espresso voice.

He smiled at me. Well, I think it was a smile; there was a change in lip shape and some teeth were definitely visible.

"Take a seat and Ferret'll find you," he said.

A tattered copy of today's *Gold Coast Bulletin* was on the table I sat down by. I did what I always did with newspapers and flicked to the sports section. There was nothing of interest.

So I read the comics. Not remotely funny.

I had a look at what movies were on. None of them took my fancy.

Finally I turned my attention to the front page.

Coast Housing Bubble to Burst? was the headline.

I read further.

Apparently, the housing market in Australia and especially the Gold Coast was in trouble. Low-collateral loans had been given to people with low incomes, but rates had risen and now those people couldn't afford the payments. Not only that, the market was in free fall, so the value of their houses was far less than their mortgages. This was so not my usual area of interest, but I couldn't help recalling what Mr. Jazy, Tristan's father, had said once about the whole of the market being one big Ponzi scheme.

And the final sentence was sort of chilling: *Could this result in the sort of civil unrest we saw during the Great Depression when people took to the streets, rioting?*

Ferret arrived with my coffee.

"That'll kick-start your day, amigo," he said which was exactly the same thing that Snake used to say. I wondered if Cozzi's had a manual of snappy sayings that each employee had to memorize.

"So Snake doesn't work here anymore?" I said. I wondered if, somehow, I had been responsible for that by uncovering the criminal conspiracy he had with Guzman and Nitmick.

Paying off the five installments had meant – what was that phrase? – collateral damage, that's it. How much collateral damage had there been?

"No, but he might as well," said Ferret, indicating a distant table with a tilt of his chin.

There were three men sitting around it: Snake, Guzman and Nitmick, and they were in deep conversation. And when I say deep, I mean deep, man; this looked like the sort of chin-wag that required scuba gear to move around in. And maybe it was entirely innocent, maybe they were discussing the relative merits of certain UFC fighters. Silva da Silva's amazing takedown rate. Or Brock the Rock's strike rate of over eighty percent. But somehow I doubted it. These guys were plotting something criminal.

And I felt a little disappointed, because I'd actually believed Nitmick when he'd told me that he was giving up crime to settle down with Eve Carides, the numismatist, and become Joe Citizen.

The three men got up and disappeared in different directions. I drank my espresso, one thermonuclear sip at a time, and as my brain synapses sparked, an electrical storm gathering in my head, I thought about Droopy Eye. Was it just a coincidence? It could be, because let's face it, anything could be a coincidence, but somehow that seemed really, really unlikely.

So why was Droopy Eye at my school?

The completely over-the-top answer to that question was: Droopy Eye was there to kill me. Other adjectives apart from over-the-top also came to mind: outlandish, ridiculous, melodramatic.

But since The Debt, wasn't that the sort of world I lived in, an outlandish, ridiculous, melodramatic one that was completely over the top?

"Youngblood!"

There was only one person in the whole world who called me by that name and, sure enough, when I looked up, there was Hound de Villiers, PI.

He was wearing triple denim again, a sartorial crime punishable with death by stoning in some countries.

"Hound!" I said.

I wouldn't say I was happy to see him – he was too scary for that – but I wasn't unhappy to see him, if you know what I mean. Maybe the way to put it is: having Hound de Villiers around made my life more interesting, it gave it texture.

"Back at school?" said Hound, taking in my uniform.

"First day," I said.

"Waste of time," he said.

"'He who opens a school door closes a prison,'" I said, quoting something he'd once said to me.

Hound smiled. "Kid, you've got a mind like a steel-trap and that's why I need you to come and work for me full time."

"Yeah, right," I said.

"I'm serious, here," said Hound, fixing me with his serious-here blue eyes. "School's just the place for some kids, but not for you."

It had never occurred to me that school was optional. And for sure, it had never occurred to my parents either. I doubted it had ever occurred to anybody but Hound de Villiers. Lateral thinker. Philosopher.

But now that he'd suggested it, now that the lose-school genie was out of its bottle, dancing its sexy dance, I was a bit excited. Maybe it was just all that caffeine, but the advantages of a school-free existence were pretty obvious. For a start, I would have more time when eventually I received the final installment.

"Youngblood, you still with me?" said Hound.

"Sorry," I said. "Got lost in my thoughts."

"Why don't you join me and my business associates?" said Hound, indicating a table nearby where a couple of men were sitting.

Actually, they looked more like gangsters than business associates, but, hey, who was I to judge?

"We've got some pretty exciting projects happening and there'd be plenty of scope for somebody with your particular skill set."

"Sure," I said, feeling flattered – despite the triple denim, Hound de Villiers had a pretty impressive skill set himself.

"Just one thing," said Hound, taking off his denim jacket. "Put this on, can you? Makes you look a bit less like a schoolboy."

I did as he asked. The jacket was about three sizes too big and I swam around in it like a goldfish in a goldfish bowl, but actually I did feel less like a schoolboy.

I shook hands with the business associates/ gangsters and we traded some small talk until I sensed it was time for me to leave.

"And remember," said Hound, gripping my hand, "that job's there waiting for you."

I went to walk off, but suddenly I remembered the jacket.

"Your jacket," I said, going to take it off.

"It's yours, Youngblood," said Hound.

All denim jackets are pretty nasty, I reckon, and this one had a touch of the stonewashed that made it even nastier than usual, but I can't say I wasn't chuffed to receive it.

I'd better get home, I thought. First day of school and all that. But as soon as I'd had that thought I had another one, which totally kicked the first thought's butt.

Why should I go home?

I'd been stabbed.

Why should I go home?

I'd been dropped in the middle of the sea.

Why should I go home?

I'd had electrical stimulation applied to my groin by two men in Shane Warne masks.

Why should I go home?

What was stopping me from heading to the spy shop, shooting the breeze with my very good Kiwi mate Hanley?

Nothing was stopping me.

So me and my nasty oversized denim jacket set off in that direction. And again, I had the feeling somebody was watching me.

Hound? I wondered. Was he having me tailed for some reason?

There were fewer pedestrians, on this street and to tell the truth it was starting to spook me a bit.

Or could it be The Debt?

Again it was a relief to reach my destination, the dinky little arcade with the spy shop and hurry inside.

The only customers were an older couple who had that typical Gold Coast sunbaked look, like a matching pair of leather sofas. Hanley was doing his usual hopeless job of selling them something.

"We're very worried about the escalating crime rate," said Mr. Sofa.

"The newspapers do tend to exaggerate a bit," said Hanley in his very entertaining Kiwi accent.

It was time for me to jump in.

"Some people up the road from us just got robbed," I said. "Actually, I think it was technically a home invasion."

The customers turned to me – this was more like it!

"A home invasion?" repeated Mrs. Sofa, keen to hear all the horrifying details.

"Apparently they came in through the window," I said.

"Was there any … any … bloodshed?"

"I'm not sure." I figured now was the time to go for the jugular. "But my dad said he was very glad he'd put in those perimeter alarms."

"Perimeter alarms?" said Mr. Sofa.

I looked over at Hanley: *time to take over, bru!*

Bru took a while, but finally he got it. "Oh, yes, we have several excellent perimeter systems here."

Hanley's cash register lived up to its name and the

Sofas left with an armful of hardware.

"You're amazing," said Hanley. "Did you know those poor people who were robbed? That sounds like a terrible experience."

"Sort of," I said.

"It's a pity you're still at school," he said. "I could do with somebody like you in here."

"Funny you should say that," I said.

I thought of that feeling I'd had, that I'd been watched. I thought of Droopy Eye, standing in the Great Hall, sworn to mortal revenge.

"*Il tuo sangue*," he'd said in Italy. *Your blood.*

"What would you recommend for personal protection?" I said.

"The pepper spray's still a very popular option – is there anything wrong?"

"No, it's for a friend of mine – she gets worried walking home through the park at night by herself."

I ended up buying the pepper spray – mate's rates, of course – and shoving it into the pocket of Hound's nasty denim jacket.

Of course, I would never need it, but I did feel a bit better with it there.

I had another mosey around the shop, and then went to check out what Hanley was doing.

He was tinkering with some piece of hardware, soldering away. Not for the first time it occurred to me how smart he was – software, hardware, he could do it all. I certainly wouldn't be running a funny little spy shop in a crappy arcade if I had sick skills like that. As I was watching him, I took in the other stuff on his desk: the other bits of hardware, the fine-precision tools, the well-thumbed technical papers.

The title of the top one caught my eye. I'd noticed the paper – "The Use of Multi-Sensor Data Fusion in Marine Archaeology" – last time, but it hadn't meant much to me then. But that was before I'd been on the *Argo*, before Felipe had told me all about a new sort of transducer, one that could transmit both acoustic waves and electromagnetic currents simultaneously.

I casually took the paper from the pile. Casually flicked through it.

The paper was heavily notated but on page five, written in the margin in Hanley's distinctive writing, was the word "Cerberus."

It took me a while to make sense of this, but when I did it hit me like a metric ton of bricks: Hanley worked for The Debt!

But of course he did. That's where their extraordinary technological expertise came from: ClamTop, Cerberus, all of that.

The spy shop was just a front.

Hanley looked up from his soldering, saw the paper I was reading, saw the look on my face, and immediately put two and two together.

"It's not what you think, Dom."

"Yes, it is – you work for them!" I said.

I wanted to test out the pepper spray right then and there, give him a face-full of it.

"I thought we were friends," I said.

"We are," he said.

I grabbed the piece of hardware he'd been working on and threw it across the shop and stormed out.

Maybe he wasn't actually part of The Debt. Maybe he just worked for them. But I didn't care – as I walked through Broadbeach, my body was hot with anger. The I'm-being-followed feeling was still there too. Was I just being paranoid? I mean, it was just a feeling, wasn't it? There was no empirical evidence to back it up, no confirmed sightings of dagger-bearing cloak-wearing men. Still, I kept my eyes peeled for taxis to hail, but it was change-of-shift time and there were none around; none that were vacant, anyway.

I joined the line at the bus stop.

The 393, my bus, approached, and then passed without stopping. The passengers at the windows all had the ha-ha-I'm-on-the-bus-and-you-aren't look on their faces. I waited another twenty minutes. Another 393 approached. Another 393 passed. Same look on the passengers' faces.

An old lady with blue hair said she was going to write a letter to the paper.

Fat lot of good that's going to do, old lady with blue

hair, I thought as I took off on foot.

Still no taxis.

But I had that same feeling, of being watched, of being clocked.

Dom, you're just being paranoid.

Maybe that wasn't even Droopy Eye you saw in the Great Hall today.

Just as I thought this they came at me, two of them, one tall, one short.

I had my pepper spray out in no time at all, was just about to give them a spray each, when the shorter one said, "Dom, it's us." Girl. Girl's voice.

The taller one said, "Don't shoot!" Boy. But still a girl's voice.

Immediately I knew who they were, but my mind was resisting that information.

No, it can't be them, it was telling me. *They stole Yamashita's Gold; they're sitting on some remote tropical island somewhere, doing whatever it is that really, really rich people do on remote tropical islands.*

"Dom, we need to go somewhere private now," whispered the person I didn't quite believe was Zoe.

"Really soon," said the person I didn't quite believe was Otto.

The evidence before my eyes – they looked like Zoe and Otto, they talked like Zoe and Otto – was getting the upper hand over my disbelief.

"Somewhere private?" I said, trying to shift my

brain up a few gears. "I know, follow me."

They kept on my heels as I hurried down one street, turned into another, down another and into a back entrance to Preacher's.

We took a couple of tracks, and pointing to the storm water drain I said, "In there."

"This is perfect," said Otto once we were inside. "How do you know about this place?"

I was just about to tell him how, but I held my tongue. That was another thing The Debt had taught me: knowledge is currency, you don't spend it unless you're in the market to buy something.

"I just do," I said.

Zoe had taken off her hoodie and even my mind was no longer resisting the available evidence: no denying her Zoeness, this was Zoe Zolton-Bander. Otto removed his cap and glasses. Same deal here: no denying his Ottoness, this was Otto Zolton-Bander aka the Zolt aka the Facebook Bandit.

For a second I allowed myself to be slightly starstruck. These were two of the most famous – or infamous – people in Australia right now, and I was with them. Not only that, they'd sought me out, and not the other way around.

But why?

There was so much we could talk about: Bones Zolton's camp, the storm at sea, the heist of the gold.

And there were a few questions I wouldn't mind asking them, either. Like had they set me up from the very beginning, because they knew their father had only the slimmest chance of bringing up the treasure?

Knowledge is currency – the shop was open, and it was their time to spend.

"So what's going on?" I said.

Otto looked at his sister. Zoe looked at her brother. There was a whole lot of wordless conversation going on, DNA conversing with DNA, none of which I was privy to.

Finally it was Otto who decided to go the verbal route. "The treasure is cursed!" he said.

"What treasure isn't?" I said flippantly, thinking of all those bad, and not so bad, movies I'd seen where the treasure always had the last say.

"No, it seriously is," said Zoe.

From the very first time I'd met Zoe, I'd pegged her as a pretty rational sort of human being – the-treasure-is-cursed didn't seem like her type of gig at all.

But there was something in both their eyes that told me that maybe I shouldn't be so flippant.

And when Otto said, "It killed my dad," I definitely knew I should take them more seriously.

It was a question that had been bothering me for a while, ever since Skip had told me that Bones jumped overboard before the *Hispaniola* had pulled into the wharf at Reverie Island.

"So Bones is dead?" I said.

Otto nodded.

"Dead dead?" I said, because Bones had been dead before.

"Dead dead," said Zoe.

"And it's touch and go with Mum," said Otto.

"Sorry, your mum?"

"She had a car accident, rolled it five times."

"She's in Brisbane, in intensive care," added Zoe.

Now I was getting to understand the the-treasure-is-cursed thing.

"So we need your help," said Otto.

My help!

These were perhaps the two richest teenagers in Australia and they needed *my* help?

That was ludicrous, for a start. But there was something else: why should I help them? I was pretty sure they'd played me like a ten-dollar Casio keyboard.

"Why me?"

"You're about the only person we trust," said Zoe.

"Plus, you're probably the most devious person we know," said Otto.

"He means cleverest," said Zoe.

If he meant cleverest, then why didn't he say it, Zoe Zolton-Bander?

Again, there was a whole lot of silence.

Finally, Otto cleared his throat and said, "We want to give Yamashita's Gold back to the owners. The treasure has brought our family nothing but misery."

"And that's why it needs to go back to who it belongs to," added Zoe.

The problem was, Yamashita's Gold had been looted sixty or seventy years ago by the Japanese forces who occupied the Philippines during the Second World War. How could you possibly give it back to the original owners, to all the people who'd had their valuables stolen? For a start, most of them would be dead.

It didn't make sense.

"So how in the blazes do you intend to do that?" I asked.

Again brother looked at sister, sister looked at brother, a whole lot of wordless communication.

"That's why we came to see you," said Zoe.

I didn't trust them, but I immediately sensed that there was something to be made from this.

I decided to string them along.

"Well, E. Lee Marx did mention this person," I said. "His name wa– I mean, is Roxas."

That much was true, but what I'd neglected to mention was that according to E. Lee Marx, this person had been killed on the orders of the president of the Philippines, Marcos.

"And you could contact this Roxas person?" asked Zoe.

"I don't see why not," I said.

And that's when they came at us, the pack of Warnies.

A PACK OF WARNIES

It happened so quickly, so unexpectedly, it took me quite a while to understand what was actually going on, to ask myself a few basic questions. Like, why were these Warnies attacking us? What did these Warnies want? And why were these Warnies Warnies?

I did have one thing in my favor as far as sorting this out went: I'd been kidnapped by a couple of Warnies during the repayment of the third installment.

In fact, one of these Warnies had applied a mild, though still terrifying, electric shock to my testicular area – not something you're likely to forget in a hurry.

I subsequently found out who one of those particular Warnies was: Cameron Jamison, resident of Reverie Island, boyhood friend of Bones Zolton and one of the major players in the obviously ongoing saga that was the search for Yamashita's Gold.

I didn't think any of these Warnies was actually

Cameron Jamison – this wasn't his type of work – but I'm pretty sure they were his employees. If my reasoning was sound, then it was probably also a fair guess that at least two of these Warnies were Mattners, Reverie Island's resident meatheads.

It was pretty obvious who the Warnies were after: Otto.

But the Zolt hadn't evaded capture for more than three years for nothing; he had long arms, long legs and some pretty nifty moves.

A Warnie moved in on him.

A Warnie copped a roundhouse kick to the head.

Another Warnie moved in.

This Warnie had his legs chopped out from under him.

Otto was outnumbered, though, and I knew that eventually they'd overpower him.

The thing about pepper spray is, it's more for self-defense than it is a primary attack weapon.

I couldn't imagine a line of soldiers advancing into battle, each holding a can of pepper spray.

But it was all I had, so I had to make do.

I'm pretty sure the Warnies had donned Warnie masks as a disguise rather than to protect them against any capsicum-based spray, but they did make my job a bit difficult.

I approached the first Warnie, the one who'd adopted more of a backup role.

"Excuse me!" I said, and sprayed him through one of the mask's eyeholes.

He screamed and de-Warnied himself, ripping off the mask.

I was right: this was one of the Mattners. Now that he was down, I gave him another dose in the other eye.

More screaming from the Mattner.

One down, three to go.

Another Warnie had Zoe in a regulation hammerlock, bending her arm up hard behind her back. There was nothing gentle about it, either.

"That hurts!" Zoe was screaming. "That hurts!"

I utilized the same technique, giving an eyehole a generous squirt.

This Warnie responded in pretty much the same way, screaming extravagantly. But unlike the other Warnie, this Warnie released the hammerlock and came at me, his arms thrashing wildly. Fortunately the spray had caused him to lose accuracy, and none of his many punches connected. I waited until he was open, got my hand through his guard, and gave his good eye a decent spray.

More screaming, and he dropped to the ground, writhing around like something you'd find in the primordial ooze.

If Hanley had still been my friend, I would've told him what an excellent product this was.

Two down, two to go.

Both the remaining Warnies had been so intent on capturing the very-hard-to-capture Otto that they hadn't noticed what had transpired in the background. I had the advantage of surprise.

I approached the bigger of the Warnies.

"Hey, you!" I yelled, hoping that he would turn so that I would have an eyehole to aim at.

He did exactly this. I aimed, I squirted, and somehow I missed, the spray hitting this Warnie in the nose and dribbling over his mouth with its shiny plastic teeth.

Then the Warnie's arm shot out and knocked the pepper spray clean out of my hand. It clattered to the ground. Rolling, rolling, rolling, it was headed for the edge and a plunge into the water.

I threw myself on the ground and just managed to lay a hand on the can before it disappeared. But now I had a problem. The Warnie was towering over me, droplets of the wasted pepper spray coming off his chin.

There was no way I could reach his eyes from where I was.

But there was somewhere I could reach.

Somewhere also known to be particularly sensitive.

I pushed myself off the ground, jammed the nozzle of the spray can against the Warnie's groin, pressed down hard, and kept pressing hard until there was no spray left.

The Warnie didn't immediately react, and I thought

I'd blown it.

But then he clutched at his groin, now soaked wet, and collapsed.

He didn't say anything, but even with the Warnie mask on I could see his eyes, see what they were saying: *How could you, a male, do that to one of your own?*

Short memory, fellow male.

Three down, one to go.

Otto was tiring now, and the last Warnie was getting the better of him.

I was thinking just how to approach this, when Zoe came out of the darkness, jumped on the Warnie's back and wrapped her arms around his eyes so that he couldn't see.

Otto then moved in and pummeled the Warnie in the guts with a series of vicious rabbit punches.

He dropped to the ground, winded.

None to go.

We were just moving in for a group hug when a voice came from behind: "Nice work, kids."

I looked around, and Cameron Jamison was there. And of course he was holding a gun and of course it was pointed at Otto.

"So, Otto, I guess you know what comes next?" said Cameron Jamison. "It's not the first time we've done this."

I could see that Otto's eyes were darting everywhere, looking for an escape route. But when the gun's aim shifted from him to Zoe he knew there wasn't one.

"He got away last time, remember?" I said.

Bang!

The gun went off. And a bullet whistled past my nose.

Whoa!

"So you think I have a credibility issue, young Silvagni?" he said.

"No, sir," I said, my heart beating like a mouse's heart.

"Let's go then," said Cameron.

I'm not sure exactly what happened next, because my eyes were mostly on Otto – I wanted to be sure he didn't make any dumb moves.

That was a real gun with real bullets that Cameron Jamison had there.

But here were footsteps, and sounds, and Cameron Jamison's gun was on the ground, and Cameron Jamison was writhing around clutching at his eyes.

And PJ was standing there, holding her can of pepper spray.

Behind her was Brandon.

"The Zolt?" she asked, looking at Otto. "Are you really the Zolt?"

Otto looked over at me.

I nodded.

"Yes, that's me," he said.

"I'm your biggest fan," said PJ, a starstruck note to her voice. "A real big fan."

Somebody's phone went off, a high-pitched drone sound, and Zoe's hand immediately reached into her pocket.

"Cops are coming," she said. "Somebody must've reported a gun going off."

We all took off, PJ and Brandon further into the tunnel, Zoe and Zolt into the bush, and I made for the track that PJ and I had taken that time, the one that led to the Preacher's car.

I hadn't done anything wrong. I hadn't broken any law.

But imagine trying to explain that to the police: *So these four Warnies came at us, okay …*

As I finally made my way back home I thought further about the Zolton-Banders. What game, exactly, were they playing? It didn't take me long, however, to decide that it didn't matter, because they could play it alone. Getting involved with those nutcases wasn't going to help me repay The Debt. Far from it.

QUITTING SCHOOL

If my fifteen-year-old son rocked up and said, "I'm quitting school," I'm not sure I'd laugh at him, like my mum did, but I'm pretty sure I wouldn't quite believe him. And if I was the older sister of that kid I would probably say something along the lines of "What a loser" too. And if I was the little brother of that kid I would also probably say something like, "Oh, how terribly dreary." Actually, I take that back – I would never, ever say something like, "Oh, how terribly dreary."

"I'm serious about this," I said to Mom as she prepared the vegetables for dinner.

"Darling, you can't just quit school."

"Why, because you've spent so much money on my education?" I said. "Or because quitting school will decrease my options in life?"

"No, because you're too young," said Mom, smiling at me. "You'd be breaking the law."

"I thought I could leave at fifteen."

"Once upon a time, maybe. But not now."

Mom would know, too, because as part of her charity work she was always dealing with juveniles, delinquent or otherwise.

She turned back to her peeling and I couldn't blame her – I had nothing more to say.

When my phone beeped, it was a pretty welcome diversion, because both my siblings were snickering at me. Maybe technically they weren't making snickering noises, but I knew that inside they were snickering like anything.

The message was from Imogen: *can we talk*

sure! when? I replied.

now?? came the reply.

after dinner was my answer.

ok was hers.

After dinner actually took much longer than I'd anticipated, because Dad arrived home unexpectedly.

"I'm afraid I have some bad news," he said, and he was definitely wearing his bad-news face.

He had everybody's attention.

"Mr. Taverniti, the old man, he passed away today."

Mom, Miranda and Toby all said the correct things.

"Oh, what a shame."

"He was such a nice man."

"He made the best gnocchi."

I don't think anybody was particularly devastated,

though. Old people die. It's mostly what they do.

But I couldn't help thinking about two conversations: the first, the one I'd had with him that night in the alley, the conversation that was still sitting on my iPhone, untranslated. And the second, the conversation I'd overheard – okay, eavesdropped – between Dad and Rocco Taverniti.

Surely they hadn't been talking about old man Taverniti. No person would ever discuss having their father "seen to." I must've gotten it wrong. As simple as that.

"The funeral's next week," said Dad. "Every Italian on the Coast will be there."

Soup was pretty somber, but during the main course the mood totally changed. Dad seemed to be on a high, cracking jokes left, right and center, making fun of everything and everybody, especially himself. I loved my dad when he was like this, we all did – he was such fun to be around.

It reminded me of when we were little kids and he'd spin us around, or he'd play zombies in the pool – "I'm going to eat your brain!" And when he was like this, Mom lightened up too.

"I'm going to give one of those planes a test spin on the weekend," he said. "Anybody want to come along?"

We all did, of course.

When Dad was in a mood like this, we'd go to the end of the world with him.

So when I eventually started walking to Imogen's house it was much later then I'd envisaged.

I was about halfway there, when something occurred to me: the last time I'd been to Imogen's room, I'd pretty much been humiliated by he-of-the-protozoan-brain, Tristan.

Why had that been? Because I hadn't been prepared. Well, even if Tristan wasn't going to be there, and I didn't think he was, I wasn't going unprepared this time.

I rushed back to my room, and downloaded a file onto a flash drive.

Now I was prepared.

When I knocked, Mrs. Havilland's voice came from behind the door.

"Who is it?"

"Dominic Silvagni," I said, though I wasn't quite sure why I felt the need to give her my full name. She had once changed my diapers, after all, wiped my bum and all that.

"Just a minute."

I could hear her unlocking the locks – there seemed to be even more than when I was last here. Eventually the door swung open and she was standing there.

The last time I'd see her it had been at Reverie Island, just before I'd been whisked away to look for Yamashita's Gold. She'd been "much better" then, though I hadn't thought she'd really looked "much better." But I guess even the fact that she'd managed to get away from the house had been a major breakthrough. But now she definitely didn't look "much better." If anything she looked "much, much worse."

"Oh, Dom," she said, and the fumes of alcohol reached out like tentacles. "Look how big and handsome you are."

I'm not sure what was so sad about me becoming so big and handsome, but she started sobbing. I didn't really know what to do except put my arms tentatively around her and say, "There, there." I wondered if Imogen was right, if finding out what happened to her husband was the key to beating Mrs. Havilland's sickness.

Could it be that simple?

I guessed there was only one way to find out.

Mrs. Havilland stepped back, flicking at her tears with her fingers. She seemed embarrassed by what had just happened. I didn't know what to do and wished Imogen would come and rescue me.

"You know you look just like your dad?" she said.

I didn't think I looked much like my dad at all, nobody did, but I wasn't going to say that.

"That's what everybody says," I said, and then something occurred to me. "What was my dad like back then?"

Something passed across her face, the same way

that a southerly storm sometimes sweeps across the coast on a warm summer's day.

"What's wrong, Mrs. Havilland?" I said.

She opened her mouth to say something, but Imogen appeared then.

As soon as she saw her mother, she moved into action.

"It's okay, Dom," she said, taking her mum by the hand. "I'll meet you upstairs, okay?"

It took her quite a while, maybe twenty minutes, to arrive, during which time I'd had a chance to check out some of the research she had done, all the newspaper clippings, the photos, the lists of names.

"Is your mum okay?" I asked.

"Not really," said Imogen, which is probably not what you expect somebody to say to a question like that. Mostly people just tell you rubbish, in order that you don't feel bad. Not Imogen, however. Or not this Imogen – the Imogen my Imogen seemed to have become while I'd been busy with The Debt. "But I gave her a shot of Valium and she's lying down now."

"You gave her a shot?" I said, holding an imaginary hypodermic.

Imogen nodded. "Nothing like a shot."

It was probably time to change the subject.

"It's incredible, what you've done," I said, indicating the papers spread throughout her room.

Imogen didn't seem to be in the mood for chitchat, however.

"Are you sure this person is your father?" she said, pointing to the figure with the hidden face in the election photo.

This was a bit strange coming from somebody who had accused my father of killing her father, but I knew where she was coming from: there wasn't much of his face visible.

"I'm sure," I said. And then I added, "So Tristan's not coming tonight?"

"Not tonight," she said, which immediately made me think that perhaps he'd been here last night and would be here tomorrow night. "How can you be so sure it's him?" she said.

"It looks like him," I said, but I could tell from her face that this wasn't enough for Imogen.

If I left it at that she would never truly believe that my dad was there on the stage the night Graham Havilland celebrated his election victory. The night he disappeared forever from the face of the earth.

I could feel the weight of the flash drive in my pocket.

My mind was a flurry of thoughts coming in from every direction, like surf in a storm. Poor Mrs. Havilland. Tristan and his putrid sports analogy. Thoughts colliding. Thoughts colluding. Imogen would never know.

My hand reached in, felt the flash drive. There was nothing extraordinary about it. Capacity 2 GB. Purchased at Woolworths. Just like millions of flash drives around the world. But I knew that what was on it could change our lives, send us both spinning off in different directions.

"I just can't find any record of your dad being there," said Imogen. "I mean, it doesn't make sense that he would be – like you say, he's always been so anti-Labor."

I brought out the flash drive. Held it out to Imogen.

She looked at it sitting there on my palm, and hesitated.

Did she know its power, too? Did she know it could send us spinning off in different directions?

She looked at me, her eyes latching on to mine. Then she dropped her gaze, taking in the flash drive. And then it was like she couldn't stand it any longer. She grabbed the flash drive and plugged it into her laptop.

There was only one document on it, a scan of the 1999 membership list.

She read it slowly, and then reread it. "Your father was a member of the Gold Coast Labor Party."

I nodded.

"He was there the night my dad disappeared?"

I nodded, but I felt I had to defend him.

"So were a lot of people," I said.

Imogen thought about this for a while.

"But why have they gone to so much trouble to erase his name from the records?" she said.

She had a good point, but I had a good response. "He was probably embarrassed, you know. Given how much he hates the Labor Party now. Like when I first went to high school, I actually joined the gamers' club for about a second."

Imogen smiled at that, but it was short-lived. She was almost immediately back into hyper-serious mode. "So where did you get this from?"

I thought of all the files I had on my hard disk at home, all the files I'd hacked from the Gold Coast Labor Party's mainframe. Who knew what else was there?

Again, that flurry of thoughts, colliding, colluding.

I thought of my dad tonight, what fun he'd been. This weekend he was probably going to buy a plane! How cool was that?

"I just found it," I said, checking my watch. "Hey, I got to go, okay?"

Imogen gave me a hug and I left. But as I walked towards my house, ablaze with light – was every light in the house on? – I was feeling guilty. Family is family. Blood is thicker than water. All those clichés were so true.

I'd owed Imogen that file, but that was all I was going to give her.

When I got back to my room I went straight to the computer, straight to the directory where I'd downloaded the Labor Party files.

And I deleted every one that mentioned my father.

But I knew that wasn't good enough, because a deleted file is easy to recover if you know what you're doing. I downloaded a program from the net called Obliterate and I obliterated everything in that directory until there was not a single byte, a single bit, left on the hard disk.

Blood is a lot thicker than water.

THE MEETING

The next day I was eating breakfast when my iPhone beeped: a text from an unknown number. All it said was *will be in touch*. Yes, it was about as anonymous as an anonymous text can be, but immediately I knew who it was from: the Zolton-Banders. *Whatever*, I thought. I'd already decided that they could work out how to give back their cursed treasure themselves.

And then my phone rang.

I checked the number; again it was *Unknown*.

Again I thought, *Whatever*, and put the phone down without answering. But it kept ringing and I couldn't help myself – I answered it.

"Dominic," said the robotic-sounding voice at the other end.

"That'd be me," I said, my mouth full of muesli. "Who is this?"

"We'd like you to come to a meeting," said Robo-voice.

We? I thought, but I didn't say it – I had a feeling I was supposed to know who "we" were.

"Sure," I said in what I hoped was a confident-sounding voice. "When did you have in mind?"

"Eleven o'clock this morning," said Robo-voice.

"I've got school this morning," I said.

Nothing from the other end, and then, "Okay, let's make it ten-thirty."

"But –" I started, but then I bit my tongue because I realized that Robo-voice had made some sort of joke.

I also realized that "I've got school this morning" was really no excuse at all, not for The Debt.

"That would suit me," I said. "And where should I come?"

"Sanctuary Cove Marina," said Robo-voice. "Pier Three."

He hung up before I had the chance to answer any questions, like where on Pier Three?

"We all ready?" said Mom. "The mommy bus leaves in five minutes."

What to do?

Feign sickness and then make my way to Sanctuary Cove from Halcyon Grove? Or go to school and then find my way from there?

"Dom?" said Mom. "You ready to leave?"

99

In the end I decided to go to school, to keep it as much like normal as possible. Coast Grammar prided itself on being the unditchable school, but I'd already dealt with that a few times.

I rushed upstairs to get my *Dummy's Guide to Ditching Grammar*, which was basically ClamTop and a change of clothes.

"Dom!" came Mom's voice from downstairs.

I shoved all this stuff into a bag and hurried downstairs.

As we drove, both my siblings had their faces in their iPhones and Mom took a call on her hands-free. Because she did this so often, these conversations had become a sort of white noise to me, sound without meaning.

But today, for some reason, my brain was actually processing what she was saying.

"Yes, Lee, I'll look into that. I'm sure it's just some electronic glitch. No, I realize how important that money is. Of course, I do. But there's not much I can do."

The call finished and Mom was straight into another one. This time the voice on the other end was more familiar to me. It was my dad's.

It still contained that tinge of excitement I'd detected in the last few days. "Sorry, darling, I've had to hold off on that payment for a while. I forgot to tell you, didn't I?"

"Forgot to tell me?" said Mom incredulously.

It was really weird to hear my parents talk about money, especially in this heated way, because they never did. We were rich – money wasn't a problem – end of story!

The conversation continued, but I think Mom must've realized that I was listening because she steered the conversation away from the financial. But when Dad mentioned the light plane he was going to test this weekend she practically blew a gasket.

"David, have you lost your grip on reality?" she said. "There's not going to be any light plane."

Actually she used another word between "light" and "plane" and I'm sure you can guess which one. Dad hung up.

Later, he said the phone dropped out, but I knew, and Mom knew, he'd just hung up.

By that time we'd arrived at the school and I really needed to get out of that car full of friction.

"Love ya, Mom," I said, cracking open the door and getting feet on footpath before Toby had even noticed that we'd arrived.

It was only as I watched the BMW wiggle its way into traffic that I realized I'd left my *Dummy's Guide to Ditching Grammar* inside.

"Crap," I said. And then, "Double Crap."

I really had no choice, so I joined the stream of students making for the front gates. Now I really did have a challenge: how to escape from school without my usual toolbox.

Ω   Ω   Ω

"Mr. Silvagni, did you hear what I said?"

Was that Mr. Travers talking to me? I looked up from my desk, where I'd been scribbling on a pad, coming up with crazier and crazier plans to get out of here.

Feign sickness?

All that would happen then was that I'd end up in the maximum security sick bay.

Pretend there was some emergency at home that required my presence?

Coast Grammar had that one covered as well – they'd fire off texts in all directions, making sure no one was telling porkies.

"Mr. Silvagni?" repeated Mr. Travers.

"Yes, Mr. Travers?"

"Did you hear what I said about a new student joining our class this morning?"

"No, sir, I'm afraid I didn't," I said, and as I did, once again it struck me how absolutely useless school was. Here I was playing stupid games with stupid teachers, while I could be doing something useful with my life, like working for Hound.

There was a rap on the door.

"That must be him now," said Mr. Travers. "Come in!"

It was the kid who used to have the neck brace

who used to have the eye patch who seemed to be now free of any such medical encumbrances. And with him was Droopy Eye.

Was I surprised?

Actually, not as much as you'd think, because I'd already figured that he could only be here for one reason: the Silvagni–Strangio feud.

I figured that he'd do anything he could – and he was obviously an incredibly resourceful individual – to get his revenge. Getting shifted to my class was a pretty logical move, I probably would've done the same myself if I'd been a homicidal nutjob like him.

Mr. Travers did his introduction thing. Droopy Eye's real name was, apparently, Francesco Strangio. Actually I already knew this, I just preferred to call him by the initial name I had for him. And even though he was a bit older than the other students in this class it had been decided that class 10T was a good fit – Mr. Travers's words – for our Italian guest. Now it was time for our Italian guest to tell us something about himself.

He was surprisingly truthful. He told us he came from San Luca. He told us that San Luca was a small town high in the mountains of Calabria.

"Do we have any questions for Francesco?" Mr. Travers asked.

Bevan Milne's hand shot up.

"Yes, Bevan?"

"What's your favorite pizza?"

"Plain," said Francesco.

"No pineapple?" said Bevan.

"No, no pineapple."

A murmur ran around the classroom – pizza without pineapple?

Other questions followed.

"Can you surf?"

"No, but I'd like to learn while I'm here."

"Why do your soccer players always fall over?"

"Because that is how we win so many World Cups."

"Mr. Silvagni, you have a question for our guest?"

"Sure," I said.

"Fire away."

"What do you know about the 'Ndrangheta?" I said. "Is it true that in Calabria where you come from they are much more powerful than the Mafia?"

"That really isn't the type of question –" started Mr. Travers, but Droopy Eye launched straight into an answer, and I'll have to give him this, Droopy Eye did not miss a beat – he really was one *cliente fresco*.

"Of course I have heard of this organization, but from my father's time. Maybe you have been watching too much television like perhaps *The Sopranos*," he said.

That got a few laughs and a huge nod of approval from Mr. Travers; Droopy Eye obviously wasn't one of those kids who "couldn't think their way out of a wet paper bag" he liked to Facebook about.

The bell went; it was time for the first class. When I glanced at my notebook and saw that it was math, my heart plummeted twenty floors.

How was that going to work? *Sorry, sir, a quadratic equation just fell on my foot and I really need to leave the school grounds.*

But then it was chemistry – something to work with at least.

By then I had it pegged anyway: the easiest, and quickest, way out of the school was in the back of an ambulance.

But to achieve that you had to have an injury that was ambulance-worthy.

Sorry, sir, but I have splitting headache, or *My tummy feels funny,* or *My stools are really loose,* just wasn't going to get you anywhere but the sick bay.

A broken leg would do the trick.

Likewise a broken arm.

But I was hoping I wouldn't have to get that broken.

Today, said Mr. Arvanitakis, we were going to reacquaint ourselves with the lab after all that time away.

First it was the Bunsen burners and he started rambling on about how dangerous they could be.

But I'd already tuned out of Radio Arvanitakis; I could see my ticket out of here.

First I had to get right at the back of the lab, away from his eyes. Not difficult – I asked to be excused to go to the bathroom and when I returned I parked myself there.

Then I had to light the Bunsen burner without anybody noticing – again not difficult, because Mr. Arvanitakis was making "elephant toothpaste" and all eyes were on him.

I got the Bunsen burner lit, and looked at the flame – so clean, almost friendly looking.

And I held out my hand so that the flame licked at my palm. *Closer*, I ordered the hand. It obeyed.

Now the flame was more than licking, it was eating, chewing my hand.

And the pain was ... well, it wasn't like the pain from the branding iron, that was sudden and brutal, and this was like pain breeding more pain breeding more pain.

My classmates were clapping: Mr. Arvanitakis and his elephant toothpaste had been a big hit.

But then Bevan Milne said, "What's that smell?"

And I quickly turned off the gas.

And I said, "Sir, I think I must've burned my hand," and I practically ran out of there because I didn't want Mr. Arvanitakis – who was a pretty cool teacher – to freak out.

Straight to the first aid room, and the school's well-oiled protocol kicked in and in no time I was in an ambulance with the school nurse and in no time I was in a hospital and in no time I was getting my burn seen to.

"Between first and second degree," said the doctor as I texted Luiz Antonio with my other hand. "You were very lucky, young man."

"Apparently your mother is on her way to pick you up," said the nurse.

"Can I go to the bathroom?" I asked the doctor.

"Of course."

I looked at the nurse.

"If you've got to go, you've got to go," she said.

From there it was too easy; I hurried past the bathroom and out of the door, to where Luiz Antonio was waiting in his taxi.

"You in the wars again?" he said.

"What are you waiting for, go!"

He went.

"So we headed anywhere in particular?" he said. "Or we just 'go'?"

"Sanctuary Cove," I said.

As we drove, that familiar song started playing and I thought, *I'm sick of this, all these charades, these games.*

"So how do you know Gus?" I said, with maybe a bit more demand in my voice than I'd intended.

"Who?"

"Don't be silly," I said. "Bad head, sick feet, you

both have the same taste in music. If it was Frank Sinatra or somebody like that, then I'd put it down to coincidence, but Brazilian samba? Not likely."

Luiz Antonio gave me a weary smile. "You probably think you've got us all worked out, do you?"

"Not at all," I replied, giving him my own version of the weary smile. "I just know that you know each other, and Gus is probably paying you to keep tabs on me, make sure I don't get into too much trouble."

"Well, if that's the case I'm not doing a very good job."

We hit a bit of traffic and Luiz Antonio said nothing as he concentrated on negotiating through it.

When we were on the other side of it he said, "If it wasn't for your grandfather I would be dead meat."

"*Carne fresca*," I said, almost automatically.

Luiz Antonio fixed me with a look that was pretty scary.

"Maybe you think Gus is one thing, but I know him as something else. I will say it again and it's all I will say: if it wasn't for him I would be dead."

By this time we'd reached our destination.

Sanctuary Cove was a gated community; like Halcyon Grove but with water.

The security guard, clipboard in his hand, peered in through the window in much the same way that Samsoni would peer in through the window at visitors to Halcyon Grove.

108

"Hello," he said. "Can I ask who you're visiting today?"

I had a complete mental blank.

He kept looking at me.

"Um," I said.

And my mental blank went even blanker. *Think of something. Anything.*

"The Debt," I said.

"You're visiting The Debt?" The polite tone in his voice had a tinge of something else now.

"That's right," I said, and suddenly it came to me: Bevan Milne lived in Sanctuary Cove.

"I'm here to see Bevan Milne," I said.

"Really?" said the security guard, and I half expected him to add, *But he's at school today* or *He's a bit of a turd, isn't he?*

But he didn't, of course, just got me to sign, and away we went.

Luiz followed the signs to the marina and we pulled up next to Pier Three.

"Today, I can't wait for you," he said.

"That's fine," I said, though actually I did feel a bit peeved: what did he have to do that was more important than waiting for me? Especially since it was my grandfather who was paying him.

The clouds that had been around earlier had broken apart and the sun was making an occasional appearance, flashing its shiny face. The air here

109

smelled so clean and fresh.

There was absolutely nobody around. Nobody. I walked down the creaking pier, checking out the boats tied up on either side. A seagull sitting atop a pylon cocked its head at me as I passed.

"I'm with you, gull," I said. "What's going on here?"

After my experiences during the last installment I'd been keeping away from boats. I wouldn't say I was scared of them, or I had a phobia about them; it was just that life seemed much simpler on land. The boats moored at Sanctuary Cove were very different from the rust-pot *Hispaniola* or the utilitarian *Argo*, however. There was a lot of gleaming chrome and a lot of shiny white leather.

I'd come to the end of the pier and had still not encountered a soul, and I wondered if, somehow, I'd gotten it wrong.

No, they'd definitely said Pier Three.

Was I being tested yet again?

I walked back down the pier, reading the name of each boat aloud.

"*Golden Lady*."

"*Boganous*."

"*Stymphalian*."

I stopped. Said it again, a bit louder this time.

A weird name for a boat, I thought, but there was

something familiar about the word. Where had I heard it before?

For some reason, Dr. Chakrabarty's face appeared on the smart screen of my mind. Okay, that much I got; I'd heard it from him, which sort of made sense – it was a Chakrabartian sort of word. But when, and in what context?

Was I going to have to go back over everything Dr. Chakrabarty had told me?

No, because I had Google!

I took out my iPhone and there was absolutely no reception.

How could that possibly be? This was Sanctuary Cove. This was the twenty-first century. And Google without reception is like a car without fuel. Actually, that's a really bad analogy. At least you can sit in a car without fuel. Make out in a car without fuel. Some chickens spend their whole lives living in a car without fuel.

No, Google without reception was like a car without a car.

So back to Dr. Chakrabarty.

And then it came to me: it was in Italy when he'd been talking about the twelve labors of Hercules.

What were they again? Slay the Nemean Lion. Slay the nine-headed Hydra. Capture the Golden Hind of Artemis. Capture the Boar with the crazy name. Clean the whatever stables in a single day. And coming in at number six, slay the Stymphalian Birds.

The sixth labor! This had to be it, I told myself, excitement mounting. This had to be the sixth installment.

"Hello?" I said. "Anybody there?"

No reply, only the lapping of the water. I took the ladder down to the *Stymphalian*'s stern.

"Hello?" I repeated. "Anybody there?"

The only reply was the water's. I tried the door. It was open. So I let myself inside.

This was a sort of lounge, with white leather couches and a bar. Again the interior was luxurious, but also weirdly impersonal, with nothing to indicate who owned this boat.

A couple more doors led from this room. I was deciding which one to choose when there was the rumble of an engine starting. The boat lurched forward. I hurried back out through the door, onto the stern.

Already we were five meters from the deserted pier, the powerful propellers churning the water into froth. I could've jumped over the side and swum for it, I suppose, but I figured that was the wet option, the dumb option.

Stay cool, I told myself. *Stay afloat*. There must be somebody else on the boat. I went back through the lounge to find them. Taking one of the doors, I followed a corridor. Through another door, and I was in the wheelhouse. The instruments were all glowing, the motors were thrumming, as the boat sped out into the open ocean.

"Is there anybody here?" I yelled, but there was absolutely no answer.

If there was somebody else on board, they certainly weren't making themselves known.

In front of us was a game-fishing boat – I could see the client sitting on the swivel chair on the back, cap on his head, rod in his hands, pot belly sticking out.

We were headed directly for them!

But just as I thought about doing something about it, like grabbing the wheel, there were a couple of whirs and the boat altered course. All very clever, but I was starting to get seriously peeved: what actually was the purpose of this little voyage?

If The Debt, if Hanley, thought it would make me marvel at their awesomeness, they were so wrong. It wasn't such a big deal; the US military used drones, unmanned aircraft, all the time. This was just an aquatic version.

"Dom," came Robo-voice over a loudspeaker.

I jumped. Not out of my skin, because that's not really possible, but I came pretty close.

"Dom," repeated Robo-voice.

This time I was able to offer an answer. "Yes?"

"You enjoying your little trip on the *Stymphalian*? There are some refreshments in the fridge should you feel like something."

Actually, I did feel like something, so I opened the fridge and helped myself to a Coke.

After I'd taken a sizeable swig I said, "So you can hear me?"

"Perfectly well."

"What is this about?"

"It's time for your final installment," said the voice.

Whoa! I knew it was coming, but it was still a shock to hear it stated so baldly like that.

The final installment, after which I would be free again.

"Okay, hit me with it," I said, and immediately regretted the unnecessary swagger.

I'd repaid the previous five installments – so what? That wouldn't mean a thing if I didn't nail this one. If I did a Gus.

My mind was racing: what would it be? Had they totally given up on Yamashita's Gold? Would I be asked to track it down? How easy would that be, I thought, given my recent meeting with the Zolton-Banders? The text I'd received only a few hours ago?

"First we'd like you to watch a little video," said Robo-voice.

As soon as he said this a screen mounted on the wall switched on. I finished the drink. I didn't usually drink Coke and I could immediately feel the effect on my body – the sugar, the caffeine, buzzing.

The *Stymphalian* continued heading out into the open sea at the same speed.

I found a seat; if I was going to watch a little video I figured I might as well do it in comfort.

The little video started and straightaway a couple of things became apparent: this was no Hollywood blockbuster screening.

It was made using old technology. No HD here. And whoever had made it was no professional; it was shaky, the zooming primitive. But they did go to some trouble to ascertain a couple of things. Firstly the setting – they actually zoomed in on the sign that said *Ibbotson Reserve*. And then the date. Suddenly we were looking at a newspaper, focusing on the writing on the top: *12 October 1983*. We kept moving, the camera shaking, through the park, down a path I'm pretty sure I knew from my running. And then we stopped.

It took a while to find focus again, but when it did, it became a bit clearer where we were. It was a sort of bush camp – I could make out a stone-ringed fire, and a type of shelter made with a tarpaulin.

The Preacher was my immediate thought. But it didn't look like the Preacher's camp. Still, it was 1983; the Preacher could've changed camps many times.

There were other questions as well. Who was the cameraman? Why was I being shown this very amateur video?

All weird, all strange – all pretty normal.

There was that whirring sound again, more urgent this time. I looked ahead: a huge ship, stacked with containers, was headed our way, but the *Stymphalian* was already veering away from it.

Thank God somebody's watching, I thought. My eyes were drawn back to the video.

A person had come into the frame now. Once again, I had that thought: *It's the Preacher.* But not for long. Yes, this person had long matted hair and was wearing dirty rags, but that would describe a whole lot of homeless people.

This particular homeless person was a whole lot smaller than the Preacher. The camera zoomed in on his face – my God, the camera work was terrible – closer and closer.

His face? It was a woman!

A homeless woman – what did the Americans call them? Bag ladies, that's right. Because they carried all these bags full of crap around with them. Actually, I'm not sure if she was a bag lady, I didn't see any bags around, but in my mind that's who she became: Bag Lady.

Bag Lady looked at the camera and smiled a gummy smile. She said something, too, but the sound quality – if you could call it that – was appalling and I couldn't make out her words. She didn't seem angry, though. Not like the Preacher, who got angry if anybody came near him. In fact, she seemed really pleased to see whoever it was who was filming her.

Then she reached out and took something, and instantly I knew the reason for the smile. It was a pizza box – I could even make out the name: Big Pete's Pizzas. She ripped off the top of the box and grabbed a slice of pizza and started cramming it into her mouth. She didn't have much in the way of table manners, but that didn't really matter – Bag Lady obviously hadn't eaten pizza in a long time; she was really loving it.

I was feeling pretty good about whoever it was who was filming, whoever had bought takeout for Bag Lady – he or she was obviously an okay person. But why did they have to film it? To show how okay they were?

Anyway, Bag Lady kept cramming pizza into her mouth and it was actually getting sort of gross.

My gaze wandered from the screen to outside of the boat. A flock of seagulls was off to the right, squawking, squabbling, dive-bombing the water. They'd obviously found a school of baitfish and were helping themselves to a feast.

When my eyes returned to the screen, things had changed. Bag Lady had stopped cramming pizza into her mouth. Although she still had a piece in her hand, it hung limply, the gooey cheese running off the end.

Her eyes were doing something weird, sort of lolling in her head. And then something was coming out of her mouth, this disgusting yellow froth. And then she was twitching, her shoulders, and her arms, and her legs.

Why wasn't the person filming doing anything? Instead of helping, he seemed to be zooming in closer and closer, capturing every horrible detail.

Bag Lady collapsed onto the ground. The twitching had stopped, but the disgusting foam was still oozing out of her mouth.

Why weren't they helping her?

Or was it some sort of made-up thing, was she some sort of an actor?

It had to be, I thought. Nobody would let another person suffer like that and not do anything.

The camera zoomed in and in.

Her face filled the whole screen.

Her eyes were closed.

The foam had stopped coming out of her mouth.

She was dead, or the actor who was portraying her was doing a very good job of playing dead.

The camera jerked back and I could see her whole body. She wasn't moving.

She really was dead, I thought. The pizza must've contained poison. Why was The Debt showing me this?

Then more shaky camera work until the camera was entirely still. Had they put it down somewhere?

All I could see were some blurred bushes in the background.

A few seconds of silence, of stillness. Some movement, and a face appeared.

The face of a teenage boy.

A face full of horror.

I knew the face, but I didn't want to know the face.

I did the math in my head.

Nineteen eighty-three.

He was born in 1968.

He was fifteen when this video was made.

I couldn't deny it any longer.

It was Dad.

And I'd just seen him murder somebody.

I moved closer to the screen.

My father ran his hand across his face, like he was wiping something away. The horror was now gone. And in its place was a mask. A blandness. He held up six fingers to the screen. Then the video stopped.

Robo-voice came back over the speaker, robotic as ever. "Dom, so you've seen our little video?"

I nodded.

"Dom, answer me!"

"Yes," I said.

"This is your sixth installment, all we need from you. We want you to prove who you are. We want you to take a life. Somebody useless, if you like. A burden on society. We don't care. But we need proof, Dom. We need proof."

With that the voice disappeared. The boat's engines cut. And there was the deepest silence, an abyss of silence, into which I wanted to fall and keep on falling until it was all over.

But then there was enormous sound. I looked up. A passenger liner was headed in our direction.

So what, I thought. *This is the best solution. Just let it come and smash me and the boat into a million little pieces.*

Because I cannot do that, cannot take another life.

I got it now. Although Dad had repaid the final installment, he'd repaid nothing. He would never be free of them, because they had the video, this proof that he'd committed murder. Any time they liked they could release the footage and he would be on the front page of every paper in Australia. They could release the video on the net and it would go viral like nothing else before it had gone viral.

Zoe had said it to me a couple of times: "You are so owned."

Not like my father is owned, Zoe. Not even close.

Another blast from the liner, this one rattling my eardrums. The *Stymphalian* rocked gently; the seagulls squawked in the distance. The liner was bearing down.

But they, The Debt, had invested too much in me to let me die.

"If you're trying to scare me, try harder," I said.

There was no reply.

"Can you hear me?" I said.

Again, no reply.

Maybe they weren't scaring me, maybe something had gone wrong, whatever technology they'd been using to drive the boat had failed them.

So I will die, I told myself. And that would be a lesson for them. They thought they could control people's lives. They thought they were omniscient. Well, they weren't.

They didn't own me.

Nobody did, except the deep dark sea.

The passenger liner kept coming.

Why didn't it stop? Why didn't it change direction?

I was still expecting there to be a sudden whirring sound and the engines to kick into life and the boat to surge, but nothing. Not even seagulls were squawking now; the baitfish must've disappeared.

An abyss of silence, into which I could fall and keep on falling until it was all over.

But suddenly Dr. Chakrabarty was in my head, talking up the labors of Hercules in that fruity voice of his. Telling me that the Stymphalian birds had beaks of bronze, that their feathers were made of metal and that they feasted on the flesh of men. Telling me that Hercules scared them out of the trees with a rattle that had been given to him by Athena, and then shot them with poisoned arrows.

Nice work, and all, Herc, but what good was that to me?

I heaved myself out of the chair and over to the controls. There were about a million of them!

First things first – I needed to start the motors. Eyes scanned the panel until they found what they were looking for: a key. I twisted it and there was a burble from below as the motor kicked into life. Now to get out of here.

I'd already noted the twin throttles and I'd been on enough boats lately to know how to use them.

Another earsplitting blast from the liner's horn.

Alright already!

I pushed the left throttle forward and the boat surged towards the liner. Not what I wanted!

Keeping the left throttle where it was, I pushed the right throttle a bit more. The boat veered to the left, away from the oncoming liner.

A bit more. It veered further away.

"Come on, boat," I urged.

The windows were full of liner, towering above me, but I knew that I was safe, that it had missed me by twenty or so meters. I didn't feel the elation I usually felt after a close shave; there was none of the usual adrenaline flooding my bloodstream.

All I could think about was the look of horror on my fifteen-year-old father's face.

COPS GALORE

Just as I was congratulating myself on my boating skills, I saw them through the binoculars, strung along the pier, waiting for me – coppers galore. Immediately I cut the engines.

I'd evaded the liner, I'd brought the *Stymphalian* back into Sanctuary Cove, and I was geeing myself up to berth the boat; it's not something I'd done before and it was a sizeable boat, but I was willing to give it a try of the red, hot and Aussie variety.

But now the cops had messed that all up.

I slowed the boat right down and thought about my options. It didn't take long, I didn't have many. The most sensible one was just to let them take me, then deal with the consequences.

Okay, that wasn't going to happen.

I couldn't get the cops involved – my life was already way too complicated, especially now that I'd been given this last dreadful installment.

Make a run for it?

The *Stymphalian* was a powerful boat, but the cops would just track it on radar, or follow in a chopper, until it ran out of fuel.

What other options did I have?

None came to mind, but I figured that a quick reccie of the boat might give me some ideas. So that's what I did, scuttling from the bow to the stern, from the bilge to the radar tower. And it worked – I found another option.

As far as plans went it was probably the craziest, the least likely to work that I'd ever had. But what choice did I have?

The first part was the decoy. I activated the EPIRB emergency beacon and tied it securely to the inflatable lifeboat. Using a corkscrew that I had found in the kitchen, I punctured the lifeboat's pontoons, four holes on either side. Then I launched the hissing lifeboat.

It floated off, the wind catching it, pushing it quite quickly away from the *Stymphalian*. Already I could see the pontoons deflating, and I wondered how long it would be until it sank, taking me with it, all the way to Davy Jones's locker.

In the meantime, while I was drowning, I had to get into my hiding place.

Ω Ω Ω

I checked my watch – I'd been in this same position for hours now, breathing in this stale, stale air, while the cops had boarded, while they'd searched the boat, while they'd brought it back to shore. My legs were killing me – *Why are you doing this to us?* they were demanding. We'd been berthed for over an hour and I hadn't heard any major sounds – cars, footsteps, people talking – for at least half of that time. So I figured it was time to get myself and my suffering legs out of this locker, or whatever it was called.

I pushed away the life jackets that had covered me, pushed the rescue flares to one side, and eased myself forward. Blood found its way back into my legs. I pushed open the door, half expecting somebody to be standing there, arms folded: a stony-faced cop who'd known I was there all along. Or a dog, one of those sniffy Alsatians.

No, the cabin was as empty as when I'd entered it hours ago.

It was probably still too early to say whether my crazy plan had worked, but I did allow myself the teeniest-weeniest congratulations; it had worked in principle anyway. I retraced my steps back out of the cabin, back along the corridor, keeping both ears open.

No sounds apart from the usual boat sounds, the creaking and the slapping of waves.

I knew we were berthed, but I wondered where.

Maybe the *Stymphalian* had been impounded by the cops and we were now in some sort of police facility.

I reached the door that led out to the open stern deck. I really didn't want to expose myself like this, but I didn't see that I had much choice – there was really no other way to get off the boat. I pushed the door open until I had a crack big enough to look through. Okay, we were at Sanctuary Cove – that had to be a good thing. But blazing bells and buckets of blood, it was just as I'd feared – there were still cops around, two of them standing up on the pier.

Why did it always have to be so difficult?

"This really sucks," I heard one cop say to the other.

"Tell me about it," said the other. "You join the police for excitement and adventure, and you end up spending most of your time standing around."

More moaning from the cops.

How to get past them? And then it came to me – their life was just about to get a whole lot more exciting.

Back down the way I came, I grabbed the rescue flares and hurried into the wheelhouse, first making sure nobody was in there. I partially opened one of the windows and then pulled the cords on all four flares. Immediately thick red smoke started pouring from them, flooding the wheelhouse.

I hurried back to the stern of the boat, again looking through the partially opened door.

The cops were still complaining. "The other day I sat at a roadblock for the whole of my shift and did nothing! Absolutely nothing!"

"Sucks!" said the second cop.

"And –" but further moaning was curtailed by ribbons of thick red smoke streaming from the wheelhouse window.

"What the blazes is that?" the first cop said, already making for the ladder onto the boat. The other cop was right behind him. This was what they'd joined the force for!

I stepped into the bathroom – sorry, the head. The two cops hurried past me and I easily made my escape, scaling the ladder and running back down the pier. It had occurred to me that there might be more coppers at the other end, but I was fine, there was nobody, just an empty cop car.

I only had one more problem: Sanctuary Cove was a gated community. Difficult to get into, difficult to get out of.

How to make a graceful exit? I searched my brain, but there was nothing there, no plans, no deviousness. Even Luiz Antonio, my usual getaway wasn't going to be much use to me in here.

I approached the gatehouse and the security guard came out, all uniform and officiousness. And I knew I wouldn't be able to explain it away, I knew I couldn't be bothered spouting lie after stupid lie. So I just ran at him, out of the blocks like an insane Usain Bolt, screaming my lungs out, legs pumping, arms swinging.

I didn't dodge, I didn't swerve, I headed straight at him, still screaming, gaining momentum.

And it worked – he removed himself from my trajectory.

I kept running through the gateway and out into the road, keeping to the shadows as much as I could. I couldn't believe how good it felt, like I was outrunning all my problems. They couldn't keep up with me; I surged to the lead.

A few taxis passed, but I didn't bother hailing one – why catch a cab when you could run like this?

Really, I shouldn't have been running as well as I was – I'd hardly trained at all. But it was like I was back at Stadio Olimpico, front-running in that semifinal, the one in which I ran my PB.

I reached Chevron Heights in what seemed like no time at all. Breath flowing freely, legs feeling fine, I actually increased the pace. I only stopped when I pulled up at the main gate to Halcyon Grove. Bent double, I started sucking up some big ones.

It was right then that Mom pulled up in her BMW.

She was out of the car in no time at all. Screaming at me.

"Calm down," I said. "Calm down."

Samsoni was saying the same thing. "Calm down, Mrs. Silvagni. Calm down."

I had never, ever seen Mom like that, she'd lost it; her composure, her temper, whatever you called it, she was no longer in possession of it.

Eventually I was able to understand what she was saying.

"I was supposed to pick you up at the hospital," she said.

For the tiniest second I actually didn't know what she was talking about, but then I saw my bandaged hand – oh, that hospital.

"It looks much worse than it is," I said.

And it was like the burn took offense at that, because straightaway it started throbbing.

"But where have you been?"

I shrugged – *Mom, you really don't want to know.*

And then she was crying, and poor Samsoni was trying to console her.

A car pulled in behind Mom's car – I think it might have been Mrs. Jazy – and its horn gently beeped.

Not a good move.

Mom picked up the umbrella that Samsoni kept just inside the door and went over and started bashing at the car.

Samsoni managed to get her away.

And then she seemed to run completely out of angry tickets. She just stood there, shaking.

"Mom, you okay?" I said, putting my arms around her.

"Dom, what are we going to do?" she said, sinking, melting into me.

And perhaps for the first time since that terrible day when The Debt came into my life I realized that it wasn't just about me, that it wasn't only my leg or my life that was in danger, it was our whole family.

"We're going to get through it," I said.

"We are?" she said.

"We are," I said, emphasizing the "we."

We got into the car, and Mom, silent, still shaking, drove slowly home.

But when we got out, I didn't make for the front door.

"Dom, where do you think you're going?" said Mom.

"Over to see Gus."

"Your dad will want to talk to you about this," she said, holding out her phone.

I'd forgotten, Dad was away for the night – some business trip to Sydney, or Melbourne, one of those places.

"He knows my number," I said. "I need to go over and see Gus."

"But –" said Mom, but the rest of her words didn't make it to me because I was already halfway there.

I could hear the techno beat even before I reached the house; I knew Gus must be out in his shed, pumping tin.

Sure enough, as I walked around the house, the music getting louder, I could see the open shed door.

"Gus, it's me!" I yelled, giving him plenty of notice so as not to scare the bejesus out of him.

"Gotcha!" came the reply.

When I walked in, he was in the middle of a set of bicep curls. Dressed in his customary tank top and baggy old army shorts, he was perched at the end of a bench. Head steady, elbows tucked in – he was a study in style as he slowly pumped the bar back and up, his bicep muscles popping.

Overhead the fan spun, but its effect was negligible; the air felt heavy, unmovable. My phone rang – *Dad calling* – but I didn't answer.

"What happened there?" said Gus, pointing to my bandage.

"Looks worse than it is," I said. "Bunsen burner. Mind if I jump in here?"

"You sure?" said Gus. "You don't want to stir it up."

"Sure, I'm sure," I said – it wasn't as if I was unused to burns, and Gus should've known that; he'd been there for five of them.

I picked up the bar and the burn burned and my immediate thought was, *There is no way I'm going to be able to do this.*

"Knees soft," said Gus.

Eight, I told myself. *If I make eight then I've done really well.*

The first three reps were okay, the next two not so okay, and at the sixth I began to really struggle.

I'm not even going to make eight, I told myself.

"Looking good," said Gus. "Keep it going."

Looking good? Really? Because I wasn't feeling good, my biceps were hurting big-time, and the burn was piling pain upon pain. And I so wanted to bring my back into it. But I toughed out the sixth, and somehow got the seventh up, and I had only one to go. Some more encouragement from Gus, and slowly the bar moved up until it eventually touched my chest.

I'd done it.

"Keep it going," said Gus. "Two to go!"

My body was telling me one thing: enough already. Gus was telling me another: two to go. Who should I listen to?

"Let's go!" ordered Gus.

I started curling the bar upwards – hurt like crazy, hurt like crazy.

"Keep your back straight," said Gus, placing his hand lightly on the small of my back.

The bar kept moving, slowly, ever so slowly upwards. Sweat was popping from my brow. And I was grunting.

Look, I've never been much of a grunter, but there was no doubt that the noise emanating from my mouth was a fairly primitive grunt.

"Almost there!"

One final effort, and I was there! I smiled at my grandfather.

He didn't smile back. "One to go," he said.

What for? What was I trying to prove?

"Just one to go," said Gus.

And, almost independently of me, and my will, the bar was starting to rise. My biceps, burning before, were now on fire. The grunting had reached French Open final levels. I looked at the bandage on my hand – blood was seeping through.

Gus was standing directly in front of me, his eyes on my eyes.

"Almost," he said. "Almost."

But it was no good, the bar was too heavy, gravity was winning, I was stuck about three-quarters of the way up.

Gus placed his index finger under the middle of the bar. "You can do it."

I summoned every last bit of energy and gave one final effort. The bar rose, and rose, and touched my chest.

I'd done it!

Ten reps!

I put the bar down with a clang, and got my high-fives from Gus.

"But I didn't really do it myself," I said, remembering Gus's finger on the bar.

"Rubbish," he said. "I was touching it, that's all. It's all in your head, son."

We sat there for a while, long enough for the techno to finish, so that there was nothing but silence. And in Gus's shed, silence was silence, there wasn't much else contributing to the soundscape, except the *whoosh-whoosh-whoosh* of the fan overhead.

Finally Gus stomped off and came back with a first aid kit.

"I better change that," he said, pointing at the bandage. "Your mother will freak."

"Freak" wasn't a very Gus-like word. But he was right about that, and she'd already done enough freaking today; any more would be unfair.

"Can you tell me about the final installment?" I said, when he'd finished.

Gus scratched the side of his face. "You're ready to know?"

I nodded. I was ready.

"It was the final race of the season," he said in his low gritty voice. "The national title, Schoolboy's Miler."

Already, I'd learned something new, something startling: Gus had competed for a national title!

He continued, "A hundred or so yards to go and there was nothing between me and the Victorian, the favorite. He was a big strong lad, much bigger than me. From one of those posh private schools

135

in Melbourne. And it seemed like everybody from Melbourne had come up and was in the stadium cheering him on. With fifty yards to go, I kicked, and I kicked hard. And the crowd, it just went silent. It was such a thing, from all that noise to nothing. He couldn't go with me. In the end I won it quite easily, by ten or so yards."

I interrupted, I couldn't help myself. "You were Australian champion?"

Gus nodded.

"Later, they disqualified me – some technicality, something to do with my registration. But, yes, I beat him fair and square, I was Australian champ." Gus took a drink of water from a plastic bottle. "I was supposed to meet a Mr. Tippett after the race, one of the Olympic selectors. They were trying to find a way to stop me going professional. You see, in those days, if you raced for money you weren't allowed in the Olympics. But a kid from my sort of background, I didn't have much choice."

"Wow!" I said. "An Olympic selector."

"I didn't meet him," said Gus. "I caught the bus home."

"To Berang Valley?" I said, thinking of the lawyer vine-choked place we'd visited a few days ago.

Gus nodded. "To the valley."

Only three words, but they seemed so ominous – *to the valley*. I could sort of guess what was coming next, and I wasn't sure I was ready to hear it, but I had to. I'd seen my dad kill somebody, and I needed to find out why Gus hadn't.

When Gus continued, his voice seemed lower, even grittier. "The bus dropped me off and I got my bike from where I used to hide it under a bush and I started pedaling. There was no moon that night, only a few stars out. And when it was dark in the valley, it was dark." Gus took another drink of water, swigging hard, smacking his lips, like it was whisky or rum, not water. But no words came.

"Gus?" I said. "What happened then?"

"Remember the church we saw?" he said.

I nodded.

"Well, I was cycling past that, but I kept my eyes on the other side of the road. I didn't want to see it. When I was well past the bridge, I risked a glance backwards. And there was this cross just floating there, shining. I'm not sure if I imagined it or it was a trick of the light, but it turned my guts to ice. And in my mind I could see Father McGrane, standing at the pulpit, his face getting redder and redder as he thundered from the Bible, 'Whoever sheds the blood of man, by man shall his blood be shed, for God made man in his own image!'"

For a second it was the Preacher, not Gus, standing in front of me.

His voice returned to normal as he said, "And then I went to check that Panda was home."

"Panda?" I said.

"Pandolfini, Greek cane farmer. Evil. His son was one of my mates, used to come to school black and blue every second day. And his sister, well ..." Suddenly Gus's face drained of all color and I wondered if I was doing the right thing provoking him like this, asking him to revisit what was obviously a horrific time of his life. "Anyway, I'd been feeding their dog every day, so he was friendly with me, no barking. Panda was there, getting drunk as usual. So I kept riding and when I got home, Alessandro was waiting for me."

"Your brother?" I said.

Gus nodded – *my brother*.

I remembered what the Preacher had said on his deathbed: *My twin was an angel*. And Gus had agreed: *An angel*.

Gus continued, and I reminded myself not to interrupt him any more. "When he found out that I won, he was so excited, of course. But that was Alessandro for you, the sweetest kid there ever was."

I thought of the photo I'd seen in the Tabori crypt – what had happened to Alessandro? Or was that something I didn't want to know?

"Inside the house, it was a different story, however," said Gus.

Again he took a swig of water, draining the bottle.

"I walked inside and Momma and Antonio were

sitting at the table, doing what they always did, studying the Bible."

"Antonio? The Preacher?"

Gus nodded and continued talking. "I hated that black book, the power it had over those two. How it would take them away from the rest of us."

Even now, so many years later, I could hear the hate still there in his voice.

"Alessandro couldn't help himself, he had to blurt all about me winning, but Momma was never interested in running. I wanted to tell Papa so I went outside, followed the path through the cane to the shed."

Again, Gus seemed lost in the past and it took him a while to pick up the thread again. "Papa had finished sharpening the cane knives and was playing the mouth organ."

I remembered what he'd told me that day in Berang Valley, how his father had been a gifted musician before they'd taken his arm from him.

"I told him about winning, and he hugged me. That was maybe the only time my father ever touched me like that. I told him that tonight was the night, that it was time to pay back the final installment. And my father, who had spent his whole life hacking at sugarcane with one arm, told me that I was stronger than him."

The tears were glistening in Gus's eyes.

"You don't have to go on," I said.

"Yes, I do," said Gus. "Just give me a second."

It took him a few more seconds, maybe twenty, before he could continue. "I went to bed that night but I didn't sleep – how could I? And at two, I got out of bed. I already had my flashlight. I went back to the shed, picked out a knife. And then I hopped on my bike. It was about a fifteen-minute ride to his house. When I got there I leaned my bike against the post and walked up the driveway. A half-moon had risen and I had no trouble seeing."

I knew I'd promised not to interrupt, but I couldn't help myself. "What were you thinking? Were you scared?"

Gus considered my question for a while.

"Actually, I was just thinking practicalities," he said. "Should I have hidden the bike? Will the knife be sharp enough? Where to get rid of it, after."

Practical stuff, I thought. Focus on the practical stuff.

Gus continued, "As I got closer I could hear him snoring. I had no excuse: he was there, I had to do what I'd set out to do. I pushed aside the burlap that served as the door. Panda was splayed out on the mattress, face up. I moved closer, tightening my grip on the cane knife. Next to Panda's head I could see an empty bottle of rum. A herd of elephants wouldn't have woken him. And then I was standing next to him, smelling his putrid smell."

Gus's noise wrinkled, as if he was smelling that smell again.

"One more installment and I would be free of The Debt forever. I thought of poor Bill's bruises. That look on his sister's face. If anybody deserved this, it was that fat pig. I knew that the police wouldn't look too hard. Panda was hated from one end of the valley to the other; there must've been a dozen men who would've gladly done what I intended to do.

"I planted my feet apart and lifted the knife up high. I'd slashed cane, I'd taken the heads off chickens; I knew what was needed. The cane knife high above my head, I hesitated. I couldn't stop thinking of that cross, how it glowed in the dark. I thought of Father McGrane's words. But one more installment. One simple act. And I would be free of The Debt forever. And the world would be rid of evil.

"I brought that knife down with both arms and could imagine how it felt meeting flesh, and gristle, and then bone. But as it came down, something dragged my arm away and the knife sliced into the pillow. Even then Panda didn't wake, didn't even stir. Again I raised the cane knife high, but it was no good. I couldn't do it. I ran out of there and got onto my bike and I pedaled and I pedaled and I pedaled."

We both sat there, said nothing. The bar at our feet, the one we'd used for the bicep curls, seemed to be looking at us, mocking us. *Not so tough now, eh, fellas?*

Gus looked at me. "Two days later, when I was swimming down at the beach, they came at me."

I knew that story, I didn't want to know any more.

"And a month later she was dead."

This, I didn't know.

"Who was dead?"

Gus looked at me, his eyes wide.

"Bill's sister, Elizabeth, the girl whose gravestone you saw in the cemetery. Panda beat her to death. His own daughter. He went to jail, and he lasted about a week in there. Rough justice, they slit his filthy throat."

DARK NIGHT OF THE SOUL

Slowly, ever so slowly, the night ticked away, getting darker and darker, blacker and blacker.

The burn on my hand ached.

I replayed my father's video over and over in my mind.

I retold Gus's story over and over in my mind.

So many times that eventually they got mixed up, like some twisted mash-up – Bag Lady became Panda, Panda the Bag Lady. One lives. The other dies. They both live, and they both die.

I had never been so utterly, terribly alone.

Who could I talk to?

My parents? Sure.

I wasn't sure who they were anymore. Was my mother Italian? My father a cold-blooded killer?

My friends? lol.

The night ticked away, getting darker and darker.

Is killing another human being ever justified?

I could google it.

Actually, I did google it.

Yes, it is, said some people.

No, it's not, said others.

How can you judge who is to live or not? said some other people. Only God can do that.

Is killing another human being ever justified?

I thought of Gus, Australian champion, before they disqualified him. He hadn't told me, but I looked it up: the Victorian he beat in that final went on to win a silver medal at the Commonwealth Games.

I thought of that gravestone, Bill's sister moldering in the ground underneath. If Gus's arm had come down straight and true, and that cane knife had sliced through flesh, gristle, bone, then she would've lived. Maybe she would be alive today; a happy old woman, somebody who had – like a lot of people – gone beyond the misery of their childhood. Maybe she would've had children of her own, and grandchildren. Maybe she'd bake banana cakes or rescue injured wildlife.

But what about Bag Lady? I was pretty sure she hadn't killed anybody, wasn't about to kill anybody, when my dad poisoned her. There was nothing justifiable about that homicide. Or was she, as Robo-voice had said, just a piece of trash, a burden on society?

The night ticked away, getting darker and darker.

Is killing another human being ever justified?

Is killing another human being ever justified?

Is killing another human being ever justified?

Light started to creep into the corners of my room. I had to do something.

A run, I thought. No, not a run, that wouldn't work. Something else.

A swim in the pool. No, too chemical. In the ocean, then.

Better. But …

And then it came to me, what I had to do, after the darkest, loneliest night of my life. I crept downstairs, and through the door, and into the garage.

Windsurfers, Jet Skis, canoes – you would not believe the crap in our garage. But it was exactly where I'd left it, a layer of dust clinging to it. And I felt a bit guilty – *why haven't I used you in such a long time, Hot Buttered Piranha? Why have I left you in here with all this other crap?*

I couldn't even remember the last time I'd gone surfing – had it been that day at Burleigh Heads when there'd been a shark alert?

As I wiped the dust off my board with an old T-shirt, I realized it wasn't the only thing I'd neglected. There, leaning against the wall, looking forlorn, looking unloved, was my bike, my Trek MTB. *Why haven't I used you either?*

I attached the board carrier to my bicycle, put the board in the carrier, but then noticed – *bugger!* – that my tires were flat. I pumped them up and away I went, rolling down the driveway. "Dom, where are you going?"

Mom's voice. I looked over my shoulder, and saw her standing at the front door, still in her nightie.

"I'll be back in time for school," I yelled, and pedaled hard. Away from her, and any objections she had.

When I reached the gates, Samsoni was on duty.

"Surfing this morning?" he said, his voice full of surprise.

"I used to surf a lot," I said, and it was true – before I started to really concentrate on the running, I surfed all the time. I'd even entered a few grommet competitions, coming third in one of them.

"I know that," said Samsoni. "It's just that the waves aren't up to much this morning."

"They're not?" I said.

"The tide's not right and the wind's offshore."

"So you surf?" I said, and I felt guilty, because this was something about Samsoni that I didn't know, that I didn't have a clue about.

"Boogie board," he said, flashing that huge Polynesian smile of his. "Shark biscuit."

I smiled back.

"We should go together one day," I said, though I

knew that would never happen.

Out through the gate and I cranked it up, eager to get to the water now, see if Samsoni was right.

Along a street with bungalows on either side. A few people out, some early-morning joggers, and then somebody I knew: Seb. Baggier-than-baggy shorts, ponytail bouncing, he was looking very strong, mowing down the joggers.

I felt a mixture of emotions, and wasn't sure which one to go with.

Anger.

Anger at how he'd tricked me.

Anger at how he'd looked at me that day I'd gone to his house.

For a crazy second the thought came to me that it was Seb whose life I should take. That would show The Debt, wouldn't it, if I took one of their own?

But it was only a crazy second.

Instead, when I passed Seb I yelled out his name and he looked up and I gave him the finger, thrusting it several times into the air just to make my point. I couldn't see his reaction – I was too far past him – but I hoped he was upset or shocked, I hoped he was something besides loose as a goose on the juice.

Ahead, between two buildings, I could see a patch of blue. And then when I crested the rise, there it was, the ocean.

Samsoni was right – there were really no waves,

none that could be surfed, anyway. Although they had shape, there was no size to them, they lacked energy.

Still, I got undressed. I carefully unwound the bandage from my hand – the burn wasn't healing that well, but I figured that salt water would do it more good than harm. I velcroed my leg rope around my ankle. I ran down to the water's edge and launched into the surf.

The salt water – surprisingly cool – washed over me. At first my burn stung like crazy, but then the pain subsided. Already I felt a million times better.

The dark, dark night was becoming the past, becoming history.

I started paddling out, and it didn't take long for my muscles to start complaining about this unaccustomed exercise.

The surf may have been crap, but there were still other surfers out there. A Japanese girl, her skin almost black. Two grommets, one I sort of recognized – did he go to my school? – and an older man, on a Malibu. As I paddled past, they all silently acknowledged me, the fraternity of the wave.

Once out back, I went to the end of the line and waited, sitting astride my board. The gentle swell rolled under me, the board rising and falling, a slow sure heartbeat. The sun had started to let me know it was there, its rays warm on my back. Why had I ever stopped surfing?

The other surfers were intent on the horizon,

looking for a rise of water, a set that could be ridden. But the waves that did pass were weak; not even the smaller grommet could coax a ride from them. The Japanese girl was the first to give up, paddling back to shore at a lightning speed. Then the two grommets decided it was time to head in, get ready for school.

So it was just me and the old guy, bobbing up and down out there.

For the next ten minutes – which is actually a very long time when you're sitting in the surf – there was no change at all, the same anemic waves. Not that I minded, I liked it out here, just bobbing up and down, getting more time between me and last night.

But then, towards the horizon, I could see something. A ripple of water. A set was approaching.

The wave grew taller, thicker.

The man smiled at me, and paddled, muscular arms plowing the water. The wave crested, and he was on.

The second wave broke too soon, but the third wave was perfect.

I paddled hard, but I was already on, already on my feet.

It'd been ages since I'd surfed, but it felt very familiar. Still, I didn't attempt anything too radical, just took it down the line.

And when the wave finished, I felt absolutely exhilarated. Punch-the-air-scream-out-something-dumb exhilarated.

And then I had two thoughts.

The first: *If they take my leg, I can't do this.*

The second: *I'm not going to let them take my leg.*

I waved good-bye to Malibu man, he waved back, and I walked up to where my bike was. As I put my shirt on, I realized how ravenous I was, hunger gnawing at my stomach like a rodent.

Breakfast, I thought. *McDonald's*, I thought.

I wrapped the bandage back around my hand. I strapped my board back on the bike, and pedaled along the bike path all the way to Surfers.

There were many people out, people power-walking, people cycling, people doing exercises at the exercise stations.

I stopped at McDonald's, chained my bike to the post.

It, too, was very busy; workers on their way to work, surfers after their morning surf, and other, more dubious-looking types.

As I joined the line, I was so glad that I hadn't brought my phone, because for sure it would've been jumping around in my pocket like a hyperactive kangaroo now, with Mom calling to find out where I was, telling me that school had already started.

I ordered a McBreakfast, and when it was ready I took my tray and went to look for an empty table.

When I saw PJ and Brandon I don't know why I was so surprised; I often saw street kids at this McDonald's.

PJ yelled out, "Hey, Dom, over here!"

I had no choice – I walked over to their table. As I sat down next to PJ I felt a little jolt to the heart. I so wished it was just her and we could sit down together and talk crap, but it wasn't just her.

She asked about my hand, but then she was straight on to the Zolt. How, without a doubt, the highlight of her life had been meeting him.

He's just a dude with a squeaky voice who crashes a lot of planes, I wanted to tell her. But I turned to Brandon and said, "How you feeling, Brandon?"

"Really, really good," he said. "Never been better."

PJ gave me a look – *Don't take any notice of him.*

"You want me to buy you something?" I said.

"You trying to fatten me up before you chop off my head or something?" said Brandon.

Now I wanted to be back out there on my Hot Buttered Piranha, riding the swell.

"Hey, check out the look on this dude's face," said Brandon, indicating me to his sister. "Yeah, I'll have a Quarter Pounder and French fries and large Coke."

"Okay," I said, getting the order right in my head. "What about you, PJ?" I asked, just as her phone starting ringing.

"Nah, food's overrated," she said, answering her phone.

I joined the line, behind two sandy barefoot grommets.

"The takeoff's a bit fat, goes into a grindy barrel,

hits the reef and really sucks dry but then turns into this long easy cutback," said the first.

"Filthy," said the second grommet. "See Mozzie's wave? Took off late, popped the fins, slipped down the face, a big slash, filthy floater, and finished with the sickest aerial."

I got Brandon's order, but by the time I got back to the table he was stretched out on the bench and appeared to be asleep.

PJ was still on the phone. "No, we're not coming to stupid Toowoomba. Not if he still lives there."

Something from the other end.

"Yeah, well, I'll believe that when I see it."

When she saw me, with my laden tray, she said, "I have to go," and hung up.

When I put the tray on the table Brandon didn't move – he really was asleep.

"Isn't school starting soon?" said PJ.

I nodded.

"So aren't you going to be late, naughty Grammar Boy?"

Her attitude was getting to me – what, she was the major badass just because she scabbed on the streets? What would she know about badass-ery? "Maybe I left school. Did that ever occur to you?"

"Yeah, sure," she said.

"Well, I'm not in any rush to get there, am I?" I said.

"But you will be," she said. "You along with all your snotty-nosed mates."

She was really, really making me angry now.

But before I could say anything, or do anything, a manager was at our table, and he wasn't happy. He had that typical loser look you need to be a manager at McDonald's: sort of greasy and pimply and round-shouldered.

"I've told you two before that this is a restaurant and not a motel," he said. He had deep-fryer breath.

"And I think I told you before that this a scummy McDonald's and not a restaurant," said PJ.

"If he doesn't sit up straight, I'm going to get security to escort him out," he said, indicating the prostrate Brandon.

"You really are a disgusting –" started PJ, but I cut her off – she was about to get us all escorted out.

"Our friend is unwell," I said.

"Unwell?" said McDonald's Manager.

"Yes, it means 'sick,'" I said.

"Well, that isn't my problem, he can go and be unwell somewhere else," said McDonald's Manager, giving the "unwell" some quote marks with his fingers.

"You ever watched *Today Tonight*?" I said.

"Of course I have," he said.

"So how do you reckon your boss would feel if he saw his 'restaurant' on *Today Tonight* because they kicked out a customer who was ..." I stumbled here because I wasn't sure how hard to play this. But PJ came to my rescue.

"… if they kicked out a customer who has a terminal illness," she said.

The McDonald's Manager backed down at that; he even sent over some free drinks and extra French fries (though they were really cold and I'm pretty sure they'd just scraped them off the floor).

"The old terminal illness," I said to PJ, my mouth full, remembering the conversation I'd had with Brandon in the hospital. "Comes in handy, eh?"

PJ gave me a look.

"What do you mean?" she said. "Brandon's got cancer."

"What?"

"Non-Hodgkin's lymphoma, but a really weird type. He's got a few months to live, probably less if he keeps going the way he's going."

"There's nothing they can do about it?" I said, thinking of all the times I'd seen Brandon looking sick and had attributed it to some sort of drug addiction – "The Needle and the Damage Done."

"No," said PJ. "I guess that's why it's called a terminal illness."

The McBreakfast now tasted McGross. I spat it out onto the plate.

"I'm so sorry," I said, getting to my feet, and getting out of there.

SHUT UP

I cycled like crazy, trying to pedal what PJ had told me right out of my head. At first I kept to the footpaths, but that was too complicated, so I veered onto the road, mixing it with the morning traffic.

People cycle a lot on the Gold Coast, in fact many elite cyclists base themselves here, so you'd think that motorists would be used to us pedalers and display a certain amount of courtesy.

Wrong.

It soon became obvious that most of the motorists hated cyclists and would have been quite happy running them over, except for a few laws that dissuaded them against this. Horns were beeped, fists were shaken, and some not-too-polite words were directed towards me.

I wasn't about to be beaten back to the footpath, however; I started returning some of what I was getting.

At the traffic lights I made sure I got in front of the first car.

I jumped the red lights.

I returned every glare I got, and with interest. By the time I arrived at the Halcyon Grove gate I was hot and I was flustered and I was full of aggro. I barged into the kitchen, and the whole family was there, even Gus. They'd been talking, I'd heard the static of conversation from outside, but it immediately stopped when I appeared.

Deduction: they'd been talking about me. To save all those tiresome questions about where I'd been, I got in first.

"I went for a surf this morning," I said. "The takeoff was a bit fat, but I got in this grindy barrel, popped the fins, slashed down the face, did the filthiest floater, and finished it all off with the sickest aerial."

Miranda laughed, which earned her some disapproving glances from the parental units.

"What?" she said. "That was funny."

Mom then went on to make some pretty obvious points about not knowing where I was, about the value of communication, about there being no excuse in this age of the mobile phone.

I didn't really respond that much, just nodded my head – she hadn't really said anything I could argue with.

I guess if that had been it, then everything would've been fine.

But for some reason Dad thought he'd have his two cents' worth, though I'm not sure about that expression; it obviously hasn't been value-adjusted for inflation.

"There really is no excuse for not letting somebody know where you were," he said, that bland TV-show-host voice coming out of that bland TV-show-host face.

I looked straight at my dad, sitting at the table, the tiniest smear of soy milk on his chin, and I said, "Shut your mouth."

There was this collective intake of breath.

Eventually Dad said, "What did you just say to me?"

"I said shut your mouth."

Nobody knew what to do, how to react.

Except for Dad. He got up from his chair and he moved over to where I was and he grabbed two handfuls of my shirt and he slammed me hard – and I mean hard – against the wall. The word that came into my head was "mongrel" – I had no idea my dad had this much mongrel in him.

I don't think the rest of my family did, either, because there was this pretty major reaction.

Toby said something and Miranda said something.

"David!" said Gus.

Mom grabbed the back of his shirt and began pulling him. "Let him go!"

But Dad the mongrel wasn't letting anybody go – he kept pressing me against the wall, his face right in mine, our noses practically touching. I should've been scared – my dad had never even smacked me before – but I wasn't.

"I saw your little film," I whispered, my eyes zeroing in on his. I could see that he didn't understand what I was talking about. "Your little snuff film."

Now he got it, and that bit of mongrel became a lot of mongrel, and he brought me back and slammed me into the wall again.

This hurt; my ribs were shaking, the burn on my hand on fire.

All during this, Mom had hold of Dad's shirt, and suddenly there was this tearing sound.

"Let him go, David!" she yelled. "Let him go!"

But Dad wasn't letting go. Not until Gus got into the act, chopping Dad's hands away with those bench-press arms of his.

I smoothed down my T-shirt; I didn't want anybody to think he'd gotten the better of me.

"I probably should get ready for school," I said.

Miranda laughed, but there was no levity in the sound, it was pure nervousness.

As I walked up the stairs, nobody said anything. I think we all knew that something had changed in our family. We all knew that something had been broken. And it would never, ever be fixed.

THE LAST DAY OF SCHOOL EVER

I'm not sure exactly when I knew.

Was it as soon as I got into the car? Was it when Mom opened her mouth several times to say something but couldn't? Was it when I walked through the school gates and Tristan came up to me and started rabbiting on about Imogen and sucking her face right off her head? Or maybe it was when I went to sit down at my desk and there across the aisle was Droopy Eye. Droopy Freaking Eye!

Halfway through homeroom I couldn't stand it anymore: I got up from my desk.

"What do you think you're doing, Mr. Silvagni?" said Mr. Travers.

"I'm going to see the principal, Mr. Travers," I said.

"No, you're not," he sputtered.

"Yes, I am – it's time for me to leave this moron factory," I said, emphasizing the last two words. This direct quote from Mr. Traver's Facebook post did the job. Yet again. No more sputtering as I made my way out of the classroom and towards Mr. Cranbrook's office.

There were already a couple of boys waiting outside, and from the glum looks on their faces I guessed it wasn't to receive any sort of commendation.

"You guys in the poo?" I asked.

They both nodded – *in the poo*.

The door to the principal's office opened and an even glummer kid exited.

"Mr. Jacks?" came the voice from inside.

Mr. Jacks stood up but I beat him to it, squeezing in through the open door, closing it behind me.

Mr. Cranbrook looked up from his desk, clocked who it was, and said, "You don't appear to be Mr. Jacks."

"Sorry to barge in like this, but it's really important." I'm pretty sure if my father wasn't a major donor to the school, then I would've been shown the door.

But instead Mr. Cranbrook shot his cuffs, adjusted his tie, and said in that pompous voice of his, "Hit me with your best shot."

I hit him with my best shot, and it *was* my best shot: all the right words coming at all the right places.

When I'd finished, Mr. Cranbrook said, "Well, you really are an impressive young man."

I wasn't sure if that compliment was major-donor related or not, but I couldn't help feeling a bit flattered.

"And I could sit here for hours and tell you all the reasons why you shouldn't be leaving school." More cuff-shooting. More tie-adjusting. "And they're excellent reasons."

I went to say something, but Mr. Cranbrook held up his hands.

"But I'm not," he said. "All I'm going to do is explain the practicalities of somebody your age leaving school."

Which is what he proceeded to do, and when he'd finished he said, "So now when you sit down tonight and discuss this with your parents you'll all know what the facts are."

Now I got it: he didn't think I was going to leave school at all, because my parents wouldn't let me.

Well, he'd soon find out.

The bell went – time for the second lesson. I thanked Mr. Cranbrook and made my way, for the last time ever, to English.

Ω   Ω   Ω

"We're going to start a new novel today," said Mr. McFarlane.

I put up my hand, and I can't blame him for being as surprised as he was.

"Yes, Dom, do you have a question?"

"Do you know the poem 'Invictus' by William Henley Ernest?"

"Yes, I do, in fact I count it as one of my favorites, but today we're going to get stuck into this wonderful new novel."

"What's 'Invictus' actually about?" I said, doing a fair imitation of a seriously annoying kid.

"Dom, like I told you –" he started, but then he ran out of steam. "You're not going to let go of this, are you?"

I shook my head. Dog. Bone. Me.

"Okay, people. Next period we start on our wonderful new novel, but this period we're going to have a look at the poem 'Invictus' by William Henley Ernest."

There was a chorus of moans, and a few comments.

"It's not about running, is it?"

"Silvagni, you loser."

"Poetry sucks."

Mr. McFarlane was on his laptop. "Now let me find the poem so I can read it out for you."

"It's okay," I said. And then adopting my best poetry voice I recited, "'Out of the night that covers me, black as the pit from pole to pole, I thank whatever gods may be for my unconquerable soul.'"

Someone wolf-whistled. Somebody else said, "What the?"

I continued. "'In the fell clutch of circumstance I have not winced nor cried aloud. Under the bludgeonings of chance my head is bloody, but unbowed.'" Nobody said anything now, you could've heard an iPhone beep, even one on silent mode. "'Beyond this place of wrath and tears looms but the horror of the shade, and yet the menace of the years finds and shall find me unafraid.'"

I looked over at Mr. McFarlane, his eyes were glistening. He gave me a nod – *keep going*.

"'It matters not how strait the gate, how charged with punishments the scroll. I am the master of my fate: I am the captain of my soul.'" More silence, but not just the usual type; it was the sort of silence where you could hear people's minds ticking.

Hey, I'm not saying it was like that bit in *Dead Poets Society* when they all stand on their desks and say, "O Captain! My Captain!"

In fact, it was probably nothing like that bit in *Dead Poets Society* when they all stand on their desks and say, "O Captain! My Captain!"

Except one kid – was it Charles? – actually did say, "'O Captain! My Captain!'"

And then there was more silence, more ticking minds.

Mr. Mac let this go on for a while, and then he said, "Let's start by looking at the poet, William Henley Ernest.

"He was born in England in 1849," he said, looking at his laptop. "When he was twelve he was diagnosed with tuberculosis of the bone and his leg was amputated below the knee when he was twenty."

Mr. Mac let the implication of this sink in.

"So basically he got legless," said Tristan, but the joke – if you could call it that – didn't raise a laugh.

"But what about the poem?" I said, continuing my impression of a seriously annoying kid. "What does it mean?"

Mr. Mac now had the poem up on the Smart Board so that everybody could read it. "Dom, you obviously know it well – you recited it off by heart. What do you think it means?"

The old turn-the-tables, number eight in a teacher's book of tricks.

I looked around at my classmates. Basically, this was my worst nightmare – everybody looking at me, waiting to hear my opinion. But – big but – this was my last day of school; most of these kids I would never see again. So what if I made a complete tool of myself?

I even stood up.

"O Captain! My Captain!"

I cleared my throat of the several hundred frogs that had taken residence there. "I reckon what he's saying is that even though the world throws a whole lot of crap at you there's no use looking for God or anything like that to help you. Basically you're on your own, and you have to deal with it yourself. Like he says, you're the 'captain of your soul.'"

Already, there were several hands in the air.

"Paul," said Mr. Mac. "What do you think?"

"Our fate is in God's hands, not our own."

This was received with several groans; it looked like Paul's born-again phase still wasn't over.

"And Derek, what do you think?" said Mr. Mac.

It was a teacher's dream: a frank and lively discussion that refused to abate even when the bell went.

Eventually an obviously chuffed Mr. Mac said, "Well, we can continue this discussion next time we meet. Maybe Dom has another poem he'd like to share with us."

Not really, I thought. *Except maybe: no more rulers, no more books, no more teachers' dirty looks.*

As the other students filed out, still talking about the poem, I lingered by my desk.

Should I say something to Mr. Mac? He was my favorite teacher, after all. Maybe even trot out the old "O Captain! My Captain!" It was Mr. Mac who had showed us the movie, so he'd get the reference.

But it was too cheesy, so instead I just said, "Thanks, Mr. Mac."

"No, thank you, Dom," he said. He was beaming so much you could've stuck him on a headland and called him a lighthouse. "And see you tomorrow."

Probably not, I thought, but I didn't have the heart, guts, whatever it takes, to tell him. So I just shuffled out, master of my soul and all that.

Next was chemistry, and weirdly enough they

didn't let me anywhere near the Bunsen burners. Poor Mr. Arvanitakis. I did my best to assure him that it was nothing to do with him or his teaching methods; I was just this masochistic pyromaniac.

At lunchtime I made my way to Hogwarts.

Knocked on that now-familiar door. That now-familiar voice came from within: "Enter."

As I walked inside, it occurred to me that it was pretty weird that my second-favorite teacher at this school had never taught me one subject.

Still, I'd learned a lot from him, stuff that I actually remembered: how Pheidippides had run two hundred and forty kilometers at the battle of Marathon, how it was the god Pan who had invented panic in order to help the Greeks win a battle, how the great earthquake of 1349 had knocked down half the Colosseum; all sorts of cool stuff.

Dr. Chakrabarty's room had always been quite Spartan – to use a word he would approve of – but it was even more so now: the books were gone, the photo of Gandhi was gone, the picture of the spinning globe was gone.

"What's going on?" I said, indicating the empty shelves.

"I'm afraid we've failed to secure a single enrollment this term," he said. Dr. Chakrabarty always had that theatrical way of speaking, as if there was an audience just behind my shoulder, but I could detect the sadness in his voice. "The classics are just not as sexy as they once were."

"I reckon they're still pretty sexy," I said, which was a pretty empty thing to say given that I, too, had failed to enroll in any of his subjects.

Dr. Chakrabarty shrugged.

"What about Peter Eisinger?" I said, naming the kid who always took all the weird and wacky subjects.

"Peter's parents, in their wisdom, have insisted that he take a more vocational approach to his education, and he's enrolled in business studies instead," he said.

"Oh," was all I could contribute to that.

"Anyway, what brings you here, Pheidippides?" he said. With the mention of the Ph word, Dr. Chakrabarty brightened up, as if it brought with it a memory of cheerier times.

"I'm leaving too," I said.

"Another school?" he said. "Brisbane Boys, perhaps?"

"No, I'm going to join the workforce," I said.

"You have secured gainful employment?"

"I'm going to work for a private investigator," I said, though I felt a bit phony saying that. Yes, Hound de Villiers, PI had offered me a job, but had he really meant it?

"And your parents have approved of this?"

"They're not that happy about it, but they respect my wishes," I said, sounding just like a character from a corny American movie. I wasn't sure how to end this, so I went with the theme of the day. "Hey, I'm master

167

of my fate, captain of my soul."

"Well said!" said Dr. Chakrabarty. "Indeed you are!"

I was just about to make my exit when he said, "Wait!"

Bending down, he rummaged in a box of books. Eventually he found what he was looking for and held out a small paperback towards me. I read the title: *The Art of War* by Sun Tzu.

"For you," he said.

I took the book and said, "What's it about?"

"War," he said. "But many other things as well."

I left his office for the last time, the book in my hand.

The afternoon sort of noodled along; I got out of the habit of saying this is the last time I'm going to do this, the last time I'm going to do that.

The last time I'm going to urinate in this urinal. The last time I'm going to sneak into the library to check my text messages.

The final bell went and that was it: the last time I'd hear that final bell. But there was one more person I felt deserved a good-bye. So I made my way down to the locker room. The very last time I'd walk through these doors.

"Here he is, captain of my soul!" said Charles.

"Ah-soul!" said Bevan Milne, making the obvious joke.

It went on like this, the usual mucking around. Towel-flicking. Yo-momma's-so-fat jokes. Eventually everybody quieted down and we got busy getting changed.

"Is this all there is?" I said, looking at the empty benches.

"Bailey's been poached by the football team," said Charles.

"Jaxon's concentrating on his swimming," said somebody else.

After we'd changed, we went outside and Coach was waiting for us by the long jump pit, wearing her faded school tracksuit, whistle and stopwatch dangling around her neck. She went through the usual early-season stuff.

Please, one last Hakuna Matata, I said to myself as she started winding down.

"Okay, let's get out there," she said.

If she wasn't going to do it, somebody had to.

"Just a minute," I said, using this new public voice I'd recently discovered I owned.

Everybody stopped.

"Remember, every morning in Africa a gazelle wakes up knowing it must run faster than the fastest lion or it will be killed. Every morning in Africa a lion wakes up knowing it must run faster than the slowest gazelle or it will starve. It doesn't matter whether you are a lion or a gazelle: when the sun comes up, you'd better be running."

I was getting quite a few funny looks, but so what?

"And remember, boys," I said, offering up another of Coach's favorite sayings, "pain is inevitable, suffering is optional."

Training was pretty standard. Given that I hadn't done much running, I actually felt pretty loose. I kept waiting for the perfect opportunity to tell Coach I was leaving, but it never came up – she was either with somebody else or we would've looked too conspicuous. It was only after I'd changed and Coach was in the parking lot getting into her crappy little Hyundai that I felt comfortable talking to her.

"Hey, Coach," I said. "I need to tell you something."

"Don't tell me you're quitting running again?" she said, keys dangling from her hand.

"No, I'm actually leaving school."

"So you'll be competing for another school?"

"No, I'm leaving for good. I'm joining the workforce."

I'm not sure what reaction I expected: disappointment, anger, but not what I got: Coach looked really quite happy.

"That's great news," she said.

"It is?"

"Yes. Toughen you up, working for a living. And you can join a serious athletes' club, not this toffee-nosed establishment. The Gold Coast Sharks – we train Tuesday and Thursday nights at the Carrara Track. You know the place, just by the football stadium. I'll send you a text with the details."

"Okay," I said, though I was thinking that the chances of me training with the Gold Coast Sharks were pretty slim.

"That friend of yours – what's his name? – has actually started training with us. Got a lot of promise, too."

"What friend?" I said, not having a clue who she was talking about.

"He was going to come here on a scholarship, remember?"

"Seb?" I said.

"That's right, Seb. And like I said, a very promising runner, ideal training partner for you, now that I come to think of it."

Been there. Done that.

Coach got into her crappy Hyundai and took off, and I made my way – yes, for the very last time – through the school and towards the gates. As I walked between those stone gateposts I looked back. Somehow, tears found their way into my eyes. More followed. And more. Okay, I was sobbing like some pathetic baby.

I didn't want to leave my school.

I loved my school.

But I had no choice, absolutely no choice.

I couldn't go to school and do what I was going to do. Take a life. Murder Brandon.

That just wasn't something a schoolkid did.

IT GOT A BIT MESSY

To say it got a bit messy that night is a bit like saying it got a bit nippy during the Ice Age. It started off okay, but that's only because my parents weren't there when I got home. Toby was parked in front of the plasma, watching some cooking show – Nasty & Nastier were in the final against Horrible & More Horrible, and may the least objectionable people win – while methodically working his way through an oversized bowl of organic corn chips. After the usual small talk – this show sucks, not as much as you, etc. – I told him the news. He actually hit the pause button just as the final judge was going to give the final mark.

"No way?" he said.

"Way," I said.

"No way?" he said.

"Way," I said.

This went on for a lot longer than you'd think until we both found some more dialogue.

"Do you reckon they'd let me leave when I'm fifteen, start a cooking apprenticeship?"

Actually, it made more sense for Toby to leave school. His grades were even worse than mine, and really, what was the use of him learning about photosynthesis or calculus when everybody knew he was going to become a chef?

"They can't stop you," I said.

He punched the air with both fists – a very un-Toby-like gesture – and hit the play button.

Miranda was by the pool, doing her tai chi.

"I've got something to tell you," I said.

"About time," she said.

"Sorry?"

"All this weird stuff that's been going down with you, there has to be some explanation."

"Okay, I'm leaving school."

Miranda glared at me. "That's not an explanation," she said. "That's just further weird behavior." So far, so good – sort of.

It was only when Mom got home that it began to get messy. She started off with a big lecture about this morning's incident, and you could tell she'd been preparing this speech all day, because nobody who isn't in a movie or Dr. Chakrabarty is that articulate off-the-cuff. Anyway, according to her, both Dad and

I had behaved BADLY, had shown a lack of RESPECT for each other as family members. And even though she expected Dad to APOLOGIZE she expected me to do it FIRST.

I let her finish her speech and then I said, "Mom, I'm actually leaving school. Today was my last day."

"That's fine," she said. "I'm sure you've made the right decision."

As if.

She launched into another speech, which wasn't so prepared and was nowhere near as articulate.

In the end, I said, "Mom, I've made my mind up – I'm leaving school." That's when she called Dad and ordered him to get home pronto.

There was this half-hour cease-fire where Mom and I just glared at each other; I could picture Dad hammering his Porsche along the freeway, his face a mask of fury.

Then with the roar of an exhaust, the screech of brakes, it was two against one.

Except it wasn't.

I wouldn't say Dad was on my side, but I wouldn't say he was totally on Mom's side either. He kept saying stuff like, "Let him see how tough it is out there, see how long he lasts." And Mom kept saying stuff like, "But he's only a child." This went on for an unbelievable amount of time: animals became extinct, ice caps melted, Windows 242 was released. As for me, I didn't shift my position.

Eventually it was agreed that it was my decision, but I would have to live with the consequences of that decision.

"And that means paying board," said Mom. "I'm not having any freeloaders in my house."

"That's okay," I said. "I'm actually going to stay with Gus for a while."

Before I said this, I hadn't considered it at all. But now it seemed like a great idea – it would give me the freedom to do what I needed to do. I hadn't asked Gus, but I knew he would say yes.

And it all ended with a big squeezy group hug?

No, not even close.

It all ended with me telling Gus what had happened and him saying, "Yes, that's okay," and me getting my stuff and carrying it to his place and taking over his spare room, the one that had cartons and cartons full of old running magazines. It all ended with me sleeping – or trying to sleep – on a bed that was nowhere near as comfortable as mine, on sheets that were nowhere near as Egyptian as mine. It all ended with me eventually falling asleep and having more dreams that were like horror movies on crack, full of amputated limbs, and murdered kids, and Bag Lady twitching to death.

Yes, it got a bit messy.

WORKING FOR THE DOG

My guess was that even if I chained my bike to the post outside it would last, say, all of ten minutes in the Block. As soon as I wheeled it through the doorway of Cash Converters, the rat-faced ponytailed man behind the counter said, "We don't need no more bloody bikes." Pointing to all the bikes in one corner, he added, "Especially not hot ones."

"I'm taking it upstairs," I said. "And it's not that hot."

I did just that, carrying it upstairs.

There were two men waiting, slouched on seats. Both of them would have been excellent contestants in the brand new TV show I'd just devised called *Australia's Worst Tattoos – Ink that Stinks*.

"Hey, you can't bring that thing up here," said the receptionist.

She was wearing a denim jacket, denim jeans; she obviously took her fashion tips from her boss. I guessed I couldn't really talk, because I, too, had embraced the denim – I was wearing the nasty stone-washed jacket that Hound had given me the other day.

"Could you tell Hound?" I said. "I'm sure he'll understand."

The receptionist picked up a phone and said, "Hey, Hound, some idiot kid's brought his bike upstairs." She listened for a while and then turned to me. "Is your name Dom?"

I nodded.

"Okay, Big Dog's waiting for you," she said, a friendlier tone to her voice. "You can put your bike against that wall if you like."

I did that, and continued on to Hound's office. I knocked, he told me to come in. But when I did, he was hanging upside down in some sort of machine.

"Whoa," I said. "What's that thing?"

"It's an inversion machine," he said. "I got a back issue, L4-L5 disc. This does wonders for it. Supposedly."

Let me tell you something – it's not that easy conversing with somebody when they're hanging upside down like a fruit bat. All those facial expressions that are so important for communication, well, they're back to front. I mean, was he smiling or was he frowning? ☺ or ☹?

We talked some rubbish for a while before I got around to what was really on my mind. "Were you serious when you offered me a job?"

"The Hound is always serious," he said.

I'd known the Hound for quite a while, and this was the first time I'd heard him refer to himself in the third person. I wondered if it had something to do with him being upside down, all that blood pooling in his head.

"Then I'd like to take you up on that offer," I said.

"You don't want to discuss salary packages, superannuation or promotion opportunities?" said upside-down Hound.

"No, I just want to leave bloody school," I said, remembering the sloshy old tears I'd shed as I walked out through the gates. "But you need to sign a form that says you're providing vocational training for me, something like that."

"Okay, you're hired," he said, still upside down. "When do you want to start?"

"What about right now?"

"Suits me," said Hound. "How about you begin by getting me out of this thing?"

So I started my working life by extricating Hound from his inversion machine.

"Nice jacket," he said when he was on his feet again. "Now let's find you somewhere to work."

Actually, it was Jodie – that was the receptionist's name – who found me a desk.

Technically it was probably a table, and it was situated in this weird little corner of the office near the men's bathroom. Just how near became apparent when one of the contestants in *Ink That Stinks* went inside. I could hear everything, all his movements, even him tearing off the toilet paper. There were no washing-hands noises though; I really hoped he didn't work in the food and beverage industry.

As well as a desk, I had a computer, an ancient desktop that looked like it'd been around when Bill Gates was only a billionaire. Still, I had a job, I had a desk, I had a computer – I was chuffed.

Now all I needed was something to do.

It wasn't long before Hound appeared, waving a piece of notebook paper. He whacked it down on my desk. On it were some names and addresses.

"Need you to do a credit check on these three," he said. "Major scumbags."

I waited for him to tell me how to do a credit check, but no such information was forthcoming. He just walked off, spurs jangling. Okay, I made that up about the jangling spurs, but Hound was the sort of hombre who should've worn spurs, even without the horse.

So it was the old leave-him-to-his-own-devices, which suited me fine.

Google, as always, was my friend. It didn't take long to find out that it's actually very easy to obtain a credit check on major scumbags, on anybody really.

As long as you are the person applying for it and can provide some ID.

As for checking somebody else's credit rating, not so straightforward.

But I guess the Zolt was right, I'm devious. And I'm pretty good on Photoshop.

So I was able to manufacture the appropriate ID and pull the credit rating for these three individuals. Not one of them made pretty reading: loan defaults, bankruptcy, fraud – like Hound said, major scumbaggery. He was very happy with my work, however.

"You're a bloody quick study, you are," he said.

For the rest of the day the work was sort of the same: a few more credit checks, and then I had to find out all I could about a list of companies that Hound gave me. Again, Google was my friend. Again, Photoshop was my friend. Again, Hound was very happy with my work. And I really felt like I'd achieved something, like I'd acquired some useful skills that I was never going to acquire at fuddy-duddy old Coast Grammar.

Something else: for stretches of time, I'd managed to keep my mind off the sixth installment. I knew I should be doing the planning – I thought of Gus feeding Panda's dog every night so that it got used to him.

But I couldn't bring myself to start. And, unlike other installments, there was no deadline.

Though I sort of wished there was.

Something to make me do this terrible thing.

After finishing work at four – Hound said I could have an easy day my first day – I took my bike downstairs. There were men lounging outside the Cash Converters, smoking, talking, being tough. Among them was Red Bandana wearing his signature headwear. He wasn't actually smoking. Or talking for that matter. But he made up for the lack of activity in these two areas by looking incredibly tough.

I kept my head down, hoping he wouldn't recognize me.

And he didn't. It was the rat-face ponytailed owner of Cash Converters who said, "Hey, Chop, isn't that the kid you've been looking for?"

Red Bandana's arm shot out and his paw grabbed a handful of my shirt. My bike fell, clattering, onto the ground.

"I've been looking –" he started, but I wasn't going to let him get the first sentence in.

"If I were you, I'd let go of me," I said.

He stared at me, and I could see the shock registering in his face – *Who does this kid think he is?*

"I'm working for Hound de Villiers," I said, though I really don't know why I bothered with his surname – everybody knew Hound. "And I don't think he'd appreciate one of his employees calling in sick tomorrow."

I wouldn't say he let go of me immediately, it actually took a while, but that's probably because it took his miniscule brain a while to process all the new information it had been fed.

Coast Surveillance didn't seem to have much of a superannuation plan, I'm not sure the promotion opportunities were great and on-the-job training seemed to consist of the phrase "You'll work it out, Youngblood," but working for Hound certainly had other advantages.

I turned back to Ratface Ponytail and gave him a taste of my patented death stare; he'd keep, the dog. Then I hopped on my Trek, and got out of the Block.

I certainly wasn't in the mood for going home, that sort of thing was for schoolkids, so I decided to go and see a movie. It seemed such an outrageous thing to do – go and see a movie on a weeknight – that I almost had to pinch myself a couple of times to make sure I was actually doing it. But I was doing it, cycling to Pacific Fair, chaining my bike to the bike rack.

As I walked in, there were all these kids from various schools in the area, including Grammar, hanging around. I recognized a couple of them, and they acknowledged me with a nod. *Schoolboys,* I thought. *Haven't they got anything better to do with their time? It's not as if homework does itself, is it?*

Up the escalators and I was in the parallel world that is the cinema complex, with its thick carpet, garish lights, arctic air-con. I scanned the board. There was nothing I really wanted to see, so I just went for the film that looked the least offensive, running the gauntlet of popcorn and soft drinks and candy, until finally I got through to the other end and found cinema 18. There was only one other person in there, so I made sure I took a seat as far as possible away from her.

The lights dimmed, the previews started. Out of the corner of my eye I noticed that a couple of other people had entered the cinema. I hadn't taken any more notice than that – people, two, enter. But as the movie proper started, they appeared at the end of my row. There was a whole cinema to choose from, hundreds of seats, an alphabet of rows, why come here?

I soon had an answer to my question.

As they shuffled along towards me, one of them said something in a hushed tone that sounded like "Dom." I looked up at them, my eyes taking a while to become accustomed to the light.

Both people were wearing hoodies and sunglasses. But I knew immediately who it was: Zoe, making one of her unconventional entrances. And with her, probably one of the most wanted people – by the television stations anyway – in Australia: her brother, the Zolt.

I would think that pretty much every one of the Zolt's 1,265,234 Facebook fans would be wet-their-pants excited to sit in a cinema near their hero. Not me, however.

"We need to talk about the gold," said Zoe.

"After the flick," I said.

"But –"

"After the flick!"

The flick was actually really, really bad – one of those high school things where all the actors look like they're about ten years too old to play the part – and normally my attention would've started to wander, but I'd made a point about wanting to watch the movie, so now I had to stick to it. My eyes remained glued to the screen while both Zoe and Otto fidgeted like crazy. Eventually, thank heavens, the movie ended and the credits started rolling.

"So that Roxas person E. Lee Marx knows?" said Zoe.

"Shhh! I really like to watch all the credits," I said.

Yes, it was a great and noble thing to return the gold to its rightful owners, but how was that going to help me with my final installment, how was that going to help me take a life?

So it was only after I'd learned the name of the very last Foley artist, that I finally dragged my eyes from the screen.

"So what do you think, Dom?" said Zoe.

I think you should go find another sucker.

I think you should ...

I think ...

I ...

Some revelations come up on you slowly; they may take days, weeks, even months. Others you have without even realizing you've had them. While others come crashing down on your head like a semitrailer of bricks.

Like this one.

I'd thought I had two problems, one major, one minor: how to pay the sixth installment, how to get rid of the Zolton-Banders. But – and this was the crashing bricks – I didn't have two problems at all, I had one problem and one solution, one yin and one yang.

"Okay," I said, my voice a bit jumpy with this sudden discovery. "Let's meet tomorrow and talk about it. How can I contact you?"

"We'll contact you," said Otto.

"Great," I said.

"Keep your wits about you," said Zoe.

Why should I keep my wits about me when I was doing them a favor?

It was a strange thing to say, but she was a strange girl, and I guessed that's what strange girls do: they say strange things.

When they left, I felt both elated: was this the answer to my problem? and wary: instead of me playing them, were they playing me? Yet again?

THE GOLD COAST SHARKS

Work the next day was the same sort of stuff – credit checks, company searches – but because I was quickly gaining proficiency, Hound gave me some more complex stuff to do.

"This fellow here has dumped his wife of thirty years and taken up with some floozy he met online," he said, pointing to the name at the top of the paper. "His wife is divorcing him, of course. But he's crying poor. And if you look at his tax return he only made forty k last year. But he's got money, orders Moët like it's mineral water. So your job is to find out where his money is. Singapore? Switzerland? The Cayman Islands? It has to be somewhere."

I spent pretty much the whole day doing this, unraveling an incredibly complex web of companies and trusts and offshore bank accounts. Eventually, however, I found his money. And Hound was right, there was a lot of it. Once again I had that sense of satisfaction, that I'd learned, or taught myself, some pretty slick skills.

After work I got on my bike and took the road towards Carrara; it was time for my very first training session with the Gold Coast Sharks.

If their clubroom was any indication of their success, then the Gold Coast Sharks didn't win many meets. At first I thought it was the public bathroom, it had that bricky, smelly look about it, but there on the side was the faded sign that said – just – *Gold Coast Sharks*. I went inside and it was the public bathroom, except for a bit added on which I guessed was the official clubroom. There was nobody else there, just a couple of cockroaches that scuttled off at my arrival.

They did have an impressive turn of speed, and the thought occurred to me that they, the cockroaches, were my future teammates. Of course, when you have a thought as stupid as this, you have to go with it for a while. So I imagined training with cockroaches, running with cockroaches, sharing the podium with cockroaches.

Once I'd finished with that, I began to feel really depressed – I'd been so proud of the plan I'd devised but it wasn't even going to reach the first stage. With a scuffle of footsteps, the door opened, and I met my first non-cockroach member of the Gold Coast Sharks.

He was in his twenties and certainly looked like a

runner – lean and sinewy. Something about him was familiar. As we shook hands, traded names, it came to me; he – Nathan – had been in that charity race on Reverie Island, the race I'd won. That pro runner, the one I'd nicknamed the Junkyard Dog, had tripped him when he'd tried to pass him.

Nathan's thought processes must've been going at the same rate as mine, because we both said at the same time, "You raced at Reverie!"

We talked a bit about the race, about the Junkyard Dog, and he told me it was very exciting to have another young runner joining the club. Just as he said this the door opened and the person who I guessed was this other young runner entered. Seb.

Seb sure had pulled a few surprises on me: luring me into Preacher's that time I got tranquilized, getting a job as our pool guy, stepping out with my sister; so it was pretty satisfying to pull one on him, to see the look of total surprise on his face when he saw me.

Nathan went to introduce us to each other, but I saved him the trouble. "Seb and I used to train together."

A few more people arrived and then Coach Sheeds walked through the door. Except here she wasn't Coach anymore, she was just another runner.

The actual coach was a man by the name of Colin; he was about Gus's age, I guess, and actually looked a bit like him, except of course he possessed the full complement of legs.

And when I told him my name he said, "Any relation to Gus Silvagni?"

"He's my grandfather," I said.

"Yeah, I can see the resemblance now," he said. "How's the old codger getting along?"

"He's good," I said.

"He was a very good coach, your grandfather. Way ahead of his time in a lot of things."

He seemed lost in reminiscence for a while, but then he slapped me on the shoulder and said, "Welcome to the Gold Coast Sharks!"

It made sense that because Seb and I were around the same age, and the same standard, that we would spend a lot of the time training together.

This suited me fine, I needed to work him over. And work him over I did.

"Okay, you two, let's have a couple of warm-up laps," said the coach.

As we ran I encroached further and further into Seb's space, and by the time we were near the end of the second lap, I was right next to him, almost stepping on his shoes, my elbows digging into his ribs. I'd become the Junkyard Dog.

"Give me some room, can you?" said Seb, swinging his arm at me.

"Come on, what you got?" I said, pointing to the finish line.

"It's a warm-up, you idiot," he said, but I knew he

wouldn't let me get there first without a race. So when I sprinted, so did he.

We reached the finish line at the same time.

Coach Colin, whistle at his lips, was about to say something but then held it back. I was pretty sure I knew what he was thinking: *there's nothing like a bit of healthy competition*.

Next was some interval work, ten 200-meter sprints.

I ran hard, treating each of these sprints as if it was an Olympic final, and Seb kept with me. By the tenth sprint we were both sweating buckets, both gasping for air. Even Coach had to tell us to bring it back a bit.

Bring it back?

To tell the truth, I wasn't actually sure what I was doing, but something told me it was right. I had to keep running Seb – and myself – ragged. Drag him into the hurt locker. And then, and only then, could I do it.

To finish, a 1500-meter race.

The coach staggered the start, runners taking off in pairs.

When it was our turn he said, "No need to bust a gut on this. There'll be plenty of time and opportunity for that.

"On your marks. Get set. Go!" He pressed his stopwatch and we took off.

Again I gave Seb no space, no room; I was the junkiest junkyard dog that ever ran. I stepped on his toes, elbowed him in the ribs, flicked the sweat off my face so that it landed on his. And I could tell that loose as a goose on the juice as he may have been, I was really getting to him.

All he had to do was slow down, fall back, and he would be in his own airspace. But obviously Seb wasn't going to do that, to let me beat him.

I hadn't run competitively for a while, and I'd never run competitively like this, so it was taking its toll on me as well. That hurt locker I wanted to drag him into, well, I was already well and truly there.

There was a lap to go, and out of the corner of my eye I saw the coach look down at his stopwatch.

The other runners had finished and were standing on the side of the track, looking on. It must've been a sight, these two sweat-slicked kids jostling down the track, going like the clappers.

There was no kick, I just kept digging deeper and deeper, using whatever I could find to increase the tempo. Somehow Seb kept up with me. There was maybe a hundred meters to go and it wasn't just about running him ragged; I wanted to beat the crap out of him, I wanted to show him who was the better runner.

Coming to the finish line, we were leaning into each other, more like two heavyweight boxers in the fifteenth round than middle-distance runners.

His sweat over me, mine over him.

The line getting closer.

I dug my elbow in hard, levering past him. His foot stomped down on my heel. I swung my fist; it found the side of his head. He swung his, I copped one on the jaw.

Limbs tangled, we lunged for the line.

Who got there first I'm not sure, but as we tumbled on the ground I grabbed a handful of his hair, dragged his head close so that his ear was right at my mouth.

"You tell them this," I hissed. "Tell them I've got a deal – lose the last installment and I'll get them Yamashita's Gold."

Seb struggled to free himself, but I wasn't going to let go, not now.

"Hey," he managed to say. "Why didn't you just say so?"

"Because you had to believe me," I said. Hands reached in then and dragged us apart.

"I gather you two have got some history," said Colin later.

"Some," I said.

"Well, I will not tolerate that sort of behavior in my club," he said.

Great, I was about to be expelled after only one training session.

"By rights I should kick you out." Colin frowned and held up the stopwatch. "But this bought you both another chance. Don't blow it."

TEXTURED SOY PROTEIN

"What is this exactly?" I asked Gus as I poked at the unrecognizable substance on the plate.

Already I was feeling pretty anxious – why hadn't The Debt contacted me yet? – and this stuff on my plate was increasing my anxiety levels even more.

"Textured soy protein," he said. "Just the ticket now that you're running again."

I couldn't help thinking of lasagna, because I knew that's what they were eating right now in my previous place of residence. Not any ordinary lasagna either. This was a recipe that had been brought by Dad's family from Italy, then improved, until it was about as close to perfection as food can get. Even Toby agreed with me on that. And accompanying that lasagna would be a crispy salad with my favorite tangy dressing.

And here I was, eating – or trying to eat – textured

soy protein, which looked and tasted like something you'd feed your third-favorite pet – a guinea pig, maybe, or even a turtle.

My phone beeped, a message from Toby. *tiramisu for sweets!!!*

There were two ways to look at this: either he missed me and was trying to lure me back home with my favorite dessert, or he was just plain old kicking me in the knurries while I was down.

At first I thought it was the second, nastier option, but I changed my mind: they actually did miss me over there. Mom had already sent three text messages. Admittedly, they were mostly about the accessibility of clean underwear. And some dentist appointment I had. But still. And Miranda had sent one as well. Again it didn't actually say, *I miss you terribly, splendid brother, please, please come back*: what it said was, *do you know where the true blood dvd is?*, but I could read the subtext.

As I forced myself to eat some of the textured soy protein I changed my mind about feeding it to your third-favorite pet – no self-respecting guinea pig, no turtle, would eat that muck. When I'd eaten as much as I could and Gus had taken my plate away I said, "What's for dessert?"

Because, let's face it, a crap main course can always be saved by a reasonable dessert.

"Dessert?" said Gus.

"Also known as sweets," I said. "Or pudding if you're Stephen Denton, because his parents are English and that's what they call it over there."

"No, I don't eat sweets," he said.

"But I do," I said.

Gus shrugged.

"I'll just have some ice cream, then," I said.

Gus shook his head.

"Sugar is poison," he said. "It will kill you."

"That's ridiculous," I said. "A moderate amount of sugar in your diet isn't going to kill you."

"No, sugar will definitely kill you," said Gus, looking and sounding like some sort of religious fundamentalist, like his younger brother.

"That's rubbish," I said.

"Sugar will kill you," said Gus.

"It's The Debt who will kill you," I said, getting more and more annoyed. "Not sugar."

"They didn't kill me, they just did this," said Gus, patting what was left of his leg.

"But they killed your little brother," I said. "They killed Alessandro."

I'd intended to detonate a hand grenade, but instead it was an atomic bomb that went off.

Its effect on Gus was instantaneous – his face flushed deep red, the veins in the side of his neck popped out, and his whole body tensed up.

"How in the blazes do you know that?"

"Because I know where he is," I said.

Shut up, Dom.

But I was too far down whatever path I was on to do that.

"I've been there," I said.

Ω   Ω   Ω

As we rattled along the highway in Gus's truck, I really wished that I'd just eaten my textured soy protein and shut up.

"Slow down," I said, which were two words I never thought I'd use when my grandfather was driving. Headlights swept over us, we swooshed past trucks, cars honked; it was freeway as dystopia, and I couldn't help but be reminded of the time I'd come along this same road on a pizza delivery scooter, during the repayment of the second installment.

Again I checked my phone – still nothing from The Debt. Yes, the thought had occurred to me that they wouldn't use anything as obvious as a mobile phone to communicate. That just wasn't their style. I still couldn't help checking, though.

Gus tapped his brake; there was a wall of vehicles in front of us, all traveling at roughly the same speed, and there was no way through. Gus leaned on his horn. None of the vehicles moved, so he came up right behind the truck in the fast lane, and started flashing his high beams. Geriatric road rage – it wasn't pretty.

"Calm down, Gus!" I said. "Alessandro isn't going anywhere." Something must've clicked in Gus's brain, because he eased his foot from the accelerator.

"How do you know his name?" he said. In the half-light from the dash, his face looked so hard, like it had been chiseled from stone.

"I heard you use it once," I said. "When the Preacher was dying."

Gus pulled off the freeway and we were on a dark road, a quiet road.

Again I couldn't help thinking of the second installment, but it was a bit like looking at a movie. I knew I was the kid in that movie, but that kid seemed so much younger, more innocent, than the kid I was now, the one sitting in Gus's truck.

I checked my iPhone. Nothing.

"I know a way in," I said, and I gave him the directions.

We drove around the back way, along the dirt roads, until we came to the rear of the cemetery.

"There it is!" I said, pointing to the gap in the stone wall, the entrance. Gus pulled up the truck and we got out.

I'm not going to say it was a spooky night, because any night is spooky when you're just about to enter a cemetery. But there wasn't much moon, and the gusty wind occasionally made an eerie whistling sound. It was a really spooky night.

Gus followed me as I made my way along the path, the gravel crunching under our feet. The last time I was here I'd been in a state of high anxiety with choppers searching for me. I wasn't sure I'd find the crypt straightaway, but I didn't even have to look for it. It was like it was dragging me towards it.

"This is it," I said, stopping in front of the boxy-looking structure.

Gus took out a flashlight, used it to read the plaque. "Tabori," he said, spitting on the ground, and added something in Italian. He tried the door; it was locked.

"Can I borrow that?" I said, taking the flashlight from him. I used it to look closer at the lock – just as I'd expected, it was new. Obviously they'd upped the security at the Tabori crypt.

"You stay here," Gus said. "I'll be back in a jiffy."

I didn't want to stay here, by myself. But I also didn't want Gus to think I was some sort of wuss, so I did as he asked.

With my eyes closed.

There was the crunch of gravel, and Gus was back, carrying a tool bag.

"Hold the flashlight steady and we'll have this thing opened in no time," he said, taking out a screwdriver.

He was right, it took only a couple of minutes for us to get inside the crypt. It was much like I remembered from last time.

"What are we supposed to be looking at?" said Gus.

I showed him where the plaque was, except it wasn't – it had gone! Gus looked at me.

"There was a plaque here!" I said.

He looked closer, using the flashlight.

"I can't really see any screw holes," he said. "But I believe you – maybe they just filled them in."

What a relief, we could go now. But why was Gus taking a crowbar from the bag?

"What are you doing with that?" I said.

"I have to see him," he said. "I have to know for sure."

I didn't get it, and even in the dark Gus must've seen this I-don't-get-it written all over my face, because he launched into an explanation. "Alessandro disappeared when he was fifteen."

"Disappeared?"

"Like that," said Gus, clicking his fingers. He jammed the crowbar into the door and started levering it back.

Snap! The door swung open and hung off one hinge.

"So you never knew if he was actually dead or not?" I said, and of course I couldn't help thinking about Mr. Havilland. And Imogen.

"I knew in my guts that he was gone, but there was no proof, no body," said Gus, and he was silent for a while before he said, "it's what sent my mother to an early grave."

He cleared away some dirt with the end of the crowbar; I could see the end of the coffin. It was very plain, unadorned, more like a wooden box than something you would put your loved one in.

"But how did he end up here?" I said, my brain in overdrive, trying to make sense of all this information it'd been fed.

"Well, I guess they did him in and put him in here."

"They? The Debt?"

Gus nodded. "The Debt."

But answers were spawning even more questions. "But why would they kill him?"

"I'm not sure about that, but Alessandro obviously upset them somehow."

"Enough to kill him?"

"You seem surprised," said Gus.

"And why would they put him in here?"

"Keep your friends close, your enemies even closer," he said. "Nobody would ever look for him in here."

"But that plaque I saw, why would they put that there? That doesn't make sense."

"Who says they put it there?" said Gus.

But if they didn't, who did? As soon as I asked myself that question, I knew the answer: the Preacher.

"Anyway, we're getting way ahead of ourselves here; give me a hand sliding this out, can you?"

"Sure," I said, as if this was the most normal request in the world, like an old lady at the supermarket asking you if you could reach the box of All-Bran on the top shelf for her.

"Easy as she goes," said Gus as we slid the coffin out.

Again, I noticed how plain it was, and how much this fitted with Gus's crazy story.

"We're just going to put it over there," said Gus, indicating a sort of stone bench with the flashlight.

The coffin didn't weigh that much, but it was pretty awkward handling it, especially in such a confined space. But we managed to get it around and up onto the bench.

Gus handed me the flashlight. "I'm just going to pry the lid off," he said.

Again, his voice was so matter-of-fact.

That's a dead person in there, I wanted to scream. *A really, really old one. And what you're doing has actually got a name: grave robbing.*

But I bit my tongue. What would I know? Gus's brother had been missing for more than fifty years; didn't he have a right to find out what had happened to him?

The lid didn't need much prying, it sort of came apart. Gus said, "Okay, let me have the flashlight."

That suited me fine, I didn't really want to see what horror was inside. He took the flashlight and played the beam around inside the coffin.

Eventually he said, "It's not my brother."

"It's not?"

"No, this is a full-grown man."

Poor Gus, I thought. "So what now?"

"I guess we put him back and get out of here," he said, the disappointment dragging his voice down low.

It sounded like an excellent idea to me: get out of this place. But I knew I hadn't imagined that plaque.

"Give me the flashlight," I said to Gus. I got down on my hands and knees and shone it into the hole from which we'd taken the coffin.

I could just make out something at the other end. Just.

I pushed myself, head first, into the hole.

Immediately, I could feel it coming at me. Cured myself of coimetrophobia, my rectum.

It was coming at me, and it was coming at me hard, icing my guts, constricting my air passage. I had to get out of there!

But I closed my eyes, steadied my breathing.

It worked.

Now the flashlight picked out wood.

"There's another coffin here," I said.

"There is?" said Gus.

"For sure," I said. "I'm going to crawl further in, you take hold of my ankles."

"You don't have to –" started Gus, but I cut him short.

"I'm already on my way."

Using my elbows, I crawled commando-style deeper into the dark hole. As I did I thought of those stories you heard: people being buried while they were still alive. The horror of that was inconceivable.

Buried alive!

I reached out, tapped the end of the hole. Just as I'd thought, it was wood.

"Pass me the crowbar," I said, reaching back with my right hand. Soon I could feel the cold metal. I brought the crowbar forward, and rammed the pointed end into the coffin. The wood was quite brittle, and by twisting the crowbar around, I was able to make a hole large enough for four fingers.

I hesitated before I reached in – what would my fingers find?

But then I thought of Gus's words: *only the vessel he inhabited.* I thrust my fingers through the hole – they felt nothing – and grabbed the wood as tight as I could.

"Okay, I've got it, drag me back," I said.

I'm pretty sure Gus hadn't done all those weights, all those bench presses, bicep curls, tricep dips, so that one day he'd be able to drag his grandson and a coffin out of some dank hole, but they sure came in handy.

Soon I was out of there and on my feet.

We carried this coffin over and put it next to the other one.

The first thing I noticed was that it was shorter, and a shiver traveled up my spine.

I'm sure Gus noticed, too, because he quickly pried off the lid while I held the flashlight. As before, he then took the flashlight from me to inspect the contents. As before, I kept my eyes averted.

Eventually he said, "It's him; it's Alessandro." In his voice I could hear sadness, and relief, all sorts of emotions.

But then it occurred to me: how did he know?

Gus must've read my mind. "He broke his leg when he was nine, fell off a tractor. I can see where it mended."

I knew Gus needed some time, but I had to get out of here now.

After waiting for what I thought was a generous period, but what was probably less than a minute, I said, "We should probably get going?"

Gus, the arch-atheist, closed his eyes and muttered something that sounded suspiciously like a prayer.

"Let's go," he said, opening his eyes.

He took a black garbage bag out of his tool bag, shook it open, reached into the coffin and brought out a bone.

"What are you doing?" I said.

"I'm not leaving my little brother in this godforsaken hole any longer."

"But, but, but …" And then I remembered: "That's

205

only the vessel he inhabited during his time on earth."

"Alessandro is coming," Gus repeated, putting the bone into the garbage bag.

At this rate, we would be here all night, so what choice did I have? I helped Gus put his brother's bones into that black garbage bag. Not his skull, though. There was no way I was going to touch that. And indeed it was Gus who dealt with the skull, placing it carefully into the bag.

When we'd finished, when there were no more remains in the coffin, Gus tied a knot in the top of the garbage bag. We shoved the now-empty coffin back into the hole, pushing it right to the end. We were just about to do the same with the other coffin when I had a thought, a really terrible one.

If this wasn't Alessandro, which it clearly wasn't, then who was it?

"Give me the flashlight," I said to Gus.

"I think we've done enough," he said, but I wasn't about to be put off now.

"Give me the flashlight."

Gus handed it over. I shone it into the coffin. Even after spending several minutes manhandling human bones, it was a shock to see a dead person like this. I had to look away, and it took a while to compose myself.

But compose myself I did, shining the flashlight onto his skull; the eyeless sockets seemed to look back at me, the jaw seemed to say, *Let me be.*

I played the flashlight down the ribs, and among them I noticed the cigarette butts. It took me a little while to understand what this meant, but when I did it shocked me more than anything else I'd witnessed on this most shocking of nights: who would be so callous as to throw their butts into a coffin?

Then I saw it, the flash of silver. Around one wrist was a watch.

I leaned over, grabbed it, and shoved it into my pocket. It felt heavy in there: solid, incriminating.

Grave robbers, that's what they're called. I'm not sure Gus saw me or not; if he did he didn't say anything.

"Let's get out of here," I said.

Gus put the lid back on as best he could, and we maneuvered the coffin back into its hole. Gus screwed the door back on.

We were out of there like bats out of – well, maybe we weren't quite bats, but that really had been like, you know – crunching back up the path, me carrying the tool bag, and Gus stomping along with the bag of his brother's bones over his shoulder. If ever there was a time for Gus to come out with his favorite saying: *blazing bells and buckets of blood*, it was this, but Gus said nothing.

Into the truck, and onto the freeway, and at last I had time to sit back and exhale, to try to process what had just happened. There was one question that needed to be asked: why did they kill Alessandro? But

I wasn't going to ask it. Not then.

There had been too much death, too much dying. I could smell it coming off my hands. Off my clothes.

I checked my phone: I had three messages, but none from The Debt.

Mom again. That dentist appointment was on Thursday.

Miranda: *it's ok I found dvd.*

And one from Imogen: *did you really leave school?*

I replied to the first one: *ok;* I replied to the second one: *good.*

I hesitated before I replied with *yes* to the third one; I could feel the weight of the grave-robbed watch in my pocket.

We turned back onto the freeway; it was less hectic now, and Gus was in less of a hurry. I looked over at my grandfather. It was hard to gauge what sort of mood he was in.

"Gus, you okay?" I said.

"I'm tired," he said. "But I'm good; it's been a long, long wait."

Again that question in my head: why did they kill Alessandro?

But now sure wasn't the time to ask it.

We took the exit off the freeway, heading for Halcyon Grove. A noise from behind, and a flashing blue light.

"Wonder who they're after?" I said.

The police car came up alongside us, and the policeman in the passenger's seat made a pull over gesture. Gus grimaced. "Might just be us."

Grave robbing. What was the penalty? Maybe not years in jail, but imagine the story on the Internet!

Grandfather and Grandson Break into Crypt

If that didn't go viral, nothing would.

My hand felt the watch in my pocket. I could drop it out of the window, shove it under the seat, but I didn't; nothing was going to make me let go of it.

We stopped on the side of the road, the police car pulling up right behind us. The policeman appeared at the window.

"Evening," he said, in a pleasant way.

"Evening, officer," said Gus, in an equally pleasant way.

"Do you mind if I have a look at your license?"

Gus took out his wallet, extracted his license. The police officer disappeared with it for a minute or so. When he came back he said, "No problems there."

"Can I ask what this is about?" said Gus.

"One of your taillights isn't working."

"I didn't realize," said Gus. "Don't take the old girl out much at night these days."

Like, derrrr, Gus! Why would you ever say that to a cop?

"You don't?" said the policeman, and I could see that he was having a look in the back of the truck. To my mind we were now goners: there was a tool bag, there was a black garbage bag, of course he was going to put two and two together and deduce that we'd used the tools in the tool bag to break into a crypt and steal the human remains that were in the black bag.

His face appeared again in the window.

"Make sure you fix the light," he said. "The good thing about these old trucks is that it's probably just a globe."

"I'll do it tomorrow, officer," said Gus.

The policeman got back into his car and drove off.

"Whoa!" I said. And Gus gave one of his low seismic laughs.

It was only when I was back at Gus's house, and in my room, that I was able to inspect the grave-robbed watch more carefully. It was a beautiful old timepiece, an Omega Speedmaster. On the back was an inscription.

To Graham from Beth. My One True Love.

Blazing bells and buckets of blood! We'd just found Imogen's missing father.

THE ASSOCIATES

You would think that after such a horrendous experience, I would be awake all night, wracked by nightmares – each more gruesome, more explicit, than the one that went before. Wrong. I slept really well. You would also think that after such a revelation – I knew where Mr. Havilland was! – my mind would be in turmoil, deciding what do with this explosive information. Wrong. I felt weirdly calm. Maybe whoever was in charge of the good ship Dominic Silvagni had decided that enough was enough, that I needed some steady-as-she-goes plain sailing. Otherwise I was going to end up wrecked on some rocky shore.

So the next day I went off to work as if nothing had happened. It was more of the same, which is not to say that it was boring – far from it. It was good to do something that had nothing to do with either graves or robbing, and I was really starting to get the hang of it now, following these convoluted money trails. And Hound seemed very happy with what I was doing.

But around midafternoon, I found myself with nothing to do. I'd done the work too quickly. Hound was out of the office; he'd gone to court for the afternoon, so he wasn't able to give me something else to get stuck into. So I was just mucking around on my computer, checking out the credit rating of a few people I knew.

Mr. Cranbrook, the principal of my school (very good, by the way).

Dr. Chakrabarty (didn't have one!).

Mrs. Havilland (very very bad!). Then I got this idea in my head of doing some digging on my father, he of the empty cobwebby office.

That swagger I'd recently acquired concerning my cyber-sleuthing – I lost it pretty quickly. My dad, and my dad's financial dealings, were elusive.

I could sense that they were there, but I just couldn't quite find them. Every time I thought I was on some sort of roll, when I'd found a trail, it came to a dead end. A couple of times I even gave up, walked away from the computer and went down to Cash Converters to annoy Ratface Ponytail a bit more. But then I'd get an idea and I'd rush upstairs again to put it into action. But that would result in another dead end, another trail gone cold. One entity that kept popping up, however, was Coast Home Loans.

So I decided to concentrate on that connection. I was really getting somewhere too – my dad was obviously a major investor in that company – when Hound came charging up the stairs, spurs jangling, and over to my desk.

"Let's go, Youngblood," he said. "We've got a business meeting."

"Where?" I said.

"The boardroom, of course," he said. "Cozzi's."

I got up, and was about to follow Hound when he said, "Why don't you slip your jacket on, makes you look older." So I slipped my denim jacket on.

It was only a fifteen-minute walk to Cozzi's, but why walk when you've got a Hummer, perhaps the world's most ridiculous car? We got on board – with a Hummer it really does feel like you're on board – and made our way there.

Unusually there was no rap playing on the stereo, but something much more folksy, like Bob Dylan.

"Who's this singing?" I asked Hound.

"Rodriguez," he said. "He was very big in South Africa when I was growing up."

"What was South Africa like?"

"For a white kid like me, it was a paradise," he said. "But maybe you should ask a black person the same question, they might have a different answer."

We pulled into Cozzi's, parking in the loading zone. As we got out I noticed that quite a few of Cozzi's customers were looking at us. I wasn't sure whether to be pleased about this – it's nice to be noticed – or a bit embarrassed – I'd arrived in a Hummer, Hound was in double denim, me single. In the end I figured that as Hound was my employer, I had to show some solidarity, so I walked alongside him. My spurs jangling.

After ordering our drinks inside – triple espresso for me, Earl Grey tea for Hound – we went outside.

"There they are," he said, pointing to a table where the Cerberus Three – Nitmick, Guzman and Snake were sitting.

"They're your associates?" I said, thinking of the first job I ever did for Hound: nabbing Nitmick, sending him back to the monkey house. Hound's only answer was a big old wink.

"Gentlemen ..." he said, approaching their table.

If the Cerberus Three held any grudges against me for effectively scuttling their project, they didn't show it. Not even Nitmick.

"How's Eve?" I asked him.

"Up the duff," said Guzman, jumping in before Nitmick had a chance to answer.

This initiated a whole lot of up-the-duff jokes, not all of which I understood. Still, it felt pretty cool to be sitting there, in this circle of business associates. Far, far away from any graves.

After a few minutes, two other associates joined

us – noted criminals, the Lazarus brothers. Again, I felt a bit nervous, because the last time I'd seen them, the mild-mannered Luiz Antonio had made them both look like a couple of big girls' blouses.

But again, they didn't appear to hold any grudges. In fact, one of them even said, "That taxi driver mate of yours, he's pretty handy with the kung fu, eh?"

"I think it's technically capoeira or even Brazilian jujitsu," I said.

After about twenty minutes of conversation, which seemed pretty much to consist of swapping insults, Hound said, "Okay, gentleman, let's get down to business."

He took out his phone, a Styxx Charon, swiped some screens and put it down on an empty seat. I could see the recorder app running.

"Somebody's got to take the minutes," said Hound. "Okay, who wants to start?"

Nobody wanted to start, and I could guess why: me. "I can make myself scarce if you like," I said to Hound.

"Nonsense, you're part of the team now," he said, looking around at his associates, daring them to oppose him. "Look, if nobody else wants to get this underway, I will."

He took a delicate sip of his tea.

Cracked his knuckles.

And said two words: "Yamashita's" was the first one, "gold" was the second one.

A feather would've been overkill; you could've knocked me down with something that had much less substance.

"But that's gone," said a Lazarus. "Those two kids got away with it."

The associates exchanged looks – *That's what we heard, too.*

But Hound smiled a knowing smile. "It's not what my intel is telling me," he said. "According to them, it's still very much in the country."

I wondered who Hound's intel was, and wondered how they knew.

It was Guzman's turn to say something. "So what, exactly, are you proposing, Hound?"

Hound took another tiny sip of his tea.

"We've got a very comprehensive range of skills around this table, especially now that we have Youngblood on the payroll," he said. "If we can't find out where that gold is, then we're not trying."

"With all due respect," said Nitmick, "you've been chasing that gold for a while, without much luck."

Again Hound sipped his tea. "Fair point," he said. "But this is different. Before it was pie-in-the-sky stuff, but we know now that the gold exists." He looked over at me. "Isn't that right, Youngblood?"

So how much, exactly, did Hound know about my involvement with Yamashita's Gold? Did he somehow know that I'd been on the *Argo* when they'd found the treasure and it had been heisted by the Zolton-Banders? I decided to play it dumb.

"It was all over the news," I said. "But I didn't take that much notice."

As I said this, my phone beeped. I took it out, checked the message. It was from an unknown sender. It said, *deal on, Y gold for 6 installment you have 48hrs to deliver.*

I looked around the table – had somebody there just sent it to me? No, of course they hadn't. It was the text I'd been waiting for, hoping for, and it just happened to have arrived in the middle of this discussion.

I felt an enormous surge of emotion, a surge that lifted me from the table and sent me hovering above, five hundred, a thousand meters high – I could get out of this without having to take a life!

The surge de-surged, and I was back at the rickety little table again, back to reality – could I really pull off this outrageous plan, align all the stars that needed aligning?

The associates talked a little bit more before Snake, his voice low, said, "We've got company, fellas. Six o'clock." I snuck a quick glance at six o'clock – cops. Two of them. They were pretending to be everyday Cozzi's customers, but Snake had it right: they had *cops* written all over them.

"So I suggest we all do some research and reconvene in a couple of days' time," said Hound.

Everybody agreed that would be a good idea.

As we drove back in the Hummer, that Rodriguez music playing again, Hound seemed to be in a very cheerful mood.

"That went well," I said.

"I think so," said Hound. "It got them thinking, anyway."

I didn't quite get his tone; it was as if he was talking about his enemies, not his associates. Which got me thinking again: how did they become his associates?

When we got back to the office Hound said I could knock off for the day.

"It's okay," I said. "I've got some more work to do."

He slapped me on the back. "That's the spirit!"

I did have some more work to do, but it was nothing to do with dubious men and their dubious credit ratings.

I tried calling Zoe's number, but I was informed it was no longer active. That, I could understand: if I was one of Australia's most wanted criminals I wouldn't have a public number either. In fact, I wouldn't have a number at all – as Hanley had said, a mobile phone is basically a tracking device. Carry one around and you're like one of those migrating whales with the electronic tag attached.

I went to the Zolt's Facebook page. He now had 1,267,987 fans.

And the comments, as before, were numerous. Most of them were complimentary, stuff like *go zolt hope your leading the good life* and *you sure showed them zolt you hero*. But there were others that were less complimentary.

zolt I hope you die you skum

Here I go again, I thought, because it was déjà vu all over again, if you know what I mean. It was back to installment one.

Back to me trying to work out how the Zolt communicated with his sister. Back to me cracking the code they used.

Except now it was me wanting to communicate with them.

Could I just put a coded message in a comment up there like before and assume they'd see it? No, I didn't think so. There's no way somebody would spend their days wading through all those comments, no way they would eventually see mine. I had to come up with something else.

And quickly.

But what?

Hound came in to say that he was going home, that his lady had prepared some sort of South African delicacy: roast zebra with all the trimmings, something like that. He said I was fine to keep working and he showed me how to lock up.

I sat at my desk, racking my brain: how do you get into contact with two people who don't want to be contacted?

The Cash Converters downstairs closed its doors. I texted Gus, told him to hold the textured soy protein because I was working late.

More racking.

It was now dark outside, and the streets were empty.

More racking.

I googled *how to get in contact with people in hiding*. But even Google, probably my best friend in the world, failed to help me.

More racking.

This time, I had an insight: how do people like the police get in contact with people when they don't have a phone number or an address or anything like that?

They use newspapers or television: "Could the person in the yellow beanie who witnessed the car crash on the corner of ..." sort of thing.

But that was old, old technology. Who reads newspapers? Who watches the news? Not people my age.

They watch ... YouTube!

So I needed to put something on YouTube that was going to go viral and get Zoe or the Zolt's attention.

I took out my iPhone, scrolled through the photos, and – lo and behold – there it was, the video I'd taken that day of the two of them heisting the gold with the stolen helicopter.

Yeah, right.

I'd done no such thing, taken no such video.

More racking.

More racking.

More racking.

Now my brain was hurting and I was thinking that it was time to go home. And I was doing just that, getting ready to leave, when something occurred to me, something pretty fundamental.

I didn't need the real video!

What I needed was something that people would think was the real video.

Armed with this insight, my friend Google and I got to work.

It wasn't that difficult to find the appropriate footage: footage of gold bars, footage of helicopters, even some footage of the real *Argo*. And there were plenty of photos of the Zolt to splice in.

I downloaded FileLab, a free video editing program, and got stuck in. Not having had much experience with editing before, it was slow going, but eventually I had something I was sort of happy with.

Especially the ending, a chopper wobbling off. (This chopper eventually crashed, but of course I didn't use that bit.)

Now for a snappy title, also a must according to the experts. I decided on *The Zolt Gets the Gold*.

But it still wasn't quite working.

Of course, something else all the experts agreed on, a stonking sound track was a must. Something to do with gold, then. It didn't take me long to find it, from that James Bond film – *Goldfinger* – sung by somebody called Shirley Bassey. It was about a million years old, but it was perfect.

Now it was ready.

I hit the upload button and away it went.

When it had finished I went to some other sites, including all the fan pages, and cross-posted the link. But just as I'd done this, I had a thought: how would Zoe and Otto know that it was me? How would they know that I wanted to contact them?

Of course, the code!

I left a comment under the clip, a comment that would only make sense to the Zolton-Banders – or maybe some *True Blood* fanatic.

came via last mail

dracula no monster

Phew!

I checked the time – it was past ten. How was that possible?

I looked out the window.

And I got scared.

Last night, I was up to my elbows in human remains. So what – the dead, as scary as they are, can't really hurt you. But out there, on those dark, dirty streets, were people who could really hurt you; they were the real vampires, the real werewolves. I was speaking from experience, from when I'd broken into this office during the first installment.

I'll call a taxi.

But as soon as I had that thought I discounted it – I was an adult, working at an adult's job, not some scaredy-cat kid.

I'd ride home. Really, really, really fast.

I followed Hound's instructions and locked up the office and carried my bike downstairs.

Only one more door to go, but I would be on the street when I locked it, my back facing the wrong way.

What choice did I have?

Putting my bike behind me as a sort of shield, I locked the final door. Now I was ready to get out of here.

"Hey, kid, you after something?"

The owner of this voice stepped out from the shadows. I knew him: he was the one I'd stabbed in the leg with the lockpick that night. But did he know me?

"Nah, I'm pretty fine," I said, trying to keep it casual.

As I threw my leg over the bike, I could see the look of recognition appear on his face.

"Hey, I know you!" he said.

"So what?" I said, stepping hard on the pedal, knowing that he had no chance of grabbing me now. "You cretin!" I added for good measure, and that's when my bike came to a crunching stop and I tumbled to the ground. I knew exactly what had happened, because it had happened to me once before at primary school, when Bryce Snell shoved a stick in the spokes of my bike.

I jumped to my feet and got ready to run, but he was on me already, and I felt the sharp point in my back.

"Okay," I said, holding up my hands like I'd seen a thousand people do on a thousand TV shows. I could see now that in fact there were four of them: vampires, werewolves, creatures of the night.

"Your wallet?" hissed the one wielding the knife.

"I work for Hound, you know," I said. Suddenly I was Billy Connolly, Eddie Murphy and everybody in *South Park* – they cracked up laughing.

I reached into my pocket, took out my wallet.

And that's when the taxi seemed to come out of nowhere, pull up at the curb. The door opened and Luiz Antonio was in the mix.

The night creatures didn't move.

"This has got nothing to do with you, old fella," said one of them.

"I wouldn't call him that if I was you," I said. Again I was the world's funniest man.

Luiz Antonio waltzed up to the first night creature and took him out with one of those leg sweeps. The second night creature came at him and Luiz Antonio disposed of him with a sort of nonchalant ease – basically he just jabbed him in the face, and the night creature crumpled screaming to the ground.

Two to go.

The third night creature took off with a speed that would have had Usain Bolt concerned.

One to go, but this one had a knife, and this one had some major attitude. I knew that he could fight too, just from the balanced posture he'd adopted. He turned to face Luiz Antonio, tossing the knife from hand to hand.

"Come on, old fella," he said. "You think a bit of karate is going to frighten me?"

I edged out of his sight, picked up the bicycle, and brought it down hard on his head.

He collapsed and Luiz Antonio finished him off, kicking the knife from his grasp, retrieving my wallet.

I chained my bike to the post and got into the taxi.

"Thanks," I said to Luiz Antonio.

But I said nothing else until we got out of the Block. "How did you know where I was? How in the blazes did you know?"

"You take too many risks, amigo," said Luiz Antonio.

Maybe, but despite what had just happened, despite the danger I'd been in, I was over being owned. I was over everybody knowing where I was.

I needed to do something about it.

And I needed to do it now!

"Can you drop me off at the hospital?" I said.

"You hurt?" said Luiz Antonio, concern in his voice, taking in the bandage still on my hand.

"No, I just need you to drop me off at the hospital," I said. I took out my phone. "I'm going to text Gus, tell him I'm okay. But he probably bloody well knows that already."

Luiz Antonio took the next right, towards the hospital, and ten minutes later we were pulling up outside Emergency.

"Don't bother waiting," I snapped. "I can find my own way home."

"I'll wait," he said. Suddenly, I felt like a bit of a grouch – he had rescued me, and here I was acting like this to him.

"Thanks," I said. "Hopefully this won't take long."

It did take long.

Emergency was chockers, and I didn't do myself any favors in the triage department.

"So what's your problem tonight?" the nurse asked me. "Is it your hand?"

"I have this other issue," I said.

"Can you be a bit more specific?"

Several things – the fact that I had once been rendered unconscious and woken to find a suspicious lump on my right hand, the fact that I now tripped scanners at airports and, most importantly, the fact that everybody seemed to know where I was – had led me to suspect that I had some sort of tracking device implanted in my body.

But I wasn't going to tell her that, because I'm pretty sure she would've triaged me straight to the loony bin.

"It's, like, this issue inside me," I said, and I wished I'd been better prepared and googled some great condition that would get me instantly to the front of the line, ahead of the people with broken legs and guts practically spilling out, but I hadn't, so I had to keep going with what I had.

She looked at me through her glasses, and I wondered if the loony bin was occurring to her anyway.

"The pain is pretty incredible," I said.

She typed something into the computer – maybe *attention seeking nutcase* – and told me to take a seat, my name would be called in due course. The thing about Emergency is that it's designed so the worst cases get seen to first, so you don't necessarily get to move up the line at all.

After over an hour of waiting, I wondered about going home, sorting this out at a later date, but something told me that now was the right time. After two hours of waiting, I'd come up with another plan:

I'd go to another hospital, but this time I would google a disease that would put me at the front of the line, probably something invasive to do with the brain. Or that thing I'd read about once where these people had huge maggots coming out of their skin.

But then my name was announced over the loudspeaker and I was in one of those examination cubicles and there was a real doctor talking to me in a lovely soft melodious voice. She didn't look very old, in her early twenties, and I wondered if she was an intern or something.

"So your hand?" she said, pointing to the bandage.

I held out my other hand. "This one."

"And what exactly is the problem?"

"I think you should X-ray it, or do an ultrasound, see if there's anything wrong inside it."

She gave me a funny look, and I didn't blame her – she was the one who'd gotten a ridiculously high score in exams in her final year at high school, who had slogged through so many years of university, who'd had to cut up smelly old corpses and all sorts of other gross stuff; she was the one who got to do the diagnosis, not me. She had another look at the piece of paper on the clipboard.

"Are you any relation to Celia Silvagni?" she said.

"That's my mother," I said.

"She's the reason I'm here today."

No! I thought. *It can't be – is she my sister?*

"I was awarded one of her scholarships," she said.

Okay – my life was not a soap opera.

"I left school when I was fifteen," she said.

Nothing wrong with that, I thought.

"If it wasn't for her I don't know where I'd be."

"Wow!" I said. "That's so cool." And I absolutely did think it was so cool, and I had that thought I'd had a few times lately, that even though Dad probably got his money in questionable ways, Mom used it in non-questionable ways. I also had another thought: I could take advantage of this. "So can you do an X-ray or an ultrasound on my hand?"

"But this hand seems fine to me, Dominic."

I took a deep breath, because I was just about to become loony. "This is going to sound really, really crazy, but I'm pretty sure there's some sort of biochip implanted in my hand. And, no, I don't think aliens put it there. Somebody else did. And I know right now you think I'm a bit loopy, but I tell you, I'm not. So all I'm asking is that you have a look for me. That's all. And if it isn't there, then I'll be fine, and I will never ever mention it as long as I live. I promise."

The doctor looked at me, and I wondered what was going through her well-trained mind. *Psychiatric evaluation? Do what he asks and get him out of here? Contact his mother – if she is his mother?*

Eventually she seemed to make a decision. "Wait here," she said.

I waited there. Would she return with a) some sort of imaging device, b) a psychiatrist or c) the security guard?

The answer, thank heavens, was a.

She plugged the machine in, turned it on, and applied some gel to the back of my hand. Then she moved the knob thing over that area. She had a nice touch, a nice manner, and a really nice voice, and I was happy my mum had awarded her that scholarship.

"It all looks very normal to me, Dominic," she said in a soothing tone.

I wondered if she'd learned that at medical school, too – the right tone to adopt with potential nutcases, just the right amount of soothe.

But then a look came over her face. She twiddled a knob on the machine. "What did you say you thought had been implanted in you?"

"Some sort of chip," I said. "It probably wouldn't be very big."

"That big?" she said, pointing to rectangular shape on the screen, about a centimeter long.

"I knew it!" I said. "I just knew it."

The doctor shook her head. "Well, I guess I've learned a lesson."

"So can you take it out?"

"No, not here," she said. "It's actually quite deep – it would definitely require anesthetic, probably a general for such a procedure. If you like, I could make an appointment for you to come back and see the general surgeon."

Did I want the biochip taken out, did I want to stop being owned by whoever it was that was owning me? Of course I did. But then I thought of all the times I'd been saved: just now by Luiz Antonio, that time when I'd been left in the middle of the ocean, that other time when I'd been almost sashimi-ed by the propellers of the supertanker.

Yes, I wanted it taken out, but I had to think it through properly.

"Can I get a hard copy of that?" I said, pointing to the screen.

"Of course," she said, hitting a button. There was whirring sound, and a printout appeared on a tray.

"I'll get my mum to call," I said, taking the printout, getting up out of my seat.

"Just wait a second," said the doctor. "This is highly irregular, and I'd like to get a more senior colleague to have a look."

But I was already on the move, ready to slam it straight into top gear. "I really think ..." said the doctor, her voice fading as I made my way quickly through Emergency.

Surely Luiz Antonio wasn't still waiting? But as soon as I had this thought, his taxi slid up alongside. And I got in.

"So what do you use, some sort of radar or something?" I asked Luiz Antonio.

He pointed to the glove compartment. I opened it, and inside was a screen. On it was a GPS map, with a red dot, a red dot that was traveling along Cascade Street, heading west.

A red dot that was me.

It all made sense now: the interest Gus had shown in the small lump in my hand, the pile of articles about biochips I'd seen on his desk that time, the fact that Luiz Antonio always seemed to know where I was. Smart old bugger that he was, Gus had quickly worked out that The Debt had implanted some sort of biochip in my hand. And he'd decided that two could play Track the Kid.

So somehow he'd worked out how to tune into the particular biochip that I had. Like I said, smart old bugger.

"Amazing," I said. "What range has this thing got?"

"Around two hundred kilometers," he said.

"And is this all you can do, track me?"

"That's all it does," he said.

I believed him, but I wondered if The Debt had more powerful, sophisticated technology, because I was sure there were occasions when they had been privy to my conversations, even to my thoughts.

I remembered that hardware I'd seen in the pump room – surely that had something to do with it.

I closed the glove compartment, and I leaned back in my seat, and I said, "Any chance of some samba?"

Luiz Antonio hit some buttons and the music started. It wasn't the happy samba, however, it was the sad samba.

Sadness has no end, but happiness does.

And it suited me fine.

CIDADE MARAVILHOSA

It was 2:35 a.m. when we got home. Gus was in his room, pretending he was asleep, pretending he wasn't worrying about me at all. But I could see the light seeping under his door, hear shuffling noises from within.

I could practically smell all that worry.

"Gus, you might as well come out," I said. "There's somebody here to see you."

It didn't take long for the door to open and Gus to appear, dressed in pajama shorts and one of his signature tank tops. This one, so it said, was from the Canggu Club in Bali.

"I believe you two know each other," I said.

Gus glared at the taxi driver, but Luiz Antonio gave a very Brazilian shrug: *Hey, what could I do?* Or whatever that is in his language.

"He saved me, yet again," I said.

Gus relaxed. "Well, that's what he's paid for."

"Paid?" said Luiz Antonio. "When was the last time you paid me, you stingy old bugger?"

Know each other? It was immediately obvious these two were old friends who probably swapped the same jokes over and over again. Did I want to overload my brain with even more information tonight?

Yeah, probably.

"So, maybe an explanation wouldn't be such a bad idea," I said.

"It's a long story," said Gus, and then he added something in another language.

"You can speak Spanish?" I said.

"Portuguese," said Gus. "The language of Brazil."

Now I definitely wanted to overload my brain with even more information. "I'm up for it," I said. "In fact, I can even pour you a couple of whiskies."

Gus and Luiz Antonio had a short conversation in Portuguese before Gus said, "Both of them on the rocks."

I made the drinks, we sat around the kitchen table.

Eventually Gus said, "I'm not sure how much your dad has told you about his childhood."

"Not that much," I said. "Except that his family didn't have much money."

"Not much money?" said Gus. "You dad is being very generous. We didn't have much money because what we had I drank all away."

"Drank it?"

"I was an alcoholic," he said, looking at the whisky swirling in his glass. "Probably still am, but I can keep a lid on it now."

He seemed lost for a while, before he continued, "My wife, your father's mother, committed suicide. And after that, I just fell into a complete hole. When your father reached fifteen, when it was his time, I was no help to him whatsoever. Blazing bells and buckets of blood, if anything, I was a hindrance." Again, the words didn't seem to be coming, but he eventually found some more. "Yet your father did it, he paid off those installments."

I looked over at Luiz Antonio, thinking obviously he must know about The Debt.

"He is a remarkable man, your dad. If he'd had any athletic talent at all, he would've won Olympic gold. Determination and tenacity, the two greatest attributes any athlete could have, and he has them in spades." My phone beeped, but I resisted the temptation to check the message. "After The Debt, he went away."

"My dad left home at fifteen?" I said.

Gus nodded. "And I didn't blame him, I was just dragging him into my sewer."

"But where did he go?"

Gus waved my question away. "Then one night, it just got too much and I decided that it was my time to go too. I was no good to anybody, especially not myself. I took the shotgun my old man used for killing rats, and I stuck the barrel in my mouth, and …"

"What?!" I said.

"Click," said Gus, pulling an imaginary trigger. "Nothing – the gun didn't work. They always say that you have to reach rock bottom before you can start dragging yourself up. Well, that was my rock bottom. The next day I went along to an Alcoholics Anonymous meeting, but that was never going to work for a nonbeliever like me. But then I was watching this old movie on the box. Ronald Reagan, yes, that Ronald Reagan, plays this character who has both his legs amputated, and during the movie somebody recites some of this poem to him."

"'Invictus'?" I said.

Gus looked at me, both surprised and amused. "You know it?"

"'It matters not how strait the gate, how charged with punishments the scroll. I am the master of my fate: I am the captain of my soul,'" I said.

Gus took a sip of his whisky. "That poem became my AA, my mentor, my guide."

"But Luiz Antonio?" I said. "How did you meet him?"

"Well, I gradually got my career on track. I had some ideas about training that were considered a bit too out-there for the conservative running scene here, so I ended up doing some coaching in Europe.

Holland, Germany and then in Italy, where I had this Brazilian kid under me. Roberto was his name. Great little runner, too. But injury finished his career. Anyway, somehow through him, or his family – I forget now – I ended up getting this job in Rio de Janeiro."

"The Cidade Marvilhosa," I said.

"You better believe it," said Gus. "Anyway, I arrived at the airport carrying nothing but a small bag, and who do you think is there to pick me up?"

"Luiz Antonio!" I said.

"Not only do we end up working for the same club, we end up living in the same house when his family takes me in as a lodger. They were good days in Rio; the Brazilian athletic scene back then was very strong, and they're a modern people, they liked my new ideas. But what I wasn't aware of, not at first, was that politically it was a whole different matter. The country was just coming out of a military dictatorship. Opposition had not been tolerated, and hundreds and hundreds of people disappeared during those times."

I remembered now that Luiz Antonio had once told me he'd come here because the military was in power in his country and it was safer for him to get out. But then he got used to living here, and his family got used to him not living there.

Gus took a sip of whisky and continued, a smile playing on his lips. "What I didn't know was that my workmate was still one of Brazil's most active Marxists."

"What's a Marxist?" I said.

"A revolutionary, somebody who wants to change the status quo," said Gus. "Brazil was a very rich country with a very unequal distribution of wealth."

"Was?" said Luiz Antonio. "What do you mean by 'was'?"

"Okay, it still is, but it was even worse back then. And at least they have democratic elections now. Anyway, to cut a long story short, for a long time the military wanted to take my Marxist friend here for a helicopter trip over the ocean, one from which he wasn't going to come back."

"Whoa," I said, immediately thinking of the swim I'd had in the ocean, the one I thought I wouldn't come back from.

"And ironically, when they started losing power, he was in even more danger. So he had to get out of the country," said Gus.

"Your grandfather risked his life to get me out of the country," said Luiz Antonio. "Without his help, I would be dead."

I looked over at Gus, and I felt an immense pride swelling up inside me. I'd always known that he was special, my grandfather. I'd always known that he was a hero. And here was the proof.

"So when he asked me if I could help to keep an

eye on you, of course I said yes."

So many questions.

But when I looked at the clock and it told me it was 4:23 a.m., the fatigue that I'd been keeping at bay suddenly got me in a hammerlock. "I have to go to bed." I said good night and left the two old men still talking, still sipping their whiskies.

I brushed my teeth and was just about to crawl between the sheets when I thought, *Why not?* I opened my laptop, went to YouTube.

Already I'd had 22,345 plays.

I did a Google search. My video was all over the net.

Viral?

You bet!

RENT-A-COP

There's dreams and there's nightmares and there's the thing I had that night. It had human bones and it had human blood and it had people getting pushed out of helicopters; it was like some desperate horror-movie maker had thrown everything into the script. Except this really was horrifying, and really was terrifying, and now there was somebody, a zombie-vampire-ghoul hybrid, trying to kill me!

Except the zombie-vampire-ghoul hybrid was Gus, and he was actually gently shaking me, waking me up. "Dom," he said, morning gravel in his voice. "You need to get up."

"No, I don't," I said. "Hound'll be totally okay if I come in late."

"No," said Gus. "There are some people here to see you."

Otto? Zoe? But would they really just rock up like that?

"Coppers," said Gus.

"Your taillight?" I said, my brain still sleep-addled. "Did you replace it yet?"

"No, these are detectives," said Gus. "I can put them off, but I think it's better if you deal with them now."

Sleep-addled, but I knew he was right. I swung my legs over, got out of bed and rushed into the shower. Hot water, cold water, hot water, cold, and I was starting to feel half awake. I got dressed – board shorts, T-shirt – and made my way into the kitchen.

There were three of them, all men – when did coppers ever come in threes, I asked myself – sitting around the kitchen table. Two were playing with their smartphones, the other was leafing through a copy of *Running World*. All three looked up when I entered the room, but I could read nothing from their blank cop expressions.

"Dominic," said the *Running World* cop, who was sporting some really retro sidies. "My name is Detective Westaway and these are my colleagues Detectives Truscott and Monroe."

Detective Westaway took a laptop from the bag that was at his feet and placed it on the table. He tapped a few keys and then turned the laptop around so that I could see the screen.

It was YouTube. And I could sort of guess what was coming next.

I guessed right.

Shirley Bassey belting out "Goldfinger," while my little video started playing.

I couldn't help checking out the play count: 88,421! This was more than viral, this was a plague, like one of those in the Bible.

The video ended, the supposedly gold-laden helicopter wobbling off towards the horizon.

"You put this online?" said Detective Monroe, who obviously had a handle on the language of the World Wide Web.

I could've told them the truth: the video was something I'd concocted, but I guess I was pretty proud of my effort – it had fooled them, hadn't it? And something told me it was in my best interests to keep the charade going as long as I could.

"I did," I said.

"Why?" said Detective Monroe.

"I don't know, I just wanted to upload something that would go crazy viral."

"Well, it's certainly done that," said Detective Truscott, who was bald.

"So where did you get the footage from?" said Detective Westaway.

"I think it was IsoHunt," I said. "Or maybe even Pirate Bay. One of those torrent sites, anyway."

Detectives Truscott and Monroe exchanged looks – that the video was already on a torrent site was obviously news to them – as Detective Westaway banged away at the keyboard. "He's right," he eventually said. "It's on Pirate Bay, and it's been up there for weeks."

Of course it was, because I was the one who put it there.

Another thing The Debt had taught me – cover your bases. Okay, two things – cover your bases, and make full use of sports analogies. Unlike YouTube, it's very, very easy to remain completely anonymous on Pirate Bay. It's also very easy to fudge the time. Otherwise all those dudes who put up movies before they've been commercially released would have the dogs of Hollywood unleashed on them.

"Have I done anything illegal?" I asked, all faux innocence. "I probably shouldn't have used that James Bond song, but it seemed so perfect."

Detective Westaway was giving his colleagues some major smile action, and it occurred to me that he hadn't been so convinced about this little trip behind the high stone walls of Halcyon Grove. I sort of guessed that he wouldn't be buying next time they went to the pub.

"Sorry to have bothered you, Dominic," said Detective Westaway. "Looks like we're barking up the wrong tree."

Right tree, wrong branch – I almost felt sorry for them, especially when Detective Westaway indicated the magazine and said, "You fellas into running?"

"Gus is a coach," I said. "And I run middle distance."

"Fifteen hundred meters?" he said. I nodded. "So what's your PB, if you don't mind me asking?"

I thought about lying, telling him something a bit pedestrian, but then I thought *why bother*? I told him my Rome time. "Four minutes flat."

He whistled. "I'll be watching out for you in the next Olympics," he said, smiling.

With those retro sidies, he didn't look much like a cop, more like the guitarist in a rockabilly band. He brought out a business card from his pocket and placed it lightly on the table.

"Rent-a-Cop," he said. "I do weddings, birthdays, bar mitzvahs, but I draw the line at pet funerals."

As he joined his colleagues and the three detectives left, I watched him carefully. He had the loose springy walk of an athlete; was he a runner too? I looked at the card, half expecting it to say Rent-a-Cop, but of course it was an official Queensland Police card. He was definitely a cool cop, though, and I slotted the card into my wallet.

Gus said, "I don't even want to know what that was about."

"You're right, you don't," I said, getting online on my iPhone, going to YouTube: 89,111 plays! But why hadn't they contacted me yet?

The visit from the cops had proven one thing, though: I was hot, and the Zolton-Banders had every right to be careful contacting me. I just hoped they weren't going to be so careful that I wasn't going to notice.

I scrolled through the comments to my YouTube video, but apart from my masterpiece there didn't seem to be any sort of coded message.

A lot of people were questioning the authenticity of the video now – cynics!

Gus turned on the radio, and the news was all about the housing crisis – apparently some mortgage provider in Brisbane called You Beaut Mortgages had gone bust and people had been picketing outside its head office. But what had started off as a peaceful protest had become violent, with doors being broken and windows smashed; the police had been called in.

As I ate my ugali, I received the usual barrage of messages from the pesky neighbors.

Mom reminding me once again about the dentist appointment. Miranda asking if I knew where the *Twilight* DVD was. She was obviously going through a vampire phase. Again. And from Toby, this: ☺

Nothing from Dad, though, and I remembered what Gus had said about him last night. The more I thought about it – mother who committed suicide, father who was a drunk, living in that dump – I realized what an extraordinary effort it had been to get through that. Was disposing of Bag Lady just more of the same, a matter of survival? A gazelle wakes up in the morning knowing ...

Just as I finished the ugali I heard my phone ding as it received yet another message.

Yes, Mom, I know, dentist at 3:45.

Yes, Miranda, the DVD is in the drawer where it always is.

Yes, Toby: ☺

I opened the message. It wasn't from the pesky neighbors; it was from The Debt.

you have until 7pm or tonight you take a life

Ice. Spine. You know the drill. I read it again and then it was gone. How do you do that, make a text message disappear?

But the ice was still there. What more could I do?

My video was now the eighth most watched on the whole of YouTube for the last twenty-four hours. Three more plays and it would catch up with the seventh most watched – a bride going a-over-t at her wedding. What more could I do?

I'd already decided that I would still go to work, that there were way more resources there. I also wanted to get my bike from where I'd chained it to a post. But after last night I was feeling a bit edgy, so when Gus offered to give me a lift I said, "Sure."

As we approached the gates, Samsoni appeared. We exchanged good mornings before he got down to business.

"Everything okay at your place?" he said. I wondered if somehow he was referring to this morning's visit from the detectives.

"Sure," said Gus. "Why do you ask?"

"We've had some small issues with the perimeter security. We've called the technician and they should be sorted out very quickly, but I was just making sure."

"No, everything's fine, Samsoni," said Gus.

We continued on our way, Gus making his usual progress – if that's the right word – through the traffic. After the revelations of last night, I had questions fighting each other to be asked, but I decided to ignore them. It wasn't as if I didn't have enough going on in my head.

We pulled up at Cash Converters and my bike had gone from the post I'd chained it to – I wasn't surprised, but I was still angry. Why did Hound have to have his office in this godforsaken – thanks, Father Antonio – place!

Although I was an hour late for work, Hound didn't seem to mind that much.

"Swings and roundabouts," he said. "Swings and roundabouts."

"Sure," I said, unsure what he was talking about.

"Did you see the YouTube clip, the one that went viral?" he said. "The two kids taking off with that gold. Priceless!"

Did I see it? I was the one who'd put it there, but obviously Hound wasn't enough of a cyber-sleuth to have worked that out. Thank God.

"So something to work with there," said Hound.

"Sorry?"

"Look, you've had a bit to do with these kids, this family. So you've really got a leg up on this thing. The gold has to be somewhere, and my bet is that it's still in the country. My contacts in South Africa tell me that none of it has found its way onto the market. So it's very simple – where would they hide it?"

Very simple? Really, Hound?

He continued, "So what I'd like you to do today is just see what you can come up with. Don't beat yourself up too much. But just have a think about where they would put it."

I'd already had plenty of thinks about where they would put it, and quite a few places had come to mind. But something told me that these were too obvious, that somebody as clever as Zoe was going to come up with the mother of all hiding places.

No, there was absolutely no way I would work out where they'd hidden that gold, which is why I needed them to tell me where they'd hidden that gold. Which is why I needed them to contact me. And now!

After Hound had gone off to do Hound things, I got back onto YouTube. They'd taken my clip down! Okay, it was a complete phony, but still: how dare they?

There was a message that said, *We have been advised by legal authorities that this video violates certain … blah blah blah.* Just when I was on my way to YouTube immortality.

I checked out the Zolt's Facebook fan page. There was nothing that looked like a message, coded or otherwise.

Of course, it occurred to me that the Zolton-Banders couldn't communicate with me for the usual reasons people can't communicate with you. Except by Ouija board.

Because they were dead.

Or they might be held captive somewhere, which wouldn't be a novel experience for the elder Zolton-Bander.

But somehow I didn't think so. They were testing me: was I clever enough, devious enough, to help them take the gold back to where it belonged?

For the rest of the day I banged my head against the wall. Well, that's what it felt like, anyway.

My dentist appointment was at three forty-five and I'd pretty much decided to give it a miss. But at three the text came from Mom – *don't forget dentist.* Okay, maybe she wasn't an American, but she sure was American about teeth! And by the time three fifteen came around, I was pretty happy for an excuse to get out of the office. Besides, I still had four hours until The Debt's deadline. Plenty of time.

Away from the bathroom, which for some reason had been in high rotation today.

I was still a bit nervous about walking the streets of the Block, even in broad daylight like this, so I asked Ratface Ponytail if I could borrow one of his bikes. He was a bit reluctant at first, in fact he told me to "rack off," but I persisted.

Eventually he said that if I left a deposit of fifty bucks I could take the "treadly" as he called it. But of course Treadly turned out to be the most beat-up machine, which somebody had given a homemade paint job.

But Treadly was actually a nice ride, and the gears worked really well. I reckon that happens sometimes – you hop on a bike, you get into a kayak, you collapse into a couch, and it just seems perfect for you. Well, it was like that with Treadly.

I got to the dentist's office, which was actually an old-style Queenslander house, probably the only one left in this area. The receptionist said I could put my bike out the back, in the shed. Then it was straight in to see the dentist.

Dr. Miller once told me that he had two passions in his life: kids' teeth and fishing, but I'm pretty sure he had that in the wrong order. There were framed pictures of fish adorning all the walls of his office, and instead of playing soothing Enya-type music while he drilled away, he played podcasts of fishing programs that had names like "Tales from the Tinny."

"Ah, Dom," he said. "Now weren't we talking about barramundi when last we met?"

Actually, Dr. Miller, you were the one talking about barramundi and I was making the usual "ah" and "ur" noises you come up with when your gob is full of hardware.

I got to hear about his recent heli-fishing excursion to Australia's Top End where he caught the biggest barra of his career.

"Ah," I said.

"Ur," I said.

Apparently I had one cavity, which needed some anesthetic.

"Would you like some happy gas beforehand?" asked the doctor.

Does a barra live in the Top End?

The nurse placed the thing over my nose and mouth and said, "Breathe deeply." I didn't need any more encouragement than that – happy gas poured into my lungs, found its way into my bloodstream and from there into my brain, where it caused the synapses of my nerves to fire in pleasing ways.

Then the doctor a stuck needle into my gum, which took away from the happiness quite a bit. But my brain was still dancing its happy little jig.

And suddenly, a turtle.

And not just any turtle, but one of those large ponderous ones that are native, I believe, to the

Galápagos Islands. Large ponderous turtle, what the Galápagos are you doing in my thoughts? Especially front and center like that. Dr. Miller was grinding away now, the soothing tones of "Tales from the Tinny" playing in the background.

Why a turtle?

What was my subconscious telling me?

Then I got why. I'd once met Zoe at the Galápagos turtle enclosure at the zoo. "Crn wo fur tor urt?"

Which is what "Can we finish this another day?" sounds like when your mouth is partially anesthetized.

"Sorry?" said Dr. Miller.

"I go now," I managed to articulate.

"Only a few minutes more," he said, and he was only a few minutes more.

I jumped out of the chair and was about to rush through reception when the receptionist said, "Mr. Silvagni?"

"Yes?" I said.

"Today's bill?"

"My mum pays that," I said.

"She informs me that because you are working you are no longer covered by her health insurance."

"She expects me to pay the bill?"

"Actually, we all do."

So I paid the bill, something I'd never done before. As I did, I understood how Dr. Miller got to go heli-fishing in the Top End. Then I got on Treadly and made for the zoo.

But "made for the zoo" doesn't give any indication of the crazy speed I went, the ridiculous shortcuts I took, the risks I risked, because I knew it closed at five.

I got there at quarter to five, out of breath.

"One kid's ticket," I said.

The ticket dude looked at his watch and said, "I'm afraid the zoo's closed for today."

"But it closes at five."

"That's when everybody has to be out of the zoo; we don't let anybody in after four forty-five."

"But when I asked for the ticket it was four forty-five, you just took ages to answer."

The ticket dude, who wasn't a dude at all, just some no-chin comb-over loser, said, "Come back tomorrow and you can have the whole day to get to know our exciting array of animals."

I could tell it was no good; he wasn't going to budge. A man in khaki walked past. *A keeper*, I thought. *I'll just sneak in behind him*.

But when the keeper came to the gate he used a key card to get access; there was no sneaking in after him.

A one-ton truck pulled up on the road behind me, on its door the amusing logo for the Zoo Poo Company. I casually walked beside the truck, and when I was at the back and hopefully out of sight, I crouched right down. As the truck took off, I hoisted myself up and dived under the canopy.

There may not have been any zoo poo in the back, but that didn't mean it didn't smell like it. I could smell chimp poo, I could smell zebra poo, I could smell giraffe poo, and was that the delectable aroma of flamingo poo terrorizing my nostril membranes? But I was inside the zoo. I'd achieved my aim, and now all I had to do was get out of this poo mobile. Easier said than done.

There just wasn't a suitable opportunity, until the one-ton pulled up to a stop and backed up. But in no time at all there were men's voices.

"This lot still looks a bit ripe, eh?"

"Well, you heard what the boss said: demand's outstripping supply. Let's just get it on board."

The tarpaulin that I was hiding under started to roll back and I got ready to make a run for it if they saw me. But it stopped, and I was still hidden. They started working, shoveling zoo poo.

No doubt there are much worse experiences in life then getting bombarded with poo – that electric shock to my testicle, for example, wasn't great, and waterboarding can't be much fun – but it was still pretty horrendous, especially since a lot of the poo was, as the man had said, "a bit ripe."

Eventually it finished and the truck took off.

Now I didn't care how unsubtle I was, I wanted out. I fought my way through the poo to the back of the truck. And I jumped out, managing to hit the ground running.

If the Zoo Poo employees saw me, they certainly didn't bother to do anything about it. Or maybe they thought I was a rogue poo, making its escape, unwilling to spend its last years fertilizing Aunt Tillie's carnations.

Fortunately for me, I picked a pretty good place get off, in the Great Cats section.

They were especially vociferous, and I wondered if me and my pungent aroma had anything to do with that.

Lion: Whoa, who did that?

Tiger: Whoever smelled it, dealt it.

Lion (with a roar): No way.

Panther: Whoever denied it, supplied it.

It took me hardly any time to get to the Galápagos turtle enclosure. And when I did they were doing much the same as when I was last here: nothing. It was a scene of such lethargy, so lacking in any sort of action, that my immediate thought was that I'd gotten it very, very wrong.

I'm not sure what I'd expected – a flashing neon sign on the turtles' shell, maybe – but I'd thought there would be at least something.

The only sound I could hear was The Debt's deadline tick-tock-ticking away.

I sat on the bench and I looked out on this dismal scene and I started to feel really, really sorry for myself. I'd thought I'd been so clever to come up with this deal, but I didn't even have the brains/balls/whatever it took to pull it off.

My eyes fell on the sign that was affixed to the fence: *The Galápagos turtle (*Chelonoidis nigra*) is the largest living species of turtle and reaches weights of over 400 kilograms and lengths of over 1.8 meters. With a life span in the wild of over 100 years, it is one of the longest-lived vertebrates ...*

I would be long-lived, too, I thought, *if I just stood around and did nothing like them*. But then I noticed something. Some of the letters seemed to have a tiny dot under them. I moved closer, so that the sign was a few centimeters from my face.

Yes, there was no doubt about it, somebody had used a marker to put a dot under certain letters.

Excitement mounting, I took out my iPhone, opened Notes and started entering these dotted letters. I was maybe three-quarters of the way through when I heard footsteps from behind – somebody was coming.

It was the same keeper I'd seen before. "Hey, zoo's closed!" he said.

I returned to the sign, copying the letters.

"Hey, mate, did you hear what I said? The zoo's closed." He walked closer, then stopped, bringing his hands up to his nose. "What is that smell?"

I thought professional zookeepers would be accustomed to strong animal smells, but apparently not – he appeared to be quite distressed.

I put in the last letter and shoved my iPhone into my pocket.

"Sorry," I said. "I'm out of here."

I ran back to the keepers' entrance and followed one of the workers out. She also gave me a none-too-subtle mate-you-stink look.

Treadly, unbelievably, was exactly where I'd left it. I jumped on and started cycling. After ten or so minutes, when I figured I was far enough away from the zoo, I stopped on the side of the road and considered what I needed to do next.

Usually people in my situation – i.e. covered in excrement – are pretty keen to have a hot shower, apply some soap to their body. But I had a bigger imperative: time was running out – I needed to contact the Zolton-Banders, decipher those letters.

I took out the iPhone, looked at the letters.

mtytdrmwrldtwrftrrrsx

Zoe, did it always have to be so complicated? Why not just a simple text message: *Meet you at Cozzi's at nine*? Or *the town hall steps*? No, with her it had to be all *mtytdrmwrldtwrftrrrsx*.

Okay, Dom, concentrate. You've been here before with Zoe and Otto's code on Facebook, with Nitmick and

Guzman's cryptic messages to each other. You cracked them, you can crack this.

What was special about *mtytdrmwrldtwrftrrrsx*?

It actually didn't take me long to work this out: there were no vowels.

So I began by adding a few of the obvious ones. *mtytdreamworldtwroftrrrsx*

And then I added another less obvious one. *mtytdreamworldtowerofterrorsx*

Every kid who has ever been to the Gold Coast knows what the Tower of Terror is: it's officially rated as one of the top ten scary rides in the known universe.

And after that the rest pretty much just fell into place: *meetyouatdreamworldtowerofterrorsix*

You know how I say I love speed? Well, I do, as long as it's linear speed, speed that pretty much obeys the known laws of Newtonian physics. Tower of Terror speed, now that's a different thing.

Actually I'd only been on it once, and if they weren't the worst five minutes of my life that was only because The Debt had come along later.

I'd spent the whole time white-knuckled, eyes closed, mouth clamped shut so my innards wouldn't tumble out.

So if Zoe Zolton-Bander wanted to meet at the Tower of Terror, I would. But I couldn't help thinking that a simple text message could have achieved the same result.

Yes, I know, how did she know my phone wasn't bugged, but you know what I mean?

Just a simple text message.

TOWER OF TERROR

There's a regular shuttle bus that leaves from Broadbeach, so I got back on Treadly, my new best friend, and hammered it. I rode down footpaths, bombed a mall, ran a few red lights, and got there just as the shuttle was about to leave.

"Don't go!" I screamed at the driver. "I've got to get on that bus."

I wouldn't have blamed him if he'd stepped on the accelerator, but he smiled at me and said, in a voice loud enough for the other passengers to hear, "Hear that, folks? That's the passion people have for Dreamworld." Most of the people on the bus looked Chinese, or Korean, and most of them were asleep, their heads lolling on their shoulders.

I locked Treadly to a post, and got on board, and watched as the driver's smile fell off his face and fluttered to the floor like a dead moth. Unfortunately for the other passengers there was only one empty seat, so me and my filthy fug of zoo poo took it. People started waking up, talking excitedly. My Chinese is pretty average, my Korean even worse, but I'm pretty sure I knew what they were saying: what is that rotten smell?

We drove through Surfers, across the bridge to Southport and then onto the Pacific Highway. By the time the bus pulled up at Dreamworld, the other passengers were almost fighting each other to get out and find some fresh air.

I joined the line to get in, and again I could see the distress my smell was causing. I think some of the problem was that it was a bad smell, but it was also an unusual smell. You drop your guts and people pretty much know what the deal is; a baby fills its diaper – same thing; but the aroma I was carrying was much more exotic – it was African, Indian, maybe even Galápogasian.

At last it was my turn to pay and as I gave the man my card it occurred to me how much it had cost my dad for me to pay back these installments: if you added up all the taxi fares, the train fares, the bus fares, the plane fares, it would probably be as much as somebody – but not Dr. Miller – earned in a year.

Once inside I made straight for the souvenir store and bought myself a really hideous Dreamworld T-shirt and a matching pair of really hideous Dreamworld shorts and took them into the bathroom and got changed. I checked myself out in the mirror – hideous on hideous and the result, actually, wasn't as bad as you'd think.

I checked my watch: 5:54 p.m. Tower of Terror time!

Just as I was about to join the end of the line I had a brain wave: if we were going to meet on the Tower of Terror, they must be in line too. Thus, we could lose the whole extremely unpleasant Tower of Terror experience. Twice I walked along the line. Either they weren't there or Zoe had gotten a whole lot more professional with her disguises.

Actually, the Tower of Terror line moved much quicker than I'd thought; there were a lot of people dropping out. Some of them saw the faces of the people who had just experienced the Tower of Terror and asked themselves: *Do I want to look like that for the rest of my life?* Like that famous painting *The Scream* by Edvard Munch. Others texted their friends, *Just about to do Tower of Terror,* and got the reply, *Can I have your skateboard when you DIE?*

And then it was my turn. Desperately, I looked around: where were they?

They said to meet at the Tower of Terror. I was at the Tower of Terror.

They said at six. It was six.

Or had I gotten it totally, totally wrong? Was the turtle just a result of the happy gas? Were those supposed spots marking the letters just fly poo or something?

"You up for it or not?" said the attendant, one of those in-your-face types who always work in places like this.

"Of course," I said, and the next thing I knew I was strapped tight in the seat and the thing I was on was hurtling along at a speed that didn't seem possible and people were screaming and my internal organs were trying to find a way up through my throat.

Stop screaming so loud! I thought, until I realized it was me who was doing the screaming so loud.

It went up high again, and then came screaming down at an even more terrifying speed.

Please no more.

But there was more.

And when it was finished, I couldn't get out of there fast enough, on my spaghetti legs, away from the Tower of Terror.

"Dom?"

"Not now," I said to whoever wanted to stop my flight from this evil place.

"Dom!" they repeated, more insistently, so I snuck a look behind me.

It was Zoe. Okay, it wasn't Zoe, it was some punk/nerd/emo, but I knew it was Zoe.

"What's the matter with you?" she said.

"The Tower of ..." I said, my voice trailing off.

"You actually went on that thing?"

"THAT'S WHERE YOU SAID TO MEET!"

"Keep your voice down," she said, hand gripping my forearm, fingers digging in to emphasize her words. She steered me away from all the rides to a plasticky little café. I sat at a table and she bought a couple of drinks.

I'd regained some of my composure by then and realized that it was okay, we were on track again, and I could take my recent ride on the Tower of Terror, scrunch it up and throw it into the trash can of history. But with the Zolton-Banders you needed to have your wits about you, and I was afraid a fair few of mine were now littering the ground below the Tower of Terror, along with the loose change those scabby attendants would pick up at the end of the night.

"Did you contact Roxas?"

"Yes," I said. "And he put me on to a woman by the name of Cory Morales – she works in the Philippines Embassy in Brisbane."

"Perfect!" said Zoe.

Google had told me there was a Cory Morales who worked in the Philippines Embassy in Brisbane.

Of course I hadn't contacted Roxas, because he was dead. And I hadn't contacted Cory Morales, either. But these lies, the first of many I would have to tell if this thing was to fly, had seemed to work okay.

"And?" said Zoe.

"She says it can be done."

"They will take the ... um ... goods?"

"They will."

"And they will use the ... um ... goods for a worthwhile cause?"

"For. schools, hospitals, for stuff like that," I said, and I hoped I wasn't laying it on too thick. "She said that it would make a huge difference to a poor country like the Philippines." Now I was definitely laying it on too thick, but why not?

Zoe said nothing for a while. "Dom, we can trust you, can't we?"

No, probably not, but who were they to talk about trust?

"Of course you can," I said. "So, here's what she said: because the embassy is technically part of the Philippines, once it's in their grounds, that's it, Australian authorities can't do a thing. It's as good as if it was in the country. All you need to do is make sure it gets there."

Zoe thought about this for a while, and then she took out her phone, opened the back and took out the sim card. She took a small plastic bag from her pocket – it must've had at least a hundred sim cards inside.

"Which one do you think?" she said.

"FunTel have got some attractive deals going at the moment."

She took my advice, found a gold FunTel sim and put it in her phone. She called a number, which I assumed was her brother's, and wandered off to have a private conversation.

After five or so minutes she returned. "We're on."

"So what time?" I said.

"Time?" she said, and I could see the suspicion in her face.

"My person has to make sure she's there when the ... um ... goods arrive, otherwise they could fall into the wrong hands."

Zoe called her brother again, wandered off again.

"Tomorrow, at midday," she said.

"Great," I said. "And what sort of vehicle will it come in?"

Again the call to her brother, the need for a private conversation.

"I'll text you just beforehand," she said, and added with a smile, "it depends on what Otto can borrow."

That made absolute sense, and as we parted company I could feel a tingle of excitement: the sting was on!

Now, I had to tell The Debt.

Athletics training was tonight. *Perfect!*

It was pretty weird: in order to converse with The Debt, I had to run fast around a circular track and get quite sweaty, but Seb seemed the most convenient conduit to them. Actually, he was my only conduit to The Debt.

By the time the shuttle bus dropped me back at my bike, it was already six-thirty; training had started. So I just unlocked Treadly, got on board and pedaled towards the Gold Coast Sharks grounds.

I was late arriving; the other runners were already out on the track, including – thank goodness – Seb. As I made my way to the locker room, Coach Sheeds came out to meet me.

"Wow, you wouldn't have been to Dreamworld, would you?" she said, which was actually quite an amusing thing for somebody with no sense of humor to say.

"No, what gives you that idea?" I said.

"Well, it's all over your clothes," she said. See what I mean?

Further conversation was curtailed by the arrival of Coach Colin himself, with whistles, stopwatch, the usual hardware around his neck.

"Hey, Dom," he said. "What say you get into your kit and get out onto the track?"

"Actually, this is my kit," I said.

"That's a funny one," he said, laughing.

I hadn't noticed before how big his teeth were, like horse teeth. "I'm not joking," I said. "I've had a bit of a funny day and –"

He cut me off. "Whatever, Dreamworld, just get out there."

I made straight for Seb, but when he saw me

headed his way, he took off down the track like a startled rabbit.

Maybe he was still spooked from what had happened in the last training session; maybe it was the Dreamworld clothes; maybe there was even the lingering aroma of zoo poo. Whatever the reason, it was pretty annoying, because the sting was on only if The Debt agreed it was on.

Coach Colin called us in; he wanted some interval training, ten 400 meters at a fast pace, with a jog in between. And he wanted us to do it in pairs.

"Seb and Dreamworld," he said, which got him a generous laugh.

I realized, with some annoyance, that he was probably going to keep calling me this, that he was one of those people who had an inflated sense of their nickname-giving ability.

The first pair took off, the second pair, the third pair, which included Coach Sheeds, and then it was the two of us on the line.

Coach Colin looked down at his watch. "Go!" he said, and we took off.

One of the reasons I'm a 1500-meter runner is that I hate the 400 meters. Actually, pretty much all runners hate the 400 meters. Even 400-meter runners hate the 400 meters; they're just masochists.

It's not like a sprint, the 100 or 200, where you pretty much go flat out. And it's not like the 800 and

1500 where you can get into some sort of rhythm, plot some sort of strategy. It's in between, and it's horrible, and I hate it, and usually I just go through the motions.

Seb, however, had the accelerator on, and in order to talk to him, I had to do the same.

"It's on," I said as we flew around the bend.

He said nothing.

"Did you hear me? It's on."

Again, nothing from Seb; he seemed more interested in the ground and how quickly he could get across it. Actually, really quickly, and when we came to the end of the first 400 meters, I was sucking some in. Not exactly big ones, but not small ones either. Sucking in the medium-sized ones.

We jogged back to the starting line.

"Seb and Dreamworld," said Coach.

I was so right about the nickname thing.

"Go!"

Again, Seb turned up the pace, and I didn't want to waste too much precious breath on words, but I had to get an answer from him.

"Yamashita's Gold will be yours tomorrow if you play this right," I said.

No response.

"And you know how much us Italians love gold," I said, hoping to get some sort of reaction from him.

He didn't respond, not verbally anyway, but we

were now sprinting towards the 400-meter line. I didn't have to keep up with him; it was a training gig, and I knew Coach Colin would wait until I was back on the line before he said "Go" for the next 400 meters.

But I wasn't going to ever let Seb beat me. Not ever. Not in anything.

We hit the line together, and Seb turned on his heels and jogged quickly back to the starting line.

I was really suffering, and the idea that there could be eight more like this didn't seem humanly possible. But there we were, on the line again, with Coach barking, "Go."

I knew I had to mix it up a bit.

Do what I did the other day and jolt Seb out of his obstinacy.

So this time I went hard, leaving Seb behind.

He quickly caught up, though, and surged ahead of me. How had he gotten so fit? And this time, he had me beat, crossing the line at least a meter ahead of me.

Again the rapid jog back.

Leave him, I told myself as I followed behind. *This is stupid.*

But as I took my position on the white line again, I knew that it wasn't stupid. This was The Debt, this was a pound of flesh, my flesh.

"Love the effort you lads are showing today," said Colin. "Go!"

We went again, and Seb hammered it once more.

I was ready for him, though.

It hurt, it was murder, but I wasn't going to let him get away again.

"The," I said, and then took a gulp of air. "Gold." Gulp. "Will." Gulp. "Be." Gulp. "Delivered." Gulp. "To." Gulp. "The." Gulp. "Philippines." Gulp. "Embassy." Gulp. "In." Gulp. "Brisbane." Gulp. "Tomorrow." Gulp. "At." Gulp. "Midday." Gulp.

We reached the line together, but I let him jog back in front of me.

One more sprint.

On the line again, and Coach said "Go" and Seb took off, even faster this time, a cross between Ben Johnson and a Formula One racing car. And I wouldn't have been surprised if he, like both of them, was on something with a higher-than-normal octane rating.

Just let the idiot go, I told myself.

But I couldn't, because there was one more thing the idiot needed to know.

I found something, I'm not sure from where, but I found it, and I made up the ground between us.

"I." Gulp. "Will." Gulp. "Text." Gulp. "Vehicle." Gulp. "Details." Gulp.

Now that I'd said it, or gulped it, I could let him go.

Yeah, right.

I noticed that the beautiful fluid form he usually exhibited was looking a bit ragged around the edges.

"I've got you," I said, managing three words in a row, as I drew up level with him.

It was probably those three words that did me in, because he beat me over the line.

There wasn't much in it, maybe a centimeter, but he definitely got me.

We both stayed there, bent double, hands on knees. And maybe, just maybe, I vomited a bit in my mouth.

"Bring it in," said Coach, but neither of us was bringing it in anywhere, neither of us had anything left in the tank.

The rest of the training was pretty much recovery for both of us. Afterwards Coach Colin called me over.

"I'd like you and Seb to go in the nationals this year."

"But it's an adult's race."

"I've had a good look at the rules and I can't see anything that stops you running. What do you say?"

"Sure, why not?" I said, and for a wonderful soaring second I totally forgot about all the other stuff in my life, and it became what it used to be, all about running.

But it was only for a second.

He slapped me on the back. "I knew you'd be up for it, Dreamworld."

AND THE BEAT GOES ON

I didn't want to go home, to either of them: Gus's or my parents.' So I cycled down to the beach, practicing riding with no hands, hands folded across my chest.

I chained Treadly up and ordered a chicken kebab – "dizzy meat" Toby calls it – from a kebab joint.

"So you've never been to Dreamworld?" said the man serving.

"Nah, but I'd really love to one day," I said. *See, Coach Sheeds, that's how it's done.*

"What sauce you want?" he asked.

"What sauce you got?"

"Hummus, yogurt, tomato, hot chili, sweet chili."

"Sounds good," I said.

"You want all of them?"

"Sure."

He didn't blink an eyelid, just gave my kebab a

decent squirt of each. As I was paying, the sound of drums came from outside.

"Great, here we go again," he said. "Ooga booga time."

I started on the kebab – the sweet chili might have been one sauce too many – and wandered onto the beach. I could see the drummers, a circle of maybe twenty or so of them, sitting on the sand. They had that Byron Bay look: half tribal, half hippie, lots of dreadlocks, natural fibers, bare feet.

The music made me stop; they were really good, this mob, not the usual drugged-out hippies making a din. Their music was disciplined: intricate, layered but powerful, the vibration thrumming through my body.

As I finished the last of my kebab, three girls, dressed in short shorts and bikini tops, appeared, spinning fire sticks in unison. As I got closer I realized that I knew one of them: it was PJ!

I had this enormous feeling of guilt – I'd actually considered killing her brother! Followed by this equally enormous feeling of relief – now I wouldn't have to.

My eyes didn't let go of her, following her every sinuous move as she twirled and whirled to the beat. When they'd finished, their fire sticks extinguished, I walked over to where she was standing.

"PJ," I said.

She looked up at me, her face smudged with charcoal, and broke into a smile. "Dom!"

"Not Grammar Boy?" I said.

"Nah, not tonight," she said. "Love your threads, by the way."

Somehow I'd forgotten the clothes I was wearing, clothes that were ludicrous to begin with, but were now stained with sweat from my battle with Seb.

"That was awesome," I said, even though I never call anything "awesome."

PJ did a little bow.

"Totally awesome," I said.

"Thanks," she said. "We get gigs every now and then around the place."

"So you've actually got a job?"

"Yeah, but the superannuation's rubbish."

Good joke; I laughed.

"Come on," she said, pulling me by the hand. "Let's sit down."

I didn't really have much choice; I joined the circle of dirty ferals. A central lantern threw a flickering light over their faces, their flashing hands. I could feel the pressure of PJ's thigh against mine; the beat got faster; occasionally somebody would say something like "Yeah!" or "Oh!" and then it came to an end.

"You want to drum?" said PJ.

"No way."

"Yes, you do," she said, taking a drum and putting it between my legs. "You just don't know it yet, that's all." She showed me how to hold my fingers. Where on the drum to hit.

But when the music started up, when PJ started drumming, my hands remained in my lap. What if I mucked it up? What if I got it wrong?

"Okay," she said. "Just listen then, get the beat."

It was pretty good advice and I did just that, sat there on the sand, PJ's thigh pressing against mine, and let the sound pulse through me.

A bottle of Jim Beam was being passed around but I just handed it on. I concentrated on watching PJ's fingers as they tapped away. And I realized that she wasn't doing anything too complicated, that she was just following a basic pattern. I looked up at the other drummers in the circle, the light flickering on their faces. They all looked so friendly, even the unfriendly ones looked friendly – maybe PJ was right, maybe they wouldn't turn on me if – when – I mucked it up.

I gave the drum a tentative tap with my right hand. Followed by another with my left.

None of the other drummers jumped and exclaimed, "He's wrecked it!" None of them even looked over at me. Except for PJ – she threw me an encouraging smile.

I tried again, left hand then right hand, remembering PJ's advice as to where to hit the drum. Again, nothing from the other drummers. Right hand, left hand, right hand – I settled into a simple rhythm. But then a pang of deep guilt – I had an installment to pay, a sting to organize, and here I was, bashing at a drum.

And, as if to rub this in, my phone beeped. I checked it. It was only Gus.

all good?

I sent him a quick reply ☺ and returned to my drumming.

But, suddenly, silence. I'm not sure what the signal was, or whether there even was a signal, but everybody seemed to cease playing at exactly the same time.

Everybody except me.

My beat kept going, so anemic, so pathetic, without the accompanying drums, until I, too, stopped.

"Ciggie break," said PJ, which didn't really make sense because a lot of the drummers had been smoking while they drummed.

Somebody picked up a guitar and began strumming.

"Bloody government's no bloody good," said somebody else. That seemed like a pretty popular opinion, everybody agreeing that the bloody government was no bloody good. And then there was a discussion on the various ways the government was no good.

"The Zolt's the only one standing up to them," somebody said.

Really, I thought.

Again, there was almost unanimous agreement – the Zolt was obviously some sort of folk hero here. They continued talking about the Zolt, according him almost superhuman qualities.

Hey, he's just a tall, skinny kid with a squeaky voice who tends to crash-land planes, I wanted to tell them.

"Pigs!" PJ muttered.

I'd been so absorbed in my thoughts I hadn't noticed the police officers – two men, one young, one old.

They're just doing their job, I thought.

"Okay, time to go home," one of them said. And tonight their job was to stop some people drumming on the beach.

"But we weren't doing anything," I heard myself saying. PJ elbowed me in the ribs – *keep your mouth shut!*

The older police officer clapped his hands. "You heard, party's finished!"

Despite PJ's quite pointy elbow in the ribs, I repeated what I'd said, more loudly this time. The police officer moved towards me, taking out a pad and a pen. He had a real old-style cop's head.

"So what's your name?" he demanded.

"Dominic," I said.

"And do you have a surname, Dominic?"

"Sure, it's Silvagni," I said.

The police officer stopped writing. "As in David Silvagni?"

"That's my father," I said.

The police officer said nothing, just closed his pad and moved away. As the other cop tried to move people on, I noticed that he was on his phone. A minute or so later my phone rang.

I answered.

It was Mom. And she wasn't happy.

"What are you doing on the beach this time of the night?" she said.

I was just about to get all defensive, to try to manufacture a plausible excuse, when I realized that I didn't have to – I didn't even live under the same roof as her anymore. "Having a pretty cool time," I said.

"And what time are you getting back to Gus's?"

"Hey, maybe not at all," I said, but then I realized what an a-hole I was being. "It's fine, Mom, I'm fine."

A pause, and she said, "Just keep your phone on, alright? And any problem, you call."

"Okay," I said, thinking I'd gotten out of that relatively unscathed. But when I thought about it, Mom had always been that sort of parent: take responsibility for your actions, that sort of thing.

I hung up and PJ said, "I guess the party's over."

"I guess so," I said. "Do you want a ride home or anything?"

"You got a car?"

"No, a pushie."

"Sure, why not?" she said, laughing.

PJ was so small it was very easy to dink her; she sat on the handlebars, keeping her legs straight out in front.

"Preacher's?" I said.

"Nah, we've moved up a bit in the world," she said. "The Spit."

"Really?" I said, thinking they must've found some place near the breakwater, one of those old sheds maybe.

It was really straightforward to get there – I just followed the cycle path all the way along the coast. As I did, something like, derr! occurred to me: how come some growly old cop had my dad's phone number?

"Dom?" said PJ.

"Yeah?"

"I just wanted to say thanks for springing me the other day."

"That's okay," I said. "It was nothing." Though having a gun pointed at you, the trigger pulled, even if it is a cigarette lighter, is never nothing.

That's when I stacked it. It wasn't anything major, I hit a patch of sand and sort of lost control and the bike clipped one of those exercise station things and we both ended up on the lawn, a tangle of my Treadly and our limbs.

"Oh, no, are you okay, PJ? I'm so sorry, so sorry."

"I'm fine," she said, and then her hand was on my face and then her face was next to my face and her lips were on my lips and we were kissing.

I felt guilty – wasn't Imogen the one that I wanted? – but when I thought of her and Tristan and all that sucking face the guilt went right away.

The kiss lasted for … several epochs … before she broke away and said, "Come on, let's continue this somewhere a bit more comfy."

What, like an oily shed? I thought, but I soon gave that thought the treatment it deserved and trashed it. I didn't care where we went, as long as I was with her. As long as I got to kiss her again. And again. And again.

"We can walk from here," she said.

I pushed Treadly with one hand and held her hand with the other. It felt warm, slightly moist; her pulse was surprisingly strong. We came to the street where I'd gone searching for Toby that night, the street with all the posh houses.

"You better leave your pushie there," she said, pointing to a fence. I chained it up.

"Keep right behind me," she said.

I wasn't sure what was going to happen, but I had a fair idea it wasn't going to be entirely legal. But really, who was I to talk?

PJ hurried across the street, stopping in front of a large two-story house surrounded by a high stone wall with a heavy iron gate. It wasn't Halcyon Grove, but it wasn't far off. How did she intend to get in there?

Quite easily, actually. First looking around to make sure nobody was watching, she took a key from her pocket and unlocked the iron gate. We both slipped inside.

"Whose place is this?" I said.

"The Bonthrons'," she said. "They go skiing in Aspen for two months every year."

I sort of knew them; they were Charles's uncle and aunt.

"CCTV?" I said.

"Sorted."

"So Brandon's inside?"

"Probably watching DVDs; that's all he ever does. We don't have to take any notice of him," she said, squeezing my hand.

The front door of the house was open. I wasn't sure if Mr. and Mrs. Bonthron were richer than my parents, but even with the lights off, I could see how much stuff they had, rich people's stuff.

I could also see the flicker of a TV from another room. Hear the biff and bang of the sound track – obviously an action movie.

PJ squeezed my hand. "I'll just check on Brandon, make sure he's okay," she said, her voice trailing off as she walked towards where the light was flickering.

I couldn't quite believe where I was, and what I was doing. The risk I was taking – this had nothing to do with The Debt. But was that just the wimp in me talking?

In a few seconds she would be here again.

Kissing again.

Somewhere more comfy.

Then came a scream that tore the night apart.

And PJ was standing at the entrance, the light from the TV on her face. "Brandon killed himself!"

"No!"

I followed PJ back into the room. Brandon was sprawled facedown on the floor, and beside him were empty prescription pill containers.

"He always said he would do it," stammered PJ. "He always said he'd get there before Paris Hilton did."

I knelt next to him, and straightaway I could see that he wasn't dead.

That he was breathing, his chest rising and falling. "He's alive," I said, taking out my phone, hitting zero, zero – but then stopping.

"They won't believe me," I said, remembering that they had my number on their database as a potential nuisance caller. "You call."

PJ ran over and grabbed the cordless. Dialed triple-0.

And then it hit me, what I had to do.

"PJ, I can't be here when the cops come," I said, and already I was on the move. "Text me."

"Sure thing, Grammar," she said, and I knew exactly what she was thinking: it was my reputation I was protecting. I had no time to explain to her, even if I could. I just couldn't afford to get involved with the cops, not when the sting was organized for tomorrow. Instead I raced out of there, back through the iron gate. As I was unchaining my bike the ambulance pulled up, lights flashing. Nobody saw me, though, and I rode off into the dark.

The first text arrived just as I braked outside Gus's house.

b ok

I sent a text back. *that's great*

PJ replied: *gold coast public ward 2d if you want to visit*

I walked inside to find Gus sitting at the kitchen table, reading a running magazine. He looked me up and down: the garish Dreamworld clothes, the sand on my feet, the burn on my hand, and said two words, "Big night?"

"Biggish," I said.

STUNG

I thought I'd keep it as normal as possible, so I rocked up to work the next day. As I went to carry Treadly up the stairs Ratface Ponytail yelled out, "Eh!"

"Yeah?" I said in reply.

"Bike," he said.

"What?" I replied, figuring that since he'd started the monosyllabic stuff I wasn't going to change it.

"Money," he said, shifting into the exciting world of polysyllables.

"Deposit," I said, seeing his two and raising him by one.

"Not enough," he said.

Ha – you cracked, Ratface Ponytail, not me. I win. "But I thought the deposit was what the bike's worth."

"Do I look like I came down in the last rain?" he said. "That machine's worth at least a hundred bucks."

"I'll give you sixty for it."

"Eighty."

"Seventy."

"Seventy-five."

"Deal."

I paid the extra twenty-five dollars and the bike was officially mine. That was, until next week when some kid on the street would recognize his crap paint job and say, "Hey, there's my bike that got stolen from the shed!"

As soon as I sat at my desk, people started arriving. Nitmick. Guzman. Snake. Lazarus brothers. I wasn't sure if they all really did need to go to the bathroom, or if they needed an excuse to say hello to me, but during the next half hour or so every one of the associates made noisy use of the men's amenities. Then they all disappeared into Hound's office; I could hear the click as the door was locked behind them.

"What's that all about?" I asked Jodie, feeling a bit miffed that I wasn't included.

"Not sure, but something's up. He plays his cards pretty close to his chest, does the Hound Dog, but I reckon it's big, really big."

In the meantime Hound hadn't given me any work, so I decided to continue my investigation of Coast Home Loans.

The more I searched, the more intriguing it became, because Coast Home Loans didn't seem to have any money, or "capital" as it's called in the world of finance. In fact, they seemed to have the opposite: they actually owed quite a lot of money, especially to some of the major banks.

And the great thing about the major banks is that it isn't that difficult to access those sorts of records.

Coast Home Loans owed 23.6 million dollars to Westpac.

They owed 3.4 million dollars to Macquarie.

And 2.4 million to Citibank.

Maybe they were called Coast Home Loans because they'd taken out so many loans themselves.

I sort of wished that like Peter Eisinger I'd enrolled in Business Studies at school, because I found it really hard to get my head around all this. Then I had a thought: there was no way I could get my head around all this, but I knew somebody who could – Mr. Jazy. And his office wasn't that far away.

I printed out some of these figures, making sure "Coast Home Loans" didn't appear anywhere on them, and told Jodie that I was popping out for half an hour.

It took no time at all to get there. Once inside I told the receptionist my name and asked if I could see Mr. Jazy. She frowned at me, but disappeared out back. When she returned it was with Mr. Jazy himself.

His beard, deforested during Tristan's coma, had returned to its former lush state. "Dom," he said. "It's wonderful to see you."

He was a very nice man, Mr. Jazy, and I wondered,

not for the first time, how he had produced such a useless son. But I'd done enough biology at school to have some idea how genetics worked: Tristan had fifty percent of his dad's genes, but had obviously acquired the idiot gene from somewhere else.

"Let's talk in my office," said Mr. Jazy.

It was a nice office, more like a family room, full of family photos and the sort of couch you could stretch out on for serious TV time.

"Tristan tells me you've left school."

"Yes, I have," I said, readying myself for the lecture that was on its way: how I'd just reduced the options I had in life, the usual blah blah blah.

"Well, school's not for everybody," he said. "Anyway, how can I help you?"

Don't think I didn't feel the tiniest bit guilty – I mean, who was it who set fire to the Jazys' pool? Who was sort of responsible for Tristan's coma? And here I was asking for help.

"Remember that time you said that the real estate market in the Coast was like one big Ponzi scheme?"

"Ah, yes, I keep saying it, but nobody takes the least notice of me. They say I'm a stick-in-the-mud, a party pooper."

"Well, I'm doing this work for Hound de Villiers – he's, like, this investigator – and he's asked me to check up on a certain mortgage supplier that I can't really name."

"Certainly," said Mr. Jazy, and I could tell he was already intrigued.

"I wondered if you could have a look at this for me," I said, taking out the paper from my pocket and handing it to Mr. Jazy.

Mr. Jazy put on a pair of reading glasses, and studied the paper for some time.

I think it's sometimes difficult to know what somebody who's got a beard is thinking, because hair isn't the most expressive stuff, but I had no trouble reading what was on Mr. Jazy's face: concern, and a lot of it.

"This is much worse than even I imagined," he said.

"It is?"

"Oh, yes, this could be catastrophic for the whole industry."

"But I don't get it – why do they keep operating, giving out loans?"

"Why? Because they're making money hand over fist."

"But how do they keep operating?"

"Here's how to look at it: imagine you have a balloon with a leak, but you keep pumping air into it, so the leak's not an issue. But as soon as you stop pumping air, then your balloon goes flat in no time."

"Okay, I totally get it now."

I took my paper and thanked Mr. Jazy. As soon

as I walked outside my phone beeped, an unknown number. I read the text: *deal on text vehicle details to this number.*

Yes, the stingaroo was working!

Then my phone rang. Hound.

"Hey, Youngblood." Youngblood? Dreamworld? What was wrong with plain old Dom. "No sweat, but when are you back in the office?"

"I'm on my way now," I said.

"So, what, ten minutes to get here?"

"Something like that," I said.

It actually took eight minutes, but that's because I pedaled flat out, feeling a bit guilty about using company time for personal business. When I got back all the associates were standing on the footpath, some of them smoking. Actually, it looked like a scene from a Tarantino movie. One of the good ones.

Hound even helped me off my bike.

"We're going on a little trip up north," he said. "Got some business to do." That, also, seemed a bit Tarantinoesque.

"You want me to come?" I said, looking at the accumulated manpower adorning the footpath.

"You're an integral part of this organization, Dom. Don't know how we've gotten as far as we have without you."

It was sort of cheesy, and sort of insincere – if that was the case, why was I excluded from the meeting? –

but it definitely worked: I felt like I really belonged, and that leaving school and joining Coast Surveillance was the best move I'd ever made.

But what about the text message? It didn't take me long to realize that it didn't matter where I was, as long as I had range, because all I had to do was forward the text message I received from Zoe to The Debt.

"So where, exactly, are we headed?" I said.

"Bris Vegas," said Hound, before he launched into a not-so-bad Elvis impersonation, "Viva Bris Vegas ..."

VIVA BRIS VEGAS

Hound, one of the Lazarus brothers and I were in the Hummer, while the rest of the associates followed in a much less conspicuous Subaru. The trip was uneventful, and the conversation was centered around rugby, a sport I knew nothing about, except that its players always left the school locker room in a horrible mess.

This suited me fine, however, because I was able to keep an eye on my iPhone, both the time and the messages icon.

It was 11:22 when we crossed the bridge, and turned right. *Fortitude Valley,* said the sign.

"We're heading for the Valley?" I said, wondering if Hound and his associates were going to make an early start on some bars, because the Valley was known as a pretty happening place.

"Never mix work and pleasure," said the Hound, which apparently was an amusing thing to say because the Lazarus responded with a guffaw.

But we'd soon passed through the area with all the bars, clubs and restaurants and were now on a street that looked like a mixture of residential and business. The Subaru pulled up on the side of the road, but we continued, pulling in a couple of hundred meters later.

I checked my watch: 11:47. "What are we doing here?" I said.

"Youngblood, in our line of work there's a lot of waiting around," he said. "Patience is the key."

"Too right," said the Lazarus.

I waited around a bit more. I checked the time: 11:51.

Why hadn't they sent me the vehicle details? Surely Otto must know – he would've stolen it ages ago. Almost as soon as I'd had that thought, my phone beeped.

Weirdly enough, it was like everybody jumped. A phone beeping wasn't such a big thing; at lunchtimes in the school library it sounded like some sort of avant-garde music was playing, with swooshes, chimes, bells and beeps. Something wasn't right here, but I didn't have time to think it through.

I checked the message.

blue van rego BYT 654

I hit the Edit button, hit the text bubble so that a red

tick appeared next to it, hit the Forward button, and entered *td* into the To field, and hit the send button.

Barely a second after I did this, Hound checked his phone. He sent a text. He then booted the engine up and pulled into the road.

Then I got it, what had been bugging me: how, when I was at Mr. Jazy's office, had Hound known that I was only ten minutes away?

Because he'd been tracking me, that's why. And not just today, ever since I'd come to work for him. Because he knew, with the sixth sense he had, that I was still involved with the Zolton-Banders, that I was still in the game.

We pulled off the road again, and there, on the other side of the road, was the Philippine Embassy. Not only had he been tracking me, he'd been bugging my conversations! I remembered what Miranda had told me, how you could stick some software on somebody's phone that could turn their microphone on and off. What a fool, what a tool, I'd been thinking he'd employed me because of my skill set.

"You bastard!" I said.

Hound's huge paw reached over the seat and grabbed for my phone. I managed to keep it from his reach, but the Lazarus's even huger paw reached over the seat and whacked me hard on the side of the head.

Chime time again.

Hound relieved me of my phone.

"It's on its way," said the Lazarus, who had a phone to his ear.

My only hope now was that The Debt would beat these chumps to it, get to blue van rego BYT 654 before they did.

There was no way I could warn them, though. I just had to sit here with my chiming head and my anger and feeling of utter betrayal and watch the show unfold.

The traffic had built up and was moving quite slowly. But then the blue van rego BYT 654 came into view behind.

I wasn't the only one to have seen it. Hound was now on his phone barking orders.

"It's only got ten or so meters," he said. "Then I'm going to pull right in front of it."

I could see what his plan was now: he would stop the van from moving, and then the others, who were right behind it, would swoop in and relieve it of its load. Simple, sort of dumb, but it would probably work.

And it did work.

When the blue van was ten meters behind us, Hound bullied the Hummer in front of it and then slammed on his brakes. The van beeped, but in vain because the Hummer was going nowhere. And if a Hummer was good for anything, it was probably this.

Just as I'd thought, the Subaru was behind it, and Snake and the other Lazarus got out. Guzman and

Nitmick were obviously staying put, doing all the surveillance, the high-tech stuff. The Lazarus used a crowbar to lever open the back of the van.

And it was right then that they arrived, two of them on buzzy trail bikes, and as before, they were dressed all in black. They sped up between the cars.

The first one took out Snake with what looked like a swinging chain. *That'll kick-start your day, amigo.* The Lazarus didn't fare much better – he copped what looked like a blast of pepper spray to the face.

But now there was a *thwocka thwocka thwocka* sound from above. *Cops*, I thought. *They haven't taken long.* But I should've known better.

A chopper swooped down low, and I could see the letters on the side: *Channel Nine News. TV news. They haven't taken long.* I should've known better.

The chopper moved over the embassy building, hanging there. I'm not sure about the next bit, maybe I imagined it, but I swear there was a crack in the clouds, I swear there was, like, this spear of pure Queensland sunlight that picked out the chopper as it started to unload its load, gold bar after gold bar, and Yamashita's Treasure was dropped into that tiny part of Queensland that is the Philippines.

My eyes moved over to the back of the van; the black-clad motorbiker was shrugging – nothing in there. Of course there wasn't, and immediately I knew how'd they played it: blue van rego BYT 654 just happened to have been traveling in the right direction and Zoe, who had been standing along the road somewhere, had sent me a text. That's why it had come so late.

So now the unsuspecting Philippine Embassy had Yamashita's Gold and I wondered if my lie would come true – would they use all that cash to help poor people?

But I knew the answer to that – of course not; it would just make rich people richer.

And the Zolton-Banders had done me again; maybe I just had to admit that they were cleverer than me.

They hadn't trusted me, but they'd been right not to.

I leaned over the seat and tried to grab my phone out of Hound's hand, but he held on to it tight. "Give it to me," I said.

He looked at me, and brought that huge paw back, but now the paw was a fist.

"Punch me if you like, I don't really care," I said.

His fist turned back into a paw, and he tossed me my phone. "Don't take it personally, it's only business, Youngblood."

I got out of the Hummer and one of the motorbikers buzzed past me. He was wearing a helmet, he had a scarf covering his face, but his eyes said it all.

You've got no options left.

Take a life.

Tonight.

TAKE A LIFE

I felt calm, calmer than I could remember feeling for a long, long time.

Which was pretty strange, because I'd just been listening to Rage Against the Machine, Miranda's favorite band, really loud through headphones. Their first album: "Settle for Nothing"; "Bullet in the Head"; "Know Your Enemy"; "Killing In The Name." It was like they'd decided to write the sound track to my existence.

Again I checked my phone to make sure a SMS hadn't sneaked through unnoticed. Especially one from PJ.

Earlier we'd had this exchange:

Me: *how is brandon?*

PJ: *still in coma*

Me: *can you let me know if there's any change??*

PJ: *sure XX*

Reading over them again, a wave of revulsion rolled through me – *Dom, what have you become?*

But then it went away – I had no choice.

I guess usually it's your brain that runs your life, that makes the decisions. Occasionally it's your heart. And a few times, when I'd been running, like that time in Rome, it was my legs that were in charge.

But tonight it was all about my gut, deep, deep in my gut. I felt – what's that hippie term? – centered. Not my legs, not my head, not my heart – it was all coming from smack bang in the middle.

I checked my iPhone, made sure it was fully charged. I checked the video function, made sure it was working properly.

I put ClamTop in my backpack with the other things I needed.

I was ready.

Not quite; though I knew it off by heart, there was something reassuring about seeing the words on the page. I read it out, not to myself, but in a loud clear voice as if I was reciting for the whole class. "'Out of the night that covers me, black as the pit from pole to pole, I thank whatever gods may be for my unconquerable soul.'" And again, it was as if the words were coming from down deep.

By the time I got to the last lines, I was ready to go out and do what I had to do. I walked through the kitchen, where Gus was sitting at the table.

In front of him a bottle of whisky and a glass, both of them empty.

I'm not sure how, but the old bugger knew.

I could see it in his face.

"Dom, you do have a choice," he said.

I looked at Gus, at his stump. *What choice?*

"If you had your time again, would've you have done it?"

Gus looked down at the floor, then up at me. "Yes," he said. "I would've done it."

But I didn't believe him.

"I'm in my room, okay?" I said. "Tonight, I never left the house."

He nodded, and I could see the tears in his eyes. We stayed like that for what seemed like ages, neither of us sure what to do. Eventually I said, "Blazing bells."

Gus grimaced. "And buckets of blood."

I walked outside, passing my house.

Lights were on inside, and I imagined what my siblings would be doing. The thought of Toby watching some cooking show, while working his way through an industrial-sized bowl of organic popcorn, made me laugh. And Miranda multitasking: phone, laptop, TV, while doing her nails. The thought of that also made me laugh.

I love youse guys.

I kept walking.

When I came to Imogen's house, I looked up at her window. Light on – she was inside.

I thought of her in there, with all her lists and her photos and I thought of the Omega Speedmaster watch, now hidden in the bottom of my drawer.

Im, I know where your father is.

But I can't tell you, not yet, not until I find out if my father was involved.

I knew he'd killed Bag Lady. But was that the only person?

When I reached the lawn, I looked around: there was nobody. I hurried across the grass until I reached the grate. I lifted it up easily, but I knew I would; I'd been earlier, armed with a hammer and chisel to make sure it was loose.

I took the headlamp out of the backpack and placed it on my head, adjusting the strap so that it was nice and tight. I put on the cotton gloves I'd bought at Bunnings Warehouse, and I lowered myself into the drain.

I wouldn't say it felt like home, but it did feel sort of familiar down here.

The right-up-your-nostrils smell wasn't so uncomfortable, and the gloves definitely helped with the crawling process. And I'd checked out the weather bureau's website – the chance of rain was negligible, so I wasn't worried about drowning like those two kids that time, or like Brandon nearly did. The irony – is that the right word, Mr. Mac? – wasn't lost on me: I'd saved Brandon's life and here I was …

When I came to the first sump, I took out the map and checked my position: I was exactly where I thought I'd be. I continued crawling.

A few times I'd wondered about the six installments. Why not twelve, like the labors of Hercules? Why not ten, like just about everything else in this metric world? Why six? But it seemed to me that six was about right. That with five installments already paid, I'd gained the experience and expertise that I needed to perform the sixth.

As I crawled, the headlamp picking out the tunnel ahead, I felt strong and confident. When I reached the next sump, I turned right, towards the hospital, not left as I had the last time I was down here. Although it was new territory, it was really just more of the same: slow steady crawling.

No need to bust a gut, time wasn't really an issue.

What had changed, however, was the smell. The dry, dusty odor had become something much more pungent. As I reached the next sump, I could see the source: the partially decomposed body of a dead cat.

I checked the map: it was time to surface. This part of my plan had been a minor concern; though the grate was situated down a little-used side alley, there was still a chance that somebody would happen to come along as I popped up, meerkat-like, out of the ground. If that happened, if they saw my face, if they somehow managed to later identify me, then I was not the professional I thought I was.

So just in case, I put on a mask. No, not a Warnie mask. Just a plastic Batman number I'd bought at the Two Dollar Shop.

I pushed the grate up and to one side. And I hoisted myself out of the drain. The Batman mask was superfluous – the alley was deserted.

This alley led onto the busy main road on which the hospital was situated. But I didn't want to go near the hospital, not yet, not until I'd cracked its security.

Just up the road from the hospital was a cluster of fast food restaurants, lots of flashing neon, a Pizza Hut, a KFC and, of course, a McDonald's. They were perfect for my needs – close enough so that I had range, but busy enough so that I wouldn't be noticed. A teenage kid munching on a burger while looking at a laptop was hardly an unusual sight. And, yes, they also had CCTV, and that burger-munching laptop-looking kid would end up on that CCTV, but I just had to wear that; I didn't have time to take out every security system in the Gold Coast.

I went into the McDonald's and ordered a Big Mac from a girl who, according to her name tag, was called Bacardee. As Bacardee took my order she was sort of checking me out, and I wondered if she knew me somehow. When she opened her mouth and started

"Is your name –" I thought my plan was about to get scuttled before it had begun; I could not afford to be recognized. But when she finished her sentence with "Blade?" I let out an audible sigh of relief.

"No, it's definitely not," I said.

"You look heaps like him," she said.

I took my tray to a table that was as close as possible to the hospital. The burger was greasy and salty and weirdly sweet: it was crazy delicious. As I opened ClamTop I noticed that the nerd of the Asian variety at a nearby table was showing an unhealthy amount of interest in me and my hardware.

I considered changing tables, but figured that would look suspicious: what did I have to hide? Instead I shifted around a bit, so the inquisitive nerd didn't have such a good view, and I got to work.

The hospital Wi-Fi was there for all to see. Getting into it was a different matter, however; it was pretty secure and the little devil had to do quite a lot of dancing before it was cracked. Once cracked, I was able to move around freely, and with a major hospital, there was a lot to move around in.

It took me a while to get my bearings, but eventually I found the security center, the place where all the CCTV feeds ended up. And, boy, was there a lot of them! But I managed to find those that I was interested in, that would track my entrance into the children's wing, to the ward where Brandon was, and into his room.

I didn't mind being seen on CCTV, there wasn't much I could do about that anyway, but what I needed to do was stop that footage ending up on a hard disk. This was very taxing work; my focus was completely on ClamTop, and I didn't realize that there was somebody standing behind my shoulder. And when that person said, "What sort of laptop is that?" I practically jumped out of my cheap plastic seat.

It was the Asian nerd, of course.

"Is it Linux operating system?" he said.

I didn't want to appear to be racist, or nerdist, but I had to get him away from here really quickly.

"Please go away," I said as politely as I could.

He stayed where he was.

"If you don't go now, I'm probably going to have to punch you in the face," I said.

This time, he did move back to his seat, a shocked look on his face. He was immediately on his phone, though, and I was worried he was calling in reinforcements, further nerds, swarms of them, who would overpower me to get to ClamTop.

I couldn't get too caught up with him, however, because I had to concentrate on the hospital. I figured that I had two options. I could get back into the system after I'd been into the hospital, get into the video files, and edit me out of them. Or I could make sure I never got into the files in the first place.

The first option seemed simpler, but I had the feeling that as soon as I'd accomplished my mission I was going to want to hightail it like crazy out of there.

The second option was the better one.

I didn't want to stop the feed saving to the hard disk completely because that would've looked suspicious, but I worked out that I needed a window in which to get through the hospital, from the first CCTV camera to the last CCTV camera.

Though these cameras themselves were pretty dumb – they just looked – the software that controlled them was very sophisticated, and had many different functions. I went through all the dropdown menus, looking for something I could use. And on the last one, there it was: "activity scheduler."

From there it was surprisingly easy, and I kept thinking that I must be forgetting something. I entered a start time, when the camera stopped saving its data to the hard disk, allowing myself ten minutes to get to the hospital from here. The end time, when the data began recording again, was tricky. I wanted to allow myself enough time to get everything done, but I also didn't want it to look too suspicious; I decided on half an hour.

By the time I'd done that for each of the cameras, I was feeling pretty pleased with myself. But then I looked over at the nerd's table. I'd been right about the reinforcements; there were about five of them sitting there, glaring at me. They were all Asian, but not all of them were so nerdish – a couple looked like they spent serious time in the gym.

So when I'd finally finished I wasted no time in packing away ClamTop and getting out of there. Though it was night, this area was well lit – lots of streetlights. I looked behind; they were following me! My attempt at anonymity was anything but; I now had five people clocking my every move.

What had I been thinking, threatening him like that? Just because violence, or the threat of violence, had worked for me in the past, that didn't mean it would work all the time.

Ugh!

Now I wished my former employer Hound had given me some on-the-job training, especially in the how-to-lose-a-tail department.

It didn't seem as if I had any choice, so I ran. When I say ran, I mean I Usain Bolt-ed out of there. And the nerds had no chance; a couple tried to keep up, but it only took me a few minutes to lose them.

Now, I had to do a complete circuit and come around to the back of the hospital again. I checked my watch; my ten-minute window of time was fast closing.

And if this plan didn't work. I didn't really have a backup one.

Back at the entrance again, and I got past the first

CCTV camera with a few minutes to spare, before it started recording to the hard disk. I half walked, half ran, and passed the second one okay.

Elevator time.

There were a lot of elevators, maybe eight, and catching one would not normally be too much of a problem. Tonight, however, it was.

What is the name of the law that says if anything can go wrong it will? Sod's law – that's it! Well, Professor Sod was spot on, and that Zen-centered feeling I'd had before, well, it was gone – my brain was buzzing, my heart was banging against my rib cage.

Finally – at last! – an elevator opened its jaws. There were only two people in it, but one of those people was on a bed on wheels, and the other was one of those funky orderlies with tribal tatts and creative hair. There was really no room in the elevator, but I went to get into it anyway.

"Hey, man," said Funky Orderly. "We're already a bit squeezy in here."

"Sorry," I said, finding some room, hitting the close-doors button. The doors closed, and I hit the 4 button.

"So, what's the big rush?"

"Somebody I know is dying," I said.

"Bummer, man," he said, and I couldn't have agreed more.

The elevator clanked upwards.

Funky Orderly was now up for a chat. "So what

ward is your mate in?" he said. "I might know him."
Awesome! Professor Sod got it right again.

I resorted to the old phone trick.

"Sorry," I said. "I have to get this." I answered the imaginary caller, "Yes, Mom. Yes, I'm aware of that." I kept it going until the elevator reached the fourth floor and the jaws opened again.

Just as I was stepping out, Funky Orderly said, "Lovely work there, mate. There is no reception in these elevators."

I walked past the third CCTV camera and I'd made it, five seconds within the time frame. Past the ward desk, or whatever it's called, where a red-haired nurse was writing in a file. I just strolled past, trying not to look as if I didn't belong here, not making eye contact. Past the last camera, and I'd made it: if my hacking had worked, and I didn't see why it wouldn't have, I was here, and I was not here.

I pushed open the door to Brandon's room. There was a woman sitting in there; a scarf covered her head.

Wrong room, I thought. *Brandon doesn't get visitors except for PJ; Brandon's a street kid*. My eyes shifted from the woman to the bed. No, it was Brandon's room alright, because there was Brandon.

Before I could make a retreat the woman said, "Hello, do you know Brandon?"

I didn't know what to say. If I didn't know him,

then what was I doing here?

"Yes," I said, keeping my answer as brief as possible.

"That's lovely," she said. "Lovely that he's got friends."

No reply. Keep it brief. I checked my watch; my window for this camera was closing, I had less than ten minutes left.

I hadn't moved from my position in the doorway, and the woman shifted in her seat. I supposed it was to get a better look at me. But I also got a better look at her.

She was about my mum's age, I guessed, but what struck me most about her was who she looked like: PJ. The same manga comic features.

I couldn't help myself, I stopped keeping it brief, and I said, "You're PJ's mother?"

"That's right," she said. "Though I know her better as Polly."

Polly? No wonder she called herself PJ.

"And you're Brandon's mother?" I said, somewhat redundantly.

"That's right," she said. "My name's Pat."

You don't think of street kids as having mothers, even though PJ had told me once that hers had a Leaning Tower of Pisa statue on her dressing table. But here she was in the maternal flesh and maternal blood.

"So how's he doing?" I said.

She shook her head, and dabbed at her eyes with a wad of tissue. "You didn't say what your name was."

"Tristan," I said, the first name that came into my head.

I checked my watch. Eight minutes and twenty seconds left.

For a few seconds my mind was completely blank – my meticulously worked-out plan had been derailed and I didn't know how to get it back on track. But then it came to me, what I had to do: there were no options, I had to get this mother away from her dying son.

Dom, you are evil.

Yes, I am evil.

Because if I failed, they would have their pound of my flesh.

I took out ClamTop.

"You young people," she said in a friendly sort of way. "You can't do without your computers, can you?"

And I did what I had to do, setting the hospital's alarm to go off in a minute.

A minute can be a very long time.

Say something, Dom. Anything.

"So you used to have a little statue of the Leaning Tower of Pisa on your dressing table?"

"How in the blazes did you know that?" she said. "Did Polly tell you?"

I hadn't given much thought to what PJ and Brandon's parents would be like – why would I? They were street kids, and that's one of the distinguishing characteristics of a street kid: lack of parents. But I guess you make all sort of assumptions. I mean, why would a kid leave home and live rough unless their parents were useless, or violent, or no-hope junkies? But Pat didn't seem to be any of these.

Again, I couldn't help myself, I had to ask her. "Do you mind if I ask a question?"

"You're going to ask me why my kids left home, aren't you?"

"Something like that," I said.

"They did the right thing," she said. "You see, I got mixed up with this fella, and basically he was no good. They knew from day one, the way kids do, but it took me a bit longer to find out." Again, she dabbed at her eyes with the sodden tissue.

One of the machines that was connected to Brandon beeped.

"Maybe I should call a nurse," said Pat.

Then the alarm went.

I think Pat thought that again it was coming from the machine, because her eyes were wide with terror; what did such a big noise mean?

"That's the evacuation bell," I said. "We have to get out of here."

"But Brandon?"

"I think if it's serious, they'll come and get him."

Pat seemed unconvinced, so I said, "Come on, we

better go." I placed my hand lightly on her elbow and helped her to her feet. And then we walked down the corridor together.

Two nurses appeared alongside us. "I wouldn't be too concerned," one of them said. "That stupid alarm goes off all the time."

When we reached the open elevator, I stepped inside with Pat. But just as the doors were about to close, I jammed my arm between them, forcing them open.

"I forgot something," I said.

I hurried back along the corridor.

Hurried into Brandon's room.

I checked my watch: I had thirty seconds left.

I looked at him, his face so thin, so white, the bandages around his wrists, the almost imperceptible rise and fall of his chest.

I took out my iPhone, put it into video mode.

Now all I had to do was take a life.

SOD'S LAW

Sod's law said there was going to be somebody in the alley.

But it was as dark and deserted as when I'd come, not even a rat to observe me removing the grate and disappearing back into the subterranean world I was getting to know so well. I put my headlamp back on, put the gloves back on, and began my journey home.

Considering what I'd just done, I felt very little at all: thoughts entered my head, but I paid them absolutely no attention, and they just wandered out again. It was the physical that I was more concerned with, that rhythmic shuffle back along the tunnel.

I wasn't in a great hurry; as far as the world was concerned, the part that mattered anyway, the part that could lock you up in jail, I hadn't moved from my bedroom all night. Why rush to get to someplace if you're already there?

I reached the first sump, stopped, had a drink of water. I reached the second sump, stopped, ate a Snickers bar. By the time I reached Halcyon Grove, pushing up one final grate, emerging into one of the Coast's most secure addresses, it was past one o'clock.

Immediately, I knew something was wrong.

Don't ask me how, but I knew.

A hundred percent, I knew.

I remembered what Samsoni had said about the perimeter security being compromised. There was somebody inside the walls who shouldn't be here. I took off, running for Samsoni's box. The light was on, but I couldn't see him.

I looked inside; Samsoni was slumped on the floor.

Dead?

I dug my fingers into his neck, feeling for a pulse.

I found it easily – strong and regular. He was alive – thank heavens. I thought about calling triple-0, but I knew how much time that could take. I knew that they wouldn't believe me.

He stirred, opening his eyes.

"You okay?" I said. He nodded. So I kept moving, ninja-ing towards my house.

Past Imogen's house. Was she in danger? Should I warn her?

No, that didn't make sense. I kept going.

Gus – was he in danger? Maybe, but Gus was a tough old bugger.

I hurried up the driveway to our house; not one light was on. That was unusual; my parents always kept at least one light burning.

I was in the right place.

I tried the front door; it was locked. I took out my key, inserted it, turned it as gently as I could. There was the tiniest of clicks as the door opened, and I slipped inside.

I stood absolutely still, and I listened. The only sounds I could hear – the hum of the fridge, the burble of the aquarium – were innocent ones. I kept moving, towards the staircase.

As far as keeping quiet, I had an advantage here; because of all those mornings I'd sneaked out of the house as quietly as possible, not wanting to disturb my sleeping family, I knew where every creaky floorboard was.

Up the stairs. Along the passage.

Miranda's door.

I turned the handle, opening the door enough so that I could see that she was in bed, asleep, safe. I kept going.

Toby's door.

I did the same. He, too, was in bed, asleep, safe.

My parents' room.

My hand on the handle.

I was about to turn it when I had another idea: there was another, less conspicuous way into their room. One us kids had used a lot when we'd been in our sneak-a-look-at-our-parents'-stuff phase.

Along the passage, and into the storage room, and there was a door that led into their walk-in closet. I slid open the sliding door, just a fraction.

And another.

It was the slightest of cracks, but enough to see the two shapes, my dad, my mum, as they slept in their canopied bed. Relief – they were okay.

It occurred to me that maybe I had this wrong, that this sixth sense was nothing of the kind; I was just on edge after what had happened tonight.

Wait, I ordered myself.

Wait.

The curtain to the side of their bed moved.

And moved some more.

And there was a person there, dressed in black, a balaclava covering his face, with some weird contraption on his head. It was so strange, so unexpected, I almost laughed.

But then he moved to the bed, and his hand came up, and something in it glinted.

"Dad!" I screamed, bursting out from between the sliding doors.

The knife came down, and Dad's eyes were open. He threw up his arm and the knife sliced into his hand.

But the knife came up again and came down again. Again, the steel plunged into flesh.

Dad screamed, and I could see blood.

Mom woke, screaming.

The knife came up again, and I knew that this time the aim would be better.

I launched myself at the intruder, my shoulder catching his chest. We both hit the floor, but the knife was still in his hand. He held it to his chest, and immediately I could see what he intended to do.

A backhand jab would get me in the heart.

But as his arm came towards me, my hand came down on his, knocking the knife from his grasp. *That's it,* I thought.

But his hand reached into his belt and came out with another knife. I reached around, grabbed the handle of the first knife.

Dad lay on the bed, moaning.

Mom was screaming; there was blood on her face.

The intruder and I were both on our feet, crouching.

"Just go," I said, waving the knife at him. "Get out of here."

He came at me low. I thought of my time in Rome, those fights I'd had in the Colosseum and in San Luca. I thought of what I'd done right and what I'd done wrong.

He came at me low, and I spun.

I knew that this thrust would miss, but I also knew that he would keep coming at me until I stopped him coming at me. So I spun, and I tightened my grip on the knife.

But when he was almost on me, there was a sound: the report of a gun.

The knife dropped from his hand, and he dropped to the ground, fingers latticed over his heart.

I turned around – Dad had a gun in his hand, and the air now had a sour metallic smell.

As I rushed over to the intruder, I took out my phone, about to dial triple-0.

"Don't call anybody," said Dad. "He's gone."

I looked at the masked figure crumpled on the floor and immediately I knew Dad was right: he was gone.

Dad's eyes were moving around the room, taking it all in. Once again I had that feeling I'd had a few times lately, the feeling that my dad was not who I thought he was, that he was capable of stuff I couldn't imagine – I mean, he'd just killed somebody, his arm was bleeding, but he was taking it all so calmly.

"We'll sort this out," he said, ripping off a strip of the sheet with his teeth and tying it around the wound on his arm. "I just need a few stitches, that's all."

"But –" I said.

"David?" said Mom, wiping the blood from her face with the corner of the sheet.

Dad opened the drawer of his bedside table, reached in, and brought out a phone – a Styxx – I'd never seen before. He started composing a text.

"Trust me," he said when he'd finished, "it's better we do this my way."

Dad moved over to the body, knelt down and ripped the balaclava off.

Both eyes were open. And one was lazy.

Droopy Eye.

He was my age. He was dead. Killed by my own father. The emotions: horror, anguish, fear, whatever, were too much, they had to get out – I screamed, a torrent of pure noise from my guts, throat, mouth.

"Now, you need to get a hold," said Dad.

He was right: I needed to get a hold. I took a couple of slow deep breaths and it seemed to work. Then I noticed what the contraption on Droopy Eye's head was: a Go Pro video camera.

And suddenly it all made sense: I was never the target; it was always my father, the one who had killed his father. *Occhio per occhio, dente per dente.* He was going to revenge that death and the camera was to show everybody back in San Luca how he, the hero, had done it.

I grabbed the Go Pro, ripped it off his head.

"You need to get rid of that," said Dad.

"I will," I said, turning the camera around so it was pointing at me, filming me.

Dad opened his mouth as if to say something, but then closed it again – could he possibly know what I was doing?

I pointed the camera at Droopy Eye, at his lifeless body, before turning it off and putting it into my pocket. And another feeling swept me up, one of utter revulsion: what had I become? Who was I?

But then there was a knock on the door, and Miranda's frightened voice came from the other side. "Is everything okay in there? What was that screaming?"

And then Toby: "What's going on?"

And then the sound of a vehicle pulling up in front of our house; whoever Dad had texted had taken no time to get here.

I almost forgot. "Samsoni," I said. "They knocked him out."

"Don't you worry, son," said Dad. "It will all be sorted." He turned to Mom. "You take the kids over to Dad's house, and don't come out until I tell you." The authority in his voice was unmistakable, and reassuring; somebody was taking control, somebody was going to fix it.

Mom opened the door, shepherding my siblings down the corridor. I was just about to leave too, when Dad grabbed me by the arm.

"He would've killed me," he said.

I nodded.

"And you saved my life."

Again, all I could do was nod.

"Don't you ever forget that," he said. "It was his life or mine."

He kissed me on the cheek, Italian-style. Something

he had never done before. "Go join the others."

I ran down the stairs and caught up with them as they were crossing the lawn.

"What happened in there?" said Toby.

"What happened in there?" said Miranda.

"We had an intruder," said Mom. "And your dad was attacked, but the main thing is that he's okay and the police are sorting it out."

"What police?" said Toby. "They don't look like police to me."

"Plainclothes," said Mom. "It's Halcyon Grove, nobody wants to create a big fuss."

I'm not really sure if my siblings bought this or not, especially not Miranda, but they didn't ask many other questions. I suppose Mom was right – the main thing was that Dad was okay, that we were okay.

Gus stomped around making us hot chocolate, and found some cookies somewhere – so much for "sugar is going to kill you."

"Okay," said Mom. "Let's get to bed."

As if that was ever going to happen; we were all wired to the max. So instead we sat around and talked total crap and when we got sick of that we watched crap TV like it was some sort of normal family get-together.

Dad turned up about an hour later, to tell us that Samsoni was fine and it had all been "sorted" and we could all go back to our bedrooms. Toby and Miranda had questions, but Dad had that amazing politician's knack of seeming to supply adequate answers while saying pretty much nothing.

Toby and Miranda got out of their chairs to leave, but I stayed where I was. Dad looked at me, and I noticed now that he had a professional-looking bandage on his arm.

"Dom, I think it's time you came home," he said.

Mom said nothing, but she didn't need to, it was on her face – *time to come home, Dom*. I knew both my parents were connected to The Debt – they had to be. But they were my parents, and tonight I couldn't argue with them: it was time to come home.

We all walked back to the house together, the five of us in a tight bunch. As for the house, it looked like nothing had ever happened. I wondered what they'd done with Francesco Strangio; now that he was dead I couldn't call him that other thing.

We sat in the living room and talked some more and then Toby excused himself and went to bed and Miranda excused herself and went to bed and then it was three-thirty in the morning and it was just the three of us.

"Well, I guess I better hit the sack," said Dad.

I couldn't believe it: he'd killed somebody, and he was going to pop off to bed. What sort of person can do that? Go through what we'd just been through, and then crawl between the sheets, and sleep like a baby?

"Don't you think you owe me some sort of explanation?" I said.

Dad and Mom exchanged looks.

"Yes, of course we do," said Dad. "We need to tell you absolutely everything, but now's not the right time."

"I know you went to San Luca," I said, looking at him hard.

I switched my attention to Mom. "And I know you're not American."

Mom look outraged. "Of course –" she started, but I didn't let her get any further than that.

"I know!" I said.

Mom and Dad looked at each other and did some of that wordless communication that parental units do.

And Dad spoke ...

SAN LUCA

"When I was sixteen, I had to get away from Gus. Rocco's family took me in," said Dad.

"You lived with the Tavernitis?"

Dad nodded.

My head was spinning: the Tavernitis were The Debt, they had to be, and Dad had lived with them? The same people who had just put him through everything, who had threatened to remove a pound of his flesh, and he moved in with them?

I knew he was connected, but this connected?

"But –" I started, before Mom leaned over and put her soft hand on my forearm. "Just let your dad have his say."

"Rocco and I were mates," he said. "We had been ever since we went to Miami State High together. Us Italians, we had to stick together in those days. So when I left school I worked at the restaurant, as a dish pig." He smiled at this, as if the idea of him with his arms elbow-deep in dish suds didn't quite seem possible. "You want to learn about hard work, there's nothing like a kitchen."

I thought about Dad's offices, the empty desks, the cobwebs – it didn't look like there was much hard work going on there.

"Then, when we were twenty-one, we were sent to Italy," he said.

Small sentence, big statement: my dad had always maintained that he'd never visited the land of his ancestors.

He must've pegged the look on my face, because he held up both hands and said, "Yes, I know. Big lie. But please let me continue. Rocco and I were sent to San Luca to learn the family business."

I'm not sure if my parents knew that I'd been to San Luca also; if they did, it wasn't me who had told them. "The family business?" I said.

"Restaurants, cafés," he said.

'Ndrangheta, I thought, because what he said didn't make sense – he was already working in a restaurant.

"Economically, Italy wasn't the place it is today, especially in a small village in the Aspromonte Mountains, but for a couple of *canguros* like us, it wasn't such a bad life." Dad paused, and I could see the glow of pleasure in his face; he was obviously telling the truth. "And then your mother arrived in town."

Mom and Dad smiled at each other.

"Arrived?"

"Yes, she'd been living in the States. Your mother was born in California, but things didn't work out, so her family came back to the old village."

So Mom was a hundred percent American, a hundred percent Californian! I felt a great surge of relief – at least she was who she said she was.

"I guess you could say it was love at first sight," said Dad, smiling at Mom again, this time upping the wattage.

"Where did you meet?" I asked.

"In the piazza, next to the fountain," said Mom.

I was just about to say, *I know that piazza, I know that fountain*, but I bit my tongue – knowledge is currency, even with your own family.

"But we had a problem," said Dad. "And here in the Gold Coast in this day and age it might be a bit hard to understand this, but remember, this was Italy many years ago, and a very traditional part of the country. My adopted family and your mother's family, well, they didn't exactly see eye to eye."

"The Tavernitis?" I said. Dad nodded. "And the …?" I had a mental block – what was Mom's maiden name, again? I was sure I knew it, but I just couldn't find it.

"Baresi," said Mom. "My maiden name is Baresi."

Before I could process that, Dad had taken up the thread again.

"There was no real issue with the Baresis; they're civilized people."

I was losing track here, genealogy had never been my strong point, but then it came to me. "So it was with Mom's mother's family?"

"You got it," said Dad.

"My mother was a Strangio," said Mom.

Though I'd been stabbed, kicked in the knurries, whacked across the ear, I'd never been punched in the face, but this is what this was: no fist, no knuckles, but *bam!* I even rocked back on my heels.

My dad had killed a Strangio.

He was married to a Strangio.

He had killed family!

"Dom, are you okay?" said Dad. "You're looking sort of white."

"The boy who died, he was your family!" I said to Mom.

"They disowned me, I disowned them," she said, her voice as hard as flint.

Now the information cat was out of the information bag, but neither of my parents showed surprise that I knew this.

"And he wanted to kill my husband," said Mom. And she had a point: Francesco had come to our house for one reason and one reason only.

Dad continued. "I wasn't allowed to see your mother, wasn't allowed to contact her, so to cut a long story short, we ran away to Australia."

I looked at my dad and my mum, the Romeo and Juliet of San Luca, and I thought: *Do you think you've raised your son to be a complete idiot? Do you think I'm going to stop believing the story you've always told, how you met in Tavernitis, and start believing that crap?*

"And this guy was going to kill you for that?" I said. "All these years after it happened?"

"Like I said, son. You have to remember how backward these places are."

Backward, but not that backward – this was the second Strangio my father had killed.

And that was on the tip of my tongue, but a voice told me that now wasn't the time, or the place, to have this out. Or give voice to the umpteen other questions that were now accumulating in my head.

I said good night to my parents, went upstairs to my room, and plugged the Go Pro into my laptop.

Download video file to hard disk? the software asked me.

I hit enter, and hit it hard.

BRANDON

The trip to the hospital later that day was much more orthodox: I asked my grandfather if he could drive me there. No headlamps, no gloves, no scurrying along tunnels like a yellow-toothed sewer rat.

"Sure," he said. "Why not, there's somebody there I wouldn't mind visiting, either."

As we got into his truck, I checked the text I'd received from PJ.

meet me at hosp urgent

Of course, I'd thought about not going.

I'd thought about running away.

I'd thought about moving to another country, making a new life for myself.

I'd thought about a lot of stuff, but I knew that I had to go to the hospital and face PJ.

It was raining, one of those light drizzles that is not as light or drizzly as you think. Gus doesn't mind an umbrella, so when we got out of the car after he had found – much excitement! – a free parking lot that was close to the hospital, he held it over the both of us.

When we got inside I couldn't help looking at the CCTV cameras. This time I would be both seen and remembered. Stored on the hard disk. We got into an elevator, Gus bound for the second floor, me for the fourth.

Gus got out. We'd already agreed to meet in the café when we'd both done what we had to do. I continued on. The elevator opened on the third floor, and who gets in but Funky Orderly?

He took one look at me, took out his phone, and said in a loud, mannered voice, "Yes, I know you're not really there but who cares, I just like to have imaginary conversations with imaginary people."

I shook my head: some people, some orderlies.

I got out on the fourth floor, past those other two CCTV cameras, past the ward desk. When I knocked on Brandon's door there were two replies of, "Come in."

I entered. PJ was sitting in one of the chairs, her mother in the other; they were holding hands.

And Brandon was awake!

Now I understood why PJ had sent the text.

"Grammar," he said. Though his voice was just a croak, it seemed a miracle that he could talk. He had come so close to dying, so close to being killed.

"No more," I said. "I've left school."

"You're still a Grammar boy," he said. "That stink lasts forever."

"Brandon, please," said his mother. "Tristan's our visitor."

"Tristan?" said PJ, looking at her mother and then at me.

"Yes, we met here last night."

"You came last night?" said PJ, and I couldn't blame her for being perplexed. "What for?"

To take a life, to kill your brother.

But I couldn't go through with it.

Just like Gus couldn't go through with it.

We sat there for a while longer, but it was about as awkward as awkward can get. Brandon may have snapped out of his coma, but he still had an incurable disease. And PJ, the girl I had recently kissed, seemed like the strangest of strangers.

I stood up. "I have to meet my grandfather."

"Thanks for coming," said Pat.

"I'll text you," said PJ.

I looked over at Brandon. His eyes caught mine and there was something in them I'd never seen, or never noticed, before: he was scared, he was terrified. I moved over to his bed.

"You're not going to hug me or anything?" he said.

"I was thinking about it."

"Yeah, well, if you have to. Let's get it over and done with."

I leaned over and hugged him as best as I could, and as I did his hand gripped my arm and gripped it tight and he whispered, "You make sure my sister is okay."

"I will," I said, though PJ didn't strike me as the sort of person who needed looking after. I stood up, and as I walked out I wondered if this would be the last time I ever saw Brandon alive.

Ω Ω Ω

As Gus approached Chevron Heights I asked him if he would mind taking a slight detour – I had something to deliver.

"Of course not," he said.

I directed him to stop outside an ordinary suburban house in an ordinary suburban street. A van, *Komang Pool Cleaners* written on the side, was in the driveway.

As I took the package from my pocket I wondered about the contents, the DVD that was inside.

I'd edited and reedited it.

I'd watched it over and over again.

Sometimes I thought it was a masterpiece: incontrovertible proof that I'd done what they'd asked. And other times I thought it was just a pile of rubbish.

But it *was* in the papers, all over the Internet:

Italian Exchange Student Goes Missing on Gold Coast

And surely that was going to help my cause.

I got out of the truck, walked up to the front gate.

Just as I was about to slot the package into the mailbox something really obvious occurred to me: I hadn't killed Francesco Strangio, but I had killed Francesco Strangio.

If I gave them the DVD, they would have that over me for the rest of my life. The same way they had Bag Lady over my dad.

A thought flashed into my mind: I didn't have to do this, I didn't have to play by their rules.

Yes, they would come after me, but I wasn't the same person now. They could come, but I would be ready for them.

This thought lasted for about a nanosecond – who was I kidding?

Bugger the mailbox – I walked past the gate, up the path, and pressed the buzzer on the intercom.

"What do you want?" came a voice from the speaker.

"I have something for you."

"Put it on the step."

I did that, turned and walked back to the truck.

PAGATO

A lamp on top of the desk threw out a weak light, leaving pockets of darkness in Gus's office. Somewhere in the shadows Dr. Roger Bannister was breaking the four-minute mile in 1954, John Landy was setting the 1500-meters world record, and Hicham El Guerrouj was setting the current world record of three minutes and twenty-six seconds.

Dad and Gus were sitting beside each other on one of the two leather couches, the ones my mum had discarded about fifty-five annoying redecorations and ninety even more annoying decorators ago.

Gus was wearing his usual clothes: a ratty tank top that showed off his ropy old-man muscles, and shorts that were baggy but not baggy enough to hide the stump.

Hey, Stumpy, I thought, looking at his funny little seamed head, like an eyeless alien from a C-grade sci-fi movie, *I could've had one of you.*

But I didn't, and hopefully I never would.

Dad's arm was bandaged.

"My golf game was never any good anyway," he joked.

Golf jokes – so not funny, but I'd laughed. Like Mom said, he was alive and that was all that mattered.

Dad and Gus were drinking whisky – straight, on the rocks – from hefty tumblers, and I had a glass of Coke. I still didn't get that: Gus had once been a hopeless alcoholic, yet he still drank occasionally. I thought one drop of the demon drink and alcoholics would immediately return to their sorry ways. Willpower, I guessed.

Outside, the wind had picked up, and occasionally, from the empty top floor of Gus's house, came the sound of a branch rapping on a window with its wooden knuckles. I remembered that there'd been the same noise on the night I'd learned about The Debt. Then I'd thought it meant evil had come into my life.

I'd been right: evil had come into my life.

And what did it mean now: that evil was leaving?

Maybe, but not all of it – according to the DVD they had, the one I'd concocted, I'd killed another human being; evil would be with me for as long as I lived.

Dad finished his drink and said, "Well, I think it's about time we got this over and done with."

Gus managed a smile, no mean feat when the grandson you love is about to get the flesh of his inside thigh branded with white-hot metal.

"We might as well." I stood up, undid the buckle on my jeans, and let them fall to the ground.

Dad took the brand from the drawer in Gus's desk and, using that ancient Zippo lighter, heated its tip until it was glowing white-hot. Many times I'd thought about this moment, many times I'd wondered if it would ever come. I'd assumed that if, and when, it did, I'd feel this incredible sense of triumph.

But as white-hot metal seared my flesh, and my whole body became nothing but raw pain, I felt no triumph at all.

Just emptiness and pain.

And emptiness and pain.

There had been too much collateral damage.

Afterwards, when the flesh had stopped bubbling and I could talk again, I said, "Can I have a whisky?"

My dad looked at his dad. "Of course you can."

Gus poured two drinks and handed one to me, one to Dad.

"You're going to drink with us, aren't you?" I said.

Gus held up his hand, and now I got it: he always stopped at one. What a tough old bugger he was – every particle in his body demanding alcohol, and he stopped at one. I sipped the whisky. This wasn't the first time I'd drunk it, but now it was different. I hadn't liked the taste of it then and I didn't like the taste of it now, but it felt right somehow. And when that fireball exploded in my stomach, that felt right too.

"Hey, Gus," I said. "Can I have a look at the original debt, that piece of paper?"

I'd already made the decision that I would never have kids. Or if I did, I would make sure they were girls. I wasn't sure about the science, but I was sure you could swing it somehow.

Gus went to his desk and returned with the document. Ancient-looking, the paper yellow, brittle; it didn't seem possible that something with a few signatures could be so powerful, cause so much pain.

For some reason I thought of what Mr. Jazy had said about all those loans, all those mortgages – they were also debts, pieces of paper with a few signatures, and if he was right they would also cause pain and heartache.

I read the title, *Pagherò Cambiaro*.

After some success speaking Italian in Italy – I'd ordered spaghetti, bought some train tickets – I sort of kidded myself that I knew my way around the language.

Yeah, right!

"So what does it say?"

Gus translated. "All male Silvagnis on reaching the age of fifteen must make six repayments on the loan."

"Sorry?" I said. "You said 'all male Silvagnis'?"

"That's right," said Gus.

"But I thought it was just the eldest son," I said, but as soon as I did I wondered where this idea had actually come from. I remembered that first night Dad had said *all male Silvagnis* too.

"No," said Gus.

"All," said Dad.

"Toby?" I said. Dad nodded. "But there is no way he could ever repay even one installment!"

"He will surprise you," said Dad, becoming all Yodaesque. "The Debt makes men out of boys."

And then I got it – of course, why hadn't I seen this before?

"Alessandro," I said to Gus. "They killed him?"

Gus nodded.

"The pound of flesh?"

"He didn't make it," said Gus.

"And the Preacher, he went mad!"

Again Gus nodded.

I didn't say anything else, I didn't need to, because it was now so clear what I had to do. My namesake had come to this country in order to make a better life for his family, and in order to do this he'd put his name to a piece of paper.

But debts do not last forever.

This one had been repaid many times over.

Toby couldn't go through what I'd been through. He just couldn't.

Never before had it been clearer to me what I had to do.

I had to extinguish The Debt.

EXTINGUISH THE DEBT

In Gus's office it had been so easy, it had made so much sense.

Extinguish The Debt.

Like some cheap slogan you'd stick on a T-shirt.

But I'd spent days wrestling with it – the enormity of it. And that morning when I woke up, the light already streaming through the window, I felt overcome, almost smothered, by the impossibility of this.

Extinguish The Debt? How could I do that? But when I thought of Toby, I knew that somehow I had to do it. He would never survive The Debt; like Alessandro he would end up dead, a cheap box full of moldering bones.

I had a shower, I got on my laptop, I checked my emails.

There was one from Imogen: *Dom, have you disappeared from this planet? I know you're a working man but it would be nice to see you every now and then!!!*

I texted her straightaway: *how about now?*

She replied: *i have school*

Home school, I thought, throwing my clothes on. I rushed downstairs and Mom and Dad were sitting at the table; they had obviously just finished a deep and meaningful.

"Dom, your dad and I think you should go back to school, now that you've ... um ... achieved your goals."

"Good luck with that," I said.

"Dom!" said Dad.

"Let's talk about this later," I said. "I need to be somewhere."

Dad stood up, and I think he actually wanted to physically impede my progress. *Good luck with that, too.* I shimmied out of his reach and ran out the door. Just in case he was after me, I gave it some gas all the way to Imogen's house.

I knocked on the door. Mrs. Havilland answered and she was so not happy to see me.

"Um," she said, followed by another "um" and yet another "um." Finally she found some words that actually meant something.

"Imogen's at school if you're here to see her," she said.

"That's okay, I can just audit the lesson," I said, using a term I'd heard Mr. Mac use once.

It was a good term, too, because it worked on Mrs. Havilland.

343

"Audit the lesson," she said. "Well, why not?"

I'd thought that because the Havilland house wasn't really a school, and didn't have science labs and all that, they would sort of skimp on lots of stuff. But Imogen was in the kitchen, in a lab coat, and she was actually dissecting a frog, while the teacher, also in a lab coat, gave her instructions.

Both of them looked up when I entered. "It's okay, I'm just auditing," I said.

The teacher smiled at me, Imogen rolled her eyes and she returned to her half-dissected amphibian. "Audit" was now my favorite word on the whole planet.

Auditing Imogen dissecting the frog was amazing; she was incredibly skillful. At my school, after an hour's dissection, you basically had a lab full of frog hamburger meat. Boys, eh? When the lesson came to an end, and the frog went into the fridge, Mrs. Havilland gave Imogen the option of using her two free periods to hang out with me.

"Your mum's a pretty tough principal," I said when we were in Imogen's room.

"What's happened?" said Imogen, fixing me with a look sharper than any scalpel.

"What do you mean?"

"You look different somehow. Did you take a get-old pill or something? What's happened to you, Dom?"

I hadn't come here with the intention of telling Imogen anything – I just wanted to see somebody from my old pre-Debt life – but now that I was here, now that she was standing in front of me, I knew, with absolute certainty, what I had to do.

"Sit down," I said.

"I don't want to sit down."

"Yes, you do," I said. "Remember that time we punked those two Mattners and you said that there was something going on in my life and I said I couldn't tell you but you had to trust me?"

Imogen nodded – *I remember.*

"This is it; I'm going to tell you everything."

Imogen sat down, made herself comfortable.

And for the first time I told somebody else what had happened to me on my fifteenth birthday, how I'd inherited an ancient family debt, a debt that could not be repaid with money.

Imogen did not interrupt, did not ask any questions or make any comments, but instead let me tell my story in one continuous flow. I left some stuff out, especially to do with the latest installment, but not that much. Her eyes told me everything, however – they seemed to get wider and wider, more and more astonished, until that's all Imogen was, just eyes and astonishment. And I knew she didn't know whether to believe me or not. Who could possibly blame her?

"Imogen, I'm going to show you something, okay?"

She nodded. I rolled up one leg of my board shorts, higher and higher, until there it was: *PAGATO*, the last letter still scabby.

Immediately Imogen brought her hand to her mouth and gasped. And then she stood up and put her arms around me.

"Poor Dom," she said.

I didn't want to be poor Dom; what I had been through had made me older, tougher, smarter, stronger. But when she squeezed me, it felt like I was melting into her, her smell, and her softness, and her girlness. Tears found their way to my eyes. Maybe she was so right: poor Dom. Nobody should have to go through what I'd been through. Nobody!

Finally she let go, and she stepped back, and her shirt was wet at the shoulder.

"I'm sorry," I said.

"Don't be," she said, handing me a towel – tissues just weren't going to cut it. "So it's finished now?"

I wiped away the tears, shaking my head. "I'm going to get them," I said. "I'm going to extinguish The Debt."

She said nothing, but it was in her eyes – *No, Dom, it's too dangerous.*

"They're the ones who killed your father, Imogen."

She shrank back. "No!"

"Wait here," I said. I rushed out of her house, over to my house, up to my bedroom, and back again.

Imogen was in exactly the same place as when I'd left.

I took the Omega Speedmaster watch out of my pocket, the one I'd taken from the coffin, from around his fleshless wrist. I held it out.

Imogen looked at it, not wanting to know what it was. Eventually, however, her hand reached out and took it. She turned it around, read the inscription on the back.

Her knees buckled slightly, and she looked like she was about to collapse. I got ready to grab her, but she managed to steady herself. "They're the ones who killed my father?" she said.

"They're the ones," I said.

"Then we go to the police."

"Not yet," I said. "Not until we've set it up right."

I wasn't actually sure what I meant by this, but I knew I had to plan this attack meticulously, and I had to attack them from all angles. I knew I'd only have one chance at it, and if I mucked that up, then ...

"And you're going to extinguish The Debt."

I nodded – *I am*.

"I want to help you."

"You will help me," I said. "But not just yet." I held out my hand. "I'm going to need that."

Imogen looked at the watch, rubbing the back of it with her thumb. "You know, it's his birthday tomorrow," she said.

I nodded, though I didn't know.

"There's this game I always play on his birthday,"

347

she said. "Things I Remember about Daddy."

"That's cool," I said, smiling at her. I had stuff to do, but I could tell that Imogen needed to talk.

"Like, I remember how he used to call me 'The Celebrated Imogen Havilland,'" she said. "How he could stand on his head. How he liked to listen to cricket on the radio. How he cut my toast into these perfect soldiers."

"Perfect soldiers aren't easy," I said.

Imogen continued, "I remember how he used to brush my hair, stroke after stroke. When he took me to swimming lessons, he always told me not to be scared." She was turning the watch around in her hand, over and over. "And I remember he used to tell me that he would never, ever leave me. Not until he was really, really old and really, really decrepit."

I reached over and took Imogen's other hand, the one that wasn't holding the watch.

"Do you remember the night he went missing?" she said.

"A bit," I said.

"I remember all the fuss about the election, how nobody thought Dad would win. And then when he did, we all went onstage together while he gave his victory speech. After we went to Taverniti's, and I ordered the spaghetti like I always did. There were people everywhere congratulating Daddy. And then he went outside and didn't come back."

I squeezed Imogen's hand.

"After that it was just this jumble. The police coming to our house every day. Your mum and dad helping us get through it all. But then it got calmer, less chaotic. Until it was really just me and Mum."

Now I didn't know what to say. I just squeezed her hand again.

"And Rocco Taverniti," she said. "He always seemed to be around our place."

"He did?" I said.

Imogen nodded. "But after a while he stopped coming, too, and it was just the two of us, and that's when Mum took me out of school."

Imogen held out her father's watch.

"You keep it for now," I said. "Put it in a safe place."

We hugged again, and I left.

As I walked back home, I thought of Prometheus, that Titan Dr. Chakrabarty had told me about. He'd been chained to a rock, eagles eating his liver, until Hercules had set him free. At last I had told somebody about The Debt, and it had unchained me, too. No more eagles snacking on my liver.

From behind came the sound of the riding mower – not unusual, as our house was surrounded by expansive lawn and it wasn't going to mow itself. I didn't take any notice, just continued on to the house, my mind in a swirl; yes, I felt freer, but it was one thing to say you were going to extinguish The Debt, another altogether to actually do it.

The mower's sound was louder; obviously it was much closer, and the air was sweet with the smell of cut grass, but I still wasn't concerned. Like I said, lawns don't mow themselves.

The mower so loud, the whir of its blades.

Something told me – *jump!*

I jumped, leaping to my left, but when I looked behind the mower was nowhere near me – false alarm much? – and Roberto was sitting on top of it, smiling.

It wasn't his usual type of smile, however; it wasn't mocking, or sneering, it seemed quite genuine, almost pleasant.

"You can probably relax now, Dominic," he said, giving my name the full Italian treatment instead of the usual sarcastic "Mr. Silvagni." What was going on here? Why was he suddenly my BFF?

I said nothing and went inside. Mom was still in the kitchen; Dad must've gone to work.

"How long has Roberto worked for us?" I said.

"I'm not sure, dear," she said. "Can we talk about school again? After what's happened, I really do think it's better to normalize everything."

Normalize? What was she talking about?

My father had killed my cousin, how in the blazes do you "normalize" that?

And for the rest of my life that dead cousin would

appear, and reappear, and re-reappear. How do you normalize that?

"So where does Roberto live?"

"I really don't know much about him," she said.

But what about when Toby went missing, and we came back and there were only the two of you in the kitchen?

So much for the new policy of honesty and transparency.

I couldn't be bothered pushing it, there were other ways to skin this particular who-the-blazes-is-Roberto? cat.

I made to move off, and Mom said, "Dom, where are you going?"

"To work," I said.

Upstairs I got changed into my work clothes: jeans and a T-shirt. I sneaked downstairs and out through the back door. I'd had enough of back-to-school crap. Onto Deadly Treadly and away I went.

As I pedaled, as my legs took on a rhythm, my mind stopped swirling so much, my thoughts became more ordered.

Extinguish The Debt: wasn't it just another installment? Hadn't the others seemed nigh impossible when I'd first gotten them?

And on this installment, unlike the other ones, I was playing for the good guys.

The usual loiterers, including Red Bandana, were standing outside Cash Converters, blocking the entrance. I pushed through them.

"An excuse me wouldn't go astray," said Red Bandana, the baddest of bad guys.

Up the stairs, and before Jodie could say anything I was knocking on Hound's door, pushing it open.

"Youngblood?" he said, his hand moving under his desk.

It took me a little while to realize that he was reaching for a gun, that he thought I'd returned hell-bent on revenge.

"Hey, it's not like that," I said, holding up my arms in mock surrender.

Hound relaxed, his gunless hand reappearing on top of the desk. "So to what do I owe the pleasure?"

"I've still got a job, haven't I?"

"You seemed a bit upset the other day."

"Oh, that!" I said, dismissively. "Purely business. Let's move on, shall we?"

"Absolutely," said Hound, holding out his paw.

"Besides, you haven't even paid me my wages yet." I took his paw, he squeezed, I squeezed; we were back in business. Soon I was at my desk, listening to the tinkle of clients' bathroom visits.

Hound arrived with a whole lot of work for me to do, handing me a piece of paper with a long list of names – the usual credit checks on the usual scumbags.

When he'd gone, I scrunched the paper up and threw it in the trash. I opened Word, and I wrote a list of my own scumbags:

Rocco Taverniti

Ron Gatto

Art Tabori

Roberto?

Seb Baresi?

I stared at the list of names for ages, wanting one of them to jump out, to put his hand up and say, *I'm the one; take me out and you extinguish The Debt.* Then I got creative, and added some more names:

David Silvagni

Celia Silvagni

Dr. Chakrabarty

I stared at this list for ages, too. And I thought the best way to do this was by a process of elimination, so I started with the least likely, with Dr. Chakrabarty.

Under his name I typed: *Against*, and under that I immediately put *Indian*.

Let's face it, whoever had heard of an Indian 'Ndranghetista?

Could you imagine Don Corleone sitting down to eat a chicken tandoori? Tony Soprano watching Bollywood films?

But then I thought about it a bit more; wasn't that sort of weirdly racist?

In *The Godfather*, the *consigliere* is Irish, not Italian. And Wikipedia told me that there had been a significant Indian immigration to Italy ever since the government had offered amnesty to illegal immigrants because of a labor shortage.

What else under *Against*?

I couldn't think of anything big, so I kept going; under *For* I typed:

speaks fluent Italian

knows heaps about Italian culture

traveled to San Luca during time of the Festival of Our Lady of Polsi

capable of composing Latin text messages

And then I added one word – well, sort of a word – at the end, in capitals: *SUSS*. There was definitely something SUSS about Dr. Chakrabarty, something about him that just didn't add up.

Time for me and Google to get down and dirty.

But we found very little – except for some obvious stuff to do with Coast Grammar. How could you live in this modern world and not leave electronic footprints all over the place? Even the Bushmen of the Kalahari have got Facebook accounts, even the Inuit are ferocious bloggers.

SUSS, and getting SUSSer.

Google and I went around in circles for a while before I asked myself a very obvious question: why was I doing this when there was a professional in the house?

Hound was leaning back in his seat, gleaming cowboy boots up on the desk, a laptop balanced on his lap.

"You should wear spurs," I said, pointing at his boots.

"Got some at home, actually," he said. "Let me ask you a question, do you remember how many gold bars they recovered from the seabed?"

"Sure," I said. "One hundred and twenty-five."

"Son of a gun!" he said, and then, reading from the screen, "*A total of a hundred and twenty gold bars were dropped into the grounds of the embassy.*"

"Hey, maybe the embassy isn't being entirely honest."

"No, some bystander filmed it, of course. There's some bystander filming everything now. Anyway, they've gone through it frame by frame and counted the bars that fell."

Nerds, I thought.

"Five bars, do you know what that's worth?"

I shrugged.

"About three million bucks," he said. "It ain't chump change."

So the Zolton-Banders had pulled yet another swiftie; I didn't know whether to laugh or cry. One thing I did know: I would never, ever trust those two again for as long as I lived.

"Anyway, what can I do for you?" Hound said.

"I've been trying to find this person, but I can't find much about him."

"One of our scumbags?"

"No, this is, like, a personal thing," I said, and quickly added, "I've been doing it on my own time."

Hound pushed a piece of paper and a pen in front of me and said, "Write his name."

I did that, making sure I spelled it correctly.

"You got a phone number?"

"I do, but I tried the reverse directory and got nothing."

"Write it down anyway."

I did just that.

Hound picked up the paper and read the name out loud. "Chak-ra-bar-ty. You sure it's not a yoga position?"

It wasn't that funny, but I laughed – I was definitely starting to get the hang of this employer/employee thing.

"Give us ten minutes," said Hound.

When I returned to his office there was an address and a phone number to go with the name. "How the blazes did you do that?" I said.

"Before Google, we had this thing called favors," he said. "I just called one in."

"Great," I said, taking the paper.

"So we're sweet now, Youngblood?"

"Sure," I said. "We're sweet."

I read the address – oh no, it couldn't be.

But although I read it three more times, not one letter of it changed.

It looked like, once more, I was going to the Malevolent Wonderland. To where hippies wanted to punch your lights out and your father spoke in a strange tongue.

THE MALEVOLENT WONDERLAND

There was no way I was going to catch a bus to Nimbin and waste all that time sitting next to some smelly backpacker.

Luiz Antonio and his farty old taxi weren't going to be much quicker. Any taxi, actually.

No, I needed to be there, and I needed to be there now.

So I called SkyFast, the company my parents always used. "Hello, I'd like to charter a small plane to Nimbin."

"For how many people?" said the woman on the other end.

"Just me."

"And for when?"

"ASAP," I said.

"And can I ask who is paying for this?" she said, and I could now hear some doubt in her voice.

"David Silvagni, my father," I said. "You can just put it on his account."

"Of course, one of our favorite customers. We'd just need a call from him, even an email would suffice, with the passenger's details."

"Sure, can you call me when it's ready to go?" I said, and I gave her my number. It took me all of five minutes to phish an email from my dad's email address, and a couple of minutes after that my phone rang: my plane would be ready in twenty minutes.

I called a taxi to take me to the airport and was just making my way down the stairs when from behind came Hound's growl: "Hey, how'd you go with that work?"

"I'm on it," I said; I could see the taxi waiting outside.

"I need it pretty soon," he said.

"I told you I'm on it," I said over my shoulder. I didn't hear what else Hound said because I was already out of the door, but something told me it wasn't that complimentary.

Into the taxi and out to the airport, and the plane was waiting for me. The pilot gave a bit of a double take when he saw how old I was, but apart from that he treated me like any other paying customer. We shook hands, swapped names, and we were up, up and away.

Luke didn't ask any pesky questions, just did what

he was paid to do: fly the bird.

I'm sure the view was spectacular and all that, but I couldn't have cared less: I was becoming more and more convinced that Dr. Chakrabarty was part of The Debt, perhaps even the boss – the Godfather – and the Tavernitis were just his foot soldiers. I'd checked the address on Google maps. It was just within the hundred-meter radius, the area that Hanley had worked out was where the last text message in Latin had come from.

The flight took no time at all, but as we were coming down to land I couldn't resist asking a question. "So as a pilot yourself, what do you think of the Zolt?"

Luke took a while to answer.

"Some of those landings have been pretty ugly," he said. "But if it's like they say and he never took a flying lesson in his life, learned everything from flight sim and by reading manuals, then he's an absolute freak."

A very rich freak, I thought. Thinking of what Hound had told me about the three million dollars.

"So Dave is your dad, right?" said Luke.

"That's right," I said, though I'd never really thought of my dad as a "Dave."

"He's pretty much my favorite customer," said Luke.

"So he flies a lot?" I said, surprised, thinking my dad only took the occasional trip to Nimbin.

"You kidding?" said Luke. "I couldn't tell you how many times we've done this run."

Once we landed, I caught another taxi back into the town I had absolutely no wish to ever return to. Nimbin and San Luca – when climate change really got serious, they were the two places to wipe out first.

Dr. Chakrabarty's address was a few blocks away from the town center, in the same direction as Coast Home Loans and the Fiends of the Earth office. I headed in that direction. A boy in a hoodie sidled up to me. "You want something?"

He looked familiar, and then I remembered why.

"Seen Anna around lately?" I said.

His face, shaded by the hoodie, was hard to see. "She's gone, man."

The sun had caught his face, and I could see his eyes now; I didn't need to ask where she'd gone.

I quickened my pace towards Dr. Chakrabarty's house.

I was going to extinguish The Debt.

I was going to take him out.

Yes, I'd lost my nerve with Brandon, but this was different.

I charged past Coast Home Loans, into the mall, past the Fiends of the Earth office. A right turn and I was in his street, and across the road was his house.

It was an old stone house with a wide verandah and a corrugated iron roof, but with a large modern garage alongside. Actually, it was a pretty anonymous-looking house, and I felt instantly deflated. Dr. Chakrabarty was who I'd always thought he was – a wacky old guy

361

who used to teach classics.

But then I had another competing thought: this house was exactly The Debt's style, wasn't it? Lose yourself in the local community, make no waves, while you wreak murder and mayhem elsewhere.

I cased his house for half an hour or so: nobody went in, nobody came out; in fact, this street made Frank Condon Drive look like downtown New York. I crossed the street, and I quickly checked inside the mailbox – there was a letter there addressed to Dr. Chakrabarty. I had the right place. "Favors," Hound's analog version of Google, obviously had its uses.

Up to the door, and I rang the bell, my heart fluttering in my chest like a budgie in its cage.

What was I going to do if he answered? I hadn't thought this through properly.

Or maybe this was the best way: confront him here and now.

He didn't answer; there was no sound from inside.

I rang again. Nothing.

There was no electronic surveillance, none that I could see anyway. This was my chance: I had to go in.

I crept along the side of the house. There were no bars on the window, and again I wondered about the lack of security. But again the answer was simple; why make yourself conspicuous? The first window I tried was unlocked.

This was feeling suspiciously easy – was I walking

straight into a trap?

Well, at least if it was, there would be a confrontation. Bring it on, Chakrabarty!

The room I climbed into was obviously the study. Like Dr. Chakrabarty's office at school, it was very neat, very tidy. Books lined the walls. I scanned the titles. Lots of classics, as you'd imagine, but there were also lots of books about ecology, biology, the environmental movement. I checked his desk, a huge old wooden number. Just a few bills and things on top, and the drawers were locked.

Into the next room, a sort of combined family room and kitchen area. There were some spooky tribal masks on the walls, some Aboriginal dot paintings. I was starting to get it now: everything here was absolutely normal; the real stuff, the nasty stuff, he did elsewhere.

It was a clever strategy.

Who would ever think an Indian classics teacher was a mafia boss, especially one who lived in a house as innocuous as this one?

I heard the sound of a garage door rising, then a car.

He was coming home!

I squeezed under the couch. The door opened and I saw a set of shoes, old-man brogues. Dr. Chakrabarty. And then a set of wheels. Somebody in a wheelchair.

"Are you sure nobody saw us?" English, posh – I knew that voice, I would recognize it anywhere:

Mandy.

"Of course not, dear, not a soul," replied Dr. Chakrabarty.

My brain refused to process the information it had just downloaded from my eyes and my ears. It was like watching *The Simpsons* and suddenly Kenny from *South Park* sits next to Homer on the couch.

Homer and Kenny, Dr. Chakrabarty and Mandy, do not belong together.

"Alpha and Thor will be here in an hour," said Mandy. "Do you think we really have time, Chak?"

Chak?

"'She walks in beauty, like the night of cloudless climes and starry skies,'" said Dr. Chakrabarty, in that hammy way he had. "'And all that's best of dark and bright meet in her aspect and her eyes.'"

"Oh, Chak," said Mandy, her voice melting like the cheese on a pizza ad. "You know how I adore my Lord Byron."

Shoes and wheels were making towards the couch and me. Then there were wet, fleshy noises – they were kissing.

But that tiny part of my brain that wasn't busy being appalled, disgusted and dismayed was working furiously to make sense of this. What was Kenny doing in *The Simpsons*? And then all the pieces fell into place: Dr. Chakrabarty spoke Italian because he was a classic scholar, he'd been on the train that day because he had been going to the Festival of Our Lady of Polsi.

As for him being SUSS, not adding up, I was dead right about that: Dr. Chakrabarty was the infamous Dr. E.! That did add up: the photo that he'd had in his office of the earth spinning in space, all the ecology books in his library, and now this, his relationship to the Fiends of the Earth.

I had two choices, stay here while they did whatever it was they were going to do and make my escape later.

Or make myself known.

I figured the first, as disgusting as it was, was the best option – there was too much explaining to do otherwise.

"Oh, Chak," purred Mandy.

"'Now therefore, while the youthful hue sits on thy skin like morning dew,'" said Chak, again with that hammy voice. "'And while thy willing soul transpires at every pore with instant fires, now let us sport us while we –'"

"Stop!" I yelled. "It's me, Pheidippides, under here!"

365

FIENDS OF THE EARTH

Déjà vu all over again: me being interrogated by members of the ecoterrorist organization Fiends of the Earth while sitting on a very uncomfortable straight back chair. Except this time their leader, Dr. Chakrabarty aka Chak aka Dr. E., was with them, and he was holding a gun, and it was pointed directly at me.

"So let me get this straight, you thought that the doctor was some sort of mafia figure?" said Alpha, and I could understand the look of disbelief that was all over his face.

How could you even start to explain something like The Debt to people, especially people who were as angry as these four? Though angry doesn't go anywhere near describing the emotional state Mandy was in. I was sure she wanted to run me over in her wheelchair, and then keeping running me over until I was a human crepe.

I nodded. "Like I said, not without some reason."

"And can you tell us what those reasons are?"

All the time Thor, Alpha and Mandy had grilled me, firing question after question, Dr. Chakrabarty had sat there, silent, revolver in his hands.

His face said nothing, his eyes even less; I could see now the ruthless man who had organized the sinking of the longline tuna boats and the sabotage of logging machinery in which a logger had suffered serious injuries.

For what seemed like the hundredth time, I told them the reasons. And for what seemed like the hundredth time Mandy said, "That's rubbish!"

We really weren't getting very far here, and if it wasn't for the gun I would've made a run for it. But was Dr. Chakrabarty capable of firing it, of actually shooting me? Dr. Chakrabarty who'd taught at my old school, the bumbling one with the shaggy eyebrows, wasn't. But Dr. E.? I wasn't so sure. We sat there in silence, the four of them looking at the one of me.

Until finally Dr. Chakrabarty lowered the gun and said, "Let him go."

"But he will go straight to the police, tell them who you are," said Mandy.

"No, I don't think so," he said in a calm, level voice.

"And you believe this ridiculous story of his?" said Alpha.

Dr. Chakrabarty nodded.

"Of course I believe it," he said. "And exactly for that reason: nobody is going to make up a story as far-fetched as that." He smiled a cold smile. "Nobody who lacks an education in the classics, anyway." He stared at me, and I suddenly had an insight into what it was like to be a fish and to be speared, flapping on a shaft of steel.

"Do you still have the last message in Latin?" he said.

It wasn't at all what I expected to come out of his mouth, and in reply I ummed and I ahhed even more than usual.

"Well, do you or not?"

"I do," I said. "But Mandy has my phone, remember?"

Mandy just glared at me, making no effort to return it. Dr. Chakrabarty threw her a look, and she tossed the phone at me. I scrolled through until I came to the text message and handed it to Dr. Chakrabarty. He sat there looking at it for what seemed ages.

Finally he said, "And you say you're sure it came from this town?"

"I'm sure," I said. "In this immediate vicinity."

He looked over at Thor, raising his considerable eyebrows. Thor shook his head: *It wasn't me.*

Dr. Chakrabarty handed me back the phone. "Dom, we are a peaceful organization, but our aims are lofty. And we can't afford somebody getting in our way, compromising our work. Do you understand me?"

I nodded, thinking of the maimed logger. If I ratted, Dr. Chakrabarty would get me – I had no doubt of that.

"Now get out of my house," he said.

I didn't need any further invitation than that; I stood up and started walking towards the door, mentally crossing Dr. Chakrabarty off the list as I did.

Next name: Rocco Taverniti. Already my brain was onto it – what did I know about Rocco Taverniti?

I went to put my iPhone in my pocket when something occurred to me. I stopped.

No, Dom, you're not – he's just told you, while holding a gun, to get out of his house. But I was.

"Dr. Chakrabarty?" I found myself saying.

"What now?" he said.

"I just wanted to ask a favor."

"You've got to be joking!" said Mandy.

Thor and Alpha, the eco-ninjas, moved towards me, ready to fast-track my exit.

"What is it?" said Dr. Chakrabarty.

"I know how good you are with languages and I just wondered if you could translate something else for me. It's a recording I made."

"You've got to be joking!" said Mandy. She really needed to come up with some new material.

But the appeal to Dr. Chakrabarty's intellectual vanity worked. "What language is it?" he asked.

"Calabrian," I said.

"As you well know, my Italian is faultless, but I do also have a passing acquaintance with Calabrian. Let's hear it."

I went to Voice Memos, found the recording and hit the play icon. Even with the volume up to full, with all the background noise it was very difficult to hear and I felt like a sizeable idiot. I looked over at Mandy – she had the smuggest of smiles.

"Alpha?" said Dr. Chakrabarty. "Can you do anything with that?"

"I can try," he said, taking a laptop out of his bag. "Your Bluetooth on?" he asked me. I nodded.

After about five minutes of frenetic keyboard and mouse work, he said, "Let's see what we've got."

His laptop started playing my recording. It was about a million times better; he'd gotten rid of almost all the background noise. It made me realize what a formidable team the Fiends of the Earth were and what a shame it was that we'd spent all this time being enemies.

Dr. Chakrabarty listened intently, scribbling in the margins of a newspaper as he did so. "And again?"

After it had finished for the second time, he scribbled some more. When he spoke, it was with a concerned look on his face. "Tell me, who is this man?"

I told him.

"I think I remember him," he said. "A few of us teachers used to go to Taverniti's in the old days."

"He's dead now," I said.

"Anyway, this is what I make of it. So you asked him about Mr. Havilland, and he replies 'the politician.' But you obviously understood that?"

"I did," I said.

"He then says '*Ha avuto troppo avidi, quello*' which I translate as 'He got too greedy, that one.' And then, '*Stava per rovinare tutto per tutti*' which I translate as 'He was going to spoil it for everybody.'" Dr. Chakrabarty looked up from the newspaper and at me. "This is Graham Havilland, of course."

I nodded. Graham Havilland, the anti-drugs campaigner. But if Dr. Chakrabarty was right, he was also Graham Havilland, the corrupt politician.

Poor, poor Imogen.

"What about the final bit?" I said. "He said one more thing."

Dr. Chakrabarty looked down at the newspaper. "'I got the boys to look after him,'" he read, and then his voice seemed to drop in pitch. "'They gave him another mouth.'"

As if that wasn't clear enough, Mandy made a slit-your-throat gesture with her hand.

"But doesn't he say some names as well?" I said. "I thought I heard him say some names."

"You have a good ear, Pheidippides," he said, and suddenly bumbling Dr. Chakrabarty with the sheep for eyebrows was back. "He said three names: Rocco and Ron and Gnocchi."

Rocco as in Rocco Taverniti, Ron as in Ron Gatto, but who was the third person? "But gnocchi is a food."

"In this case I'm sure he's referring to a person; it's probably their nickname." Dr. Chakrabarty looked to be deep in thought. Finally he said, "Sun Tzu said that all war is deception. If you need help, contact us. We just can't be involved, if you know what I mean."

"Thank you," I said.

"Now get out of my house," he said, but there was the faintest hint of a smile on his face.

This time I did get out of his house, hurrying back along the street, turning into the mall. I passed the Fiends of the Earth office; I was totally convinced now that the text message hadn't come from there.

Ahead of the mall were the Coast Home Loans offices. *Why Rent When You Can Buy? Loan Approval within the Hour!* yelled the sign outside.

I was becoming more and more convinced that somewhere inside those garish offices were at least some of the answers to the countless questions that were cartwheeling through my head.

But I'd already broken into the building – well, sort of broken in, because I'd managed to copy the office keys and had just let myself in – and I'd found nothing suss. I did remember, however, that I'd had one key left over. One key that didn't fit a lock. At the time I'd explained it away: locks are changed, doors are demolished, people don't remove the orphaned keys from their rings.

But now I wasn't so sure.

I looked around – nobody was within sight, so I started a circuit of the building. Just as I'd hoped, there was a door on the other side.

No writing, no nameplate, just an anonymous unpainted door.

I tried the handle – it was locked.

To think that I'd once had the key for this very door but had tossed it into a drain, worried that it would incriminate me.

So what to do now?

The answer didn't take long to come: visit the hardware shop, buy some stuff, go to the library, find a comfortable beanbag, wait for dark, and then return to this place. That's exactly what I did.

Remembering my encounter with the security guard the last time I'd broken into this building, I took everything very slowly, very carefully. The last thing I needed was some knucklehead mucking up my plans.

Eventually me and my pocketful of hardware were in front of the mysterious door. Without The Debt I would never have become proficient at lock-picking. And that was one irony I actually liked – they had taught me something that might help cause their downfall.

I set to work, remembering what I had read in the lock-picking manual: *Project your senses into the lock*

373

to receive a full picture of how it is responding to your manipulations.

This particular lock responded very quickly to my manipulations. With the tiniest of clicks, I was away.

I quickly pushed the door open and immediately saw the flashing light on the alarm box on the far wall. My guess was that I had thirty seconds to feed it a code.

I turned on the light, scanned the room.

There on the desk was a framed photo of me, Toby and Miranda.

This was so my dad's office!

There were bookshelves full of books.

This was so not my dad's office!

There on the desk was a framed photo of Mom.

This was so my dad's office.

I hurried over to the console and punched in Dad's code, the one he used for everything: credit cards, Apple account, PayPal, everything. It worked – the light stopped flashing. I was in.

This office was such a contrast to his generic office at home with its handful of management texts, or his office in the city, Cobweb Enterprises. This was a real office, and I was gobsmacked.

Firstly there was hardware galore: screens and servers and printers and scanners. There was the art on the walls, moody black-and-white photos, stuff I had no idea that Dad liked. But what I couldn't take my eyes off were the books. There were hundreds of them. I moved over for a closer look. Books on anything and everything arranged in what looked like a crazy jumble. *The Fountainhead* by Ayn Rand was next to a book called *The Wealth of Nations* by Adam Smith which was next to a book called *Metamorphoses* by Ovid.

There was something about that last book that seemed familiar. I took it off the shelf and opened it.

One of the pages had the corner turned over, the laziest of bookmarks. *An appalling habit*, Mom called it. I went to this page. Some text was underlined in pencil: *atque ita semineces partim ferventibus artus mollit aquis, partim subiecto torruit igni.*

I took out my iPhone and swiped through the messages until I came to the one I was looking for: *atque ita semineces partim ferventibus artus mollit aquis, partim subiecto torruit igni.*

The logical part of me got it immediately: it was my father who had been sending those scary messages. But every other part of me didn't get it at all: how could he?

I mean, HOW COULD HE?

The door opened and my dad was standing there.

I wasn't that surprised to see him: it was his office, after all, and there were a number of ways he could've found out that I was here: SkyFast, the biochip.

But just because I'd been sprung in his office didn't mean that I was going to back off. "You sent those messages!" I said, my logical part winning the battle.

"Okay, Dom," said Dad in his lifestyle-program-presenter voice. "Let's you and I have a civil discussion about this. Father to son."

What freaking father? What freaking son? I fumed for as long as I needed to fume and then I thought – why not?

Dad indicated that I should sit in a chair. Then he fetched two bottles of fancy mineral water from the fridge, handing one to me. Switching off the room light, turning on a desk lamp, he sat down in the other chair. I drank the water in one swig, the fancy bubbles running up my nostrils.

Finally he spoke. "I had to keep you on your toes, Dom. Stop you from getting complacent."

Complacent? What was he talking about? But when I gave it some further thought, I realized that those messages had definitely kept me on edge, had definitely kept me guessing. So, maybe my old man was right. Definitely right.

"We believed in you, we all did," he said. "But I just had to throw something extra in."

We?

And then I got it, the biggest got-it of them all.

I guess there had been signs, and lots of them, but I'd refused to go in the direction they'd pointed me in. But that "we" had done it. I got it. Blazing bells and buckets of blood, did I get it.

I looked around this office, at this side of him I didn't have a clue about.

"You're The Debt?"

Dad smiled. "It's not that simple, nothing ever is."

"You're The Debt," I said. "You would've taken a pound of my flesh. Your own son's flesh!"

"That was never going to happen, Dom. Not to somebody as capable as you."

"But you and the Tavernitis?"

"If it wasn't for the Taverniti family I wouldn't have made it, Dom." He must've read the doubt in my expression, because he said, much more forcefully, "If it wasn't for the Tavernitis, I would've ended up a useless peg-legged drunk like your grandfather."

My instinct was to jump to Gus's defense, but I held my tongue; Dad was in a talkative mood and I wanted more answers.

"When you were in San Luca, you killed somebody," I said; it was a statement, not a question.

I could see the surprise in Dad's face – *how did I know that?*

"It's a long story," he said. "But yes, a man died."

"It was his father, the boy who tried to kill you."

Dad nodded. "That would add up."

"And in San Luca, they caught you and kept you underground in a cell."

377

"Eight months in that hellhole," he said.

"'Out of the night that covers me, black as the pit from pole to pole,'" I said.

"'I thank whatever gods may be for my unconquerable soul,'" said Dad. "That poem was about the only thing your grandfather gave me that was any bloody good."

He stood up, his eyes scanning the bookshelves. "Ah, there it is," he said, reaching for a book. He handed it to me.

The cover was blank. I opened it and read the first page. *Book of Verses* by William Ernest Henley, 1893.

"The first time the poem appeared in print. It didn't even have a name then," he said.

I wasn't about to get sidetracked. "In San Luca, why did they let you go?"

Dad smiled ruefully. "A deal was done, a very complicated deal."

"And Mom, was she part of that deal?"

The color rose in Dad's face. "Your mother and I fell in love the first time we laid eyes on each other," he said. "Don't you ever forget that, okay?"

"Okay," I said, and I had absolutely no doubt that Dad was telling the truth, and it made me feel good – at least their love wasn't some sort of lie.

"And Roberto?"

Dad sighed and said, "I need a drink."

He took a bottle of single malt whisky from the bookshelf, splashed some into a glass and took a gulp.

"Roberto is from the old country – he's family, Dom."

"Family?"

"He's your mother's brother," said Dad. "Your uncle." And another piece of the puzzle fell into place – Seb's surname was Baresi.

"Our gardener?"

"They wanted to be near each other," said Dad. "That just seemed to be the simplest way."

More pieces fell into place: that closeness I'd noticed between Mum and Roberto, how they'd stopped Seb and Miranda dating. "And Seb is Roberto's son?"

Dad nodded.

"So Seb's my cousin?"

Again Dad nodded.

"Does he know?"

"He does now."

My guts felt like mush, like ugali; I collapsed into myself. The office was swirling. The whole world was swirling.

"You need some more water, son?"

I nodded, and Dad took off, returning with more fancy mineral water again. I finished the contents in one gulp. He got me another bottle. This one I took much more slowly. Dad looked on approvingly.

When I had finished he said, "Better?"

I nodded. "Better."

The light from the desk lamp was now falling on his face in a way that made him look sort of, I don't know, magnificent, or mythical. And when he spoke again his voice had this tone, this resonance that was deep and commanding. "Dom, you did incredibly well. Better than anybody expected. Now you're *pagato*, you can do absolutely anything you like. Stay working where you are if you like. Go back to school if you want, any school you wish. If you want to keep going with your running, then why not go to the States and train there? Or Kenya, even? Anything you want, you can do."

"I can?" I asked, imagining myself running in the thin air of the Rift Valley of Kenya, home to more champions than anywhere else in the world.

"You're *pagato*," he repeated. "The world is yours."

The world is yours – it was an intoxicating thought, even more intoxicating than the whisky I had drunk that day on the *Hispaniola*.

"And Toby?"

"Toby will be tested, like you were tested."

"But … but … but he's not capable."

"You don't know that, you don't know what he's capable of. You didn't even know what you could do yourself until you did it."

He was right – I didn't have a clue. "But Dad, he's your son."

"Exactly!" he said. "That's why I have to let him have the opportunities that I had, and that you had."

"Opportunities?" I said. "You mean the installments?"

"Of course, opportunities to show what you are capable of." Dad looked off towards the wall, and then back at me. "Our culture has gone soft, Dom. We don't allow boys to become men anymore. We mollycoddle them. Pack them in cotton wool. And then we wonder why they never grow up."

I was exhausted; he'd spun an elaborate web of logic and reason around me and I couldn't move.

"So whatever you're doing, Dom, you're going to stop," said Dad, getting some mongrel in his voice. "I dragged this family out of the gutter and nobody's going to let it go back there again."

All I could think of was running barefoot in the thin air of the Rift Valley.

"So let's go home," said Dad, taking me by the arm.

I went to put the book back, but he said, "No, it's yours now."

I followed him as he set the alarm, as he locked up his office. "I'm not even going to ask how you got in here."

"It wasn't easy," I said.

Dad's Porsche was parked right outside. We got in and he hammered it through the town and he hammered it over the range, through all the twists and turns. I mean, really hammered it. I remembered how I used to think he was a useless driver – he had been a useless driver – but that was yet another lie.

He was a gun.

It felt both exhilarating and relaxing, like I was literally in very safe hands.

When we were about a hundred kays from the Coast, on a long straight piece of the freeway, he pulled into a turnout.

"Bathroom break?" I said.

"No," he said. "I'm a bit sick of driving."

What, so we were going to sit here in this stinking turnout while he had a nanna nap?

"Why don't you take the wheel for a while?" he said.

Um, because I'm only fifteen.

Um, because I don't know how to drive.

Um, because I don't even have my learner's.

"Seriously?" I said.

"Sure," he said, opening his door.

"What about the coppers?"

"Superfluous to our needs," he said dismissively.

What fifteen-year-old boy wouldn't want to drive a 911, a car that appears on every one of those best-sports-cars-ever lists, a car that *all* the revheads on *Top Gear* like? So I got behind the wheel, and Dad taught me how to drive.

In the beginning it was pretty ugly: bunny hops, gears crunched, nosebleed braking, but I soon got the hang of it.

"You're a natural," he said. "Open her up a bit."

"Really?" I said.

"The road's empty," he said. "Kick her in the guts."

While the Rolling Stones sang "Hot Stuff" I kicked her in the guts, the needle creeping past 100km/h, 110km/h, 120km/h, 130km/h.

When it touched 140km/h, I eased my foot off.

"Come on," said Dad. "Let's go for the ton."

"The ton?"

"Yeah, a hundred miles an hour; it was always the magic number when I was your age."

"So what's that, around one sixty?" I said.

Dad nodded. I pressed my foot down, the needle crept past 150km/h, getting closer and closer to 160km/h.

My father had killed three people: Bag Lady, Francesco Strangio, and Francesco Strangio's dad.

He was a murderer. He was a monster.

But when I looked over at him, the dashboard light soft on his face, that's not what I saw.

I saw my dad smiling at me.

I heard my dad saying, "That's the ton, I reckon, Dom."

And we blasted into the night, my father and I.

OLD MAN'S FUNERAL

The next day I woke late. Lying in bed, I came up with plenty of reasons not to go to old man Taverniti's funeral. As for all the revelations of yesterday, I'd managed to keep them at arm's length. Actually, it hadn't been that difficult – it was like they didn't want to bother me too much, either. The only thing my mind seemed to want to engage with was this idea of me running in the thin air of the Rift Valley of Kenya.

Why not? I thought.

The benefits of high-altitude training are indisputable. And I already had a head start with the ugali. And as Dad said, I was *pagato*, I could do absolutely anything I wanted to do.

Hungry, I went downstairs, where everybody was dressed and ready to go to the funeral.

"Wow, you're wearing black," I said to Miranda. "That's so unusual."

"Isn't it?" said Mom.

"Haven't you heard? Black's actually the new black," said Miranda.

Dad looked up from his iPad and rolled his eyes.

Now that I saw everybody there like that, I forgot all the excuses. I wanted to be with them. Or I didn't want to be by myself. Either way, the result was the same – I scoffed my cornflakes and had a quick shower and got changed. Taking Miranda's lead, I dressed in black too. Then we piled into Mom's car and made for the church.

It was one of those magical Gold Coast days, one that makes you glad you're where you are and not where old man Taverniti is.

The footpath outside the church was already crowded. Dad had been right – every Italian on the Gold Coast was there. If nothing else, the old man's death gave them a chance to catch up again, swap *sugo* recipes.

Dad and Mom went into total meet-and-greet mode. "And these are our three children, Miranda, Dominic and Toby."

Eventually Rocco Taverniti made his way over to us, a cigarette in his hand. He looked, I don't know, coarser or something. He took a last greedy suck of the cigarette and flicked the butt into a gutter.

You pig, I thought. The next rain would wash that butt down the storm water drain and into the open ocean where some poor little Nemo fish would eat it and die a horrible fishy death.

Dad and Rocco hugged, Italian-style, and when they came apart tears glistened in both pairs of eyes.

"He loved you like a son," said Rocco to Dad.

"He was like a father to me," said Dad.

Wow, I thought. *They really need a new scriptwriter.*

They talked some more, but I didn't hear what they had to say because Mom dragged me away to meet some people I would probably never see again.

After that had finished, I saw Rocco and Dad shaking hands. "We'll talk," I heard Dad say to Rocco. And then Rocco did a strange thing: he tousled Dad's hair, like you do to a kid, and he said, "Aye, Gnocchi."

When he'd gone into the church, I moved closer to Dad as we followed suit.

"Did Rocco just call you Gnocchi?" I said.

"Sure," said Dad, laughing. "It was the old man's nickname for me – I couldn't get enough of the stuff when I was a kid."

The service was starting and people hurried inside to their seats.

Not me, though. I stayed where I was. Soon I was the only one left on the footpath.

The weather was still perfect, not one cloud spoiling the sky's unbroken blue. And the soft breeze smelled like the sea.

Rocco Taverniti had killed Graham Havilland.

Ron Gatto had killed Graham Havilland.

And David Silvagni had killed Graham Havilland.

They had killed the father of my best friend, they had given him "another mouth." And all I could do was dream of running in the Rift Valley.

A bushfire of anger swept through me.

I took out my wallet and found the business card Rent-a-Cop had given me. I took out my phone. I punched in his number and was about to hit dial, when I stopped. Was this the way to do this? Tell a cop about the coffin in the Tabori crypt? Play him the recording on my iPhone?

By doing that, would it achieve my aim: would it extinguish The Debt?

All war is deception, said Sun Tzu.

I deleted the number, digit by digit; this wasn't the way to go about it. I sat down in the gutter. I needed some legal advice, but not from a cop. I scrolled through my contacts, stopped at the one I wanted. Hit dial. He answered straightaway.

"Dom! I was asking myself if you'd ever call me!"

"Sorry, Mr. Ryan," I said. "There's been a lot going on. But I need some advice and wondered if I could talk to you."

"Over the phone?"

"I think it's better if we actually meet," I said.

"Sure, I'm having a mental health day today – why don't you just pop in?" He gave me the address, and I put out my hand to hail a taxi.

Mr. Ryan's apartment building was right on the

beach, one of those enormous white high-rises the Gold Coast is famous for. I rang the buzzer and Mr. Ryan answered immediately. "Is that you, Dom?"

"Yes."

"Come right up," he said, and there was a click as the door unlocked.

As I took the elevator, I wondered if I'd been a bit hasty. I mean, what did I know about Mr. Ryan? He was a teacher, he'd been a lawyer. So what?

Maybe he was part of The Debt too?

Maybe I was walking into a big old trap.

Maybe. Maybe. Maybe.

Dom, you're getting paranoid. The 'Ndrangheta in chinos?

Yeah, right.

I knocked on the door, and Mr. Ryan opened it, and he was wearing ... a sarong! I think it had frangipanis on it. Not just a sarong, also a lilac T-shirt, but it was the sarong that demanded my attention.

"You've caught me in a casual moment," he said. "Can I get you a drink?"

"Water would be great," I said.

Mr. Ryan's apartment was nice – large and airy, with views straight out over the Pacific Ocean.

There were a lot of photos on the walls: Mr. Ryan graduating as a lawyer, another one of him graduating as a teacher, and all sorts of group photos. It seemed like my old civics teacher belonged to a lot of organizations.

He came back with a glass of water and we sat on the balcony. Mr. Ryan in a sarong, the beach spread out down below; it was so not the day to talk about what I wanted to talk about. So we sat there for a while and just sort of smiled benignly at each other.

"What's boppin' ya pod these days?" I eventually said.

"Well, inspired by your good dad, I'm still exploring the Stones' back catalog. Untold riches there. Yourself?"

"Rage Against the Machine," I said. "Mostly their first album."

"I'm afraid I'm not familiar with them," he said. "In what genre would you classify them?"

"It's angry music," I said. "They're pretty pissed off."

"Fascinating. I'll have a listen." Finally Mr. Ryan said, "Is there anything on your mind, Dom?"

"You're a lawyer, right?"

"Well, I was."

"And so you know about criminal stuff?"

Mr. Ryan nodded.

"Murder?"

He adjusted his sarong; I so wished he'd go and put some chinos on.

"I'm no expert, but maybe I can help you," he said,

and I could detect the change in his tone; this was no longer about boppin' ya pod.

"So what if somebody found a body?"

"Okay, well, that's not unusual; bodies are found much more frequently than you'd think. And in all sorts of unusual places."

"What if the body was, like, more than ten years old?"

"Again, not unusual. Especially in more remote areas where there aren't as many people around."

"What if there was something suspicious about where this body was found?"

"How suspicious?"

"It was found buried in a crypt where it had no right to be."

Mr. Ryan looked at me hard. "The question, as a lawyer, I would ask is this: how do you know it had no right to be there?"

"Because I know whose body it is."

"You have identified a body that is more than ten years old? How? Dental records? DNA?" There was a toughness to his voice now.

"No, he was wearing a watch with an inscription on it."

Mr. Ryan whistled. "That'll do it."

As soon as he said this, I realized how dumb it had been to grave-rob that Omega Speedmaster.

I was also starting to wonder how smart it was divulging all this stuff to Mr. Ryan.

He could very well be The Debt!

After Hanley, you'd think I would've learned my lesson.

"So if the police found such a body, what would they do?" I said, figuring it was okay to just ask questions.

"They would look for evidence of foul play. The obvious things are bullet holes, of course. Hands or legs bound. That sort of thing. And they would look for traces of a third party. Evidence of another person's involvement."

"What sort of evidence?" I said.

"There's a famous law of forensics called Locard's principle – basically what it says is that every contact leaves a trace. In this day and age, it's all about DNA. Blood, even the saliva on a cigarette butt would be enough."

"Even after more than ten years?"

Mr. Ryan nodded.

I drank my water and looked down at the sea, at the surfers bobbing in the waves.

"Whatever is going on, Dom, I strongly advise that you get the police involved."

That definitely didn't sound like something The Debt would say.

I thanked Mr. Ryan and was getting up to go when I noticed something: one of the group photos was from an organization called Gold Coast Youth Alliance, an organization I knew Mom was involved in. I walked over to get a closer look and, sure enough, Mom and her big hair were in the photo. Not only that, she was standing next to Mr. Ryan.

"So you know my mum?" I said, changing my mind yet again – he was The Debt!

He did that thing, that mouth-open-and-close-like-a-fish thing bad liars do when they're about to let rip with a major one.

But he just didn't have it in him. "Yes, I know your mother very well. We've worked together on a lot of projects for disenfranchised kids. She's an incredibly capable woman."

Something occurred to me.

"Did Mom ask you to look after me?" I said, thinking of all those times that Mr. Ryan had come to my rescue.

"She's an incredibly capable woman," said Mr. Ryan, with a half smile.

So she had asked him! I felt a surge of affection for my mum – maybe I hadn't been as alone as I thought I'd been as I'd battled to repay those six installments.

As I took the elevator down I took out my phone.

Already a plan was forming in my head.

I ran my fingers over the back of my hand.

There was something that needed to be done right away.

And I knew just the person to do it.

DEBUGGED

When I rang the doorbell, Imogen answered. Her face was so white.

"Where's your mum?" I said. Imogen shrugged. "*Where?*"

"In the hospital," she said.

"Is she okay?"

"She took all these pills. She had to have her stomach pumped."

"When?"

"Yesterday."

Something occurred to me. "On your father's birthday?"

Imogen nodded. I felt like such a heel – Imogen deserved several truckloads of sympathy, but I'd come here for something else. "The chip in my hand?" I said. "I need to lose it now."

"I don't know if I can do it," she said.

"I don't know if I can, either. But it has to be done."
I took her hand it and squeezed. She squeezed back.
"It'll be okay, I promise you," I said, and I wanted to
promise myself the same thing.

Still lightly holding hands, we went upstairs and
into Imogen's room, locking the door behind us.

That familiar smell, girl smell; those familiar
colors, girl colors. Imogen was playing with her hair,
twisting it tighter and tighter.

"I don't have a lot of time," I said.

More twisting.

"These are the people who killed your dad,
Imogen."

She looked at me hard. "What happened to you,
Dom?"

"You saw – I got branded. Either you do it or I'll do
it myself."

A change came over her face, her posture stiffened,
and she moved over to her desk. When she came back
she was holding a scalpel, the one she'd used on the frog.

I took the ultrasound image from my pocket and
held it out to her. "That's it there," I said, pointing to
the image of the microchip that was buried deep in
my hand.

She went into the bathroom and returned with
some white towels, a bowl of what I assumed was
warm water, and a bottle of disinfectant. She laid one
of the towels on the desk.

"Okay, if the patient would like to pop his hand here, we can begin," she said, lightness returning to her voice.

But now it was me, so gung-ho one second ago, who was having serious second thoughts about this. Wasn't there another way?

Actually, no.

I spread my hand on the towel. Imogen turned on the desk lamp and adjusted it until my hand was bathed in light. She swabbed it with the disinfectant. For somebody whose only previous surgical patient had, as far as I knew, been a dead amphibian, she was remarkably professional. She took the ultrasound image and used the point of some scissors to make a small hole in the middle of the microchip. Then she placed it over my hand, making sure it was a perfect fit. Using a felt-tip pen, she made a mark on my hand.

"Stay there," she said, and once again she disappeared into the bathroom. This time I could hear water running, and she returned wearing latex gloves and a surgical mask.

"Are you sure?" she said.

"Maybe you could do my appendix while you're here."

Not the funniest joke, but it did the job: we both relaxed a bit. Until she took out the scalpel, that is, and replaced the old blade with a new blade. It looked so shiny, and so sharp, and so unambiguous – this thing was made for one thing and one thing only – that I couldn't stop looking at it, imagining the pain it would cause me.

"Dom, you've gone really, really white."

"Do it, Im."

"You're shaking!"

"Do it, Im."

"But …"

"Do it, Im."

She turned to my hand.

"Wait!" I said. "I need something to bite down on."

She grabbed a tartan scarf and I fed some of it into my mouth.

And then Imogen did it: she clamped my shaking wrist with one hand, and with the other she sliced deep into the back of my hand with the scalpel. I bit down hard on the scarf, and the scream didn't get any further than that. Immediately, blood started welling up out of the incision. Imogen was ready; she flooded the incision with disinfectant, mopping up the blood.

"I can't see," she said. "I'm just going to open it a bit."

She did that, spreading the wound with her latexed fingers, and this time there was nothing the scarf could do, tartan or not. The scream escaped, instantly turning Imogen's bedroom with its girl colors and girl smells into some sort of House of Horrors.

"I can see it," she said excitedly, tweezers hovering.

The tweezers delved into the cut. Another scream joined the previous one.

"It's not coming, it's sort of stuck," she said. "I'll have to cut just a bit more, Dom."

"Do it, Im. Do it."

The scalpel went back into the incision, and the scalpel cut some more, and this scream made the previous two seem weak, halfhearted.

Again the tweezers, and this time a triumphant, "I've got it."

"Be careful," I said. "Don't drop it."

Imogen was careful, placing the blood-smeared microchip on a tissue, putting it into a small ziplock bag. "Do you mind if that stays here with you?" I said.

"Of course not," she said, as she set to work on my wound, dousing it with disinfectant and using butterfly closures to stop it gaping.

"You promise to get it stitched?" she said.

"I promise," I said. "Tomorrow, when it's all over."

She went to wrap a bigger bandage around my hand, but I said, "No, I don't want them to suspect anything. A small one like this they might miss, but not something like that."

She went with just an ordinary bandaid.

"And would you have an aspirin?" I said, wondering if that could possibly have any effect on the skyrockets of pain that were shooting from my hand.

"I can do better than that," she said, and she

disappeared from the room for a couple of minutes, returning with a small pill container.

"Mum's," she said, shaking two out onto her palm. "These should help."

I took the container and tossed the two pills down my throat.

"Don't you need some water?"

"It's my superpower," I said. "Pills without water."

I checked my watch: ten forty-five. "Im, I just need one more thing," I said.

She reached under her pillow and brought out her dad's watch.

"You'll get it back one day," I said. "But right now it has a job to do."

Remembering what Mr. Ryan had said about DNA traces, I used some of Imogen's disinfectant to swab it clean and then put it in a fresh ziplock bag.

"I have to go now," I said, going to kiss Imogen on the cheek. She turned her head towards me, however, and our lips met.

We kissed, and then she drew away.

KRYPTONITE

As Luiz Antonio drove, sun splashed in through the window. I was actually a bit put out – if everything went to plan, this was going to be the most tumultuous of days, and I guess I'd expected some correspondingly tumultuous weather: the rumble of thunder, flashes of lightning, that sort of thing. Meteorologically, this wasn't so outrageous, either, because according to the weather report there was a huge low pressure system skulking around the coast. But here it was all sunshiny.

We pulled into the parking lot of the Gold Coast Necropolis. I'd been there so many times I reckon I could've started my own business: Dom's Spooky Tours.

"If I'm not back in half an hour," I told Luiz Antonio, "maybe you better come and look for me."

"Sure," he said.

As usual, he hadn't asked any questions. I wondered if he'd been born without an inquisitive gene. Or if it was something he'd lost along the way. Whatever the case, I guessed it was for the best – ask no questions, get told no lies, that sort of gig.

Backpack on my back, I followed the now very familiar path towards the now very familiar crypt. Without the good old cloak of darkness I had to be extra careful. I'd brought my lock-picking tools, but take it from me, there is no unsuspicious way to unlock a crypt door. I decided that I just had to go for it – if somebody happened to come along I would skedaddle.

For somebody with my now considerable lock-picking experience, this one was pretty straightforward, and I was inside in less than a minute.

I had to go through the same grisly process that Gus and I had endured, except there was only one of me. Now that I knew all about Locard's principle – every contact leaves a trace – I'd brought disposable gloves to wear.

I made slow progress, but eventually was able to slide Mr. Havilland's coffin out far enough so that I could open it.

Poor Mr. Havilland, I thought, looking at what was left of him.

But I remembered what old man Taverniti had said, or what Dr. Chakrabarty had translated: *he got too greedy, that one.* I would never, ever tell Imogen that her father had been corrupt. But if I did what I intended to do, it seemed inevitable to me that this would come out. I hesitated.

And then put the Omega Speedmaster back where I'd found it, around Mr. Havilland's left wrist.

I was no longer a grave robber – it felt right.

Again I noticed the cigarette butts inside the coffin. I'd seen Rocco Taverniti smoking at the funeral. When I'd visited the Labor Party office, I'd seen an ashtray on Ron Gatto's desk. And my father didn't smoke, and never had, as far as I knew.

That felt reassuring – maybe Gnocchi hadn't been there, after all.

I slid the coffin back in. Replaced the little door. Just when I was thinking how well it was going, how Professor Sod was keeping his law to himself today, there was the scrape of a key in the lock.

They'd found me – I was still owned. What would they do? My fight or flight (or maybe even both) instincts were ready and raring to go.

The door opened. An old Italian lady who looked like she'd just come from that piazza in San Luca poked her head in and said, *"Mi scusa."*

I didn't need any more opportunity than that. *"Mi scusa,"* I said, squeezing past her, but then I remembered something: I took out my iPhone, went to Maps and stored my current position. Then I hurried back down the path. I checked my watch: forty-six minutes. Why hadn't Luiz Antonio come looking for me?

When I went outside, his taxi wasn't even there. I called him. "Where are you?"

"Heading towards you," he said.

"Great," I said.

"But you could've told me."

"Told you what?"

"That you went back to Halcyon Grove."

What? But then I got it – of course, Luiz Antonio didn't know that I'd removed my tag! I got something else: having two Dom Silvagnis was a very powerful thing; more powerful than I'd thought. I just had to work out how to use it to my advantage.

He took half an hour to return; it was pretty annoying, because I had so much to do.

"Back to Halcyon Grove?" he said.

I shook my head. "The Block."

It was time to unleash the blogs of war!

WHO LET THE BLOGS OUT?

It was after two when I arrived, and it was just as I hoped: Hound was at his usual Wednesday meeting at Cozzi's.

I could've done all this at home, but I'd figured that by using Hound's network and IP addresses I would remain more anonymous.

I powered up my work computer. I put in my earbuds. I put on Rage Against the Machine. And I put it on really, really loud. Miranda's favorite band – phooey! Her love for Rage Against the Machine was nothing compared to how I felt about them.

Ron Gatto, local member for the Gold Coast, was my first target.

I didn't know much about politics, but from what I'd read online, Ron Gatto seemed to have a real talent for "dodging bullets," as one journalist put it. The betting scandal. Dodged. The credit card scandal.

Dodged. The lewd text message scandal. Dodged. I wasn't firing bullets, though. I was launching drones that would take him out wherever he was.

I created a blog in WordPress, and gave it a very simple title: "Ron Gatto, Member for Gold Coast – Crook?"

My work checking the credit rating on Hound's scumbags had given me some pretty useful skills. And when I reexamined the data I'd downloaded from the Labor Party mainframe, I found out a few interesting things about Ron Gatto. For example, he kept two sets of personal MYOB accounts. I could tell that one of these sets was entirely for the benefit of the tax office. The other set, however, detailed a whole lot of extra income that came from various companies up and down the coast. I googled some of these: just as I'd expected, they were all involved one way or another in tendering for government projects. I'm no accountant, but this income was looking a lot like kickbacks to me. I posted this data to the blog.

Oh yeah, there was one more fascinating thing about Ron Gatto, happily married man, proponent of family values.

He was gay.

Okay, maybe he wasn't, but for a married man he sure spent a lot of money on male escorts. About a thousand bucks a month, according to one of the seven credit card accounts I examined. I wasn't going to make a judgment either way; I'd let the wider Internet community decide on that one. I posted those details on the blog as well.

And then, using an anonymous email address, I sent the address of this blog to a few people I thought might be interested. The leader of the Queensland Liberal National Party was the first one. And the editors of the *Gold Coast Bulletin*, the *Brisbane Courier-Mail* and *The Australian*. And finally I thought, why not, and sent it to an email address I found for *Today Tonight*.

Rocco Taverniti was next on my list.

I took out the card Rent-a-Cop had given me; his real name was Stewart Westaway. Just out of interest I googled Stewart Westaway. It was exactly as I'd suspected: he was a middle distance runner. Not such a bad one, either, if his times were any indication.

Again I used a phished email address. And I kept it really simple.

The body of Graham Havilland can be found at the Tabori family crypt at the Gold Coast Necropolis, I typed. I took out my iPhone and found the coordinates I'd stored and typed those in as well.

Then I added, *Please find attached an mp3 of a conversation with Luigi Taverniti (deceased), former head of the Gold Coast 'Ndrangheta concerning the murder of Graham Havilland.*

From my iPhone I downloaded the mp3 of the conversation with old man Taverniti, the one Dr.

Chakrabarty had translated. I copied it and uploaded this copy into Audacity, a free audio editor. Played it a few times.

I knew that my father was a killer, that he'd killed at least three people. Had he killed Graham Havilland, too?

According to old man Taverniti he had. If that was the case, then didn't he need to be held to account for his actions?

Didn't he need to be arrested?

Didn't there need to be a trial?

Didn't the court need to then determine whether he was innocent or guilty?

And if he was guilty, then he would be punished – sent to jail, maybe for the rest of his life. And I would be responsible for that, for my family losing its father.

I thought of the amazing house we lived in. The cars we drove. The stuff we bought. All the charity work Mom did. *She's the reason I'm here today*, that doctor had told me. I thought of all the great times we'd had as a family. I thought of what Dad had said the other day: that I could do anything I wanted to do. Finally, I thought of running barefoot in the thin air of the Rift Valley in Kenya.

Right then, the love I felt for my dad was so real, so intense, it seemed to envelop me, wrap me in its octopus arms.

I turned my attention back to the screen, to the

mp3. I edited it, cutting out *"e Gnocchi."*

"Ho ottenuto i ragazzi a prendersi cura di lui. Gli hanno dato un'altra bocca," it now said. *"Rocco e Ron."* I attached this edited version of the mp3 to the email. And I sent it.

I went to the bathroom, even though I really didn't have much to offer. I washed my hands for several minutes.

When I returned, I put the earbuds back in. I cranked the volume up to the maximum. The brutal chords hammered into my brain, the brutal lyrics extolling me to take back the power, to not put up with any more lies.

Didn't Dad need to be held to account for his actions?

Didn't he need to be arrested?

Didn't there need to be a trial?

Didn't the court need to then determine whether he was innocent or guilty?

I took out my phone. Maybe he hadn't been there after all, I told myself, thinking of those cigarette butts. No phishing. No phony accounts. No hiding behind anything.

I sent the mp3, the unedited version, to Rent-a-Cop.

Two down, one to go.

I brought up the document again, the one I had shown to Mr. Jazy. The one he said would cause the whole coast to melt down. It didn't seem possible that those numbers would have such power, but I believed Mr. Jazy and his beard.

Maybe what I'd done already was enough to extinguish The Debt. Ron Gatto was a goner, I had no doubt about that. But Rocco Taverniti? With his money he would hire the best lawyers available.

But he was all over Coast Home Loans, his name was on everything. How could he get out of that? But Dad's name was there also; not as prominently as Rocco Taverniti's, but he was still a major player.

I leaned back in the chair, tuned back into the music.

No more lying, demanded the lyrics, over and over again.

I created another blog in WordPress. This one I called "Coast Home Loans = Ponzi Scheme." And below that I posted the contents of the document I'd shown Mr. Jazy, the one he'd said was enough to cause a meltdown. As before, I emailed the address of this blog to the editors of the major newspapers.

The blogs of war had been unleashed; in the meantime I had a race to run.

I stood up, turned and found Hound standing right behind me. I took out the earbuds, cursing myself for having them in and not hearing him sneak up on me like this. This was Scary Hound, the one who had caused my head to ring like a bell that day.

"What's going on here?" he said.

"I was just catching up on some work," I said.

His eyes scanned the screen. He sat down, clicked on History, saw what else I'd done this morning. "You've got to be joking!" he kept saying. "You've got to be joking!"

If there was a time to take him out, it was now, while he was engrossed in the screen, while his back was to me.

"Ron Gatto is the best thing that ever happened to the Gold Coast!"

I looked around for a possible weapon; there was a sad-looking plant in the corner. I could smash him over the head with that.

"This joint was a joke before he took over," continued the outraged Hound.

Or what about all those guns in his office – surely one of them was loaded?

Who was I kidding? I was so not the taking-somebody-out sort – Brandon had shown that. Hound knew it too, arrogantly keeping his back to me like that. But the blogs of war had been unleashed and there was no restraining them now. Over Hound's shoulder I could see that already the blog was generating traffic.

"I'm calling Ron right now," said Hound, taking out his phone.

I wasn't the taking-somebody-out type, but I was the running type. Not running as in "running away" but running as in "running to." Running to whatever future I had just created.

So this was the end of my job, which was sort of sad – it had been my first real one. But if I stayed working for Hound I would inevitably become like him: arrogant and cynical and bent.

It was time to run.

But I did have one more thing to say. "Hound?"

"What?" he demanded.

"Triple denim is so not okay."

I took off, out of the office and down the stairs, and straight into a wall of Lazarus. The two of them, smoking.

"Hey, what's the big rush?" said one of them.

Quick thinking was needed. They, obviously, didn't know that I was in total disgrace. Not yet, anyway. I noticed the flash of silver in his hand.

Keys.

"Hound asked me to get something out of the Hummer," I said.

"Sure, Bloodyoung," he said. *Nice try, meathead.*

I took the keys and hurried over to the Hummer and unlocked it and got into the driver's seat. Keys into the ignition, engine started. But unlike the Porsche, it was an automatic. I'd sat in the front seat of Mom's BMW enough to know what the deal was, however.

I stuck it into drive, and was about to move off when Hound appeared at my window. He was holding a gun, and it was pointed at me.

Whoa!

And he was *so* the taking-somebody-out type.

But then I remembered something: Hound bragging about how his Hummer was totally bulletproof, even the windows.

Either he'd been lying (not unusual) or he'd been telling the truth (less usual). There was an easy way to find out.

I put my foot down.

As I did, I braced myself, expecting the shattering of non-bulletproof glass and the disintegration of a non-bulletproof head.

Nothing, except Rodriguez – was that his name? – started singing about someone called Sugarman.

For once, thank God, Hound had been telling the truth.

HUMMER

Despite being only fifteen, despite being behind the wheel of one of the most ludicrous cars on the Gold Coast, I didn't feel that conspicuous. I'm not sure what it was – the tinted windows, perhaps. Or the fact that there was so much vehicle around me. It actually reminded me of the night I drove the bulldozer, the night I rescued Zoe Zolton-Bander from her own uncle.

And the Hummer, despite its size, was an easy vehicle to drive. No gears to change, and the power steering really was powerful. So instead of ditching the Hummer straightaway, which was what I'd originally intended to do, I decided to take it for a spin.

I headed away from the beach, away from all the traffic, away from all the police, and towards the hinterland.

The Rodriguez CD finished and the next one was

some of the gangsta rap that Hound loved so much. Rodriguez and gangsta rap – he sure was a weird contradictory dude, but, hey, maybe everybody is a weird contradictory dude. What was that line that Mr. Mac put up on the board that day? *I am large, I contain multitudes.*

I passed a Coast Home Loans office and there were quite a lot of people milling around outside.

Surely not, I thought. *The blog went live less than an hour ago.* No, it had to be a coincidence; Coast Home Loans must have some sort of deal going, the deposit-less loan, something like that.

The thought had occurred to me that my blogs would just fizzle, that nobody would believe a word of them. People post all sorts of rubbish on the Internet – in fact, that's what the Internet is, a place where people post rubbish. And most of it, 99.9 percent of it, just gets ignored.

My phone rang: Imogen.

"Have you done it?" she said.

"Who let the blogs out?" I sang tunelessly, Baha Men style. "Who let the blogs out?"

"The watch?"

"It's done, Imogen." I wondered what it was I'd done exactly.

"So what do we do now?"

"We play the waiting game," I said, an idea flashing in my head. It was a pretty outrageous one, and

I wasn't going to give it any airtime. But something gripped me, a sort of recklessness, devil-may-care-ness.

"You want to go for a drive?" I said.

"With your parents?"

"No, just the two of us."

"Okay," she said, totally calling my bluff.

"I'll pick you up at the end of Chirp Street in ten minutes."

"Where?" she said.

"Byron Street," I said.

I was sure she wouldn't be there, that she thought I was crazy or something, but ten minutes later, when I pulled into Chirp Street, she was standing there. She was wearing scruffy denim shorts and a white short-sleeved shirt and flip-flops. But she still looked … Imogenesque.

I drew up next to her, and she took a couple of steps back – *What the Hummer!* I wound down the passenger window. "Imogen, it's me!"

She moved closer and peered into the Hummer, the doubt written all over her face in CAPITALS with **bold** and <u>underlining</u>.

"So do you want to go for a spin?" I said. "It's your choice."

Imogen had always been the goodest of good girls; when she did go to school, I could never remember her getting into any type of trouble whatsoever.

But the **DOUBT** on her face had been replaced by something less certain. "You're a safe driver?"

"So far."

"You don't go over the speed limit?"

"No, I'm really slow."

"And you haven't been drinking?"

"Of course not."

"Drugs?"

"Don't be crazy."

She continued staring at the inside of the Hummer, and then she sighed, and then she got into the front seat. "If at any stage I don't feel comfortable with your driving I'm going to ask you to let me out," she said as she buckled the seat belt.

"That's fair enough," I said as I pulled out onto Chirp Street.

"And is there any other music besides this misogynistic rubbish?"

Miso-what?

"There's Rodriguez," I said.

"Well, it has to be better."

I punched a couple of buttons and Rodriguez came back on.

A little while after turning onto the main road, four police cars, lights flashing, passed us in the opposite direction.

"They're in a hurry," I said, glancing behind.

"Keep your eyes on the road!" said Imogen.

415

As we began to ascend into the hinterland, Imogen started to relax. Maybe it was my driving, maybe it was Rodriguez, who knows?

"This is fun," she said. "Whose car is this, anyway?"

"My boss's," I said.

"And he lets you use it, even without a license?"

"Yeah, he's a pretty loose sort of guy," I said.

I had no destination in mind; it was just a drive with the girl I adored, that was all. Something to do while the blogs did their work. But I found myself following the same route that Gus and I had taken, past the winery, the organic farm, and down into the Berang Valley.

"What is this place?" said Imogen.

"It's where my dad grew up," I said.

We passed the church and Imogen said, "Stop, I want to take a photo."

So I pulled over and we got out and I sat on an old concrete bench while Imogen took a whole lot of arty photos of the church with her iPhone. If only she knew, I thought, remembering Gus's story about the cross just floating there in the night sky.

About how he couldn't kill Panda.

Would I tell her one day?

Tell her the truth about the final installment?

Tell her that I'd considered killing another human being? That I'd even gone to the hospital with that very intention?

Imogen came over and sat next to me and showed me the photos she'd taken.

When she'd finished she said, "It's going to get messy, isn't it?"

I nodded – she didn't know the half of it. And neither did I.

"But at least Mum can bury Dad, at least she can do that."

I put my arm around Imogen's shoulder and she leaned into me.

"I'm pretty sure the cops will find out who killed your dad," I said.

"They will?" she said.

"I hope so," I said, though I wasn't sure, despite all that I'd done, that I really did.

"Thanks for what you've done, Dom."

I didn't say anything for a while, and when I did I wish I hadn't – it sounded so puerile. "Tristan helped too, though?"

Imogen smiled.

"Rap is crap," she said. "Sharks are cool, under no circumstances should dads ever be allowed to wear Speedos and …"

I knew straightaway that all the practically-sucked-her-face-off stuff Tristan had said about him and Imogen was crap.

The final line we said together, "And Tristan Jazy is so not okay."

Imogen reached up with her hand and placed it on the side of my face.

It was such a weird place to be, but I wanted us to stay just like this, with the sun on us, the pigeons cooing from the church. I wanted us to stay like this forever.

"I love you, Dominic David Silvagni," said Imogen.

"And I love you, Imogen Rose Havilland," I said.

My phone rang, but it kept ringing and ringing.

I wanted us to stay like this forever.

Before it got messy.

But I couldn't help myself, I glanced at the face of my iPhone. *Hanley calling* ... What did that traitor want? I let it ring out.

Immediately it rang again. *Hanley calling* ...

"Sorry, I have to get this," I said.

Imogen sighed. "Phones," she said, sounding like some sixty year old.

I stood up and walked away as I answered, "What do you want?"

"They're coming after you!" he said.

"What are you talking about?"

"Rocco, Ron, Art, all of them. They're coming after you and your family."

Here I was in a forgotten valley, pigeons cooing, and he was sounding like somebody from *The Godfather* – all "Luca Brasi sleeps with the fishes."

"Why should I believe you?" I said.

"Have a look around you, don't you see what's going on?"

"What do you mean?"

"Every Coast Home Loans office has been torched, every one. Other companies, too. It's chaos out there. Rocco's already had people throwing homemade bombs at his house. They'll come after your father, too. All the Coast Home Loans directors."

There was the sound of glass shattering. "Do you hear that?" said Hanley, and there was terror in his voice. "It's getting out of control! You have to believe me, Dom. Rocco is coming after you and your family. They've got traces on all your phones."

I'd heard enough. I hung up.

"Imogen, we've got to go!"

Ω Ω Ω

I hadn't been drinking; I wasn't on drugs; I didn't break those promises. I broke the other one, though. I drove fast, tooling the Hummer around the curves as we quickly left the valley behind us.

"Imogen, can you do me a favor: can you get my dad on the phone?" I said.

She tried.

Engaged.

Engaged.

Engaged.

As I passed the lookout point, the one where Gus and I had stopped that day, I stole a glance to my left. There were plumes of smoke rising up from the coast.

It's not possible, I thought. The effect was disproportionate to the cause. But then I remembered what Mr. Jazy had said: if people found out that their houses were worth nothing, there would be a meltdown.

As we drove through the outer suburbs, police cars passed us in all directions, bells blaring. Imogen turned on the radio.

"What started as a few isolated events, angry mortgage holders venting their frustration, has now become a full-scale riot. Police are warning people to stay home and not to go out into the streets. Anybody traveling to the Gold Cost today is advised to turn around now."

We reached Halcyon Grove, and I parked the Hummer outside, and Imogen and I ran up to the entrance. Samsoni came out of his gatehouse in his uniform and suddenly everything was normal again.

"Not a good idea to be out there now," he said, a look of relief on his genial face.

"Samsoni, what's happening?" said Imogen.

"I've seen it back home," said Samsoni. "A few people get excited, get angry, and it spreads like wildfire. It's like now people have permission to fire up about all the stuff that's been getting to them for years."

He looked at both of us and I could see the affection in his face.

"Don't take this personal, but there's a lot of money on the Gold Coast, a heck of a lot of money. But there's also a lot of people who don't have much. Maybe that's their fault, maybe they're lazy, or unlucky, or just plain dumb, but they're the ones out on the streets now." Samsoni flashed us one of his trademark smiles. "You're safe in here, though. The two of you better get home."

A year or so ago I would've believed Samsoni when he said we were safe in Halcyon Grove. Not now, though.

I saw Imogen home and ran back to my house.

Mom and Miranda and Toby were crowded around the plasma, looking slack-jawed at shots of the main street at Surfers Paradise. Shops were on fire. Police were in riot uniforms. A mob of people, some with T-shirts hiding their features, were throwing stones at the police, surging and receding like the surf.

"Thank heavens you're here," said Mom, jumping up to embrace me. "I was so worried."

"Where's Dad?" I said. "We have to get out of here."

The concern returned to Mom's face. "I've tried calling; he's not answering."

There was the screech of a car from outside.

The door opened.

And there was Dad, wearing his usual suit. Except half of it had been ripped from his body.

His lip was smeared with blood.

"We have to get out of here," I said.

"It's just a few bogans," he said. "They'll calm down."

"No, it's not them," I said. "It's The Debt, they're coming after us."

He looked at me hard, his body tensing. "We are The Debt," he said. "Surely you understand that now: you and I, we are The Debt."

"Not me," I said. "Not ever."

"What are you two talking about?" said Miranda.

"All of us have to get out of here now," I said. "I pulled the pin."

Dad just stood there, torn suit, bloodied lip, not saying anything, a look of incomprehension on his face.

"David?" said Mom.

It took him a while to answer, but when he did the authority had returned to his voice. "Dom's right, we need to go."

"But how?" said Mom. "It's not safe on the streets."

"I know a way," I said. "You get ready, I'll go and get Gus."

PUMPING TIN

I heard the techno techno-ing, and found Gus in his shed, sitting at the end of the bench. The bar was lumpy with weights, and I did the math: 77.5 kilos. Two and a half kilos more than he'd ever lifted before.

"Gus, they're coming after us! We have to go!"

He didn't move.

The old bugger must be getting deaf. I turned off the power to the ghetto blaster. "We have to get out of here, now," I said. "The Debt, they're coming after us!"

"You stirred them up?" he said.

I nodded. "A bit."

"At last," said Gus.

"Come on, we have to go."

"I've got tin to pump," he said.

Deaf *and* senile. "Are you crazy? They're coming!"

"I'm not running, not this time," he said, scratching at his stump. "I'm too old for that." I looked at him, and I knew it was no good, that he wasn't coming.

"I just reckon today might be the day for a PB," he said as he lay back on the bench and reached up for the bar.

I couldn't go, not now.

His sinewy arms lifted the bar off the rack.

There was no way he could do it, his arms were already shaking. But he brought the bar down to his chest.

"Go on, Gus!" I yelled. "Get that baby up!"

Back arching, he began to heave the bar upwards, millimeter by millimeter.

"Go on, Gus!" I yelled. "Get that baby up!"

His arms were shaking violently, but the bar got higher and higher until it dropped with a clang back into the rack.

There was no celebrating from Gus as he sat up, just a sort of wry look on his face.

I knelt by him, embraced him. "Now you can come!" I urged, though I already knew what his answer would be.

"I'm staying put."

"Ciao, Gus," I said.

"Ciao," he said, kissing me, Italian-style, on each cheek.

I got up, went to hurry off, but I thought of one more thing that I had to say. "And Gus, I think it was the right thing to do, not killing Panda."

I ran out of the shed, across the lawn and into our house. Everybody was ready.

"Gus isn't coming," I said.

"I'll go across and get the stupid old bugger," said Dad, making to move off.

"It's his decision," I said, standing in Dad's way.

He looked at me, and shrugged. "His decision."

"Follow me," I said. "We're going underground."

We walked out of the front door.

Roberto was standing on the lawn, a machine gun in his hands.

"Back in the house," he said.

My lovely Uncle Roberto, I thought. *The Debt.*

Nobody moved. Dad said something to Roberto in Calabrian.

Whatever it was, it didn't work. "Back in the house, now!" said Roberto.

Mom stepped forward. "Roberto, we're not going back in there."

"Stop!" he said, and now the gun was aimed directly at her.

Mom kept walking.

"Mom, don't," said Miranda.

But Mom just kept walking slowly and steadily towards her brother.

From outside the walls there were the sounds of explosions. Smoke billowed in the air. Two choppers flew overhead.

"Stop," said Roberto. "I will shoot you, Celia!"

But Mom kept coming, slow and steady; she was only a meter from him now.

And then the sound of a gun; a bullet whizzed overhead. Coming up the road was a motorbiker, dressed all in black. He shot again.

Dad screamed and clutched at his arm.

Roberto turned around with a burst of machine gun fire, and the motorbiker flew from his bike.

There was a rumble of thunder, jagged strikes of lightning. It was just as I had wanted: tumultuous weather on a tumultuous day.

"Go!" said Roberto. "You've got to get out of here now!"

So blood is thicker than water.

And I wondered if my uncle had just signed his own death warrant.

Mom was by Dad's side. "David, are you okay?"

"I'm okay," he said, turning his shirt into a type of sling.

"Everybody, this way," I said.

Past Imogen's house, and the door flung open and Imogen was there.

There was an almighty bang to our left.

"Come with us!" I yelled. "It's not safe here."

Another bang, and a portion of the perimeter wall tumbled inwards and the bull-barred front of a truck appeared.

Holy crap, The Debt!

But the three men, T-shirts tied around their faces, who got out and ran into Halcyon Grove, spreading in three directions, were not The Debt.

They were looters. Or they were even worse.

"You have to come with us," I said to Imogen.

"And Beth?" said Mom.

"She's in the hospital," I said.

Imogen hesitated, and started towards us.

But then another thought. "I need the microchip!" I yelled. She disappeared back through the front door, reappearing twenty or so seconds later. "Let's go."

We'd reached the recreation area when there was the sound of a car horn. I looked up: a taxi.

Luiz Antonio.

"Who's that?"

"Gus's mate," I said. "Luiz Antonio."

"Perfect," said Dad. "He can take us. Come on, everybody."

"No!" I said. "My plan is better." All eyes were on me now – why was my plan better? I thought of how we'd flushed that rat Nitmick out of his apartment. How we'd nabbed him in the street. "They might be waiting outside the gates, ready to just pick us off. That's why they only sent one biker in."

Dad thought about this. "Dom's right, we follow his plan."

I ran over to the taxi and quickly explained to Luiz Antonio what was happening.

427

He agreed – it was too risky.

"Imogen, the chip?" I said. She handed me the ziplock bag.

Immediately Luiz Antonio knew what it was. "Ah, my favorite customer. Destination, please?"

"I was thinking Nimbin," I said. "Maybe you could leave him at the McDonald's? He really loves it there."

Luiz Antonio took his favorite customer, tossed him onto the passenger seat and said, "Gus?"

"Old bugger doesn't want to come." I almost added he was going for a PB, but even on a crazy day like this that sounded way too crazy.

"*Gringo malandro*," growled Luiz Antonio, and he took off with a squeal of tires, making for the gates.

Dad and Mom had already removed the grate.

"Who's first?" I said.

"I'll go," said Toby.

Showing surprising agility, he was quickly through the hole and into the storm water drain. I couldn't help but think about what Dad had said the other night, that I didn't know what Toby's capabilities were.

Maybe, he was right.

Maybe, there'd been no need to unleash the blogs of war.

But I knew that that wasn't just it – The Debt had to be extinguished.

Miranda and Imogen scampered down next. Then Mom.

"You go, Dad," I said.

More thunder thundered. I noticed, now, that Dad's shirt was soaked with blood, and I could see that his arm was next to useless. I helped him down as best I could.

As I lowered myself into the hole, a drop of rain caught me right on the end of my nose, where it dribbled down to my lip and then onto my chin.

"You go first, Toby. Mom. Miranda. Imogen. Dad. And I'll go last. No rush, just slow and steady. And keep talking to each other, because it'll get really dark. When you come to the first sump, stop and wait for me."

"What's a sump?" said Toby.

"You'll know when you reach it," I said.

I took out my iPhone and scrolled through my contacts until I had the one I wanted. I was going to text, when I thought: *sometimes it's just better to call.* Amazingly enough, she answered almost straightaway.

"Geez, are you okay?" Zoe said, the worry in her voice genuine. "It's the only thing on the TV now, the whole Gold Coast is up in flames."

"Where are you?" I said.

"As if I'm going to tell you that."

"I really need your help."

"You got it," she said.

"I have?"

"Yes, of course. You risked your life that day to get us off that boat."

"Okay, listen closely," I said, and I told her my plan.

A few minutes later, when I'd finished the call, I turned my phone off – I was off the grid now, they couldn't trace me. But I'd forgotten to tell the others to do the same.

I dived into the tunnel and crawled like mad. It didn't take long to catch up to Dad.

"Hey, Dad, pass it on ahead – everybody needs to turn off their phones."

I heard him say, "Miranda, you need to turn your phone off."

Dad was making slow, awkward progress. And when I experimented, crawling with only one arm for a while, I could see why. Still the Silvagni train kept chugging down the tunnel. And then from ahead Toby's voice echoed, "I'm here. I'm here. I'm here …"

Soon we were all at the sump, the grid above letting in light which fell in lattices on the faces of my family, of Imogen. From above we could also hear sounds: the wailing of police bells, the shattering of glass, footsteps.

"So everybody's turned their phones off?" I said.

There were five "yes" responses.

"We could just wait it out here," said Mom. "It's not that bad."

I thought of the raindrop that had landed on my nose. "That's probably not a good idea," I said. And not wanting to freak everybody out, I went with a lie: "There are issues with the air in these places, especially with so many of us."

"And remember those kids who drowned in one of these a couple of years ago?" said Miranda.

Well done, Miranda.

"And it had just started to rain when we left," said Mom.

"Let's get a move on, then," said Toby. "Which way is it?"

I pointed to the drain to our left. "We've got about another hour, and then we come out at Preacher's."

"And we'll be safe there?" said Mom.

That was the problem: The Debt had always been able to find me in the past. Always. And yes, I know I'd been electronically tagged then, and I know my phone was now off the grid, but I still had this sense that they could find me. That they had these extraordinary, almost supernatural, powers. We had to go somewhere where they would never find us.

"I've got a plan," I said. "Trust me."

Dad moaned and grabbed at his arm. The shirt was completely soaked in blood.

Then I remembered the pills that Imogen had given me. I felt in my pocket: they were still there. "Dad, hold out your hand."

He did as I asked, and I shook four of the pills into it. "Painkillers," I said.

Dad threw them into his mouth. I took a couple, too. My hand was throbbing.

"I'm outta here," said Toby, diving into the hole.

Was this really the same person who had been scared about going on television because he might get his pipe of tempered chocolate wrong?

Mom followed him.

Miranda.

Imogen.

Dad hesitated.

"I'm just holding you up," he said.

"Please, Dad, don't go all midday movie on me. Gus reckons you're the most tenacious, most determined person he ever met."

"Gus said that?"

"Gus said that."

Dad clambered into the drain. As I followed, I felt another drop of rain on the back of my neck. I looked up at the grate; rain was falling heavily.

"Whoo-hoo!" I said, probably the first time in ten years that I'd attempted a train noise. "Let's get this choo-choo going."

I could hear the "whoo-hoo" progressing from carriage to carriage.

With Dad making such disjointed progress it was impossible to fall into any sort of rhythm with my crawling. Despite the painkillers, my hand had started sending out those skyrockets of pain again and I wondered if the butterfly closures had come loose.

I soon had my answer when blood began to seep from under the bandaid. After that, it didn't take long for the bandaid to drop off. There was the wound, gaping. And as macabre as it was, I couldn't help thinking that it looked like some sort of mouth, like Mr. Havilland's extra mouth.

"Whoo-hoo!" I yelled, and again it progressed up the carriages, but this time the volume was noticeably less. Train Silvagni was running out of steam.

When I felt the moisture under my hands, I thought it was blood, either mine or Dad's. But when I brought my moist fingers to my nose it was rainwater I could smell.

I checked my watch. There was perhaps half an hour of crawling to go.

Dad moaned, and stopped. "More painkillers."

"You had four already," I said.

"Give me another four!"

I shook some more pills out of the container and passed them to him. "It's not long now."

Dad started moving again, but it was obvious that he had very little left in the tank.

That stupid treadmill, I thought. Why didn't he do some real exercise? Why wasn't he fitter?

Water was flowing freely now; it completely covered my hands. "Full speed ahead," I said to Dad. "Pass it on." He passed it on, but that's about all he was capable of, repeating the words.

What could I do? Somehow, crawl past my dad, and make sure that at least I made it? It didn't make any sense for two of us to drown.

I remembered the last time I was in the drain, the last time it had been raining. How PJ and I had managed to drag her brother out. All that effort, I thought, and what for? Paris Hilton was going to get him anyway.

Dad had stopped completely.

"You keep going," he said.

What in the blazes was wrong with me? I'd risked my life, busted an absolute gut, to drag Brandon out and I didn't even like the little turd. This was my dad!

The water was rising rapidly; it was now up to my elbow level. But remembering how we'd half dragged, half floated Brandon out, I realized that was a good thing.

"Dad, listen to me. I have to crawl over you, okay? I have to get in front of you."

"Of course you do," he said.

"So you lie down flat and I'm going to crawl over you."

Dad did that, arching his neck up to keep his head out of the water, and I clambered over him, trying not to touch his arm.

Then I turned around so that we were head-to-head.

"Dom, I want you to know that –" started Dad, but I cut him short.

"Enough of that crap, okay? I'm not going anywhere. You need to roll over so that you're on your back."

With my help, he managed to do that.

"You need to sort of push with your legs," I said, grabbing him by his shirt collar. "You ready? One. Two. Three."

But when I yanked, Dad screamed, the most horrendous sound I'd ever heard come from a human being.

"My arm!" he moaned.

How dumb can you get? The shirt was also his sling. But where to get purchase? I had no choice.

"Sorry, Dad," I said, as I grabbed a handful of his thick lifestyle-presenter's hair. "One. Two. Three. Go!" I pulled, and this time it worked, the same way it had worked with Brandon, the water actually in our favor, lifting Dad up, reducing the friction. Using this technique, we made very slow but steady progress down the drain. At the same time, the water level was rising just as steadily. I wondered about the others – surely they'd made it by now. And what about the other end? What then?

Something grabbed my ankles and the scream that came out of my mouth made Dad's effort seem puny.

"Dom, it's me."

"Toby, what in the blazes are you doing?"

"I came back to help," he said. "It's not very far, only about ten minutes."

435

With Toby helping, pulling me back, we caterpillared our way down the drain.

He was right, it was only about ten minutes and then we were there; it was the place where I'd slept next to PJ, the place where the Preacher had died. And here I was again. Who gave such a crappy place permission to play such a significant part in my life? There were still remnants of PJ and Brandon's camp: some tatty old blankets, a filthy foam mattress.

Mom was comforting Dad. There was no color at all in his face and his breathing was labored.

"We need to get him to a hospital," said Mom.

"Doesn't anybody know first aid?" I said, thinking that there must be something we could do.

In the movies they always put a tourniquet on, but maybe that's only because it's sort of exciting. Everybody shook their heads: not one iota of first aid between us.

"Great," I said, taking out my iPhone. It was still dry; that waterproof case had been the best thing I'd ever bought. I went to turn it on.

"What are you doing?" said Miranda. "You said to keep our phones off or they would find us on GPS."

I actually hadn't said anything about GPS, Miranda had worked that out herself.

"Doctor Google," I said, looking at my fading father. "It's our only hope."

"You sure there's a signal here?" said Toby.

"Yeah," I said. "This place is like a second home to me."

The joke, if you could call it that, was wasted on this audience.

When I turned on my phone, three messages downloaded. I couldn't help but notice that they were from Rent-a-Cop's number. The wheels were already in motion. Why not just call him? But I thought of what Dad had said – you never know.

I opened Safari, got onto Google and typed *how to treat a gunshot wound to the arm*. "The Survival Doctor – What to do when help is NOT on the way" had the answers.

"Elevate arm above the heart," I said.

Miranda and Imogen helped Mom to remove Dad's arm from his homemade sling and gently raise it until it was above his heart.

"Apply direct pressure to wound," I said.

"Really?" said Toby.

But Mom was already gently tearing Dad's shirt open so that she could see the seeping wound more clearly. "Anybody have a hanky?"

"Here," said Toby, handing her his, a black and gray number that had *YSL* embroidered in one corner.

She folded it over a couple of times. "You ready, darling?" she said to Dad. He nodded. She pressed the handkerchief against the wound. Dad grimaced but didn't scream.

"If this doesn't work we can also try a tourniquet," I said.

"It's working," said Mom. "It's already bleeding much less."

I noticed, too, that Dad had more color in his face.

"Maybe you should turn your phone off now, Dom," said Miranda.

I considered sending Zoe a text, or calling her again, but realized it was a waste of time. Either they were going to let me down yet again, or they would turn up.

"Why don't you just call the police?" said Toby. "Tell them to come and get us?"

My God! I'd been so anti-cop, I'd completely forgotten what their role in society was. It was as simple as that.

"Don't!" said Dad, his voice a broken thing. "Rocco has too many friends in the police force."

I took Miranda's advice: I turned off my phone. "We should probably move," I said. If they had fixed my position on GPS it made sense to get out of there right away.

But at the end of the drain, I could see the heavy rain slanting down outside. And Dad, though better, was in no state to go anywhere. I just had to hope that they hadn't triangulated my position.

Because if they had, we were *carne fresca*.

HEARSEY

Two-twenty in the morning and it was my turn.

We'd decided that each of us kids would take it in turns keeping watch, eyes on that circle of concrete, our window onto the outside world, while the others tried to steal some sleep.

"Just like the movies," Toby had said.

I hadn't pointed out the obvious: in the movies the people keeping watch are usually armed. There was absolutely nothing we could do to stop The Debt from waltzing in and sticking a bullet in each of our heads.

But something really obvious occurred to me: The Debt didn't know we weren't armed. As far as they knew, each of us could be toting an AK-47. So why risk getting shot when you could just play the waiting game? Sooner or later we would have to come out. And they would be there to pick us off, one by one.

Or maybe my ruse had worked and they'd hightailed it all the way to Nimbin to find a Dom-free McDonald's.

The others were all sleeping, the drain full of their sleeping sounds. Even Dad's eyes were closed. I knew that Mom had been determined to stay up all night, to apply constant pressure to that hanky, but she, too, had dropped off. I'd already checked Dad's wound – the blood was no longer flowing freely – so I figured it was better to let her rest.

Somebody stirred.

"Dom?"

"Imogen?"

"You okay?" she said, shuffling closer to me.

"Sure," I said, keeping my eyes on the concrete circle.

There were a thousand questions Imogen could have asked, but she didn't. Instead, looking over at Dad, she said, "Your father's very brave."

How long until the police came after him, I wondered.

How long until there was a court case, the details splashed over the papers, over the Internet?

How much longer would Imogen think that my father was brave?

"Yes, he is," I said.

And then, from outside: a noise!

"What's that?" said Imogen.

"Shhh!" I said. Had they realized that we were unarmed, and were now coming after us? I went to grab something, anything. But there was nothing.

More noises. Rustling, shuffling noises.

And then a silhouette at the end of the drain. And then a person. A person I knew.

"PJ?" I said.

She was carrying a small backpack. She quickly took in the scene, the slumbering bodies.

"What happened?" she whispered.

"They came after us," I said. "They smashed their way into Halcyon Grove."

She nodded – *I understand*. But the what-the-blazes-is-going-on-here? look on her face said otherwise.

"Brandon?" I said.

She didn't have to say anything, her face said it all: he was dead.

"I'm sorry," I said.

PJ shrugged. "I'm going back to Toowoomba with the old girl, try and work it out. She says she's going to get rid of that dipstick." PJ then noticed Imogen. "Ah, the beautiful girl," she said.

"Hope it works out with your mum," said Imogen.

PJ shrugged. "I just need to get my stuff."

What stuff? I looked at all the garbage strewn around the place. But PJ tiptoed through the bodies until she came to a huge valve. She reached behind it, and brought out a plastic bag. Ah, that stuff.

As she tiptoed back, she stumbled slightly, and the bag flew out of her hand and onto the concrete, some of its contents spewing out. Among them was the Leaning Tower of Pisa statue, the one I'd bought for her in Rome. As she grabbed it and put it back into the bag, our eyes met.

PJ gave me a little smile. And, one eye on the outside, I gave her a little one back.

"Okay, Grammar," she said. "I'm out of here."

"Okay," I said, not having a clue what to say, what to do.

And then she was gone.

It had all happened so quickly, I had to ask myself if it was real, if she'd been real. But when Imogen said, "Is that the girl you were with in Halcyon Grove that day?" I knew it was definitely real.

And I knew that Brandon had definitely died. And in my chest, there was this flower of sadness, spreading and growing, spreading and growing.

"Yes, that's her," I said, wiping the tears from my eyes.

"She just sort of wandered in and wandered out," said Imogen. "Maybe there's nobody outside?"

Imogen's question was just what I needed – *let's focus on the practical*. Again, I tried to look at it from The Debt's point of view. Why wouldn't they let PJ wander in and out like that? It was us they were after, not her. In fact, it might even lull us into a false sense of security.

No, it was better to assume that they were there, and that they were armed to the teeth.

There was the buzz of a watch alarm, and Toby was upright and awake.

"My turn now," he said.

My first instinct was to say, "It's okay, I can take this." But it didn't take me long to realize that this wasn't a great idea. I needed the sleep, needed to be as alert as possible when daylight came. And Toby had already shown how capable he was.

"Okay," I said. "Then it's Miranda after you."

I found a place to stretch out. Imogen did the same. My hand searched for hers, and we went to sleep holding each other.

Ω   Ω   Ω

I woke, and the first signs of daylight were appearing. Outside, birds were in full voice. A kookaburra let rip with its signature mad cackle.

Miranda was sitting up, eyes on the entrance.

"All good?" I said.

"All good," she replied.

The sky was still overcast, the clouds gray and heavy, but the rain had ceased.

Mom and Dad were already awake.

"Reckon we're over the worst of it," said Dad, pointing to his wound.

"Not so sure about that," said Mom.

I waited until we'd had an hour of light – enough time, I figured, for the Zolt to steal a chopper – before I turned on my phone again. *Beep. Beep. Beep. Beep.* SMS city.

From PJ: *in toowoomba – you ok?*

From an unknown number: *You ok pheidippides?*

From Hound: *I will hunt you down Youngblood*

And from Zoe: *airfield 7*

Immediately, I switched my phone off. And I slumped back. Airfield? They'd let me down yet again. Otto was supposed to steal a chopper. He was supposed to land it right outside here. The disused airfield, the one on which we'd landed the plane during the first installment, was at least three or four kilometers away. Even without Dad I doubted whether we could make it safely. But with him?

"Dominic?" said Mom. Her eyes were bloodshot, her tangled hair hung over her face.

"Yes, Mom?"

"You did the right thing, you really did. All the lies, all the deceit, all the violence, they had to stop. And you've done that."

Not for the first time, I wondered how much Mom knew.

"But look at this," I said, looking around helplessly. "Look what I've done." Again a kookaburra let rip with its mad cackle.

I turned on my phone again.

"I'll be back in a while," I said.

There was no way out but through the end of the drain. I imagined the gunman waiting outside, gun poised, finger ready. And as soon as a figure appeared, framed in that circle like some sort of arty photo, they would squeeze.

I crouched down like a sprinter on the starting line, fingers spread.

Ready! Set! Go!

I took off, all legs at first, and then brought arms into it, swinging hard. When I reached the entrance I was at top speed. They could shoot, but I wasn't going to make it easy for them. I burst out of the drain and into the day.

Any second a gun was going to go off, a bullet would rip into flesh.

But there was no noise, except for the *squish squish squish* of my runners on the sodden ground.

The sudden movement had caused the cut on my hand to start bleeding again, my swinging arms causing the blood to splatter over my shirt.

I tried to remember the way I'd come with PJ that morning, where we had turned off the main track. They all looked the same now. Blazing bells and buckets of blood.

I wondered how Gus was, whether he'd upped his PB even more.

Where was that turnoff?

That was it, the tree with the split trunk!

I turned left, building up my pace again. This track was rougher, but the bush it went through was much thicker and I felt less exposed. The ground was slippery, though, and I stumbled a couple of times.

In the distance I could hear police sirens. Was all this my fault, all this destruction, this chaos? I hadn't started the Ponzi scheme, but I sure had let out all its air.

Suddenly the bush thinned out and I was at the back of Preacher's, in those badlands with their burned-out car shells. But where was the hearse?

There was the hearse.

I felt under the back tire for the keys, the way PJ had. And that's when the mutant bee sound of a two-stroke motorbike engine rent the air. And then another one. I unlocked the door, got in the driver's seat, jammed the key in the ignition.

The mutant bees got closer.

I turned the key. The starter motor whirred, but the engine didn't start. "Come on, Hearsey!" I said borrowing PJ's nickname for, and familiarity with, the Preacher's vehicle.

Two motorbikes burst into the clearing just as the hearse responded with the throaty roar of an internal combustion engine.

Thanking Dad for the other night's impromptu driving lesson, and Hound for the run in his Hummer, I slotted the gears into first and eased the clutch.

The hearse stalled.

There was the sound of a gun, and the front window disintegrated completely, shards of it accumulating in my lap.

Again I turned the key in the ignition; this time the hearse started.

Straight ahead, one of the motorbikers had stopped, his machine side on to me. He was taking careful aim with his pistol, using his forearm as a steadying brace.

I pressed my foot hard on the accelerator; the motor roared. Slumping right down in my seat, I let the clutch out.

This time the hearse spun its wheels, and then they gripped, and it rose up and surged forward like a speedboat.

A bullet ripped into the upholstery where my head had been a second or so ago.

Both hands gripping the bottom of the steering wheel kept it going in a more or less straight line. The mutant bee sound again. The hearse roared. There was a *thud*, and the mutant bee became even more mutant.

I pulled myself up in the seat and risked a look behind. The motorbike was on the ground, the back wheel spinning furiously. The motorbiker was also on the ground, squirming. One leg looked fine, but the bottom half of the other one stuck out sideways at a right angle.

I felt sick – I'd done that to him! But this thought didn't last long – one down, one to go. I couldn't see the other bike. But I knew that was only a temporary situation.

There was no way into Preacher's from here, so I had to get back onto the main road and then come in through the main entrance.

I turned the radio on.

"The Gold Coast is in total lockdown," said the news reporter, "with roadblocks on all roads in and out of the city. All flights due to land in Coolangatta Airport have been diverted to Brisbane. Police have said that despite the extensive looting there has been no reported loss of life. The Prime Minister is due to give a press conference to discuss what has now become known as the Gold Coast Riots. There has been talk of mobilizing the army, which would be unprecedented in modern Australian history."

I turned the radio off.

I slowed for the T-intersection ahead but forgot to change down gears and the hearse started bunny-hopping again. I managed to bring it under control just before the junction, and wrenched the wheel to the right. How had tiny PJ ever managed to drive this monster of a thing?

The hearse drifted across the intersection before it responded to my steering. We were now heading more or less in the right direction.

A straight road, and I floored the accelerator. My concern now was that the other motorbiker had gone straight to the drain, to where my family was hiding.

The hearse built up momentum; I wondered whether it had ever gone this fast. The needle crept up: 60km/h, 70km/h, 80km/h. At 90km/h it was rattling so much that I decided to ease back a bit.

Ahead, I could see the sign that indicated the main entrance to Preacher's. So far I hadn't seen any other cars; the lockdown was obviously working well. But as I managed to turn the hearse into the drive to Preacher's I saw two all of a sudden. Both of them were white with lots of blue checks over them, with a strip of lights on top. Of course it made sense to have a roadblock at Preacher's; from there you could get to practically anywhere in the city.

Two policemen were standing by the roadblock, both busy on their phones. This obviously wasn't one of those boring days the copper at Sanctuary Cove had complained of.

There was no question about busting through the roadblock, not when there was even the slightest chance of a cop getting hurt. The old stone wall on either side of the gate, the old stone wall that ran around this half of the reserve, looked about as solid as a wall could get.

If I was in Dad's Porsche, no way; even in Hound's Hummer I would have had second thoughts, but Hearsey? Sure, why not?

The police were on the bullhorn: "Stop now!"

I checked that my seat belt was tight as I veered away from the roadblock, stepping down hard on the accelerator.

The hearse hit the wall hard, my forward momentum arrested by the seat belt. For a split second it seemed like we were going nowhere, that the old stone wall had won, but then the hearse seemed to find a way through. Debris flew through the broken windshield and into the front seat. Fortunately, none of it did me any harm.

We barreled along the road for a while, and then it was time to go cross country. Fortunately this was more parklands than bush, and the hearse coped easily with the grassy terrain. I avoided the bigger trees, but just plowed on through the smaller trees and the bushes. I kept waiting for the familiar sound of a police siren but I figured they couldn't leave their post, especially now that the wall had been breached.

Up ahead, the stub of drain poked out. I pulled the hearse as close as I could to the entrance.

I knew that there was no way of getting everybody in the hearse, without being exposed. The other motorbiker was lying in wait somewhere. But how to do this? How to play it?

I was struggling with this conundrum when I saw a figure break from the pipe and run towards me. He ran in a crouch, zigging this way, zagging the other, but Toby still made a sizeable target. I waited for the gunshot, for my brother to catapult through the air like in a Tarantino film. I cracked the passenger door open. Toby launched himself through it, and onto the seat.

"That was a crazy thing to do," I said.

"Somebody had to go first," he said, and he was absolutely right: somebody had to. "Is this what I think it is?" he said as he clambered into the back of the hearse.

"Don't worry, no customers today," I said, and as I did I realized what a pathetic attempt at humor it was. No customers yet.

Miranda was the next to break. Keeping low to the ground, she seemed to float across to us: the Arrogant Squirrel, the Swooping Goose, they were all paying off.

"Get in, sis," I said.

Imogen followed her. I'm pretty sure she did absolutely no tai chi, but she showed the same sort of ninjaesque capability as she flew across the ground and into the hearse.

"Does Mom need a hand with Dad?" I asked.

But our parents were already out of the drain and on their way. No crouching, no zigzagging, they just made steadily for the hearse, Mom supporting Dad as best she could, until eventually they both squeezed into the passenger seat. Now I noticed how white Dad was, how thin his breathing. Mom said nothing, but she didn't need to – her look said it all: *hurry, he's dying!*

451

I crunched it into gear, gave it some juice, released the clutch and we were away.

"We're going to make our getaway in this?" said Toby.

Actually, why not? At least then I wouldn't have to rely on anybody else. Captain of my destiny, master of my soul and all that.

"Not with that fuel gauge," said Miranda.

I haven't given the gauge a glance, but she was right: the needle was touching empty. But if I remembered correctly, hadn't PJ once said that it didn't work properly? The disused airfield wasn't far, but would we have enough fuel to make it?

We bounced over the rough terrain, and I don't think any of us could quite believe the situation we were in. At least I understood what was happening, but Miranda and Toby?

"Geez, I could kill for a latte," said Toby. Okay, it was pretty funny, but it got a much bigger laugh than it deserved.

I checked my watch. It was a couple of minutes before seven, we were almost at the airfield. I scoured the sky. The heavy clouds had broken up and there were patches of blue. Nowhere could I see anything that resembled a plane, however.

Why had I trusted the Zolt yet again?

Then two sounds, both high-pitched, came from different directions. I didn't know which way to look.

"A plane!" said Mom.

From behind a stand of trees a light plane appeared, taxiing towards us. The Zolt! I put my foot down.

"Motorbike!" said Toby.

And from the other direction, the motorbiker, the mutant bee, also heading towards us. If only we had a gun, I thought. And somebody who could shoot it.

I could now see Otto sitting up in the cockpit.

"It's the Zolt, isn't it?" said Miranda.

"That criminal?" said Mom.

Criminal?

"Right now he's all we've got," I said.

"Who's that next to him?" said Dad.

I hadn't noticed. What was Zoe doing there?

Otto motioned for me to pull up on his left. I did just that, making sure there was room for the car door to open. I noticed now how beat-up it was, like the aeronautical version of the *Hispaniola*; definitely not up to Otto's usual high standard. Mom and Miranda helped Dad into the plane. Imogen climbed in next, followed by Toby.

"Come on, Dom!" yelled Toby, his hand outstretched, ready to give me a boost up.

The motorbike flashed past, and a gun went off as I dropped down low, the side window of the hearse shattering. I sat up again, saw the motorbiker clutch at his right thigh, before both bike and rider crashed to the ground.

I looked up at the cockpit; Zoe put down the rifle, and smiled at me.

I killed the motor and gave Hearsey a silent good-bye before I climbed into the beat-up plane. Immediately Otto went into his takeoff routine.

Yes, the ground was ridiculously bumpy.

Yes, the plane was old and beat up.

But I had no doubt that the Zolt would get this bird off the ground.

Landing it, however; that was a different matter.

DROP IN SOME TIME

The Zolt had borrowed the plane from a parachute training school. Hence its age and beat-upness. Hence the longitudinal bench seats. And hence the parachutes everywhere. He seemed pretty happy with it, though.

"It might not look like much, but they're tough little units, these," he said in that incongruously high voice of his.

Miranda and Imogen didn't seem to mind it; they both looked at him with adoring eyes, hanging on his every word.

"We've got ourselves a full tank, so what say I drop you nice people in some little out-of-the-way place like Barcoola, or Marcoola, or Yarcoola, somewhere with coola in it?"

As far as jokes went it wasn't much but Miranda laughed like a hyena. She was quickly becoming a major embarrassment.

"We have to get your father to a hospital, and fast," said Mom. "Otherwise he's not going to make it."

Otto turned around so that he could see Dad. Dad was slouched against some parachutes, his arm over his head, and Mom was applying pressure to his wound with that YSL hanky. Obviously, it had started bleeding again.

"That'd be Brissie, then," said the Zolt, immediately banking the plane to the right.

Down below I could see smoke rising from the Gold Coast; it was still on fire. No cars moved on the roads. Still in lockdown.

It was only a half-hour run to Brisbane, and way before we'd gone that far we started getting grief from the control tower.

"Aircraft approaching eleven miles to the north of Brisbane airport at altitude one thousand feet, can you please identify yourself?" demanded the woman. "Can you please identify yourself?"

Otto let her talk to herself for a while before Zoe said, "Stop playing games, Otto."

Otto decided to identify himself. "Control tower, this is that plane."

"Please squawk ident." Otto pressed a button, which I guessed was the ident squawker. "Okay, I have you now. Please identify yourself, pilot."

"Otto Zolton-Bander, also known as the Zolt, also known as the Facebook Bandit, also known as a modern-day Robin Hood."

I was pretty sure he was showing off in front of Miranda and Imogen.

"Do you intend landing in this airport?" the woman demanded.

Otto's tone changed instantly. "I have limited fuel and I also have a seriously injured man on board my plane who needs immediate medical attention."

"So are you declaring a medical emergency for a priority landing?"

"He has a single gunshot wound to the upper arm," said Otto.

"I repeat my question – are you declaring a medical emergency for a priority landing?"

Otto looked at me, and there was the tiniest flicker of doubt on his face – *Have I bitten off more than I can chew this time?*

But it didn't last long.

"Yes, that's right, I am declaring a medical emergency for a priority landing."

Control Tower went quiet for a while, but when she came back on air she had good news.

"Please join a five-mile final for runway nineteen," she said. "You are clear to land."

There was a cheer from inside the plane, followed immediately by an uncomfortable silence. We all knew – well, all of us kids anyway – that the Zolt had taken off successfully plenty of times, but he hadn't nailed many landings.

And this was the Big Dance, this was a major airport.

"We'll be fine, Otto," I said. "We'll nail it just like we did the other time."

Mom and both my siblings were staring hard at me – what was this "we" thing about? Control Tower came on again with some more instructions that Otto acknowledged.

"You know there'll be a welcoming party waiting for you?" I said.

"Yes, I know," he said. "But do you know what, I'm actually sick of hiding out, of always having to look over my shoulder. Law of averages says I have to get nabbed one day, so why not today? Give myself up, instead of being hunted down like a mongrel dog."

I looked over at Zoe. She didn't seem so convinced, but kept quiet.

The landing was just like last time, except instead of two impossibly tense people there were eight of us.

As the ground came up to meet us, Otto talked to himself; and just like before, his voice seemed to have dropped several octaves. "Keep the nose level," he kept saying. "Keep the nose level."

The wheels kissed the tarmac, and what we had was pretty much a textbook landing. Miranda clapped. But she would. Before the plane had rolled to a standstill, a couple of fit-looking paramedics had jumped on board.

The cops tried to come on board too, to nab one of Australia's most wanted criminals, but the paramedics waved them away. Let me tell you, I would have done anything they said too.

As one performed his medical magic on Dad, sticking a drip in him, putting his arm into a real sling, the other asked Mom all the usual questions.

"Smoker?"

"Not anymore," said Mom.

"Dad was a smoker?" said Miranda.

"It wasn't something he liked to advertise," said Mom.

All I could think of was those cigarette butts in the coffin.

When they'd finished, this paramedic said, "Your mum did really well; your dad's going to be absolutely fine."

Was my dad really going to be absolutely fine?

The paramedics, accompanied by Mom, stretchered Dad out of the plane. I could see how impatient the police were – they were itching to get their hands on the infamous Zolt. I looked over at Zoe and then Otto, who had a sort of smile on his lips.

Sick of hiding out, my butt.

Didn't want to get hunted down like a mongrel dog, my rectal passage.

Otto gave her a nod and Zoe slammed the door shut just as the first of the policeman tried to board.

Then we were taxiing again. Control Tower, as you can imagine, was going ballistic. But in the end she had no choice, she couldn't afford any sort of accident, so she gave us our takeoff instructions.

As usual, Otto had no problem with nailing the takeoff.

But as we all know, takeoffs had never been an issue.

In the absence of the moral authority provided by the parental units, Miranda leaned over and kissed him, practically sucking his face clean off his head.

"I hope Gus is okay," said Toby, looking towards the smoke-smudged Gold Coast.

"He's as tough as they come," said Miranda.

"Your grandfather, right?" said Zoe.

I nodded – *our grandfather*.

However, Zoe must've noticed where I was looking, straight at the parachutes. "Let me guess," she said. "You want us to fly over Halcyon Grove so that you can parachute in and check on him?"

I nodded; she was scarily smart sometimes.

"So you know how to parachute?" said the Zolt.

"Not really," I said. "But I could google it."

I didn't need to google it, though, because Otto knew practically everything there was to know about parachuting. He told me how to strap it on. How I wouldn't need to pull anything because I'd be using a static line. How to open the emergency chute in case the main chute didn't open. How to steer using the steering toggles once I was airborne.

I wasn't actually that scared. That might sound a bit try-hard action man, but it's the truth. It seemed like it was actually quite a safe thing to do, even for somebody with zero experience.

"What do I do if I land in somebody's swimming pool?" I said.

"Don't ask me," said Otto.

Then I got it. "You've never actually jumped yourself, have you?"

"Not exactly, but I'm all over the theory," he said as we swooped low and made towards Halcyon Grove.

I hugged my sister and my brother. Hugged them hard. Who knew when I'd see them again? If ever. I told them to enjoy Barcoola, Marcoola or Yarcoola, whatever coola they ended up in.

I hugged Imogen.

And hugged Imogen.

And hugged Imogen.

"You better let go of her now," said Otto. "We're almost there."

I didn't want to un-hug Imogen. Not then. Not ever. But reluctantly I let go of her.

"You don't have to do this," she said. "It looks crazy down there."

I peered through the window – she was right,

461

Halcyon Grove was now Scorched Grove.

But I had to find out if Gus was okay.

And I had to face The Debt.

I attached the static line just like Otto had taught me. Just as I was about to climb out onto the wheel Otto said to wait, and dug into his pocket. He held something out to me.

Something I knew very well.

A Saint-Gauden's Double Eagle.

"For good luck," he said.

I wasn't exactly sure how lucky the coin was, but I sort of got where he was coming from. I took it, and put it in my pocket.

"I guess we're about even now," I said to the Zolton-Banders.

They looked at each other, and then at me. *Yeah, about even.*

I climbed out onto the wheel just like he had taught me. And when he said, "Jump!" I pushed myself out and away just like he had taught me.

One, two, three seconds, and the parachute opened and I was floating down like an autumn leaf. I got the theory of the steering toggles fine, it was just that in practice they weren't so easy to use. So, to answer my own question as to what you do if you land in somebody's swimming pool: well, you just get out of your harness as quickly as you can before your parachute drags you to the bottom and you drown.

It was the Jazys' pool, ironically, but I couldn't see any of the Jazys, and when I looked inside the house I could see why: it had been completely trashed.

"Anybody there?" I yelled, but nobody answered.

I walked past Imogen's house – also trashed: the windows broken, the front door torn off its hinges – and towards my house and my first thought was that I'd actually gone in the wrong direction because my house wasn't there.

But then I saw the rubble, and the twisted metal, and the deformed plastic, the smoke twisting into the sky – they'd burned my house down. And I felt like I should cry, but there were no tears.

I kept walking.

Gus's house was still there, the front door on its hinges, the windows intact.

And as I got closer I could hear the sound of techno techno-ing from the shed.

Gus was still pumping tin, the crazy old fool. It was like that old Roman dude who kept on playing the fiddle while Rome burned around him.

I walked into the shed, expected to see those sinewy arms shaking, eighty kilos on the bar, yet another PB.

A man was sprawled on the concrete, on his back.

Rocco Taverniti.

He's dead, I told myself.

But when I got closer and I could see the rise and

fall of his chest I felt a sense of relief – dead men don't go to court.

One side of his head looked like a Big Pete's Meatlover pizza, and a kettlebell lay next to him, the six kilo by the look of it. He had a gun in his hand.

I kept walking.

Gus was pretty much where I'd left him, stretched out on the bench. I looked up at the barbell, did the math – I'd been right. Eighty kilos, a new PB.

But Gus wouldn't be lifting it, not today.

The front of his tank top was stained red.

So Rocco had come at him, Gus had brained him with the kettlebell, but Rocco had managed to get a shot away before he'd kissed the concrete.

I turned off the techno, and then I could hear footsteps.

Standing at the entrance to the shed was Seb.

He reached down and took Rocco's gun and pointed it at me.

I looked over at Gus. No, that wasn't Gus, it was the vessel he'd inhabited during his stay here on earth.

I moved towards him.

"Dom!" said Seb. "Look at me."

I knelt down next to my grandfather, and I put my hands on the rough stubble of his face.

"Dom!" screamed Seb.

"Gus, I love you," I said, and the flower of sadness in my chest burst out again, growing and spreading, growing and spreading.

The sound of a gun, and a bullet whizzed over my head.

I turned away from Gus, and faced Seb.

"Why did you do it, you idiot? See what you've done! Why did you do it?"

"'It matters not how strait the gate, how charged with punishments the scroll. I am the master of my fate: I am the captain of my soul.'"

Seb waved the gun at me.

"We're cousins, you know?" I said.

"Yes, of course I know."

"Shame about you and Miranda. Hey, but nobody wants three-headed kids."

Again he waved the gun.

"What is wrong with you, Dom? Don't you understand, it's all finished. You've ruined it all."

"Ruined what, Seb?" I said.

"You paid the installments, you had it made. And now we could've worked together, you and me."

I got it now – Seb had been there to test me, too. To help me, like at the Colosseum, but to test me.

"I mean, what is there to do now?" he said.

"Well, we could go for a run," I said, looking at Gus, my coach – he pretty much thought running was the answer to everything.

"Are you crazy?"

"I'll race you to the beach."

"It's madness out there."

"They won't catch us," I said.

I started jogging up and down on the spot, just like Seb used to do outside Big Pete's when I'd meet him on our morning runs.

"A gazelle wakes up in the morning knowing that –"

"Shut up, Dom!"

"– it must run faster than the –"

"I said shut up!"

"– fastest lion."

"Shut up!"

"Come on, Seb," I said. "It's time for a run."

I started moving off, still jogging, out of the shed. I wasn't sure if he was behind me or not, but when I turned around, there he was.

He was running like one of those no-style marathoners, knees hardly lifting, feet dragging, and the gun was still in his hand.

I waited for him to catch up and gently took the gun from him, tossing it onto the ground.

"Come on, Seb," I said. "Race you to the beach."

I found some pace, and when I glanced behind it was to see that he had, too. I didn't bother with the gate, just ran through the hole the ram-raider truck had made in the wall.

I turned into Chirp Street, the birds eerily quiet.

And then across the bridge and onto Chevron Heights.

Most of the shops had been looted, but Big Pete's looked like it was still open for business.

I looked through the window and I could see why – Big Pete himself was standing there, a shotgun cradled in his hands.

I could sense that Seb was behind me, keeping his distance.

But I struggled up the Gut Buster; my hand had started bleeding again. I really did need to get that stitched, I thought.

When I was about a third of the way to the top, Seb powered past me, in the effortless languid style that he had.

I wasn't going to let him do that, however. I found another gear, and I caught up to him. We crested the hill abreast of each other.

"Hey, cuz?" I said.

"What?"

"Loose as a goose on the juice?" I said.

"Loose as a goose on the juice," he said.

We cruised down the descent together, building speed, the wind in our faces, heading for the sea and the distant horizon.

ACKNOWLEDGMENTS

It takes a team to write a series such as this, and I would like to thank mine. Firstly, to my agent, and coach, Margaret Connolly, for your encouragement, for the many pep talks. Thanks to my Australian publisher, and indefatigable team captain, Anna McFarlane; your knowledge of story is second-to-none. To my Australian editors, the tireless midfield trio of Julia Stiles, Hilary Reynolds and last, but certainly not least, Rachael Donovan. Rachael, without your tenacity, perspicacity and extraordinary eye for detail, this series would not have even made it onto the field. I would also like to thank my son Gabe Gwynne, skater extraordinaire, my nephew Luke Dowd, pilot extraordinaire, and Maxine Denton, diver extraordinaire, for your technical advice. Lastly I would like to thank my family, especially my gorgeous wife Eliza McCann. I owe you, darling. Big time.

THE DEBT
PHILLIP GWYNNE
INSTALLMENT ONE
CATCH THE ZOLT
LESSON ONE: DON'T MESS WITH THE DEBT

THE DEBT
PHILLIP GWYNNE
INSTALLMENT TWO
TURN OFF THE LIGHTS
LESSON TWO: NEVER GIVE ME LEVERAGE

THE DEBT

THE DEBT
PHILLIP GWYNNE
INSTALLMENT THREE
BRING BACK CERBERUS
LESSON THREE: YOU NEVER KNOW WHO'S LISTENING

THE DEBT
PHILLIP GWYNNE
INSTALLMENT FOUR
FETCH THE TREASURE HUNTER
LESSON FOUR: SOME ROCKS CAN'T BE RUN

THE DEBT
PHILLIP GWYNNE
INSTALLMENT FIVE
YAMASHITA'S GOLD
LESSON FIVE: ALL THAT GLITTERS ISN'T GOLD

THE DEBT
PHILLIP GWYNNE
INSTALLMENT SIX
TAKE A LIFE
LESSON SIX: HE THAT DIES, PAYS ALL DEBTS